PENGUIN BOOKS

MIRACLES

Ranjit Lal has written fiction and non-fiction for both adults and children. His books for Puffin include *The Caterpillar Who Went on a Diet and Other Stories*, *When Banshee Kissed Bimbo and Other Bird Stories*, *The Battle for No. 19* and *Faces in the Water*, which won the Crossword Best Children's Book Award in 2010 and the Laadli National Media Award.

PENGUIN BOOKS

USA | Canada | UK | Ireland | Australia
New Zealand | India | South Africa | China | Singapore

Penguin Books is part of the Penguin Random House group of companies
whose addresses can be found at global.penguinrandomhouse.com

Published by Penguin Random House India Pvt. Ltd
4th Floor, Capital Tower 1, MG Road,
Gurugram 122 002, Haryana, India

Penguin
Random House
India

First published in Inked by Penguin Books India 2013

Copyright © Ranjit Lal 2013

All rights reserved

10 9 8 7 6 5 4 3 2

ISBN 9780143333036

Typeset in Jonana Mt Std by Eleven Arts, Delhi

Printed at Repro India Limited

www.penguin.co.in

MIX
Paper from
responsible sources
FSC® C047271

mate digitally printed version of the book and therefore might not
have certain extra finishing on the cover.

MIRACLES

Ranjit Lal

PENGUIN

An imprint of Penguin

CONTENTS

CHAPTER ONE

MOTORCYCLE MOM

'Trish, are you ready, sweetheart?'

'Coming, Mom! Come on, Shivi, Mom's busting a gut.' Sixteen-and-a-half-year-old Trisha Bhave grabbed her younger sister's hand, picked up her school bag and hurried out to the porch.

'I don't want to go to a new school!' Shivi protested, sticking out her jaw. 'I want to go to our old school!'

'Just come on, Shivi!'

Actually, even Trisha was nervous—first day at a new school always made your stomach a little wobbly. Strictly speaking, it wasn't a new school—it was just a different branch of their old one, Ridgewood High, but with its own principal. (The Bhaves had moved from Gurgaon to Delhi that summer.) She remembered her interview with the principal, Mrs Krishnan—who she thought had put on far too much face powder and a much too red a shade of lipstick. Mrs Krishnan had eyed her and her mom sceptically, but Trisha's straight-A academic record and the glowing report from the principal of the Gurgaon branch had given her no option but to admit her—and Shivi—into their Central Delhi branch.

Trisha bustled out of the house, banging the door shut, dragging the pigtailed Shivi along and stopped short.

'Mom! Are we going on Smelly Beast?' she asked in disbelief.

'Yes, now put on your helmet quickly, we're running late.'

'But . . . can't we just take the pickup?' Trisha pointed to the four-door black, four-wheel-drive Toyota pickup in the driveway.

'Battery's flat. And you know Tikka and Komal are on leave. Come on, darling!'

'Bb . . . but . . .'

The deep-throated throb of the Bullet's engine cut off Trisha's protestations as her mom expertly kicked the bike to life.

If you saw Trisha's mom you wouldn't believe she could ride a bike, a Scooty maybe, but not a bike, and a Bullet—never—not in a million years! Slim and delicate as a reed she was, with curly jet black hair wriggling down to her shoulders, and light as a thistle. But if you took a closer look at her face, maybe you'd change your mind. She had huge metallic black eyes, which held the purple gloss of jamuns in them (and which could soften to shimmery mush, but only Trisha and Shivi knew that), and a jaw that brooked no nonsense. One cool stare from those eyes, framed by those oh-so-supercilious eyebrows, a tilt of the head and that firm jaw, accompanied by a husky, icicle 'yes?' and you'd shut up quickly and mumble 'but *of course*, ma'am, sure you can'. She could do wheelies on a bike—even the big Bullet, no problem, man; she had sinews of steel . . .

Trisha thought her mother was drop-dead cool and envied her; she knew she'd never have the guts to do all the crazy and often hugely embarrassing things her mom did—like ride Smelly Beast all over the Himalayas (right up to Ladakh as they had done last summer) with her and Shivi and a tent for company. Actually, that wasn't entirely true, because Tikka Singh and Komal—the husband-and-wife team who had been their household help ever since she could remember—had followed them in the Toyota as backup, but still.

'I look like a frumpy lump beside you, Mom, and just look at my bum!' Trisha would often complain, 'I'm like a waddling hospital matron from 1940!' Sometimes she really felt that things were topsy-turvy—that *she* ought to have been the slim, hip chick in skin-tight jeans clinging on to hunks on the backs of bikes (well, not that her mom ever did *that*, but you get the drift) and her mother the more conventional, plump kind who tottered after her and nagged her about boyfriends. But Trisha had a kind face with flawless skin and soft lines and a smile that could make a whole roomful of sourpusses light up. She had a good height, about 5 feet 4 inches, tipped the scales at 60, well 62 kg ('I'm at least 10 kg over the limit!') and a full figure. She had thick, wavy dark brown hair that bounced attractively from her shoulders and those smiling brown eyes that she'd got from her dad. And when she sang (only in the bathroom) she could easily hold an auditorium full of frenetic breakdancers spellbound; her low notes, husky and deep, ran clear and true.

Shivi by contrast, just six, was skinny and dark and volatile and twitchy as a mouse with hiccups and took after their mother. After a couple of bites of chocolate she became as hyper as a Tom and Jerry cartoon.

'Shivi, do you want to ride up in front or sandwich behind?'

'Up front, up front!'

Mrs Bhave strapped on Shivi's scarlet helmet securely and hoisted her little girl up in front of her. 'Put on your shades, sweetheart.' Shivi happily put on her virulently purple and gold sunglasses and leaned forward over the petrol tank, racing style.

'But Mom! We can't go to school on the bike!' Trisha wailed, 'not on the first day! It's so embarrassing.'

'Nonsense, Trish, lots of kids come to school on motorbikes. Now hop on!'

Of course a lot of kids did. But they were driven by their dads. And some—usually obnoxious—guys rode their own bikes to school. No one she knew had a motorcycle mom. Trisha and Shivi's dad had disappeared many years ago, just after Shivi was born. Trisha still vaguely remembered—always with a pang of sadness and longing— that laughing, jolly man who had taken her around on his shoulders or plonked her on the petrol tank of his bike, with her mom at the back. And no, he hadn't died in some horrible motorcycle crash—his ship had gone down in a typhoon in the Philippine Sea and they said there had been no survivors and that was that. Trisha's mom had been sad and quiet for six months—hoping for a miracle—but finally, one Sunday morning, she had swallowed hard and started up the silent silver Bullet they had nicknamed Smelly Beast (because it always reeked of petrol and oil). Tikka Singh, who had been her father's manservant, had assiduously maintained and polished the bike all those silent months, but had never actually started it. It had made a huge fuss about being woken up after so long, but like Tikka,

Mrs Bhave could coax it into doing anything. With Trisha clinging to her back and baby Shivi squashed between them, the three of them had gone for a long and glorious ride, and they had been calmed and comforted by the steady, deep bass heartbeat of the engine. They'd gone on several motorcycling holidays after that, swooping up into the mountains, riding serenely through the mustard fields in the plains. Dhaba owners and truck drivers always did a double take when they realized that a wisp of a woman was riding the big bike—and after that they always got preferential treatment—the most comfortable chairs or charpoys and extra ghee on their paranthas. It was a bit different in Delhi sometimes. While most other bikers gave Mrs Bhave the thumbs up and an admiring grin as she passed them, there were some who whistled and followed her, unable to accept that a woman could be riding such a brutish bike. Mrs Bhave just ignored them and sailed on calmly as they followed on their tinpot machines, buzzing peevishly like flies. But usually she just had to let Smelly Beast growl and they dropped back embarrassed.

But going to a new, rather snobbish school on the back of a silver Bullet, driven by your mom, who looked like a model for a biker's magazine . . . What would the kids think? What would those prissy teachers say? At the moment there was no time to think because Mrs Bhave had turned the bike around and indicated with her thumb that she hop on pronto. Trisha sighed, stuffed her thick brown hair under her helmet and climbed on.

It was all very well for her mom to be a motorbike maniac (as Papa had been), but not that great for her. That starched and blanched Mrs Krishnan and the other teachers would think that she was some kind of female Hells Angel freak (she'd worn a black leather jacket for the interview because they were going for a ride and a picnic afterwards!) and an irresponsible parent who probably drank and smoked and grew weed in her garden. As for the kids . . . they'd probably snigger and smirk at her as they got down from their swank, chauffeur-driven cars. Even the Toyota pickup was a bit much—it was big and black and had massive tyres, with a row of headlights mounted on its roof. It looked like 'a mafia hitman's wheels', as Trisha had once remarked. Why couldn't they have an ordinary car like everyone else?

They couldn't have made a worse entrance. A long line of cars had drawn up on the road outside the school, dropping kids off at the gates one by one; the buses had parked along one side of the road and were still disgorging kids and teachers. Trisha's mom on her big dazzling bike throbbed, *dhabadhabadab*, coolly past them all up to the head of the queue. Just behind her a turquoise Swift pulled up and the security guards rushed up to open its doors. As Trisha got off and helped Shivi down, she saw Mrs Krishnan disembark from the Swift and glance disapprovingly at their thumping bike. It promptly stalled, and the sudden silence was like as if the whole world had been switched off.

Mrs Bhave took her helmet off and kissed her daughters. 'Bye, sweethearts, I'll pick you up in the afternoon,' she called and strapped it back on. She kicked the bike and it started obediently, then she gunned it gloriously and rode off down the road.

Trisha smoothed down her hair and straightened her tie. 'Good morning, ma'am,' she mumbled as Mrs Krishnan walked frostily past her. At the gates a gaggle of kids stood around, smirking. Trisha sighed. 'Come, Shivi, I'll take you to your class and then find mine ...'

'Hi, I'm Gulnar.' The chubby girl with the frizzy hair and round face sitting next to Trisha dimpled and held out her hand. 'Was that your sister who dropped you off this morning? Did you see old Papad-Face's expression! Superbly constipated, I'd say!'

'No, it was my mom, believe it or not. By the way, I'm Trisha Bhave.'

'Wow, that is so cool! Your mom rides a motorbike! Mine wanders around in a petticoat and flip flops all day.' She rolled her eyes. 'Say, have *you* ridden that bike? If you have all the boys will be chasing you like anything.'

'Um yes, Mom taught me in the holidays, but not on the roads or anything—she said it was good I learn, in case there's an emergency, but it petrifies me. It's so heavy, and if you let it lean over just a little too much, you've had it; it just *wants* to fall over, preferably on top of you! I don't know how Mom manages it.' She smiled. 'When it comes to me and the motorbike it's sometimes a bit like Calvin and his bicycle. But when it allows you to ride it and is in a good mood, it's pure heaven!'

A burly, pimply fellow with thick lips and a leer on his face stopped by her desk.

'Hey, who was that cool chick on the Bullet who dropped you off?' he asked without preamble. 'Will you introduce her to me?'

Trisha eyed him up and down and wished she had her mom's cold snake stare and ability to cut people up into little pieces when they were insufferable. 'My mom,' she said softly.

'Your mom rides a Bullet? Wow, and your dad? A dumpster? A tank? A bulldozer?' He whistled. Two of his friends who had joined him laughed coarsely.

'My dad's dead,' Trisha said quietly. 'And right, my mother rides a Bullet.' She stared at him, 'So?' And Nana *had* driven a tank in the army and bashed the hell out of the enemy in some distant war and been decorated from head to toe for that—before he had gone to war with Trish's mom and disowned her because he couldn't stomach the fact that she had run off with a shippie who was a motorcycle maniac.

'So . . . so . . . er, nothing . . .' the boy shuffled off awkwardly.

And now, willy-nilly she had started thinking about Nana again and how beastly he had been about her mom's legendary romance. Trisha never tired of listening to the story. It was quite the most romantic thing she had ever heard!

Apparently her dad (to be), rugged and charming First Officer Kartik Bhave, had come to Kasuali on a biking holiday and had met her mom in the garden of Ros Common. They fell in love and after six months, decided to get married. But when Trisha's dad very correctly asked her mom's dad for her hand, the curmudgeonly old general went through the roof like a tank shell and threatened to shoot the 'shippie sailorboy' for his gall. He coldly informed him that his daughter had been spoken for (a blatant lie) by the son ('that fat, pasty Vipul Namdev') of his commanding officer.

So the young couple eloped dramatically at night and rode to Delhi on Smelly Beast, where they got married. The vindictive old general cut off her mom from his will, and even after all these years, still hadn't forgiven her.

The story always gave Trisha goosebumps and she often wondered how her mother would react if she ran away with someone like that. But then, she'd be in no position to argue!

'Oh, I'm sorry to hear that,' Gulnar was saying now, 'hello, are you there? You're looking a bit spaced out! Excuse me! Anyone home?'

'Oh! Sorry!' Trisha shook her head and smiled at her new friend. She had warmed to those round black eyes and the cherubic baby face immediately.

'I hope that fool didn't upset you,' Gulnar went on.

'Thanks, that's okay. He didn't know any better.'

Gulnar made a face. 'Avinash is wholesale gross. Period. Come on, Trisha—let me show you around and introduce you to some of my friends here.'

It wasn't as bad as she had feared, not with Gullu at her side. During recess she checked on Shivi. She was amused to see that her little sister had taken charge of a little Sardar boy in a blue topknot and slipping shorts and was dragging him around the playground by his tie, talking non-stop.

'Hi Shivi—who's your friend?' she asked.

'He's Daljeet, but everyone calls him Bobby. He's new too.'

'Hi Bobby,' Trisha smiled. 'Would you guys like an ice cream?'

'Yes, yes, yes . . . I want a choco-bar and so does Bobby,' Shivi said firmly.

Bobby nodded shyly; he knew he had no choice.

'Okay, Shivi, now after class you stand by the gate, right here, and wait for me. Mom will pick us up. Okay? Don't go anywhere from there.'

'Oof, okay, okay.' Shivi took Bobby's hand and moved off. 'She's like a mother hen. She thinks I don't know anything,' she complained earnestly.

Mrs Bhave, in black jeans and a matching denim jacket stunningly embroidered with scarlet and yellow hibiscuses, waited for them at the gates, standing by the Bullet, her helmet dangling from the handlebars and her sunglasses perched over her forehead. She smiled at the kids surging out to their buses and cars and waved frantically as she caught sight of Shivi first, still clutching Bobby by his tie as she made her way out. Shivi saw her mom, dropped Bobby like a hot potato and ran into her arms.

'Hi sweetheart, how was your day?'

'Fine, Mommy, but the teacher said I talk too much. I was only talking to Bobby so I don't know what her problem was.'

'Bobby? Oh I see, you mean that little boy who came out with you?'

Likewise, Bobby had spotted his own mother and had gone charging off to her, Shivi forgotten.

As Trisha walked out with Gullu, she noticed that a small crowd of boys had gathered around the bike; it wasn't so much the bike itself that had drawn them (though there was always that) as the slim and glamorous looking lady, surely a top model or DJ, who was standing next to it.

'Come on, Mom, let's go!' Trisha urged, strapping on her helmet. 'Everyone's looking at us!'

'Nice bike, ma'am,' one of the boys commented and a ripple of laughter went through the crowd.

Mrs Bhave smiled at him brilliantly. 'Thank you,' she said and sat Shivi on her perch in front of her.

'Er . . . how do you control it, ma'am?' the boy continued cheekily. 'Isn't it too heavy?' He grinned, 'or does it control you?' More sniggers, louder this time.

'Mom, let's go! Please.'

Mrs Bhave pinned the boy with her eyes. 'I control it like I control everything else—including little boys with bad manners,' she said sweetly. 'It's no problem when you know exactly how to.' She got astride the bike and strapped on her helmet.

'Vroom . . . vroom!' Shivi called happily from the petrol tank, leaning forwards and sideways, her arms outspread airplane style. 'Let's go, Mommy!'

And yet again Trisha wished the bike didn't make such a thunderous announcement when it started. It sort of stopped everyone in their tracks. An ordinary Bullet was bad enough, but Tikka had done things to it which made it sound even more like some bestial, growling carnivore of the Jurassic age or an approaching thunderstorm. All eyes automatically swivelled to it. And her mom didn't seem to notice anything!

Trisha decided she'd have to have a chat with her mom when they got home. In the meanwhile she might as well enjoy the ride.

And a ride it was, because they weren't taking the usual route home; they were soon on the lovely road running through the Ridge, past Buddha Jayanti Park. At a traffic light, Trisha raised her visor.

'Where are we going, Mom? This isn't the way home!'

Mrs Bhave glanced back at her and nodded. 'I have to pick up my test reports from the Tulsidas Hospital,' she said.

For several weeks now, her mother had been off her food and complaining of feeling 'liverish', whatever that was. Dr Khurana, who had been referred to them by their old Gurgaon doctor and had his clinic in the same colony as theirs, had examined her and ordered a battery of blood tests.

They burbled gently into the hospital parking lot, as the attendants and drivers gaped.

'This shouldn't take long,' Mrs Bhave said after they disembarked.

'This is like a railway station,' Trisha said, holding Shivi firmly by the hand. She wrinkled her nose. The hospital smelled of the usual nauseous mixture of sweat, disinfectant, phenyl, medicine, urine and—she thought with a pang—of blood and pus and the pain and frightened people . . .

'I just hope the reports are ready.'

They were. Mrs Bhave glanced at them briefly before stuffing them back into the envelope.

'What do they say, Mom?' Trisha asked, as a nurse passing by smiled at Shivi, who scowled back at her.

'All clear.'

'Are you sure? Can I see them please?'

'I'm sure as I can be,' her mother replied, squeezing her hand. 'But we'll show them to Dr Khurana, of course. Come on, you guys must be famished—let's raid Big Chill, shall we?'

'Yay!' Shivi grabbed her mom's hand and led the way. She didn't like all these strange sick people milling about—some in wheelchairs,

some with bandages on their heads, some lying flat on beds
with wheels with bottles hanging over them, looking like they
were dead.

'What are you having, Mom?' Trisha asked, as they sat down and
glanced at the menus.
    'I'll have an iced tea, I think,' Mrs Bhave said and shook her curls.
    'Squidgie for me!' Shivi declared, nodding firmly.
    'I'll have the blueberry cheesecake.'
    'Why don't you order?'
    'Mom, please . . . you know I hate doing that!'
    'Just tell the fellow what we want. He won't eat you up, sweetie!'
    Trisha hated doing things like ordering; what if she made some
embarrassing goof-up? And her mom was always doing things like
that to her. It was just so much more . . . relaxing . . . to let her mom
do the choosing and ordering and everything. Even shopping—she
hated being asked to shop, and more often than not, her mom would
send her into some shop while she waited in the pickup or on the
bike. Now she raised her hand tentatively at a passing waiter.
    'Um . . . excuse me . . . sir, we'd like to order . . .' She bit her tongue
and blushed. For heaven's sake, you didn't call waiters 'sir', they called
you sir or ma'am. But poor guy, he had to take orders and be polite to
obnoxious customers all day; he must be longing for the day when
he'd be the one giving instead of taking the orders.
    'Trish, sweetheart, you're daydreaming again,' her mother said
softly. 'He's waiting.'
    'Oh, sorry,' she blushed again and looked up. 'Okay . . . ummm.'
    'I want squidgies and a Coke with chocolate ice cream!' Shivi said
and Trisha stammered out the rest of the order.
    Mrs Bhave leaned over the table. 'So how was the first day at
school, babies? Shivi, you go first. Tell me everything—leave nothing
out! Copy that?'
    'Mommy, this fellow Bobby—he was crying in a corner in the
class and these other children were making fun of him because his
patka had come undone and they said he looked like a girl.' Shivi
took a breath.

'And?'

Shivi's eyes opened wide and innocently. 'And I told them they shouldn't make fun of him.'

'That's good. And then?'

'And then they stopped. Bas, that's all.'

Mrs Bhave frowned and leaned back. 'Aha . . . I think I smell a rat . . . You just told them to stop teasing him and they listened to you? I think something's missing here.'

Shivi nodded then shook her head. 'They're good children, really,' she said virtuously.

'You didn't middle punch them . . .'

'Only two, bas. The others ran away and tattled to the teacher.'

'Hmm. Well, I suppose it was for a good cause.'

'So then I told Bobby he should learn karate like us. Then he'll be able to fight himself. I asked him to join Mr Singh's class.'

'I'm sure Mr Singh wouldn't mind that.'

'But then all the other kids were calling me a fighter-cock and tattled to the teacher. So I talked only to Bobby all day.'

'And what did your teacher say?'

Shivi shrugged. 'Nothing.'

'Ah, I see. And how was your day, Trish?'

'I met one really nice girl—well, you met her too—Gullu. And she sort of introduced me to some of her friends.'

'That's nice.'

Trisha grinned. 'And one of the boys wanted to date you!'

'What? Ah . . . what's he like?'

'I don't think you'd like him. He was pretty awful.'

'Boys at that age usually are.'

'And how was your day, Mom?'

'Oh, I missed you guys. I finished the presentation for the farmhouse project and they loved it—so that's done. Then I saw to the pickup—it's gone for service too. They said they'd deliver it by the evening.'

'Good. Going to school on Smelly Beast is a bit much.'

'I like going to school on Smelly Beast!' Shivi said. 'It's fun.'

'Okay now, why don't you ask for the bill?'

'Uh,' Trisha raised a hand nervously and this time the boy (whose name tag said 'Manav') was at their table in a trice. 'We'd like our bill, please,' she said.

Her mother fished out her credit card and handed it over. 'You do the honours, dear,' she said, smiling brightly.

If there was one thing Trisha hated more than giving orders it was paying the bill; for some reason it always made her nervous. And now her mom was getting reading to scarper.

'Mom, please! First you made me order, now you make me pay the bill . . .'

'Can I pay, can I pay?' Shivi asked, scrabbling about in her pocket for her little red purse.

Her mom smiled. 'Sure dear, that's how things go normally, you order, you eat and you pay!'

'But . . . but Mom!'

To her dismay Mrs Bhave had already got up and was now walking out of the place with Shivi, who looked back and waved gleefully.

Two minutes later, 'Manav' returned, smiling regretfully.

'Sorry, ma'am, our machine isn't working at the moment,' he said, handing back the credit card. 'It'll take a little time to fix, but you could pay cash if you like . . . or wait and have a soft drink on the house.'

'Oh . . .' She delved frantically into her purse, wondering if she had enough cash. What if she didn't? Would he allow her to go out and fetch her mother—or would he think she'd do a bunk? Well how was she to know that their card machine was kaput? And why couldn't places like this have backup machines? But how could he let her out of the place without paying? What if she did do a bunk? He'd lose his job! And what if she didn't have enough cash and her mom took off with Shivi . . . she'd be left here to do the dishes all evening! Idiot, Mom would never do that . . . would she?

'Ma'am?'

'Oh, yes, uh, just a minute.' She scraped around and managed to rustle up just enough cash. 'Here you go,' she said, relieved, and then her heart sank. 'I'm sorry . . . I don't seem to have enough for a tip . . .' she stuttered, going crimson. 'Look, could you call my mom—she's parked outside, down to the right—it's a silver Bullet.'

His eyebrows shot up. Then he smiled. 'No problem, ma'am—not your fault our machine is out of order.' He held her chair back. 'Have a nice day!'

Outside, her mom was astride the bike with Shivi up front, waiting.

'Mom, it was so embarrassing! Their card machine didn't work and I barely had enough cash and couldn't tip the poor fellow!'

'And Mommy nearly dropped the bike,' Shivi said. 'She was dreaming like you and it fell over.'

'What happened? Mom, really, this bike is too heavy.'

'Nothing happened. I just didn't balance it properly when I took it off the stand, that's all. Now hop on, we have to collect the pickup from the service station. They can't deliver it after all.'

TWO BAD BOYS

They rumbled into their driveway at Semul Enclave, with Smelly Beast now silently 'piggybacking' on the gleaming pickup. There was a courier boy standing outside their front door, ringing the bell.

'Darling, collect the letter, I'm going in.' Mrs Bhave took off her sunglasses and disappeared inside.

'Mrs Bhave?' the boy asked. Trisha nodded.

'She went in. Can I sign?'

'What is it, Mom?' Trisha asked a little while later as her mother slit the thick manila envelope and scanned the contents. Mrs Bhave smiled.

'Good news! You know that resort project in the hills—near Kasauli? Well, I've got it! They want me to redesign it from scratch: the interiors, gardens, landscaping, everything! It's great money too.'

'That's awesome!' But then Trisha's face fell. 'Wait . . . Kasauli?' That was where Nana and Nani lived . . . and her mom had never gone back, not even after Papa had died.

'It's okay, Trish. Nana doesn't own Kasauli. We can go there any time we like. It's a free country.'

'Will that mean you'll be gone a long time?' Shivi asked in a small voice.

'Well, for a bit, yes . . . but we can all go together for short weekend trips when I check out the place . . . like during the Diwali and Dusshera holidays maybe . . . and for long weekends even.'

'Can I bring Bobby with me?'

'We'll see about that . . .'

'When do they want you to start?'

'Well, I have to meet them here in Delhi first . . . but they do seem to want to get on with it quickly.'

While Shivi and Trisha shared a bedroom (painted a happy sunshine yellow and white), Trisha had a small study to herself, where her books and computer were kept. Their mother had her own bedroom just along the corridor, which led to the drawing-cum-dining room. On a small walnut-wood table were three framed photographs—of Trisha's dad, dadi and dada (both of whom Trisha had, sadly, never got to meet) and one family group, taken a few days after Shivi had been born. Huge windows along two walls flooded the house with light, and both the bedrooms opened up into balconies which led to the small, neat garden outside, crammed with leafy potted plants. When her dad had been around, they had lived in Bombay, but Trisha's mom had shifted to Gurgaon a year after he had disappeared—trying to evict the tenants of this house, which had been Dada's and then their dad's. They had finally got out just six months back, leaving it in a complete mess, and Mrs Bhave had spent four months redecorating and renovating it. Only that summer had they shifted into the ground floor. Trisha's mom used the first floor as her studio-cum-office.

Trisha took her school bag to her study and kicked off her shoes. Usually she'd change into jeans and a T-shirt and then check on Shivi who would have switched on some computer game. It was Komal who took control of Shivi—saw that she washed and changed and took her out to the park across the road. Trisha had accompanied her on several occasions hoping to make friends with some of the kids who hung out there but had been too shy to approach them. So she had stuck around with Shivi and Komal, glancing enviously at the knots of kids as they or tossed a frisbee or played badminton, shrieking loudly; they hadn't seemed particularly keen on saying hello to her either.

Now her mom stuck her head around the door.

'Trish, could you take Shivi to the park?'

'Okay, why don't you come too? We could go for a walk.'

'I'm a bit tired, sweetie.'

At the park, Shivi headed straight for the swings. 'Higher! Higher!' she squealed happily, as Trisha pushed her. Two boys, about sixteen and fourteen and just about as tall as her, wearing khaki cargo pants and dark blue T-shirts were flicking a frisbee at each other some distance away. Trisha glanced at them from time to time and wondered where they lived. They looked like brothers. Both had glossed black hair standing up in short spikes from their foreheads and slightly jug ears and toothy smiles. The younger boy was clearly trying to get the better of his brother and threw the frisbee with great energy and verve, though his brother was light on his feet and caught the disc every time. Nearly.

'Watch out!'

Trisha had just given Shivi a good push and stepped back for a breather, when she heard the shout. She turned too late. The yellow frisbee hissed a curving trajectory as it spun unerringly for her. It struck her hard on the forehead, sending her reeling back with a squeal. She tripped over a brick used for bordering and fell sprawling on her back.

There was a burst of muffled laughter from the boys. She struggled to her feet, as Shivi twisted on her swing complaining, 'Trisha, push me, why are you lying down in the mud? I'll tell Mommy!'

The younger of the boys, who had thrown the frisbee, darted in, picked it up, flashed a cheeky grin at her and made tracks towards where his elder brother stood, gawping.

Trisha propped herself on her elbows trying to get over the shock, and wanted to yell at them but the words would just not come out of her mouth. She glared at them as they took to their heels, casting backward glances at her.

'Bloody idiots!' she gasped, swallowing the frog in her throat and getting to her feet, sudden tears in her eyes.

'Trish, you're just standing there waiting for a fly to go into your mouth—push me!' Shivi commanded.

'Hang on, Shivi. Oh come on, learn to swing yourself!'

'But I like you pushing me!'

'Okay, okay!'

They returned home as the shadows of the big semuls stretched across the park. Trisha felt her forehead—she was sure to have a bruise.

'How was the park, dears?' their mother asked, still ensconced in her Lazy Boy.

'Two stupid boys threw their frisbee at me!' Trisha recounted what had happened.

'Why don't you show your bruise to Dr Khurana? He'll be coming to see me in about an hour's time.'

'Oh. Mom, are you feeling okay?'

'Oh yes. I called him with the results of my test and he very kindly said that he would be passing by later in the evening and would pop in. Would you be a sweetheart and tidy up the drawing room?'

'What about me?' Shivi demanded. 'What can I do?'

'You could dust the coffee table, Shivi, and pick up your books and felt pens and take them to your room. And Trish, we're having pizza for dinner. I don't feel like cooking.'

It was about eight o'clock when the doorbell rang. Shivi went charging off to open it. She put on the safety chain and peeked out.

'Who's there?' she demanded. 'Beware! I have a ferocious dog with me!'

'It's Dr Khurana, silly,' Trisha hissed, by her sister's side, slipping off the latch and opening the door. The doctor, a trim silver-haired gentleman with a ruddy complexion and gold-rimmed spectacles, complete with white coat and black bag, nodded briefly.

'Good evening, I've come to see Mrs Bhave.'

'Um . . . good evening, Doctor, please come in. Mom's in the drawing room.' She led him in and stood hovering close as he read her reports and examined her.

'I've lost my appetite completely,' her mother said. 'And occasionally feel nauseous . . . and itchy sometimes too. Also, I get tired very quickly now . . . I'm not half as active as I used to be.'

The doctor turned to Trisha.

'Will you do me a favour? My ECG machine is in the car outside— a white Zen. My boys are in the car; tell them to bring it in, please.'

'Oh, sure!'

She slipped out through the driveway, past the Toyota. Sure enough, just outside the gate, a white Maruti Zen was parked. She went up to it and peeked in. There was nobody inside and she didn't want to check if the doors were locked for fear of setting off the alarm. She looked around; maybe the doctor's 'boys' had stepped out for a quick bidi or something.

There came a sudden clunk and a muffled exclamation, and she jumped, staring back into the driveway. Someone was in the back of the Toyota . . . were they trying to steal it—or Smelly Beast? Her heart beating fast, she crept back silently into the driveway; she had to make it back to the house, pass the Toyota unseen and then raise the alarm. She got on to her hands and knees and began crawling past the pickup.

'Hold it straight, you idiot, don't turn the handlebars, it'll fall, bloody heavy monster!'

Beside the rear wheel of the Toyota, Trisha froze.

'Shit, we've had it! Oof! Oww! Get this thing off me, Jai, dammit!'

Slowly, Trisha stood up and peered over the Toyota's side. Two young boys were in the back of the pickup, struggling and wrestling with the bike. It had leaned over at an alarming angle and pinned one of them against the opposite side and the other boy, with his back to her, was trying valiantly to pull it back. The boy who was pinned down and on his knees saw her and his eyes widened. 'Help!' he squawked, 'get this thing off me!' The other boy, now attempting to push the bike up instead of pulling it, saw her too.

'Hey, help me get this up! It's bloody heavy.'

'You!' she gasped. He was the younger of the brothers who had thrown the frisbee at her. He was gaping at her, now horror-struck as recognition dawned.

'You both followed me home?' she squeaked, the dread in her stomach settling like a cannonball.

'No, no . . . we didn't know . . .'

'You're stalking me!' She turned to flee. These fellows were obviously hardened delinquents, really bad boys.

'No, please . . . our dad . . .' the fellow jerked his hand towards the house, and the bike leaned over even more alarmingly.

'Yikes! It's falling on me . . . it'll squash me!'

'Serves you right!' she wanted to say, but didn't. He did look quite scared and she knew exactly how heavy the bike was: 185 kg! His brother was now trying to push the bike upright, but it had leaned over too much. He grunted with the effort, but it made no difference. Suddenly she realized that if he released his grip, the bike really would flatten the boy; it could injure him nastily—it could maim him for life and it would be her fault for not helping in time . . . and how would she sleep every night, knowing she had been responsible for ruining someone's life?

She vaulted into the bed of the truck. 'Okay, you push now and I'll pull. On the count of three: one, two . . . three!'

Between them they got Smelly Beast vertical and pushed it back into its stand. The elder brother wriggled away and sidled next to his sibling, rubbing his shin. Too late she realized that she had opened the barn door, so to speak. They just had to jump down and disappear into the darkness. Idiot!

'Wh . . . what are you doing here?' she stuttered. 'I'm . . . I'm going to tell my mother and she'll call the police!'

The elder brother raised a hand in surrender. 'Pl . . . please . . . no, just listen a sec, will you! Our dad—he came to see a patient here and we were waiting in the car. Then we saw the bike . . . and . . . and just wanted to take a closer look . . .' His eyes widened. 'Is it yours?'

She nodded. Then she frowned. 'Your dad . . . he's Dr Khurana?'

They both nodded. 'He's seeing a patient inside. He told us to wait in the car.'

She nodded, the colour returning to her face. 'Yes, I guess you would need a doctor as a father,' she said tartly, suddenly finding her courage. 'Considering how you keep hitting people on the head with frisbees.' She touched her forehead lightly.

'Sorry about that,' the older boy said. 'By the way, I'm Akshay and this is my brother, Jai. And thanks for helping.'

'Wow, your dad rides this bike?' Jai asked, his eyes round as coins.

'It's my mom's bike,' Trisha informed him. 'And the next time you want to have a look at it, ask. That's the usual way.'

'Er . . . sorry, look, could you, um, not mention this to anyone?' Akshay jerked his hand towards the house. 'Papa will be very mad at us.'

'Maybe,' she said sweetly, beginning to enjoy the situation.

'Your mom rides this?' Jai asked, still wide-eyed.

'Uh-huh!' She tossed her head and nodded. 'And sometimes I do too! We've ridden all over the Himalayas on it.'

'Trisha! Where are you? Doctor wants his machine!' Shivi came charging out of the front door. 'What are you doing talking to strange boys in the pickup?' she asked. 'I'll tell Mommy!'

'Oh, shit,' Trisha said. 'Your father wants his ECG machine.'

'Right, no problem!' The brothers leapt off the back of the Toyota and went to their car.

'What took you so long?' Dr Khurana asked irritably, taking the case from Akshay. 'Fooling around as usual?'

'No . . . nothing, Papa!'

He turned to Mrs Bhave. 'These are my sons—Akshay and Jai.'

'Hello boys, nice to meet you! Would you like something to drink?' Mrs Bhave offered. 'Trisha, get them something to drink.'

'Actually,' Trisha said sweetly. 'We'd met in the park earlier this evening.'

'They were playing with a frisbee!' Shivi chimed in, blinking angelically.

'Okay, everybody out!' Dr Khurana ordered.

'Come on,' Trisha said, leading the way to the kitchen.

'You said your mom rides that bike?' Akshay asked, sipping his Coke.

'What about your dad?' Jai asked, 'is your mom divorced?'

'My dad died a long time ago. It was his bike actually. Mom didn't want to sell it and then one day just decided to ride it. Papa had taught her, but she hadn't really practised. Anyway, now she rides it all over the place.'

'We went to our new school on it today,' Shivi said, crossing her legs like a proper lady and slurping up her Coke. 'You should have seen everyone's faces.'

'Actually, it was quite embarrassing!'

'Wow, cool! Imagine going to school on the back of that!' There were stars in Jai's eyes.

'So you must live close by?' Trisha asked, hopefully.

'Yup! We're in D block, on the other side of this one.'

'Um . . . would you . . . or could she . . . uh . . . someone . . . take us for a ride someday?' Akshay asked hesitantly.

'Sure I could!' Trisha said, still amazingly gung-ho, though the first of the doubts had already begun gnawing at her. Of course she could ride Smelly Beast perfectly well, but with a schoolboy sitting pillion? 'Anytime!'

'It'll have to be someplace away from here.' Akshay said.

'Oh.' She was surprised. 'I thought I could take you around the park here—the road is usually deserted most of the time.'

Akshay shook his head. 'No, someone will see us and tattle to Papa and he'll be mad.'

'Why? You're only riding pillion. I'll be riding the bike, so if anyone wants to complain it will have to be against me! Besides, I'll have to ask Mom. She'll probably say yes, but have Tikka to supervise or something. Still, you'll get your ride. Why should your dad mind?'

Akshay shook his head. 'It can't be here,' he said stubbornly.

And suddenly she realized why: sixteen-year-old guys do not ride pillion (on a Bullet, for Christ's sake!) behind sixteen-year-old girls! If someone saw him, it would be all over the neighbourhood and he'd be roadkill. She took a deep breath and smiled mischievously.

'If you like,' she said gently, 'we could always pretend that you were teaching me how to ride and not the other way around. You could keep shouting instructions at me or something.'

'Thanks,' he said.

'Well, think about it.'

'I love the way it sounds, *dhubdhubduhb*!' said Jai, beating a tattoo on the kitchen table. 'Like a tribal drumbeat! I can never make my drums sound like that.'

'See!' Shivi said to Jai, running into the kitchen, wearing her helmet and shades. She had put on her special scarlet motorcycle overalls too. 'This is what I wear when we go biking!' she said excitedly. 'I wear knee and elbow pads too.' She put them on. 'Mom says I look real cool!'

'You look like a miniature Ferrari pit stop mechanic!' Jai grinned. Like his brother he had an engaging (if more toothy) smile.

'Akshay! Jai! We have to go!' Dr Khurana called from the other room.

'Is Mom okay?' Trisha asked nervously as she followed the doctor back into the living room, where her mother was now sitting up. Dr Khurana looked at Trisha and pursed his lips.

'She's okay for the moment,' he said. 'But it seems that there may be a slight blockage in your mom's bile duct. An ultrasound would show that, so she ought to have one done soon.'

He picked up his bag and indicated to Akshay to carry his ECG case.

Trisha saw them out and went back to her mother, where Shivi was explaining earnestly: 'Mommy, those doctor's boys were the same ones who hit Trisha with their frisbee. And they were up on the pickup like they wanted to steal Smelly Beast. They want Trisha to take them for a ride but not here.'

'Shivi, when will you learn not to blabber like NDTV!' Trisha exclaimed, going red. 'Just shut up!'

'But it's true!'

In her bedroom Mrs Bhave removed all the makeup from her face and stared at her reflection in the dressing table mirror. Her complexion was pale, and ever so slightly yellow tinged, like the pale yellow wash that she sometimes saw in her eyes. She was happy she had managed to drop and pick up the girls from school on the bike, but riding had tired her more than it ever had before. Well, perhaps the ultrasound would reveal exactly what was wrong with her, though she suspected Dr Khurana probably already knew . . . She went to her writing bureau and opened her letter pad. It had been years since she had written a letter in longhand. She unscrewed the cap of her fountain pen and stared at the writing paper. Should she? Or should she wait? Perhaps she could write after the ultrasound, when hopefully everything would be a lot clearer.

'Shit man, that was a narrow escape! That bike nearly squashed me!' Akshay glanced at the bruise on his shin that Smelly Beast's chromium leg guard had given him and grimaced. Admiration had quickly given way to a bruised ego, and he was still trying to get over the humiliation of being pinned down by the bike and then getting caught and rescued by a girl.

'I bet she can't ride that bike. It's far too heavy!' he said. 'I bet she was just trying to impress us!'

'Yeah, yeah, like any chick would want to impress you! Lying squashed there like a pasty maggot under the bike, yelping for help!'

'Only because Superman here didn't have the muscle to keep the bike upright! He needed to be helped by a girl!'

'Thank your stars she helped. Otherwise you would be a smear on the floor of that Toyota. And also, thank your stars she didn't run home and tattle. You know what Papa would have done to us.'

'We'd have been grounded for six months at least!' Akshay agreed dolefully.

His brother looked at him. 'So do we want to make friends with her?'

'I think,' said Akshay nodding portentously, 'Operation Bullet will be under way tomorrow.'

CHAPTER THREE

OPERATION SMELLY BEAST

The second day was much easier—already a routine of sorts had set in—and Trisha liked what she had seen of her class teacher, Ms Sonam. She was a tall, gangly lady, with teeth that stuck out a bit and stringy hair, but she had a very practical attitude and stood no nonsense. That afternoon, Tikka turned up in the pickup to collect them.

He grinned as Shivi rushed to him, squealing happily. He was a stocky, solidly-built Garwahli with a G.I. cut, enormously versatile and could 'fix' virtually anything using a mixture of charm and force of personality and if necessary, sheer physical strength. He had a disarming 'golden-toothed' smile and adored kids; Shivi and Trisha he protected like a Rottweiler. His wife, Komal, a round, rosy-cheeked tomato of a woman, usually rushed around the children, clucking like a distraught hen.

'Shivi baby!' Tikka lifted the little girl up, a wide grin on his face, 'What have you been eating? You've got so heavy!' He put her down and took her satchel.

Trisha smiled at him. 'Tikka—I need to practise riding the Bullet.'

'Okay, baby!' He grinned and winked. 'You'll come to school on the Bullet to scare your teachers?'

'Mom, we're home!' Trisha called as they entered, and Shivi charged off to the kitchen to hug Komal. Komal staggered out, Shivi on her hip, and smiled. 'Memsahib's in the studio,' she said, kissing Shivi on the cheek.

Trisha went up to the first floor, which had been converted into her mom's office-cum-studio. The whole floor had been partitioned into two rooms, well, actually three if you counted Mrs Almeida's (Mrs Bhave's secretary) glassed-in cabin. The smaller room through which you entered (after being vetted by Mrs Almeida) was where her mom met her clients; it had her desk and laptop at one end with chairs arranged opposite, and funky but comfortable leather and stainless steel armchairs and a sofa around a glass-topped coffee table, at the other. Along the partition wall was what her mom called her 'presentation table', where she displayed finished designs of her projects: sketches, photographs, models in clay and cardboard and thermocol. A door from this room opened out into the huge studio, with floor-to-ceiling glass windows on two sides, and cluttered with its drawing board and huge tables, many staggering under the weight of paints, modelling clay, sheets of cardboard and all the interesting and unusual raw materials and implements Mrs Bhave used for her work. In a cubicle in a corner of the studio was her fabulous Mac.

Trisha glanced into Mrs Almeida's cabin; it was empty and her computer was off—perhaps she was in the office. She knocked perfunctorily and poked her head around the office door. Her mom was lying on the settee, fast asleep. Trisha's eyebrows shot up and she looked around: no Mrs Almeida anywhere. She walked up quietly to her mom.

'Hey, Mom, wake up, we're home!'

Mrs Bhave's eyes fluttered open. 'Oh . . . oh . . . I must have dropped off . . .'

Trisha raised an eyebrow. 'So how's the Kasauli project coming along?' she asked mischievously. 'Hard at work on it? And where's old Almirah?'

Mrs Bhave sat up. 'Oh, she couldn't come in today.' She rubbed her forehead, looking a bit bemused, her eyes still heavy with sleep. 'I don't know what happened . . . I just lay down here for five minutes and dropped off.' She seemed surprised and a little annoyed. 'Well, yes, the Kasauli people came to see me this morning and signed the contract, so that's pucca in the bag; they even paid a fat advance.'

Shivi burst into the room and flung herself on her mother.

'Hello, sweetheart! How many kids did you beat up today?'

'None! I only put a pencil up that Ghanshyam's nose!'

'Mom, I want to practise riding Smelly Beast,' Trisha said, as they sat around the dining table. 'You said I should know how to.' Her mother raised her eyebrows.

'Oh? Sure . . . but you'll have to ask Tikka to take you somewhere safe.'

'He's fine with that.' Trisha looked hopeful.

'I know why she wants to ride! She only wants to show off to those two boys,' Shivi said, swinging her legs under the table.

'Shut up, Shivi, you don't know what you're talking about.'

'I do!'

'You don't!'

'Do too!

'Don't!'

Komal bustled out of the kitchen with a steaming pile of poha and crisp matar-aloo samosas.

'Wow!' said Shivi, rubbing her hands.

'Aren't you going to have some?' Trisha asked her mom, crunching into a samosa soaked in ketchup. Mrs Bhave shook her head.

'No, dear. Don't feel like it . . .'

'Memsahib's only had a little khichchiri since the morning,' Komal said, her beady black eyes flashing.

'You've got a bad tummy?'

'Well, not exactly, just not very hungry.'

They went across to the park after tea, and Trisha wondered if she'd meet Akshay and Jai again. They were there, just as she'd hoped—playing cricket with other boys, and they ignored her. She was too shy to wave and say hello herself, so she put her head down and walked on.

'Trish, aren't those the boys who came yesterday?' Shivi asked, pointing. 'Your new boyfriends?'

'Shivi, it's rude to point,' Trisha could feel the colour rise in her cheeks. 'And they're not my boyfriends.'

'Why aren't you saying hello?'

'Just shut up and let's go to the swings.'

'Oh, because then their friends would tease them that you're their girlfriend?'

'Shivi, you talk too much. Just get on the swing now.' She flinched when she heard the solid 'thunk' as the cricket ball was hit and a ragged cheer went up.

Of course it had to happen sooner or later, and it did. Some idiot thwacked the ball solidly and it bounced and rolled right up to the swings. Trisha picked it up as Akshay gave chase. He was red and sweaty as he pulled up some distance away from her.

'Hi,' she said, tossing the ball over-arm casually at him, spinning it with her wrist. He lunged and missed as it dipped, bounced and spun viciously at right angles to him.

'Oops, sorry!'

His eyes popped. 'Can . . . can you do that again?'

'What?'

'Spin the ball like that'

'I guess . . . why?'

He tossed the ball at her. 'Just do it again.'

She swung her arm around and tossed the ball. His eyes bulged some more. He could see it spinning viciously as a top as it climbed and dropped. Again, it took off virtually at right angles when it landed.

'My God!' he said, 'even Shane Warne couldn't do that!'

'Who's Shane Warne?' she asked.

From the pitch, the catcalls and crude laughter had begun.

He gulped. 'Can you bowl? Will you give it a shot?'

'Give what a shot?'

'Bowling. I mean cricket.'

She shrugged. 'I don't know. Why?'

'Because if you can spin the ball like that . . . please, just give it a shot?'

'Right now? In front of that lot? No, thanks.'

'Okay, okay, see the game's almost over. When they've gone, will you bowl to me or Jai?'

'Fine, I guess.'

'Thanks. I've got to go!'

He turned and ran back, as jeers and whistles greeted him.

About twenty minutes later the cricket game finished and the boys dispersed. Very casually, Akshay and Jai made their way over to her, as she sat on a bench with Shivi who was whining now that she wanted to go home.

'Okay,' Akshay said, glancing around to make sure his friends had disappeared. 'Come on. We've left the stumps on the pitch. Let's see you bowl. Jai, you keep wickets.'

She shrugged.

He showed her the bowling crease. 'You know what to do, right? You have to try and hit the stumps there with the ball. Just toss it over-arm like you did to me back there.'

'What can I do? What can I do?' Shivi demanded.

'You field. If I hit the ball, you run after it and collect it.'

'I'm always fetching!' Shivi grumbled, but hunkered down to field like she had seen the boys do.

Akshay took his guard and tapped his bat. 'Bowl.'

Trisha was quite flattered. It was nice to think that he thought she could bowl—or heck, was he just flirting? Of course it would all come to nothing; she'd miss hugely, or he'd thwack the ball through someone's window and that would be the end of it. There was no point taking it too seriously; she'd just end up being disappointed. But she liked the feel of the ball and its rough seam in her hand. She glanced at it; it was old and leathery: poor thing, she thought suddenly, what a fate it had—to spend its existence being thwacked all over the place till it came apart . . .

She looked down the pitch and squinted, measuring her distance. Then she trotted up to the wicket and rolled over her arm, rotating her wrist and fingers as she released the ball, sending it into a humming high arc, her eyes glued to the spot where she wanted it to land. At the other end, Akshay tried gauging its trajectory—it was far down the leg side—way too far. He swatted as it looped down, dipping suddenly, bounced in a puff of dust, and then maliciously like a driver darting across lanes, cut viciously across and cannoned into his stumps.

'Bowled first ball!' Behind the wickets, Jai was dazed and ecstatic.

Akshay looked equally stunned. A slow grin lit his face. There was no doubt about it: the chick could bowl.

'Fluke!' he snorted, tossing her the ball. 'Do it again!'

By the time they turned in, she had taken four wickets, including one near hat-trick, and her fingers were getting sore and her wrist had started to twinge.

'How did you learn to bowl like that?' Akshay asked. 'Who taught you?' She looked at the ground diffidently.

'Actually, I never learned. This is the first time I've tried it. Well, you know what you're supposed to hit; you know if you spin the ball, you need to land it at a particular spot . . .'

'But the way . . . the amount you spin it . . . the control you have . . .' He stared at her wrist. 'Show me your wrist, twirl it . . . wow!' He watched as she spun the ball up dizzily. For a moment he held her wrist delicately as she turned it around almost full circle to show him. 'It's so supple, it's amazing! Like that old fogey, Chandrashekhar.'

'Akshay, she should play in our team,' Jai said. 'Ask her if she'll play in our team!'

'Abbe are you mad? Can't you see she's a girl?' Akshay glared at his brother.

Jai shrugged. 'So what? There's nothing in the rules about girls not being allowed.'

'Maybe Trisha could cut her hair and pretend to be a boy!' Shivi said helpfully.

'Shivi, don't be nuts! As if I want to cut my hair.'

'It's for a good cause! Mommy says you should do things for a good cause.'

'Even if I do, it wouldn't work.'

'Why?'

'Why don't you shut up?'

'You shut up!'

Trisha glared exasperatedly at Shivi. Sometimes she could be really tiresome. She was nodding wisely now and wagging her finger. 'I know why! It's because you've got big, round boobies!'

Poor Akshay and Jai went scarlet and quickly looked away. Trisha too turned a deep shade of plum and hoped the ground would open and swallow her.

'I told you to shut up!' she hissed at her little sister. 'Can't you listen?'

'What?' Shivi said, cocking her head and cupping her hand to her ear. 'What? Come again?'

They had entered their driveway, the boys nonchalantly accompanying them. They gravitated automatically towards the Bullet, gleaming silver in the late twilight and parked just in front of the garage. Trisha glanced at them. The bike drew them like a magnet—that's why they had followed her home, she thought suddenly. It was the bike they were gunning for, and her ability to spin the cricket ball. It was nothing to do with her or, for that matter, her big 'boobies'.

'When . . . when do you think you'd be able to take us for a ride?' Akshay asked diffidently.

'I'll ask my mom and let you know,' she replied. This Saturday, she thought, this Saturday she'd have to shanghai Tikka and get him to take her for a practice session. Then, maybe on Sunday, or more likely the following weekend, she could take the brothers.

Early that Saturday morning, she snuck out of the house with Tikka. They drove quietly out of the gates, with Smelly Beast in the back of the pickup. (Tikka had very cunningly, late that night, driven the pickup a little way off, wheeled the bike to it and then ridden it up into the pickup.) Actually it was only poor Shivi they were avoiding, because if she knew they were going biking, she'd want to come too, and Shivi, early in the morning, could really be quite a hideous child—cranky, sleepy and petulant and prone to throwing tantrums. Of course, there would be hell to pay when they returned and she confronted them. But even Mrs Bhave had conspired with them.

Now, in the predawn cool, they drove through the nearly empty roads towards Kalindi Kunj, near the Okhla barrage. They stopped in the huge empty parking lot there and Tikka rolled the bike down from the back of the pickup and indicated that she climb on. Trisha was wearing a tough old denim jacket and jeans and had strapped on knee guards, elbow and arm pads and put on her scarlet and yellow helmet.

'Okay, baby, start it,' he said, standing at her side and holding the bike. She kicked it, once, twice and then the third time, the engine rumbled to life. Using the optional electric starter was more convenient but infra dig—especially in front of Tikka. She'd learnt the basics and ridden the bike before, many months ago, at first with her mom sitting pillion, yelling instructions in her ear and Tikka hovering close. Then of course, much too quickly, her mom had got off. 'Okay, dear, on your own now,' she had called, standing back and crossing her arms. Trisha still remembered the sheer thrill the first time she got her clutch, throttle and gear-change coordination perfect after endless tries (with the bike being plain cussed and stalling or threatening to rocket off till she wanted to kick the damn thing to pieces) and it sailed off majestically without racing, stalling or wobbling. It was a top-of-the world feeling but it didn't last, because at the end of the run while trying to U-turn, she slowed too much, stalled the engine . . . and dumped it, scraping her knee and the palms of her hands painfully. To her annoyance, Tikka was grinning like a monkey as he rushed up and helped her to her feet—and then proceeded to show her how to lift the heavy bike back upright.

'Try again,' he urged, though she was ready to go home. 'You have to try till you get it right—we will only leave when we win.' She was very nervous, but bit her lip and got on the bike again. And eventually had succeeded. She had practised diligently for nearly two months every day during those holidays—and had fallen off at least four times. And then school re-started and they shifted to Delhi, so biking was relegated to the background. Astride now, she was surprised how easily it all came back.

'Don't you dare dump me, Smelly Beast!' she muttered as she got a feel of the throttle and clutch and engaged the first gear. Gently, she released the clutch and revved the engine just a fraction. She set off cleanly, weaving and wobbling just a bit at first, the bike throbbing beneath her, the wind beginning to brush her cheeks. Tikka ran alongside, shouting encouragement. Carefully she banked into the turn as she approached the end; one leg automatically stuck out to brace herself on the ground if necessary, but the bike behaved beautifully. Soon she was doing steady laps of the parking lot, wanting to open the throttle more. A small motley crowd collected to watch her, slowly beginning to nod their heads in approval.

'Stop!' Tikka shouted, and she came to a halt, putting both her feet down and keeping the bike upright.

'Wow!' she said, thrilled. 'I haven't forgotten!'

'Now I'll put the cones.' Tikka went to the pickup and lifted out the set of six orange traffic cones he'd brought along. He set them down at fairly wide intervals and grinned at Trisha.

'All right, baby, go!'

She weaved past the first, overshot the second, knocked over the third (and almost lost her balance), missed the fourth, but weaved between the fifth and the last one okay.

'Do it again!' Tikka yelled, setting up the dropped cone.

At last she did three flawless rounds on the trot and Tikka grinned. 'Fust clash, baby, furst clash!' he shouted as she rode up to him, a huge grin plastered across her face.

'Now you'll ride on the highway?' he asked.

'What!'

'Don't worry, it's a private highway,' he grinned, his gold molars winking.

They crossed the Okhla barrage and drove past Noida for some way. Suddenly they veered off down a narrow, rutted two-lane road and bounced along it for about fifteen minutes, a huge cloud of dust billowing behind them. And then, suddenly in front of her, in the middle of nowhere as it were, the track ended, with massive boulders set across it. Beyond the boulders, like some immense runway, an empty six-lane highway stretched to the horizon. It was part of an ambitious unfinished highway project that had run into trouble with the courts—and all work had stopped several months ago. Tikka swung the pickup off the road down the steep verge, lurched dead slow over and through tussocks and rocks, and then roared back up the steep embankment on to the abandoned highway.

'It's dead straight for twenty kilometres.' She looked around, amazed. The sun had just come up, vividly orange: in a few moments it would turn the countryside to gold. The land was flat and barren, interspersed with big rocks and clumps of high, silver-fronded grass on which small birds clung and yelled their heads off. Above, the sky was pink in the east, but still dark blue in the west. Ahead, the highway stretched till it merged with the horizon. She looked at its surface: it seemed quite smooth but there were already signs of erosion and potholes here and there.

She started riding, enjoying the clean breeze in her face and the steady thump of the engine beneath her. The bike ran rock steady, and behind her Tikka kept pace in the pickup. She grinned and opened up the throttle. The speedometer swung from 30 to 40 and then to 50 kmph. Soon she was doing 60 and was thrilled to bits. She had never ridden Smelly Beast so fast; she narrowed her eyes and watched the road ahead as the ground whizzed past her. It was a bit bumpy and gravelly in places where the surface had started disintegrating but the heavy bike just steamrolled over the imperfections. At 65, Tikka swung wide and passed her, waving his hand and indicating she should not go any faster. Then he swung in front of her and began slowing down, making her slow down too.

'Oh . . . oh,' she thought, 'he's going to do the slow-motion routine.' He wanted to see how slow she could ride without having to put her feet down or wobble the bike too much or God forbid stall and fall over.

They rode and drove up and down that entire 20-km stretch, by which time Trisha had begun feeling completely at home with the bike.

'Next time we'll take that road,' he said, pointing to a furrowed path that ran across the fields. 'Your control is fine on a straight road and through the cones, now we'll see on a crooked and broken road.' He grinned wickedly. 'And then in Delhi's traffic!'

'Tikka, can we come tomorrow?' she asked. 'I want to bring some friends along.'

He raised his eyebrows and frowned. 'Those boys who were looking at the bike yesterday?' He distrusted teenage boys around big bikes.

She nodded. 'Haan—yes, they only want to ride pillion. They've never been on a Bullet.'

'Okay, if Memsahib permits it.'

She was tired but exhilarated as they reached home.

'Mom!' she yelled, 'it was just great! That bike is fabulous! I could ride it all day!'

Shivi came charging out, all fired up. 'Why did you go without me? I hate you, I hate you, I hate you! And Tikka too! I hate you both! I hope you die!'

'You were fast asleep.'

'So wake me! You wake me for school but not for this! I hate you!' She charged at Trisha and beat her fists against her. 'You only want to have all the fun by yourself!'

'Hey, hey, easy. Baby, what can I do? You're always so cranky in the mornings and anyway Tikka was just teaching me.'

'I'm not cranky!' Shivi burst into tears. 'You don't love me! None of you love me! You have all the fun without me!' she bawled. 'You leave me alone every time! I hate you all!'

Mrs Bhave came out of her room and picked up Shivi and wiped her cheeks.

'Hey, hey, Shivi baby, that's okay. You know, you really are getting heavy. Listen, Trish will take you to the bank this morning—how would you like that?'

Shivi swallowed a sob.

'On Smelly Beast?'

'No, you know she can't ride Smelly Beast on the roads as yet. The police will catch her and put her in jail.'

'Good.'

'But if you're with her, they'll catch you too.'

'Oh.'

'So have your breakfast now, and later on Trisha and Tikka will take you to the bank. How about that?'

Trisha pricked up her ears, her heart dropping down a deep well. 'Er . . . Mom? What's this about the bank?'

'I want you to cash a cheque for me, that's all.'

Trisha shook her head and put up her hands. 'No, no . . . oh no, not me, Mom. I've never done that before. I wouldn't know what to do—I'm allergic to banks—they always look at you as if you're going to rob them.'

'That's exactly why, sweetheart; it's time you got rid of your allergy.'

'Mom, please.'

'Sweetheart, there's nothing to it.'

'I want to cash a cheque too!' Shivi said. 'Why should only Trisha be allowed to?'

'You will—when you're older. Now you can watch Trisha and see how it's done.'

'Mom, I need to see how it's done,' Trisha said dismally. What if she made some sort of blooper?

'Actually,' her mother went on, going into her room and coming out with her cheque book. 'You can write and sign the cheque too. It's our joint account. Remember I'd made you sign when we opened the account?'

Trisha eyed the cheque book as if it would bite her.

'How much is the cheque for?' she asked.

'Twenty thousand.'

'Twenty thousand bucks?! I can't carry twenty thousand bucks!'

'Darling, Tikka will be waiting outside. Nothing will happen. Now bring a pen and come to the dining table.'

Laboriously and in her best handwriting, Trisha wrote out the cheque.

'Now sign it, darling.'

For a second her pen wavered, then she swallowed, got a grip and signed: Trisha Bhave. 'Done!' Her mom crossed her arms and smiled. 'And now sweetheart, guard that cheque with your life. If anyone finds it lying around, they can go to the bank and cash it!'

'What?' Trisha squeaked, grabbing the cheque. 'Mom! You're horrible!'

Shivi, of course, was hugely excited as they set off later that morning. A ball of dread had settled in poor Trisha's stomach as they approached the bank, the cheque snug in her handbag. What if something went wrong? What if someone snatched the cheque from her hand and said it was theirs? What if someone snatched the money as she walked out of the bank? What if the bank fellow said the signature did not match and called the manager and then the police? No two signatures could be identical. What if they arrested her?

'Tikka,' she pleaded. 'Will you come with me inside the bank, please?'

He shook his head. 'It's a tow-away zone, I'll have to keep an eye on the cops.'

Shivi, of course, was in a lather of excitement. They entered the gleaming bank, through the metal detectors which beeped frantically and made her jump (must be her bangles and hoops . . . oh, why didn't she take them off? And maybe the buckle of her skirt's belt . . . but she couldn't have taken that off!). Inside she looked around uncertainly as Shivi stared wide-eyed. Ah, there they were—the teller windows, six of them altogether, two with a 'Use the Next Counter' placard outside. She could see just the heads of the tellers behind the glass partitions. She took a deep breath and stood behind a fat, sweaty man in a safari suit in the third row because there was just one person ahead of him. She rummaged in her bag and took the cheque out, hoping her sweaty fingers wouldn't smudge the signatures.

At last her turn came, and she thrust the cheque through the window at the scrubbed-looking young man behind the glass.

'What's happening? What's happening? I want to see!' Shivi stood valiantly on tiptoe, but the counter was just too high. 'Pick me up!'

'Shivi, please! Behave yourself!'

'Pick me up, Trisha, I want to see! I want to *see*!'

'Oh okay, but stop whining, will you? You're such a nuisance!' She lifted her little sister up, so she could look through the glass.

'There,' Trisha said, with a sudden gush of affection, giving her an impulsive peck on the cheek, 'now you can see, okay, baby?'

Shivi's eyes were like saucers as she watched the teller pull out a fat wad of notes, yank out a handful and begin to count them. Trisha's lips had started moving automatically and silently too as she counted along. He twined a rubber band around them and put them into the automatic counting machine, which went *whhhrrrrr*, making Shivi's eyes nearly fall out in surprise and delight. The machine stopped obediently at 40 and the man repeated the process.

'Sign at the back twice, ma'am,' he said, pushing the cheque back at Trisha.

'Yes . . . listen, Shivi, I'm going to put you down—I can't sign otherwise.'

'Bhhhrrrrr!' Shivi said, entranced, 'that machine counts so fast! Bhhhrrrr!' She could watch it all day. Trisha signed and handed back the cheque, her heart beginning to beat fast again. The man glanced at it and nodded and handed her the wad of notes which she stuffed in the deepest recesses of her bag.

'Can we buy ice cream now?' Shivi asked. 'You've got so much money!'

Suddenly Trisha felt great . . . she could do anything! She could cash cheques all day! There really was nothing to it. 'Okay, Shivi, let's have ice cream!' she said, as they climbed back into the Toyota where Tikka had been listening to old Hindi film songs on the radio.

That afternoon Trisha wondered if the boys would be in the park; she could ask them if they'd like to come for a ride on Smelly Beast and maybe they'd ask her to bowl again. But then her mom asked her to accompany her to the clinic where her ultrasound test was to be done.

This time Shivi didn't mind too much being left behind: she didn't like going to hospitals. 'I'll say hi to your boyfriends,' she said, waving to them as they drove out. 'And tell them that you miss them!' Trisha glowered.

There was a crowd milling around the reception, waving reports and receipts and folders in the faces of the girls manning the counters.

'Trish, will you show the girl this? I have an appointment at 5.'

Trisha quickly occupied a spot vacated by a fat woman and thrust Dr Khurana's note at the girl.

'Fill in the form,' she said, jerking her head towards a table where two heaps of forms lay. 'Yellow one.'

Trisha paled. If there was one thing she hated more than going to the bank (well, not anymore really) it was filling in forms. They filled her with dread. What if she made a mistake? Would they make her fill it up again and again till they closed for the day? Would a bell suddenly ring and someone shout, 'All those who haven't filled in their forms are disqualified!' She hated them.

'Mom, we have to fill this first,' she said, taking the form to her mother and holding it as if it were infected with the plague.

'Will you do it, darling?' her mother said glancing at it. 'It seems simple enough.'

'Mom, you know how I hate forms!'

'They won't bite you, sweetheart,' her mom said, picking up a tattered copy of *Society* magazine.

Actually it really was quite easy. Suddenly Trisha bit her lip and smiled. What if she filled in her mom's age as 394? And her name as Drew Barrymore? And her husband/father's name as 'None of Your Business'? Well, this was a medical matter, so she'd better fill it up correctly. She filled it up and showed it to her mother who glanced at it and smiled. At the counter, the girl didn't even bother; she scanned it swiftly, scribbled something and asked: 'You are the patient?'

'No, my mom.'

'Okay, pay Rs 600 to the cashier and tell your mother to drink one bottle of water. Her name will be called.'

Trisha bought a bottle of water and sat down next to her mother. The TV was showing the news, and people kept drifting in and out. A young mother in a shocking pink salwar suit tried pacifying her tiny baby, as her husband looked on indifferently. Occasionally a door would open and a technician would bark out a name and someone would get up hurriedly and follow. So many people needed tests, she thought. They all had something wrong with their insides. What was wrong with that tiny baby? Why was she here?

Mrs Bhave's name was eventually called and twenty minutes later, Trisha and her mom were walking out of the clinc.

'Did it hurt, Mom?'

'No, dear. All they do is put a microphone on your tummy and it takes a picture of your insides using echoes, I think—rather like what happens in a submarine.'

In the pickup on the way back home she asked:

'Mom, can I take Akshay and Jai for a ride on Smelly Beast tomorrow morning? I want to take them to that fabulous empty highway I told you about.'

'Okay, but don't let them ride. And make sure they've got permission and they wear helmets.'

'Pillion,' she said firmly. 'They'll be pillion.' She frowned. 'There's only one thing. I don't think Shivi's going to let me out of her sight again. She'll go ballistic if I ditch her a second time.'

'Hmmm . . . I think you'll have to take her this time. Usually she behaves better when there are other people around.'

It was about 6.30 by the time they got back home, and Shivi and Komal were just heading back from the park.

'Where are you going? We're going home, can't you see?'

'I'm just going for a walk,' Trisha replied. She glanced quickly into the park. Today's cricket game was just about winding up again, amidst much acrimonious shouting and yelling. Obviously someone was objecting vociferously to being given out.

'Those boys,' Shivi said scornfully. 'All they do is fight and shout. They hardly play.'

Trisha grinned. 'They must have seen you.'

'So?' Shivi looked at her suspiciously.

'So they know a champion fighter-cock is watching them and wants to show off.'

'Hah! I'm not a fighter-cock.'

'Abbe, you were out . . . right in front, plumb lbw!'

'Abbe, are you blind? Did you see where the ball pitched? And where it was going? You're blind or what? Kanya!'

Trisha gave a sudden snort of laughter. 'I'm telling you they've got influenced by you, Shivi. You could start a war in no time!'

'The umpire's decision is final. You're out. We've won! We've won!'

'The bloody umpire is in your pocket!'

'I'll show you what's in my pocket.'

'You can't bat to save your life. And when you're out you yell and scream like a girl.'

'I can bat. Better than you at least. Scored a big fat duck and talking!'

'You can't bat. I bet a chick can get you out!'

'Hah! Let's see.'

And suddenly, Trisha found that the whole sweaty, dishevelled group was looking at her and Shivi. The batsman who was refusing to vacate the crease was a tall, fair boy with light brown hair; he was

striding about the crease, swinging his bat about. He grinned and
pointed his bat at her.

'Hey, man—there's a chick, ask her if she can get me out. Hah!
Do you have the guts to even ask her?'

'Ravi—that's the same girl Akshay was line lagaoing yesterday.'

'So? Call her.'

'Okay, I will.' Akshay came running up.

'Hi, um . . . will you do me a favour?'

'Hi . . . what?' Her eyes opened wide. 'Oh, no—no I don't play
cricket.'

His eyes were pleading. 'Please! Just one ball. Like you bowled to
me yesterday! If you get him out . . . man oh man!'

'I can't.'

Akshay glanced at the group, who were beginning to guffaw and
jeer. 'Please,' he said hoarsely. 'Just . . . just imagine you are bowling
to me.'

'Oh.' That was just so sweet, she thought suddenly, warming to
him, and that must have hurt his ego—to admit that she could get
him out easily. 'Umm . . . okay, is he good?'

'He's more a big mouth than a big hitter. Come on!'

She trailed behind shyly as he led her to the group.

'Okay, guys, this is Trisha. She's agreed to bowl to Ravi and get
him out as he wants!'

Jeers and wolf whistles rent the air. Ravi swaggered up; he picked
up the ball and tossed it to Trisha. 'Hi, ever thrown a ball before? Ever
held a cricket ball?'

'Okay, here's the deal,' Akshay said, his eyes alive again. 'If Trisha
gets you out, you will swear never to argue with the umpire again,
no matter how bad his decision is.'

'Oye, chal! And if I hit her for six, then I get to bat three times
in every innings.'

Ravi sauntered back to the wicket and took guard, tapping the
bat menacingly.

'Okay, Trisha—just imagine it's me,' said Akshay with a lopsided
grin. 'You got me three times yesterday!'

'What kind of field would you like?' one of the boys asked as Jai
went behind the wickets.

'What do you mean?'

'Where would you like us to stand?' the boy said as the others burst out laughing.

'Oh, anywhere,' she shrugged. 'What difference does it make?'

There was much snorting and shoving as the boys took their positions. At the other end, Ravi licked his lips and grinned, raising the bat halfway to his shoulder like a weapon.

Trisha took a deep breath, suddenly wondering how she had got herself into such a pickle. She gripped the ball and twirled it in her hand. The boy who was the umpire lowered his hand. 'Bowl,' he said.

She looked at the leering batsman. He was standing cheekily out of his crease, looking as if he wanted to swat a fly. Well, she knew how difficult that could be. She trotted up to the wicket, rolled over her arm and twirled her wrist, her eyes once again fixed hypnotically at the spot where she wanted it to land.

Ravi's sneer grew wider as he saw the ball arc high and far to the legside. He stood up straight and put his bat on the ground.

'Abbe, can't she see the stumps are here . . . not in GK!' he sneered, as the ball landed and jinked sharply and headed like a homing missile into his wickets.

'Bowled!' The whole team was jumping up and down yelling, as Ravi goggled at his shattered stumps.

'B . . . b-but . . .'

'Bowled first ball! Abbe, nikal! Get out!'

Akshay charged up and exchanged high fives with her.

'Abbe, I wasn't ready!' Ravi shouted. 'Didn't you see I wasn't ready?'

After much shouting they agreed (Trisha very reluctantly) to give Ravi another chance.

Trisha turned around and squinted down the pitch. She glanced at Ravi and then fixed her eyes on where she wanted the ball to land. She trotted over and as she began raising her arm, Ravi came dancing down the pitch, leering and raising his bat. But she only saw the spot where she wanted to land the ball, and Ravi was nowhere near it. The ball sailed past him as he tried to get in line, pitched, spun and missed the stumps by a whisker, only to be collected gleefully by Jai who whipped the bails off as the whole team went up again in delight.

'Howzzat?'

Stranded halfway down the pitch, Ravi looked like an even bigger fool than he had when she had bowled him out.

'Oye, Ravi, would you like her to get a hat-trick?' Akshay yelled.

But Ravi was eyeing her speculatively. Damn woman had got him out twice in succession, both flukes of course. But if it happened again, he wouldn't be able to show his face here ever again.

'Bah!' he snorted, slouching off.

'Go! Go home!'

Some of the other boys were eyeing her with respect.

She took a deep breath. 'Listen,' she said softly to Akshay. 'Do you want a ride on Smelly Beast tomorrow morning?'

'What?' Akshay's eyes lit up even more. 'Oh, sure!'

'You'll have to get permission from your parents.'

'Sure, no problem. Where?'

She fixed up the pick-up time (5.30 a.m.) and place (outside her gate) and walked home feeling light and happy. On an impulse she decided to call Gullu too—it would be fun with her.

Gullu was gobsmacked.

'Trish, was your mom a hippie or flower girl? She's letting you go biking on a Bullet with two guys! My mom's a housecoat!' Poor Gullu glanced at her mother, stomping around in flip-flops, her hair like a squirrel's nest, wearing an ancient dressing gown, yelling at the cook as the pressure cooker went nuclear yet again.

Trisha giggled. 'I'll tell Mom you think she's a hippie!'

'Don't you dare!'

Trisha put down the phone to find Shivi glaring at her. 'I'm coming too,' she said. 'You have to take me!'

'Okay, okay, sure! Keep your hair on!'

'My hair is all right,' Shivi felt her curls. 'Promise?'

'I promise. But you have to be good.'

'I'm always good.'

'Ya, of course.'

At dinner that night, Trisha glanced at her mother's plate. It was virtually empty.

'Not hungry again?'

'Uh-huh.'

'Mom, Trisha played cricket with the boys in the park,' Shivi said. 'And she got one fellow out twice.'

'Shivi . . . shut up!'

'That's good, dear.'

'All the boys were doing high fives with her then.'

Mrs Bhave yawned and pushed away her plate. 'Now sweethearts, I'm off to bed. Goodnight. Shivi, it's your bedtime too! Have a good time tomorrow and be careful on the bike.'

'Goodnight, Mom!'

CHAPTER FOUR

'If We're History, You're Toast!'

Akshay and Jai were outside Trisha's gate at 5.25 the next morning, glancing at their watches and looking anxious. She went out to greet them and raised her eyebrows. They were both dressed in white and Akshay had a kitbag over his shoulder.

'Hi! We're going biking, not to play cricket,' she said. He grinned sheepishly.

'Papa thinks we're going to school for net practice,' he said. 'We said we'd be picked up from the main road.'

Shivi emerged, kitted out in a bright orange jumpsuit, helmet and purple stardust shades, followed by Komal staggering under the weight of a picnic hamper.

'Let's go!' Shivi called excitedly. 'Let's go!'

The two boys gleefully leapt into the back with the bike. They picked up Gullu, who squashed in with Shivi and Trisha in the front, and set off. At the turn-off point, Tikka stopped.

'Tell them to close their noses, it's going to get dusty!'

Both the boys rammed their baseball caps hard down over their foreheads and masked their faces with handkerchiefs.

A few minutes later Tikka drove the pickup on to the deserted highway and parked. 'Right!' said Trisha, 'We're ready to go riding!' They gathered around Smelly Beast, which Tikka had quickly brought down and dusted.

'Who wants to come first?' She leaned the bike slightly towards her, climbed on expertly and kicked it to life.

Gullu went first, helped aboard by Tikka. She clung to Trisha like a leech.

'Relax, Gullu, put your feet on the footrests there. Just sit back comfortably. Okay, here we go!' Trisha sang happily. Gullu screwed her eyes shut and screamed faintly as they sailed off. Five minutes later they were back and Gullu's big black eyes were shining.

'Wow! That was so cool! I love it!'

'Trisha, I want to go next!' Shivi said, jumping up and down. 'Can I sit up front with you?'

'No, not in front. Come on at the back.' Tikka helped Shivi up; beaming, she wrapped her arms around Trisha's waist and off they went.

Jai took his turn next, and she took him for a longer ride.

'Her mom taught her! Can you imagine?' Gullu told Akshay as they waited. 'They go on biking holidays to the Himalayas! What a mom! Mine teaches me to make kaddu ki sabzi!'

'My dad would have a fit if he saw us now,' Akshay grinned. 'We'd be grounded for life! He thinks bikes should be banned altogether. He was shocked when he saw the bike in the back of the pickup when he went to see Mrs Bhave.'

Smelly Beast rumbled up and stopped. Jai hopped down and took off Mrs Bhave's helmet. His eyes were shining. 'Wow, that was great, thanks!'

Trisha glanced at Akshay. 'Is this your first time on a bike too?' she asked.

Akshay nodded, the colour rising in his face. To admit to a girl who rode a Bullet that he'd never been on a motorbike before . . . 'Papa doesn't allow us,' he mumbled.

'Come on then, hop on.'

'Could you point out the controls to me, first?' Akshay asked.

Feeling like a million bucks she pointed out the levers for the throttle, front brake, clutch, and the gear and footbrake.

'Basically, you have to get your coordination of clutch, throttle and gear right,' she explained. 'See, this light means it's in neutral, now you pull the clutch lever towards you like this, slightly increase the throttle, engage first gear and gently, gently engage the clutch and off you go . . .' Of course, just to spite her, Smelly Beast stalled and she had to put her feet down hastily. 'Dammit!' she said, kicking it alive again. 'It always does this to me.'

She glanced at Akshay. He was looking at her as if she had just descended from the clouds or something, which made her feel very good indeed. She had junked her denim jacket and was wearing a summery lemon yellow top, with a rather risky U-shaped neckline—cool for a hot day. Akshay thought she looked just great.

'Okay, climb aboard, let's go.'

He got on, just touching her shoulders lightly with his fingertips in the process. 'Here we go!' Behind her, Akshay stared at her dark bouncy hair and those tanned arms stretched out towards the handlebars. She turned around and smiled and he became a puddle again.

'How do you like it?'

'Great!'

'Would you like to learn how to ride?'

He just nodded, grinning like an idiot.

'I could teach you.'

'When?'

'After the demo?'

She took him down the straight road for about 5 kilometres before dropping gears, slowing down and turning around perfectly, and returning. At one point she'd gone up to 70 kmph and was feeling rather kicked about that. As always, there was a serenity and calmness that came with the rhythmic throb of the engine—it seemed unstoppable as time itself. And then she had a crazy idea. They had just passed the place where Tikka had pointed out the rutted track leading off the highway, where he said he'd take her. She did a wide U-turn and headed back towards it, slowing down as she approached. 'Let's go cross country,' she yelled. 'Hang on, it'll be a bit bumpy!' She changed down to second and guided the bike down the embankment, both her feet just flicking the ground from time to time. As the front end dipped, she felt Akshay's hands grip her shoulders and his chest bump against her back as he leaned forwards against her.

Sitting in the pickup, Tikka noticed the change in the note of the bike's engine and turned off the radio.

'Oye!' he yelled. 'Trisha baby, where are you going?' Then he grinned. The bike had clambered down safely and was bumping its way along the kachcha road, with Trisha baby sitting straight-backed and in perfect control and the chokra clinging on to her. Occasionally it disappeared behind the high fountains of silvery moonj grass that grew up from the sides. To Trisha's delight the road surface suddenly improved and she accelerated. On both sides, rainwater from a recent thunderstorm gleamed in narrow ditches that ran alongside, mossy green and evil looking, the pools fringed by the whispering silver grass fronds.

'I love biking,' she yelled. 'There's nothing like it. It's much better than a car. Isn't it beautiful?' Behind her, Akshay nodded, bumping his helmet against hers and still lightly holding on to her shoulders. The Bullet throbbed on steadily.

'*Bloody goats, where did they come from?*' Trisha yelped as a swarm of goats suddenly materialized from the surrounding scrub and high grass and decided to cross the road all at the same time, just as they rumbled towards them. The animals saw them and promptly panicked and went skittering hither and thither, some taking flying leaps off the road to avoid the bike, some galloping down it, some charging stupidly towards them, bleating manically. Trisha braked, using more front brake than she ought to have. The front wheel skidded on the gravel and turned at right angles . . . and met an inundation. The bike stopped abruptly and tipped over on its side, with slow deliberation.

'JUMP!' Trisha screamed and leapt clear of the toppling bike and behind her, Akshay had the presence of mind to follow suit. Trisha flew headlong over the edge of the road, her arms and hands spread out protectively, and landed on her tummy with a resounding splash in the muddy ditch at the bottom. Akshay rolled down and landed right beside her in the squelch. From three sides, the feathery silver grass leaned over them, concealing them from the highway.

For a moment neither of them moved or spoke. The only sound was that of Smelly Beast's engine still rumbling. Gasping and spluttering, Trisha pushed herself up on her hands and knees. The mud was soft and slithery at the bottom, and she was elbow-deep in the water. She got on to her knees and levered her helmet off, shaking her hair

loose. Her bright yellow top was soaked through and stuck to her, and
the bow of the strap had come undone off one shoulder. She stared
at Akshay, who seemed dazed. He just sat there propping himself up
with his hands, his legs stretched out in front of him. His cricketing
whites were ruined.

Oh God, what had she done! What would he be thinking? On his
very first ride she'd deposited him in a ditch full of mud! Big fancy
biker she was! Really, she ought not to have showed off like that.
Now he'd develop a phobia against bikes for the rest of his life and it
would be her fault. He would hate them with a passion . . . and would
obviously stop being friends with her. He might think she'd done this
deliberately, like it was some stunt—or to show him exactly where he
got off with her. Why hadn't she just stayed on the highway?

'Hey Akshay, are you okay?' she asked, her heart thudding. Up on
the road, Smelly Beast was lying on its side, still rumbling quietly like
an incipient volcano. She leaned forward and gently prised his helmet
off his head and tossed it to the edge of the pond, next to hers. He
had a funny glazed look in his eyes.

He nodded bemusedly. 'I think so. Whew,' he said rubbing his
head. 'That was close! What happened?'

'I'm so sorry, I really am! Stupid goats! I should have seen them
earlier! Are you sure you're okay?'

'I'm fine,' he said as his hands slipped in the soft mud at the bottom.
'Yikes!' He lost his balance and fell back with a gloopy splash.

'Hey, take it easy!' She leant forward and caught his arms and
pulled him up. 'Come on up, we better get out of this swamp. You're
stuck!' She tugged again. He floundered for a moment, like a fish
in the shallows, the soft sticky mud sucking him back. Suddenly
he plopped free and sat up in a rush, falling forwards against her.
She felt his chest thump against her and instinctively they clung
together for balance, cheek against cheek and their arms around
each other. They remained like that for a long, teetering moment,
and when he tightened his grip around her for support, she did
the same. Then they let go and rocked back simultaneously on their
heels and for another long moment eyeballed each other in their
little mud pool, perfectly screened from the world. He was goggling

at her, going red in the face and suddenly, yikes, she realized that her top had slithered halfway down her body. She blushed crimson and adjusted it hastily, not that it made too much difference now that it was soaked through. But what would he be thinking? She couldn't really blame him if he picked himself up and made for the horizon post-haste.

In the pickup, Tikka was frowning. Again there had been a change in the note of the Bullet's engine . . . and then it had stopped. He stared at the road Trisha had taken—the bike had vanished—perhaps it had gone behind one of those tall clumps of grass. He got out and walked a little distance, staring at the road. And then he spotted the chrome glinting in the sun as the bike lay on its side.

'Chalo! Come on!' he roared, startling poor Gullu and Jai and Shivi, who were playing French cricket to pass the time. 'Get in!' The pickup raced down the road.

In the ditch Akshay and Trisha struggled to their feet and waded out.

'Now what?' Akshay said, as they emerged, soaked and covered with mud and leaves, dangling their helmets in their hands. He looked at the bike, still on its side. The engine had shut down.

'Now we pick it up and hope it starts and ride back,' said Trisha. 'Come on, give me a hand. God, what a mess!' She glanced at him. 'You're sure you're not hurt anywhere? I'm really sorry.'

'No, I'm okay. Thanks. It's fine.'

'The soft mud saved us.'

Between them they hoisted the bike up. 'Right,' Trisha panted, 'let's hope it starts.' She looked the bike over for a moment. 'It seems okay, it was a soft, slow tumble. No petrol or oil has leaked. The mirror's gone a bit crooked but it was mostly useless anyway. Okay first, we have to turn it around.' They swivelled it around and she got on and grinned at him mischievously. 'Want a lift, mister?'

'Look, the cavalry's on its way too,' he said, suddenly pointing to the highway. The Toyota pickup was racing towards the turnoff. He stared at Trisha—he had never met someone so beautiful (even when covered with mud and dead leaves) and wonderful and plain gutsy before. And he couldn't forget the wonderful soft feel of her against his chest. He climbed up behind her and diffidently put his hands on her shoulders. 'Let's go.'

The bike started on the third kick, just as the pickup drew up at the turning, and Tikka charged out. The rugged track was too narrow for the vehicle. Then he stopped as he heard the deep-throated baritone of the engine. He stared at the two ragamuffins riding towards them.

'Oh my God! What happened to you two?' Gullu screamed.

'Bakri—goats!' Trisha explained to Tikka who was looking very concerned as he rushed up and helped them off. 'They came so suddenly!'

Tikka heaved a sigh of relief when he saw they were okay.

Shivi looked them up and down and screwed up her nose. 'Now you are the smelly beasts,' she declared. 'You'd better sit in the back when we go home.'

Like a magician Tikka vanished into the pickup and emerged with a huge green towel. Akshay had taken off his sodden shirt and spread it out on the bonnet of the pickup. Trisha glanced at him surreptitiously: he was quite sturdy and had a cute belly button, she thought, hiding a grin, but there was no hair on his chest as yet!

'It should dry quickly,' he said. 'But what the hell am I going to tell Mama?'

'That you were practising diving catches in a pond!' Jai said with a snort of laughter.

'Baby, should we go home?' Tikka asked. Trisha wrapped the towel around her shoulders and shook her head.

'Let's have our picnic!' She grinned. 'Then Akshay wants to learn how to ride.'

'How many times have you fallen off the bike?' Akshay asked her, taking a huge bite out of a ham and cheese sandwich and stuffing some chips into his mouth at the same time.

'Counting this time, five.'

'Did you ever get hurt?'

'Bruised and scraped, yes—quite nastily once! No bones broken or anything—thank God.'

'And your mom lets you ride regardless? Wow!'

'Well, she says it's better I learn to ride properly with her permission rather than slyly behind her back. Of course she doesn't want me to ride a racing bike or anything like that.' She grinned. 'Actually she's probably scared I'll take off on the back of a bike of some ghastly Hells Angel stud type.'

She glanced at Akshay and flashed him a mischievous grin. 'But I think I'll give you your first lesson next time. We're not properly dressed for that. How does next weekend sound? Make sure you wear a thick jacket or something, or you'll get horribly scraped if you fall.'

'Mommy, do you know what happened?' Shivi yelled excitedly, charging into the house. 'Trisha took that Akshay fellow piggyback on the bike and they fell into a pond! She's all muddy and stinky!'

'Shivi, will you please shut up?' Trisha hissed.

Mrs Bhave came out of her room and looked at Trisha. 'Are you all right? No cuts and bruises . . . or worse?'

'No, Mom, I'm fine, really!'

'Good, be careful, darling . . .'

'Mommy, she's going to teach Akshay how to ride next time!' Shivi informed her and went on virtuously, 'but Dr Khurana doesn't want them to ride bikes!'

'Shivi, will you shut up? You're not coming next time!'

'Man, that was cool,' Jai said, sitting down at his drums later that morning and trying to produce Smelly Beast's beat. 'Doesn't this sound like the bike, Akshay?'

'Rubbish! But yeah, what a bike! Can you imagine riding up on a bike like that for a concert?' He sat down at the piano and thundered out a few chords. 'All the chicks will be swooning over us.'

'Yeah, like you're swooning over Trisha.'

'I'm not swooning over anyone!'

'Man, have you seen the goofy look on your face when you talk to her?'

'Don't talk bull!'

'You like her, don't you?'

'I don't. Shut up! But she is different from other chicks.'

'Yeah, she's different all right.'

'You know, she might like jazz and reggae too. Let's ask her if she knows who Miles Davis is next time . . . or Ella Fitzgerald . . . or Bob Marley.' Akshay got off his piano stool and picked up his saxophone.

'Come on, man, we'd better practise a bit.'

The loud plangent sounds of a saxophone punctuated by frantic drumming filled the house. Their parents were still out. Suddenly Akshay stopped.

'Hey,' he said, 'maybe we should call Trisha over to listen. I mean, we hardly know if we're good or not . . . hardly anyone likes this stuff anymore . . . so maybe she can tell us.'

Trisha was surprised. 'Oh . . . wow, you guys play jazz? You have a piano at home? What do you call yourself?'

'Um . . . we haven't yet thought up a name actually. Maybe you could help us!'

'I don't know, but hey, sure I'll come and hear you! What do you play?'

'Oh, just stuff, you know . . . any old-time tune that we sort of jazz up, and sometimes we just make up stuff as we go along. And reggae—Jai loves it. Okay, it'll be really great if you'd come.'

'When do you practise?'

'Usually at night—about 8 or so. We eat at 9.'

'I'll have to ask my mom; anyway, I'll let you know.'

That evening, when Shivi was safely away at the park with Komal, Trisha tackled her mom. Mrs Bhave smiled.

'Well, I have to meet Dr Khurana at 7.30 tomorrow at his clinic with my reports, so we could go together.'

'Can I stay on for dinner?'

'Sure, darling. I'll get dropped and send Tikka to fetch you at around 10 then. No later, it's a school night, remember.'

'Thanks, Mom. You're the greatest.'

'I know!'

Dr Khurana's clinic adjoined his residence. The waiting room was brightly lit with immaculate brass lamps wearing Chinese hat shades;

the walls and furniture and floor were all a pristine white. A money plant, which obviously had been polished three times a day, gleamed in a brass plant holder, and at one end, multicoloured tropical fish twirled in an aquarium. Even the receptionist was dressed in white from head to toe, as was the nurse who stepped out of the doctor's room every now and then to call a patient. There were already three people waiting, softly talking into their phones or flipping through the magazines.

'Mom, this is like coming through heaven's door,' Trisha giggled as they sat down. 'There's a lot of white noise here!' She went on: 'Hey Mom, did I tell you . . . Akshay and Jai play jazz too!'

'Really? Why don't you go and join them?'

'It's okay, I'll wait . . .'

Dr Khurana too was all white-coated, his hair perfectly groomed, his moustache trimmed. 'So how are you feeling today, Mrs Bhave?' he asked as they sat down in front of him. At one end of the room was a bed, with a curtain that could be drawn across for privacy. 'Would you lie down, please?'

Five minutes later, he scribbled something on a pad. 'It'll be best if you have an MRCP done,' he said, 'as they've suggested in the report. We'll see that and then decide a further course of action.'

He glanced at Trisha who was looking anxious. 'So you are the girl my wife tells me the boys have been raving about. You play cricket very well she said.'

Trisha blushed. 'Where are they, Doctor? They called me over.'

'They'll be at the house . . . just ring the front door bell.'

She waved her mom goodbye and rang the bell and waited, admiring the pretty hanging plants in the porch. A tiny, wizened old woman opened the door and let her in, smiling toothlessly.

'I'll call them,' she said and vanished. Trisha sank into an armchair and looked around. Huge, obscenely expensive oil paintings hung on the walls and heavy cut-glass glittered in cabinets. One wall had bookshelves, floor to ceiling—and every book was a fat, glossy hardback. A flat-screened TV set and an expensive sound system occupied another corner.

'Hey, hi, come on in!' Akshay materialized suddenly, grinning at her. He led her through a corridor and then opened a door.

'We've been given the basement; we can make as much noise as we want down here,' he said. They went down a flight of stairs into a large dimly lit room painted white. A gleaming tobacco brown upright piano stood against one wall, and Jai's drum kit was arranged at one end, with the drummer boy himself thudding away and nodding to the beat, hitting the cymbals every now and then. A saxophone gleamed golden, standing up against another wall, next to a keyboard. From the ceiling, fighter planes hung, swinging slowly, and a pickup and mike were placed on a table, their wires snaking across the floor. One wall was festooned with posters of great jazzmen and musicians: Miles Davis, Herbie Mann, Ella Fitzgerald, John Coltrane, Bob Marley . . .

'Wow,' Trisha said, 'you've got quite a den here!'

'It's not bad, but the acoustics could be better. Hey Jai, just stop it for a sec . . . listen, you want a Coke or something?'

'Sure, thanks!'

She smiled sweetly at them. 'Now, play me something!'

Jai whispered something into Akshay's ear. He nodded, grinning. 'Okay, here goes,' he said, sitting down at the piano.

A storm of music exploded from the piano, kept company by the drums that appeared to have gone ballistic. Trisha winced and then cocked her head. Somewhere within the cacophony, a melody was twinkling . . . it was a tune she knew, plinking itself out of the piano, stringing itself together, then vanishing and reappearing again . . . 'Scarborough Fair!' she said, smiling. And then 'Scarborough Fair' effortlessly morphed into 'Bridge Over Troubled Waters' . . . 'Fly Me To The Moon' . . . 'It Takes Two To Tango' . . . 'Big Spender' . . . 'Return To Me' . . . all pretty ancient tunes which she recognized thanks to her mom. She listened raptly, her eyes widening with amazement at first and then with entrancement. One thing was clear: both the boys had tremendous talent. Who would believe that these were the boys who ran away after bopping you on the head with a frisbee!

Sometimes when you want to believe in miracles, they smile

and happen just like that. And that's what happened to Trisha that evening.

Akshay flashed her a grin and launched into another melody and she had it in the first few notes; it was a huge favourite of her mom's and Shivi's, though the boys were playing it with a funky honky-tonk beat. No problem, she'd cottoned on to it pretty quickly . . . and before she had quite realized what she was doing . . .

Akshay's eyes grew round and large as he stared at her and tried to concentrate on his piano. He gave her a sidelong look, then shut his eyes and went on playing, softer and slower now so that her voice took flight above the instrument. Jai took it easy on the drums, muffling his beat, his ears almost perpendicular with shock.

'Somewhere . . . over . . . the rainbow . . .' Trisha's voice started a deep down G, so deep they could barely hear it first and then soared huskily, each note as clear and deep as well water, making both the boys break out in goosebumps.

Something magical took over, something none of them could control; Trisha just shut her eyes and went on, full-throatedly, without pausing to 'What a Wonderful World', and the boys matched her effortlessly. None of them noticed the door of the room open, as Mrs Khurana put her head around it to check on them. She stood there stupefied as Trisha filled the room with her vibrant voice, and withdrew quietly, not shutting the door properly, so she could still listen.

At last they stopped and Trisha put her hands against her cheeks, suddenly acutely embarrassed and blushing furiously. Akshay and Jai were goggling at her.

'Wha . . . what other numbers do you know?' Akshay whispered.

'So how come you guys are into this jazz stuff and not the usual?' Trisha asked about twenty minutes later, sipping her Coke. They were taking a break after having belted out four more numbers non-stop.

'Well, Papa put his foot down. He said if we're good, we might as well learn and play something that's really worthwhile, not all this "rubbish modern stuff full of bad language".' He grinned. 'It's not

that we don't play the other stuff . . . we just disguise it as jazz and
Papa doesn't know the difference! Actually it's fun and some of those
old numbers are cool.'

'And,' Jai added suddenly, 'if everyone plays the same sort of stuff
it's no big deal. Ours is different.'

'Do kids like it?' Trisha sounded doubtful.

'If they stick around long enough they begin to like it; usually
they just start booing and throwing things because it's something
they haven't recognized or are familiar with. Or . . .' he grinned, 'it
reminds them of their parents or grandparents! Anyway so far we've
only played in school.'

'Wow, you guys have guts . . .' Imagine being booed off a stage
. . . what did it make them feel like? Especially when you knew you
were good at what you were doing.

Dinner was a very informal occasion, but Trisha suspected that was
because Dr Khurana was still seeing patients. Mrs Khurana was a
cool, sophisticated lady, who looked like she knew everything you
were thinking the moment she glanced at you. But she was sweet and
seemed affectionate too.

'Hello, beta,' she greeted Trisha with a hug. 'Come along and help
yourself.'

Trisha helped herself to the wonderfully fragrant mutton pallau,
studded with almonds, and rajma and karkar bhindi and baingain
aloo and raita. They had just about finished with the kulfi, when Dr
Khurana came in and sat down.

'Okay, children, you may be excused,' Mrs Khurana said as she
bustled around her husband.

'Come on, Trish, let's play some more,' Jai said.

'I've eaten too much. If I try to sing now, I'll be sick!'

'Seriously, we should form a group, you're the missing link,' Akshay
said and then went red.

'Sure, with the kind of stuff we like and play we'd be history before
we start!' Jai snorted.

'Well, if we're history then they'll be toast!' Akshay said mutinously.
'It'll be their loss.'

Trisha's eyes sparkled. 'Say, that's a great name for a group.'

'What?'

'If We're History, You're Toast!'

'That's brilliant!'

'That'll shut them up and make them listen.'

They sat around in the basement for a bit, riffling through the boys' CDs and then Trisha glanced at her watch. Oh damn, in five minutes Tikka would be waiting outside.

'Okay, I'd better be going. Tikka is picking me up. I'd like to say bye and thanks to your parents.'

She waited in the corridor as Akshay disappeared to find them. A few minutes later he returned.

'Come on—they're in the drawing room,' he said in a voice so subdued she hardly heard him. She glanced at him, puzzled.

She followed him and shyly thanked and wished his parents goodnight.

'Goodnight, my dear, you must come again and sing, it's such a pleasure having you over,' Mrs Khurana said. 'And next time bring your little sister too.'

The doctor looked at her. 'Yes,' he said quietly, 'you must come again.'

Outside, Tikka had just drawn up and was about to start hooting when she emerged from the gate with the boys.

'Bye,' she said, shaking their hands awkwardly turn by turn. 'I had a great time. Thanks.'

'Great?' Jai said. 'That was awesome!'

They waved as she drove off. Then Akshay gripped his brother by the shoulder.

Jai looked up, surprised.

'What's with you, man? Your current address should be Cloud 9, Seventh Heaven! She sings like an angel!'

Akshay gulped. 'When I went in, I overheard what Papa was telling Mama.'

'What was he saying?'

Akshay told him.

It was Jai's turn to turn pale now.

'No . . .'

Back home, Trisha was humming with happiness. 'Mom, I had a great time,' she said and chatted non-stop (rather like Shivi) about her evening. Her mother was reclining in her Lazy Boy, her eyes closed, the TV still on.

'That's lovely, darling,' Mrs Bhave smiled. But if only the dull heavy ache in her stomach would recede . . . She took Trisha's hand and squeezed it. 'Darling, will you ask Komal to bring me a hot water bottle, please?'

CHAPTER FIVE

CA 19-9

At school the next day Trisha buttonholed Gullu and told her about the impromptu jam session she'd had with the boys.

'What did you play?' Gullu asked.

'I sang!'

'You never told me you sang.'

'Only in the bathroom . . .'

Gullu's big eyes grew round. 'You sang in the bathroom with those two guys?'

'Idiot!'

'You have a vacancy for a guitarist?' Gullu asked sotto voce.

'What?'

'I play the guitar, only I have a voice like a parrot with laryngitis.'

Trisha's eyes gleamed. 'I'll fix it up with the guys asap—we'll all jam together. It'll be fun. How does Saturday evening sound? Then maybe we can go biking on Sunday morning and you can stay on for the day.'

'Sounds good!'

Trisha waited impatiently with her mother at Dr Khurana's all-white clinic, idly wondering why she had not objected when she had said she'd like to come along. Excitedly, she had told the boys she'd pop in afterwards but hadn't told them about Gullu. That, she thought, would be her surprise for them. Akshay had seemed a little subdued on the phone—not his usual ebullient self, maybe he'd flunked a class test or something and got yelled at. Well, she had news that might cheer him

59

up. At last the nurse ushered them in; Dr Khurana greeted them and bade them sit. He glanced at the MRCP and read the accompanying report and steepled his fingers together on the table.

'Mrs Bhave, as I was telling you, I think it's time you saw a specialist. Dr Sameer Phadnis is the best person for this: it's his specialty. Most probably he'll suggest an ERCP . . .'

'A what?' Trisha looked up, surprised.

Dr Khurana ran a hand through his hair carefully and leaned forward. 'Trisha, your mother has a problem with her bile duct, it's called cholangitis. You know—you must have learned in biology that the liver produces bile, which is used for digestion, specifically for breaking down fats and getting rid of the waste that the liver filters. It's a pretty foul but very vital liquid. Well this bile is stored in the gall bladder and used by the body as and when required. Now your mom doesn't have a gall bladder because it was removed when she had gallstones some years ago . . .'

'You were about two years old then.' Her mom took her hand reassuringly.

'So, what's the problem?' She knew her mom had suffered from tummy trouble for a long time—it sort of came and went.

'Well, normally there isn't a problem. The liver produces the bile and in absence of a gall bladder, the bile just flows into the intestines where it aids digestion. However, in some cases, like that of your mother, a growth develops in the bile duct, blocking it, and blocking the flow of bile. The bile sort of backs up into the liver and manifests itself in jaundice-like symptoms—which your mother has. It is absorbed by the body, giving the skin and eyes the yellow tinge. And naturally digestion and appetite suffer, and the liver can get infected. The patient may suffer from nausea and itching and fever . . .'

'A growth?' Trisha whispered her face ashen. 'What sort of growth? And how does one get rid of it?'

'There are various ways, including surgery and radiation and using drugs. But looking at your mother's case I don't think they're viable or at all useful. However, Dr Phadnis can take the call on that. What he would probably recommend is an ERCP.'

'What's that?'

'Well, the full name is Endoscopic Retrograde Cholangiopanceatography, quite a mouthful really. Basically, a stent is pushed through the bile duct, opening the passage again and pushing the growth against the walls of the bile duct. A stent is quite simply a tube made of metal or plastic. So once the flow of bile is normalized the patient recovers . . .'

'Oh,' Trisha breathed. 'Thank God for that.'

Dr Khurana shook his head gently. 'The trouble is that eventually, like a creeper, the growth extends over the ends of the stent, blocking it again, so a new one has to be inserted.'

'Can't you get rid of the growth itself?'

'I think Dr Phadnis will be the best person to judge that, but personally, I don't think it's possible in your mother's case. The growth is not in a place it can be easily or safely reached or removed.'

'Oh.' Trisha looked at her mom. 'You knew this?'

He mother nodded. 'The doctor explained it to me on the phone.'

'So it's an operation then?'

'It's a procedure. No incision is made. The stent is pushed down via the gullet, through the stomach and into the intestine.'

It sounded grotesque, and involuntarily Trisha shivered; just what on earth did these doctors get up to and how did they think up these ghoulish 'procedures'? She'd hate to have something stuffed down her throat like that. And with a prickly chill, Trisha suddenly realized why her mom had not objected to her keeping her company this evening. What Dr Khurana had just told them was specifically for her benefit. He'd been talking to her, not her mom. She'd already known.

'But . . . but . . . if it grows again . . . you can push it aside with another stent, can't you?' she whispered.

Dr Khurana hesitated. 'Yes . . .'

She knew it was an open-ended reply. This business could go on and on, until . . .

'See, there's nothing to worry about at the moment. Let's see what Dr Phadnis recommends and take it from there. Step by step . . .'

She nodded dumbly. The question was looming up malevolently, evilly as a pus-filled boil—but there was no way she could ask it. Was it . . . Trisha was too afraid to even form the word in her mind. What if it was and the doctor hadn't told her mom? Or what if he had and her mom knew and wasn't raising the subject for fear of upsetting her? And how did it feel to be a doctor and have to tell someone something like that?

'Sweetie, why don't you find Akshay and Jai and play some music?' her mother suggested gently. 'I'll be fine, don't worry.'

Dr Khurana nodded. 'Good idea. Those two have done nothing but talk about you,' he said. 'You've made a big impression on them!' He looked at Mrs Bhave. 'Right, I'll fix up an appointment for you right now.' He rang his bell and the receptionist came in. 'Don't worry—I know Dr Phadnis very well. He is the best in this field.'

'Thank you, Doctor.'

Outside, the receptionist handed her mother a piece of paper. 'Your appointment with Dr Phadnis is at the Tulsidas Hospital and Healthcare Centre on Thursday—day after tomorrow, at 7.30 p.m. You are patient no. 23 . . . Here's his telephone number for reference. It's room P 34.'

'Thank you.'

Trisha's palm was clammy as she took her mother's hand and they walked out. 'Why don't you go and say hello to your friends? I'll get dropped and send Tikka back for you.'

'I think I'll just come home, Mom.'

'Sweetie, they're probably waiting for you.' Her mother looked at her. 'At least let them know. It'll look bad if you don't tell them.'

'Okay . . .' Trisha walked up the driveway and rang the bell. Akshay opened the door and grinned at her. 'Hi,' he said. 'We were waiting for you. Come in!' She shook her head.

'No, not today. I've got a lot of homework . . .' She tailed off. She knew she was a hopeless liar.

'Oh!' His face fell about a mile and Trisha felt a sudden pang.

'Just for a bit,' he pleaded. 'Jai's already sitting at his drums.'

She glanced at her mother and took a deep breath. 'Okay, for just as long as it takes Tikka to drop Mom and return.'

'Great!' He stared at her. 'Say, are you okay?'

'Yeah, yeah, I'm fine. It's just . . .' She took a deep breath. 'Akshay, I don't think I can sing tonight.'

'Oh.' He sounded disappointed. 'Okay . . .' he shrugged. 'We'll play for you. You'll listen at least, won't you?' he added a little anxiously.

'Sure!' she said, suddenly feeling bad. 'I'm sorry.'

'It's cool.' He glanced at her diffidently. 'Is everything okay?'

She nodded. 'Yes, everything's fine. I'm fine.' She took a deep breath and gave him a small smile. 'Remember Gullu?'

'The girl with the round face and curly hair, the one who came along with us on Sunday?'

'Yes. Well, she plays the guitar.'

'Oh wow! Is she any good?'

'I don't know. I haven't heard her, actually.'

'Well, call her over some day.'

'I have. I told her Saturday.'

'Great!'

And yet again the magic of their music took over. Trisha just listened, swallowing and wiping away the tears that had welled up without warning and begun rolling down her cheeks. Both the boys pretended not to notice, though their music was becoming slow and sweet and rather mushy . . . they were playing the blues . . . Akshay, she thought, with a huge surge of affection, was a born performer (and such a sweetheart); he'd sensed her mood and set his music to it. And then he nodded briefly to Jai and they picked up the tempo, moving to perky, cheerful stuff that lifted her and made her smile and want to dance. She smiled at them both through her tears and sniffed embarrassedly.

'Thanks,' she whispered after they stopped. Jai jumped off his drums and scooted out of the room. Trisha raised an eyebrow. 'What's with him?'

Akshay shook his head. 'He can't bear anyone crying,' he said. 'He starts crying himself . . . but what's the matter?' he asked. 'Why are you crying?' He looked stricken. 'Is it something we . . . I . . .?'

She wiped her eyes. 'I'm sorry. No. It's Mom. She's not well at all.'

'Oh.' He avoided her eye.

'Your dad's referred her to some expert.' She was looking at him pitifully. 'It's just . . . I'm so terrified—I don't know what to do.'

He squeezed her hand and gave her a lopsided grin. 'You shouldn't be terrified. You weren't scared when the bike went over. You just picked it up and got on again.' And of course, what he really wanted to do was to take her into his arms and crush her and miraculously make what had been upsetting her vaporize forever. Though if he did that, she would probably scream and give him a couple of tight ones and storm out, and where would that leave him then?

'That's different. Nothing happened.'

'Yes, but something could have.'

She got up and glanced at her watch. 'I guess Tikka should be here any moment—I'd better go.'

In the driveway, Jai rejoined them as if nothing had happened and they waited at the gate for Tikka. 'Bye,' she said, as he drove up and stopped next to her. 'I'll let you guys know about Gullu.'

Akshay turned to his brother. 'Shit,' he said, 'she pretty much knows, and now she's going to stop singing and we'll be both history and toast before we start, man!'

Two evenings later, Mrs Bhave and Trisha arrived at the Tulsidas Hospital and stood around uncertainly in the tumultuous entrance lobby.

Trisha pushed her way to the reception desk, using her elbows effectively. She was becoming quite good at this sort of thing, she thought wryly, but heck, if you didn't shove you just remained at the back.

'Room P 34?' she asked, wishing Tikka was with them.

'Second floor, right side.'

They took the stairs: there was a queue a mile long outside the lifts. The stairs opened up into another busy lobby and Trisha stopped, surprised.

'My God, Mom, there's a coffee shop here, and a Chinese takeaway!' Automatically her eyes ran down the menu displayed outside. Had Shivi been with them, she would have demanded noodles and ice cream right away! The lobby led to corridors running to the right and left and in front. 'The fellow said "right side".'

They entered the corridor and looked around. There was seating for patients in large open cubicles, with the doctors' rooms along one side.

'P 24 . . . P 28 . . . Mom, this is like finding an address. Here it is . . . room P 34.'

A chunky-looking peon was outside the doctor's room fielding queries from agitated patients and ticking off those who had turned up for their appointments from a list.

Trisha's mom went up to him. 'I'm Mrs Gitanjali Bhave . . . I have an appointment for 7.30 p.m.'

'Number, madam?'

'23.'

He glanced at his pad and nodded. 'Please wait—we'll call you.' It was already 7.25 p.m.

They sat down on the gleaming stainless steel chairs, and were immediately scrutinized by the other patients.

'Mom,' Trisha whispered, 'it seems like every patient has about six relatives with them.'

'I hope he sees us quickly.'

At 7.45 she asked Trisha to find out how long it would be. So far, not a single patient had either entered or left the doctor's room. The peon told her the doctor still hadn't come.

Dr Phadnis finally showed up at 8.15. He was tall and good-looking, and reminded Trisha of Richard Gere. He strode into his clinic, causing a flutter amongst the patients waiting outside. At 9.10, the peon finally called their number. 'Imagine, he's made us wait nearly two hours!' Trisha grumbled as they went in. The doctor was on the phone but took Mrs Bhave's reports and scanned them swiftly. He finished his call and nodded.

'Would you lie down, please?' he said, indicating a bed to one side of the room. He drew the curtain perfunctorily around the bed and examined her, checking her eyes and tongue and palpating her stomach gently. Then he returned to his desk.

'Dr Khurana's already briefed me . . . yes, Mrs Bhave, we'll have to do an ERCP; it's a simple procedure. Will Tuesday be all right? I'll be out of station till Monday.'

'Tuesday?'

'Yes. At noon. You'll have to come on an empty stomach. Room 243 on the 2nd floor of the old wing.'

'Can I go home straight afterwards?'

'We'll have to keep you for a night or two. I'll have the room assigned to you, don't worry about that.'

'Er . . . Doctor? How long will it take?' Trisha whispered. She looked at him and blushed. Bloody hell, how could he look like Richard Gere and have a name like Phadnis and stuff tubes into people's intestines for a living?

'Fifteen-twenty minutes at the maximum. Bring all your reports and prescriptions and get this blood test done too . . . and let me have the report on Monday. You can get yourself admitted on Tuesday morning and they'll bring you to the ERCP room.'

Trisha brightened; surely it couldn't be too bad or serious if the whole thing would get over in fifteen or twenty minutes. She had one more question she wanted to ask but just then there was a faint scrabbling sound from behind. There appeared to be a rugby scrum going on just outside the door. People were peering in through the porthole window, looking over each other's shoulders. Maybe the peon had been overwhelmed. Maybe they had killed the peon . . . Maybe they were gouging out his gall bladder and feasting on his liver . . .

'So Trish, what are your plans for the weekend?' Mrs Bhave asked as Tikka drove them back. Trisha shook her head and stared out of the window. 'Nothing, Mom. You're going to hospital on Tuesday.'

'Sweetie, that's three days later!'

'I know . . .'

'Why don't you take Smelly Beast for a spin and have another picnic? Or have your friends over?'

'No, Mom. Don't feel like it.'

'Sweetheart, there's no point in brooding over it. It's just a fifteen-minute procedure, like maybe having a filling put in . . . I'll be fine.'

'But . . .'

'No, you listen to me: you take your friends and go for a spin on Smelly Beast. Only this time, don't fall into any ponds. Or go for a swim or play music with Akshay and Jai. Darling, I'm going to be

very busy this weekend with the Kasauli project anyway; I've called
Mrs Almeida over for the weekend.'

'Oh. You're *sure* you're okay?'

'Positive.'

'Anyway, I'm coming to the hospital with you on Tuesday.'

'Darling, you can't miss school. Besides, I'll be taking Mrs Almeida
with me.'

'Mrs Almeida is not a relative. They always want a relative around
for these things . . . I'll tell Ms Sonam.'

All the same, Trisha was immensely relieved that Mrs Almeida was
coming along. Whatever else she may be (inquisitive, prudish and
starchy) she was an efficient and capable woman who could handle
all the paperwork, which terrified Trisha.

Shivi came flying out to meet them as they walked in.

'You both don't love me!' she bawled, 'you always go away together
and leave me alone!'

'Darling, we'd only gone to the doctor's,' Mrs Bhave said, trying
to pacify the little girl.

'You both hate me! I'm going away! I'll go away forever and then
you'll know!'

'Shivi, we went to this hospital where all the nurses were walking
around with huge needles and injections, which they were poking
into everyone.' Trisha said, opening her arms wide to indicate the
size of the injections. 'They were celebrating Big Injection Day today;
that's why we didn't take you.'

'What?' Shivi's eyes widened, and the tantrum stalled. 'Did they
poke you and Mommy?'

'We escaped, thank God!' Trisha rolled her eyes. 'Just before they
were about to, the doctor called us, and we ran into his room.'

Shivi gave the matter a little thought. 'But didn't the doctor give
you an injection?' she asked hopefully.

Trisha grinned. 'Oh no, Shivi, we begged and pleaded on bended
knees and he took pity on us.'

Shivi frowned and screwed her eyes shut. 'Nah!' she said, 'you're
just trying to fool me!'

'Come on, darling, time for bed,' Mrs Bhave said. 'What would you like me to read to you tonight?' With an effort she picked up the little girl and kissed her.

Shivi smiled angelically and whispered: 'Mommy, you love me more than Trisha, don't you?'

Mrs Bhave nodded vigorously. 'Of course I do! But don't tell Trish that.'

'And even more than Smelly Beast?'

'Yes. I love you most of all, Shivi.'

'I like that!' Trisha said indignantly. 'She put Smelly Beast before me!'

Her mother grinned and put an arm around her. 'Darling, you ride Smelly Beast a little more and see what happens. You'll forget all about me.' She leaned over and kissed her.

'Mom, you're kissing her and not me!' Shivi wailed. 'You have to kiss me ten times now!'

Trisha gave Akshay and Gullu their first riding lesson that Saturday morning. Tikka took them to a wonderfully remote spot this time. For a while they wound up and down a road that cut through rugged rocky Wild-West-like country (the Aravalli mountains actually) and then turned off on to a rutted track which suddenly passed through a narrow gorge between high cliffs and dramatically opened out into a large, flat sandy lakebed. The lakebed was surrounded by high rocky cliffs, festooned with thorny bushes. At the far end a thicket of thorny scrub struggled halfway into the lakebed like a hedgerow. They lurched down the track to the edge of the lakebed and disembarked, looking around in amazement.

'Tikka, how do you find these places?' Trisha asked in wonder. She scanned the high rocky cliffs surrounding them and the edges of the lakebed; there was not a soul (or goat) in sight. The ground was baked hard and cracked like crazy paving, but it was layered with powdery dust and crumbled; it would cushion any falls nicely.

'There used to be a lake—I used to catch fish here,' he said with a smile. 'The water dried up and now it's good for motorcycling.'

This time they had come properly attired, with heavy-duty jeans and jackets, elbow- and knee-pads and helmets, of course; it was hot but it was better to be hot than hurt.

'I could teach them,' Tikka offered, but Trisha shook her head. 'No, I'll teach them,' she said, and Tikka grinned delightedly.

Again, she pointed out the controls to her pupils and then quizzed both of them. 'Right, Gullu, you'd better use the electric starter,' she told the nervous girl as she got astride. 'First, just get a feel of the weight of the bike; this is one heavyweight champion, so you have to watch it and make sure it doesn't tilt too much and use its weight against you. Okay, put your hands on the handlebars and let me explain. Right, so this is your front brake, this is the throttle, this is the clutch, which you pull when you change gear . . .'

Gullu was hugely nervous, and Smelly Beast bucked and bolted as she screamed. Trisha clung tight, yelling instructions and Tikka ran alongside, ready to catch the bike if it tilted over too much.

They stalled several times but to Gullu's credit they didn't fall off when they actually set off, wavering and wobbling a bit. After about half an hour she decided that she had had enough.

'Whew,' she said, stripping off her jacket. 'It's so hot! But I can't believe I actually rode the bike . . . even if it was for twenty feet! But it'll be ages before I can ride properly.'

'Practice—that's all it takes. The more you ride, the easier it gets.' She glanced at Akshay who was looking just a little apprehensive.

'Okay, Akshay, your turn!'

He was a quick learner, and determined to not disgrace himself in front of her.

'Okay, so you want to kick-start her?' Trisha asked as poor Akshay bounced up and down like a pogo stick and Smelly Beast made a rude gurgling sound. 'Don't just kick randomly, get the pulse of her . . . hey, that's the way . . . now hang on, I'm getting on board!' She climbed on and leaned over his shoulder.

'Let's go . . . you're in neutral now . . . pull the clutch, into first, throttle . . . and . . . release clutch slowly and away . . . ooops!'

'Shit, man!'

At his fourth attempt, they finally got going, legs dangling frantically, feet brushing the ground and then settling on the foot pegs. When she glanced at the side of his face, she could see a huge grin plastered on it.

Akshay couldn't believe it. He was actually riding a big chrome

Bullet, with a knockout girl sitting pillion—all right, she was yelling instructions, but still. There was the glorious staccato throb of the engine being echoed back by the cliffs, the breeze against his cheeks, and most of all, Trisha looking over his shoulder and grinning at him. He glanced at the speedometer—shit, it had to be wrong—they were doing just 30 kmph! Okay, so big deal, not bad, this was his first time, after all, and they were on a kachcha surface. There was a huge cloud of blond dust billowing behind them. But man, this was the life; he could ride this bike all day . . .

'Hey man, you'd better start turning or we're going to hit the cliffs,' Trisha yelled, and he nodded. Very gradually he turned the bike in a wide arc along the circumference of the lakebed. 'And slow down a bit, put her into second . . . oops, not so jerky, and watch the ground, it's pretty bumpy here . . . look out for those rocks and hoof prints. Steer away from those bushes, Akshay . . . *Akshay watch out for the thicket in front!*'

But Akshay, who'd been concentrating hard on the ground just ahead of his front wheel in order to avoid the deep holes and ruts at the edges of the lakebed, hadn't looked up to see exactly where the bike was heading and so, they rode straight into a thick and rather prickly stretch of thornbush with a splintering sound as the dry but very well-barbed branches caught them. Both of them put their feet down at once, and the bike remained upright as it juddered to a halt about a yard deep in the bush, which clutched at them from either side. The engine stalled and it was suddenly very quiet.

'Oh shit,' Trisha giggled, 'I put you into a roadside ditch and you drove me into a bush—now we're quits!'

'Heck, I'm sorry . . . I was concentrating on the ground . . .' He was mortified.

'That's okay . . .' She'd taken her helmet off and he could feel her silky hair blow against his cheek.

'Now what?' he asked, looking back at her.

'We'll push backwards with our feet . . . okay, together now, one, two, three!'

Bit by bit they backed out of the bush as it clawed at them, trying to hold them back.

'Ow!' Trisha exclaimed suddenly as a barbed branch got caught in her jacket. 'I think a thorn's gone into my back! I've been stabbed in the back!'

'Take your jacket off, maybe it'll come out with it.'

'Have a look at my back. If it's there just pull it out . . .'

'Okay.' Sure enough, there was a thorny twig stuck horizontally across the back of her jacket.

'Hang on, I'll pull it out.' He levered the twig out and she winced again.

'There! Okay now?' He held up the twig.

But it wasn't okay. It was still there, stabbing, stinging and burning her like hell.

'Look,' Trisha said desperately, looking around. 'There's no one around—I'm taking my top off . . . it's still there!

Akshay goggled as she unbuttoned her top and took it off, draping it over Smelly Beast's seat and keeping her back firmly to him. She was wearing a white bra—but he spotted the cause of her distress straight off. A sliver, small and nasty and black jutted out from the middle of her back, surrounded by a red weal like a gigantic mosquito bite. Her bra strap was chafing against it, making her squirm every time she moved.

'There's a thorn . . .' he said, going deep red and looking around hastily. 'Your strap is rubbing against it, which is why it's hurting you.'

'Please, can you take it out? It's burning like hell.'

'I'll try . . .' He rummaged in his pockets and took out a penknife. She turned her face towards at him. 'What are you doing?'

'I've got a pair of tweezers,' he said, taking a small pair out of the penknife. Gingerly he poised the tips of the tweezers over the red spot on her back.

'Ow!' she exclaimed.

He shook his head. 'I can't get at it—it's sort of half behind your strap. Look, maybe we should go back and Gullu can take it out.' At the same time he didn't like the look of it; it was red and angry and beginning to swell.

'Just take it out, please,' she said. She took a deep breath. 'Don't freak and don't peek but I'm taking my bra off now. I can't bear it anymore.' She reached back and unhooked her bra strap. 'Oh, whew, that's better, what a relief. Now can you get at it, please?' She dropped her bra on her top and looked back at him, colouring and crossing her arms over her breasts.

He stared at her bare, smooth back. 'Okay, here goes,' he said hoarsely. His hand was shaking slightly as he poised the tweezers over the spot.

'Hang on, I'll have to dig it out a bit to get a grip: it's gone in with hardly any bit sticking out . . .'

She squealed a bit, but he was firm and gentle; at last the tweezer closed over the protruding thorn and he smoothly pulled it out.

'Ow!' she cried.

'Done!' he grinned.

A bead of blood swelled up from the spot and he took out his handkerchief.

'Wait a sec . . .' Gently he dabbed the spot. 'How does it feel?'

'It's still burning and itching a bit, but it's better.'

He leaned forward and blew gently on the spot.

She squirmed. 'Oh, that's lovely and cool, do it again, please . . .' she breathed blissfully. 'Thanks.'

'When we get back you can put some antiseptic or Betadine on that. That spot will still be tender though.'

She shrugged on her top and turned around, doing up the buttons with one hand. 'How is it that every time we go biking something like this happens to us?' She rolled up her bra and stuffed it into her jacket pocket.

She leaned forward to take a look at the thorn still in his palm and their heads bumped gently together. She'd done the buttons of her blouse all wrong and his eyes widened as he glimpsed her full breasts, nestling against each other inside her blouse. They drew back simultaneously, blushing furiously.

'Let's get back,' she said, quickly looking down and turning around again to re-button. 'Right, Rambo, back on the bike, on the double!'

'Say, can we do this again tomorrow?' he asked. 'Ma and Dad are going to Dehradun tonight for a couple of days.'

'What?' she asked, grinning. 'You want to drive into a thicket again and make me do another striptease?'

'Shit, no, I mean just ride this bike around . . .'

She tapped his shoulder reassuringly. 'I know . . . I'll ask Mom, I guess it should be okay.' She yelled, 'Now look in front, please!'

'Yes ma'am!'

And again, Gullu looked at them sceptically. 'What happened this time?' she asked, hiding a grin. 'You disappeared behind that thicket for ages. We were getting worried you might have eloped!'

Back home Gullu ragged her unmercifully about the incident.

'Jai told me Akshay's got the hots for you.'

'Bullshit! What does he know?'

'Well,' Gullu rolled her eyes dramatically, 'first you fall into a pond together, then you drive into a thicket together . . . I mean . . . did he kiss you?'

'Hey Gullu, play something!' she said, changing the subject.

'If you sing along.'

Suddenly Trisha sighed; all this would soon be over, she knew. All too soon it would be Tuesday and her mom would be in the hospital having 'procedures' done to her. It was like some malevolent cloud hanging over them.

But Gullu had taken her gleaming black guitar out of its case and was now strumming a few chords. Shivi came running in on hearing her.

'Can you play "Old MacDonald?"' she asked breathlessly.

'Here goes,' said Gullu launching into the chords to Shivi's hand-clapping delight. 'Sing, Trisha, sing!'

'So do you think she'll be able to play?' Akshay asked Jai sceptically as the boys waited for Trisha and Gullu to turn up that evening. 'I hope she's not hopeless . . . and then if we say no she'll start crying. You know what girls are like!'

'Well, Trisha is a girl too . . .'

'Not that kind of girl, she's different. I mean, she rides a bike!'

'And you've fallen for her hook, line and sinker.'

'Don't start that rubbish again, Jai, I'm warning you.'

They heard the doorbell ring and Akshay rushed out, leaving Jai grinning. He sauntered up to his drums and started his soft, deep beat, nodding his head in time. Ah, if that chick Gullu could play

. . . God knows she looked like a diminutive pop-star, what with her wild curly hair and sparkling eyes, and she had said she knew all the songs he'd mentioned to her that morning.

'Hi, come on in,' Akshay said breathlessly, staring at Trisha. She'd changed into maroon capris and a sleeveless pink and white top, with her midriff peeking out, and looked devastating.

'Um . . . we've brought Shivi along,' Trisha said apologetically as Shivi stepped in a little shyly behind her. 'She refused to be left alone.'

'That's okay. Hi Shivi. How're you doing? Would you like some chips?'

'I'm good!' Shivi perked up. 'Yes, thank you!'

They gathered around their instruments a little self-consciously and argued about what to play.

'Play *Wizard of Oz* music—that above the rainbow song!' Shivi demanded. That was what her mom had been reading to her at bedtime.

Jai grinned. 'Okay,' he said good-naturedly as Akshay launched exuberantly into 'Over the Rainbow' again. He'd heard Trisha sing it once; he could hear her sing it a million times . . . he could hear her sing it forever! It took a while for Trisha to really launch herself into the song though. At first she was terribly self-conscious and made several false starts, smiling sheepishly and blushing, as the boys and Gullu played on. But then it caught . . . and her voice soared as she just shut her eyes and sang. Gullu's eyes nearly popped out with surprise. Outside, Mrs Khurana had stopped in her tracks again; she'd been on her way to ask the kids if they wanted anything to eat or drink. She scuttled away and returned, pulling her husband along, her finger on her lips.

'Just listen to that voice . . .' she whispered. 'That girl is going to be famous.'

The doctor nodded. 'It's good for Jai and Akshay,' he said. 'She'll make them appreciate jazz more now.' He sighed and shook his head. Really, it was too bad . . .

'Whew! I'm beat!' Trisha moaned after the last chords had died down. They all stared at each other.

'You were awesome!' Gullu screamed.

'She sings like this in the bathroom,' Shivi complained. 'The old man and his wife next door stand out in the balcony and listen with their mouths open even before they put in their teeth. She doesn't even hear other people banging on the door.'

'Listen,' Akshay said earnestly. 'Right, so we're a group now. There's a talent competition coming up next year, sponsored by this new radio station—FM Forever—and they're already auditioning for it. Entries have to be in by the end of the year and then groups in various zones play and the finalists from each zone get picked . . . and will be broadcast live! The winners get to have a concert at the Jawaharlal Nehru Stadium at the end of next year. If we win, we might even cut an album!'

'Hold it, Akshay . . . I can't possibly sing in public!' Trisha shook her head firmly. 'Besides, I have my Boards next year.'

'See Trisha, first you sang only in the bathroom. Now you're singing here—take it step by step. And anyway, they factored the exams in; the serious selections only start next summer—after the exams. Haven't you sung in school?'

Trisha shuddered. 'No.'

'They're idiots if they haven't heard you as yet.'

'So, can we ride again tomorrow morning?' Akshay asked her quietly as Jai and Gullu played a 'jugalbandi' together and Shivi danced. 'It'll only be me; Jai has his karate class in the morning and tuitions in the afternoon.'

'I guess it should be okay,' Trisha replied, 'provided Mom doesn't need Tikka. I'll call you, okay?'

Her heart was beating in a little fluttery way: it would be so nice, just the two of them on Smelly Beast—and of course Tikka, but he was the perfect chaperone—he just sat in the pickup and listened to his old Hindi film songs on the radio. Later that evening, Trisha dropped Gullu to her house and Tikka took a diversion on the way back home.

'We have to collect Memsahib's report,' he explained succinctly. It was the report of the blood test that Dr Phadnis had asked for. Trisha waited while he disappeared inside the pathology lab and returned and handed it to her. Curious, she opened the envelope and scanned the contents. It was the report of something called Serum CA 19-9.

Her mother's score was 3459 and was starred. The blood drained out of her face as she stared at the normal range: 0–32. That couldn't be good . . . Idly, she scanned the back of the report: there were explanatory notes about various blood tests: Allergies . . . something called Amenorrhoea . . . Allergies Panel . . . Cancer Markers . . . Trisha almost fainted: there it was—CA19-9 (GI, Liver, GB).

There was no doubt anymore.

Her mother had cancer.

'Is everything okay, baby?' Tikka asked, glancing at her.

'Haan—yes,' she said in a small, dead voice. 'Everything's okay.'

CHAPTER SIX

One Hell of a Day

'Baby, will you be riding the motorcycle tomorrow?' Tikka asked as they arrived home. 'Should I put it in the back?'

'What?' she said blankly. 'No . . . I don't know.'

At the moment all she wanted to do was rush into her mom's arms and howl. But come what may, she couldn't be the one to tell her mom. Surely it was Dr Phadnis's job. (What a hateful job it must be.) And anyhow, maybe she'd interpreted things incorrectly; maybe that obscenely high figure was actually a good score . . .

Her mom was up in her office, fast asleep again.

'Mom, wake up, I got your report!' Suddenly Trisha panicked. 'Should I put it with your other medical reports?' Maybe her mother ought not to see it right now. It would upset her—and ruin her work at least till the time she saw Dr Phadnis.

'Thank you, sweetie.'

'Now you better eat something.'

Mrs Bhave made a face. 'I'm really not very hungry. The very thought of food makes me feel sick.'

'Mom, that's why you keep falling asleep all the time!'

'Have you had dinner, Trish?'

'I'll have it when you have it.'

'Oh, very well, come on, let's go down.'

'You feeling all right, Trish?' her mother asked, as they watched the news on TV after dinner.

'Yes, Mom, why?'

'You keep looking at me as if you want to say something . . . everything all right?'

'Sure, Mom, everything's fine. How's the Kasauli project coming along?'

'Oh, fine—but it's tiring. We'll plan a visit after this procedure thing is over. Maybe in August.' Trisha glanced at her. She was pale, and the yellow tinge on her cheeks was quite discernible. 'Well, I'm turning in. Goodnight, sweetheart.'

'Goodnight, Mom.'

Five minutes later Trisha followed. She changed and climbed into bed. Next to her Shivi slept blissfully, arms and legs spreadeagled. Lucky thing, she knew nothing. For Trisha, sleep was impossible, and the questions buzzed around her head like dervishes. Did her mom really have cancer? It couldn't be—this sort of thing happened to other people! You read or heard about this sort of thing . . . but if so, if by some horrible chance, she did have it, could it be cured? There were always miraculous cures one read about—people who had been given up for dead making complete recoveries. And yes, she thought, she believed in miracles. And maybe it wasn't such a bad form of cancer anyway. How did they treat it? Chemotherapy? Radiation? Surgery? But Dr Phadnis had ruled those out and suggested this strange ERCP thing. What if, what if in spite of everything her mom died? What would happen to them then? What would happen to poor Shivi? Would they live here or . . .? Nana and Nani were out of the question—they'd washed their hands of them. The beasts! She hated them.

Trisha tossed and turned. She glanced at her bedside clock—it was just 9.45 p.m. Oh shit, she'd completely forgotten to ask her mom about tomorrow morning—not that that was very relevant anymore—but she ought to have told Akshay. Poor guy, he must have been waiting for her call.

'Hi,' he said, and with a twist of anguish she heard the hope rising in his voice. 'I was going to call. I thought you'd forgotten! Hey, what's the matter?'

She just heard his voice and blubbed. 'Akshay . . . it's Mom . . . I picked up her blood report this evening . . . she's got cancer.'

'Oh. Shit.' He took a deep breath. 'Are you sure?'

She gulped. 'There was this CA 19, a cancer marker thing, and her score was way above normal.'

'Shit. Hell, are you okay?'

'Sort of,' she sniffed dolefully. 'I guess.'

'Listen,' he said, 'don't worry and don't jump to conclusions. They've found all sorts of cures for cancer these days . . . it's not as scary as it used to be.'

'Thanks, Akshay, but I'm so scared.'

'Listen, I'll come over tomorrow,' he said, 'you shouldn't be alone at a time like this.'

Through her tears she smiled. 'You're very sweet, Akshay . . . I'm fine.' She took a deep breath. Maybe she should give him his second lesson in biking tomorrow, after all. Her being away for a couple of hours would not make any difference to whether her mom did or did not have cancer. If the monster was there, it would remain there, gloating and waiting to pounce on her when she returned, a little bigger and more evil perhaps. She took a deep breath.

'Okay, Akshay. I'll pick you up at 5.30.'

'Are you sure?'

'Yes.' Stuff the cancer or whatever it was; they were going biking tomorrow.

Quietly Trisha peeked into her mother's darkened bedroom. Her mother was fast asleep. She went to her study and wrote a note in her neat hand:

Dear Mom,
I forgot to tell you . . . I've taken Akshay for a biking lesson on Smelly Beast (he's getting addicted!) with Tikka. Will be back soon; eat breakfast!
    Lots of love,

                                                    Trish

She left the note on her mom's bedside table and went back to her bedroom.

Akshay was looking quite sombre as he climbed into the pickup beside her the next morning; he really didn't know what to say to her. He was carrying a padded brown windcheater over his shoulder. Tikka gave him a cheery smile. He was beginning to like this bright-eyed, wiry-haired fellow.

'Hi, how're you doing? You okay?' Akshay asked her. She nodded, her eyes holding his.

'Yeah, I guess.'

'You sure you want to go?'

'Yes.' She took a deep breath and gave him a small smile. 'You need to work on your gear changes.' She felt his windcheater.

'Good; this will cushion you if you fall off.' She flashed him a smile, 'I brought the first aid stuff too,' she added.

'Baby, we'll go where we went yesterday?' Tikka asked. She nodded. 'Yes.'

'Right,' she said as Tikka wheeled Smelly Beast down from the pickup after they'd reached. 'Today, you'll ride solo . . .'

'What?' he yelped. 'Already?'

She nodded firmly. 'Yes, you have to develop a bond between yourself and the bike and the only way to do that is by riding solo. Pillions distract you. You have to have a one-to-one relationship with the bike. Listen to her rhythm, her heartbeat, her movements, what she's telling you, how she's responding to your touch, how she banks into a turn . . .'

'Oh.' The 'she-bike' in this case was a growling, somewhat temperamental steel monster, all 500cc and 400lbs. of her!

'Okay, get on!'

He gave her a crooked smile: 'I just hope she doesn't tell me to get off pronto!'

She squeezed his arm and gave him that funny, searching look again. 'You'll be okay,' she said. He zipped up his windcheater and nodded. 'Right, here goes! Wish me luck!'

He got off to a wobbly, shaky start, his legs flailing and flapping, stalling several times but managing to stay vertical. Trisha watched him and kept quiet. It was better not to distract him by shouting instructions—he'd get the hang of it eventually. At last he was riding up and down the lakebed quite steadily, his grin getting wider by the moment, even managing very wide turns at the ends.

'Okay,' she yelled. 'You can ride at a constant speed all day, now accelerate and decelerate through the gears.' She looked at Tikka, who had an equally broad grin plastered across his face. 'When should we put the cones out for him?' she asked innocently. In spite of everything, she had begun to enjoy herself. Screw you, cancer, she thought. Screw you. And also, deep inside her, something had stirred.

'Let him practise a little more—it's only his second day today.' Tikka said. 'But he rides well.'

At last Akshay pulled up, with his big schoolboy grin. 'How was I?' he asked. 'Wow man, this is like being in *Easy Rider*. Wow, oh wow, seriously, I could do this all day!'

'Good.' She wagged a warning finger at him. 'But watch it. Just when you think you're a hip dude the bike will dump you.' She put on her helmet. 'Okay, now get behind, I want to ride!'

She took him around the lakebed twice, then drew up alongside the pickup. Tikka was in the pickup listening to the radio as usual. 'Tikka, is there any other road here?' she asked. 'I'm getting bored going round and round this lakebed.

'Yes, baby.' There was a circuitous route, he explained, that went around a couple of the hills they had driven through and wound back to the far end of the lakebed. It was an un-metalled track, but quite smooth and all right for a motorcycle.

'Tikka, we'll go alone; if we follow you we'll be covered with dust,' she said. 'Just tell us where it is.' Tikka frowned. He didn't want to let Trisha out of his sight—if she fell—well, if she fell he wouldn't be able to catch her even if he was around. Besides, he knew she would only become really confident on the bike by going solo, or well, even with a greenhorn chokra as pillion.

'Okay, baby. You have your phone?'

It was a beautiful route, dusty but stunningly scenic. It curved through the rough hills, many devastated and scarred by mining, rising and falling. The rock faces glittered with mica and the acacias, all twisted and gnarled, thrust out their branches in tragic, beseeching gestures. Trisha kept the bike at a steady 35 to 40 kmph and her eyes on the track ahead. Bushes of deadly thorn apple and prickly Mexican poppy were interspersed by wanton lantana: not comfortable stuff to fall into. The deep thump of the Bullet reverberated off the rock faces like gunfire.

'Isn't it fabulous?' Trisha yelled and Akshay nodded, his hands on her shoulders. He'd been watching her like a hawk: the way she pulled the clutch and changed gears and twisted the throttle—he was in heaven. Eight minutes later they were back on the lakebed. 'Another round?' Trisha asked, intoxicated by the fresh breeze and Smelly Beast's steady bass heartbeat. Her gloom-and-doom mood had dissipated temporarily at least and she was grateful for it: cancer seemed completely unreal here. Akshay nodded. She waved at Tikka as they passed him. They came around yet again, and stopped by the pickup.

'One more time,' she said, 'I want to take some pictures . . . Mom must see this place!' She rummaged in her bag and took out her shiny maroon Coolpix. 'We'll take a little while,' she told Tikka.

She stopped the bike at a point where the track passed between two towering, jagged cliffs. Ahead, and below them, was the lakebed, and they could see the pickup parked there in the shade of a great rock. She angled the bike stylishly and crouched down so that it stood against a clear sky, glittering in the sun.

'Wow, this is so cool! Silver and blue! Mom will love it. It's just so awesome!'

She took several pictures of the bike against the sky and the cliffs.

'Okay, dude, get on and look macho.'

'Just don't show them to Papa,' said Akshay and rakishly unzipped his windcheater halfway down.

'Now it's your turn,' he said, after she was done. 'You get on the bike and I'll click you,' he suggested. He grinned. 'Take your helmet off so your hair can blow in the wind like that woman in *Titanic*.'

The breeze indeed had picked up suddenly, and the dust had started blowing around in swirls. She posed dramatically on the bike, dangling her helmet nonchalantly and grinning.

'Great!'

'Hey look,' she said, pointing at the lakebed. 'Dust devils . . . twisters!'

'It is pretty blustery, isn't it?'

'Come on, we'd better go. There's a dust storm brewing.' She waved at Tikka far below, who had got out of the pickup and was indicating that they return. She waved back, got on and started the bike and flashed her lights to let him know they were on their way.

There was indeed a dust storm roiling, and the sky changed colours with startling rapidity first to mustard yellow and then a rather malevolent, glowering orange grey. It pounced on them just three minutes later, nearly unseating them from the bike.

'Oops!' Trisha squealed as a rude gust nearly blew her off her seat and the bike wove around drunkenly. Promptly she stopped, as the dust boiled all around them in opaque orange clouds.

'We'd better wait till it blows over,' she yelled.

Akshay nodded and pointed to a deep rocky overhang, some way off the track.

'We can take shelter there!' he shouted. They wheeled the bike under the overhang. The dust was still everywhere, but at least it wasn't sandblasting into their faces there.

'Whew! That's better.'

'God, it's really blowing crazily—I can hardly see my nose!'

She dug into her jacket pocket and took out her mobile.

'I better call Tikka—poor guy will be worried sick.'

They sat side by side, their backs against the rock, knees drawn up, with Smelly Beast parked in front of them.

'I . . . I don't know what to do, Akshay,' she said, suddenly looking at him.

'About . . . oh.'

'If . . . if something were to happen to her . . . Mom, I mean.'

He gulped. 'She'll be all right.'

'She has cancer, Akshay. I can't believe it.' She turned to him with stricken eyes. 'We can't live without her. Not me, not Shivi.'

He turned to her; she was shocked to see that his black eyes were glistening suspiciously. He nodded. 'I know. All night I tried to imagine how things would be for me and Jai if something happened to Papa and Mama,' he said, 'I couldn't.' Tentatively he took her hand and squeezed it. 'Listen,' he said gruffly, 'you just keep telling me all this stuff—all this stuff that you feel when you're upset and all, okay?'

She squeezed his hand back. 'You're very sweet, you know that?'

'Nah!' He glanced at her. 'Third time,' he said suddenly.

'Third time what?'

'That we've been stranded together . . .'

'Smelly Beast,' she said with a wan smile. 'It's all Smelly Beast's fault!'

He took a deep breath. 'So tell me about yourself, Trisha,' he said softly.

She shrugged. 'What do you want to know?'

'Everything,' he replied simply.

She smiled. 'You sure? Okay then . . . stop me if I'm boring you!'

'Shit,' he said after she had finished. 'It must have been awful for your mom! Er . . . she didn't want to get married again? I mean, she's . . .' he went red with embarrassment. 'Sorry!'

Trisha grinned. 'She used to tease me about that, and say that if we didn't behave, she'd run away with some guy on a bike and leave us. In the end, she said that none of the fellows who came running after her could match up even quarter-way to dad.' She looked at the boiling clouds of dust and the acacias bent back by the howling wind. 'This is quite a storm.'

Akshay looked around, feeling the grit against his teeth. He spotted what appeared to be a split in the rock face; a long dark cleft about two feet wide at its base and which tapered off about fifteen feet up. He scrambled to his feet.

'Where are you going?'

'Just checking this out . . .'

The crack seemed too narrow to squeeze through—at least while standing up. He got down on to his tummy and peered inside.

'Akshay, watch it—there'll probably be snakes there!' Trisha looked quite alarmed. But Akshay was rummaging around in the pockets of his cargo pants again. He took out a slim Maglite.

'My God,' Trisha said, 'penknife, tweezers and torch . . . what else do you carry when you come biking with me?'

He flashed a grin. 'You'll be surprised. Now let's see . . .' He switched on his torch and peered inside the crack again. And then began wriggling inside on his back, feet first.

'Akshay, what are you doing?'

'Recce!' His voice came out muffled. A few minutes passed. Trisha started getting really alarmed—had he been bitten by something? She was about to call out to him—when suddenly his head popped out of the crack.

'Come on in, you've got to see this!'

'What?'

'Just come in. You won't believe this.'

'Are there bats?'

'No, I don't think so. But come on . . .'

She tied up her hair, got down on to her back and wriggled in. He took hold of her hand and guided her. Slowly, she sat up and stared, blinking. It was pitch dark except for two sources of light—one from the crack through which they had just crawled, through which an ethereal dust-filtered golden light entered, and the second from Akshay's torch beam. Then her eyes got used to the dimness. The crack had opened up into a cavern, about as big as their drawing room. It was musty and damp, but cool. She could feel a faint current of breeze on her cheek. Akshay had taken his windcheater off and tied it around his waist.

'Akshay, what's that glimmering down below?' She pointed downwards.

'Water . . . it's an underground pool!'

'Wow! I don't believe it!'

'Look, we can go down from here. There's like a path going down along the sides . . . it's like a natural baoli.' He flashed the torch along the rocky ground—the rocks were flat and curving down in shallow steps. He guided her down, holding her hand with one hand, feeling the wall of the cavern with the other. They sat down at the edge of the water, dangling their legs over the side, the suffused golden light from the entrance falling on them. They stared at the trembling amber-gold ripples quivering in the water and stole glances at one another. Their fingers were still interlocked.

'It looks quite clear,' she said as he played the torch over the water. 'Not scummy and mucky.' She tried to keep the tremor out of her voice and wondered if he could feel the great waves of heat coming off her.

'Yes, you can even see the bottom in the shallow parts . . .'

Trisha swallowed hard. Her heart was thudding like one of Jai's drums.

'Akshay?'

'What?'

'Umm . . . want to paddle?'

'In there?'

'Where else?'

'Sure. Leave your phone on the rocks—it might get deep.'

He rolled up his jeans and took her hand. Together they waded in, slightly over knee-deep.

'It's lovely.'

He stared at her; gilded by the strange gold-dust storm light filtering through, surrounded by velvet darkness, her ears lit translucent pink. He cleared his throat.

'You are too . . .' he whispered hoarsely—and hoped she hadn't heard him.

'What?'

'Nothing!'

'Uh.'

'The light here—it's beautiful. Your ears are pink and I can see every eyelash of yours.'

Her grip on his hand grew tighter as they took another tentative step ahead.

'I wonder how deep this gets; it's up to my tummy now——hey, can you swim?'

'Ya, not too well but I can.'

'Akshay . . . have you ever . . . I mean . . . kissed . . .?'

'Kissed? What?'

'I mean . . . a girl . . .?'

Dumbly, he shook his head.

'Would you like to?'

'Don't mind . . .' he tried sounding nonchalant.

She was staring at him, her eyes big.

'I haven't either . . . but . . . maybe . . .' Her voice tailed off.

They turned and drew together, as the water sloshed musically around them.

'I think it's supposed to be like this . . .' she said, holding his face in her hands and put her lips on his.

'Ummfff.'

They sank to their knees, the water lapping their chins, their arms fast around each other.

'Trisha—we'll be soaking wet . . .'

'What do you expect? It's pouring!'

'Yes, of course!'

She drew back, the water cascading off her like liquid gold.

'What?' he asked, alarmed.

She shook her head vigorously and then simply floated right up to him, her skirt swirling around her waist and took his face in her hands and kissed him again. 'I've fallen for you, Akshay Khurana . . . ever since I saw you in the back of the pickup trying to steal Smelly Beast.'

'Me too!' he whispered back staring at her, wonderstruck. He grinned. 'Ever since Jai brained you with the frisbee . . . that's when . . . headlong.'

'Oh shit,' she said suddenly, 'Tikka! He'll be worried sick!'

'Call him.'

She retrieved her phone.

'Take it to the entrance,' he said. 'You won't get a signal in here.' He stared at her as the light silhouetted the curves of her body. She lay down on her tummy and peered outside. 'It's still blowing madly . . . it's pouring now . . .' She dialled and took a deep breath. She told a very relieved Tikka they were fine, and that they'd wait for the rainstorm to peter off before riding back.

It was amazing, she thought; this beautiful, miraculous thing that was happening to them.

The storm subsided as suddenly as it had struck. 'Look,' she said, pointing to the slit through which they had entered, 'blue sky. The storm's over . . . we'd better go back. Tikka will be having kittens.'

Outside, Smelly Beast gleamed, raindrops like diamonds glittering on the chrome body, pearling the handlebars and mirrors. The sky was pale blue, and towards the south a few tattered clouds scattered. Puddles glinted and wisps of vapour rose off the warm rock faces. But the breeze was cool and fresh. She called Tikka again and told him they were on their way.

Safely back in the pickup, she turned to Akshay.

'Would you like to come over for a bit . . . have breakfast? I'm sorry I didn't bring anything to eat this morning.'

He nodded in delight. 'Sure.'

'Hi Shivi, we're home!' Trisha bustled in with Akshay in tow. Shivi, who was watching TV, glared at her and turned her back on them. 'Shivi, is Mom in her office?'

'I don't care! Find her yourself . . . you left me secretly and went.'

'I know, but you would have been bored—Akshay was learning how to ride Smelly Beast.'

'But I could have played with Jai and Gullu.'

'They didn't come . . . you can ask Tikka.'

'Oh.'

'Here,' said Akshay, suddenly delving into his pockets again. 'I got this for you.' He gave the little girl a tube of Polos. Shivi brightened up.

'All for me?'

'Sure.'

'None for Trisha?'

'No! She left you alone, na? Bad girl!'

Shivi ripped open her mints and put three into her mouth. She looked at Trisha and Akshay. With great deliberation she took another mint out.

'Here,' she said, offering it to Trisha with big, meaningful eyes. 'But only one.'

'Thank you.' Trisha took the mint and kissed Shivi. The little girl had pulled out another mint. 'Give this to Mommy,' she said. And then a third and handed it to Akshay. 'That's for you.'

'Shivi, you'll need another packet soon,' Akshay said, rummaging into his pockets again. 'Let's see . . . hmm, yes, I have a couple of sticky éclairs. Here you go.'

'Come on,' Trisha said, 'Mom's probably in her office—let's go up.'

Halfway up the stairs she stopped on the landing and turned to face him. 'Penknife, tweezers, Maglite, peppermints, eclairs . . . what else do you keep in your pockets?' She pinned him against the wall.

His eyes sparkled. 'That's for me to know and you to find out!'

'We'd better behave when we're with Mom. She's very sharp.' Akshay leaned forwards and kissed her full on the lips. 'Mmm.' A door on the floor above opened and they sprang apart.

'Mom?' Trisha called, colouring richly.

A tall, spare grey-haired lady in a printed pink salwar kameez peered down the stairs, her spectacles dangling from a chain around her neck. Her pale grey eyes were fixed on Akshay and her eyebrows had disappeared up her forehead in surprise—and suspicion.

'Oh! Mrs Almeida! Hi, is Mom upstairs?'

'Hello Trisha—yes, your mother is here.'

'Um . . . this is, um, Akshay . . . you know, a friend . . .'

'Hello Akshay.'

'Hello ma'am.'

Mrs Bhave was sitting at her desk surrounded by prints and plans and papers. She looked pale and harassed. Trisha rushed up to her.

'Hi Mom, did you see my note-anyway we're back-there was this huge storm and we had to take shelter and have you had breakfast?' she gabbled breathlessly, suddenly nervous. Her mom smiled.

'Yes, dear, I did see your note. Did you have a good time?' She looked up at Akshay. 'Hi Akshay—I hope your father doesn't mind you learning how to ride?'

'Um . . . no, ma'am. I guess not,' Akshay murmured, going red. 'Trisha's a great teacher.'

'Hmm.' she glanced at them amusedly. 'I see.'

'Flattery will get you nowhere, boy!' Trisha riposted, grinning. 'Now, Mom, have you had breakfast? We're starving!'

'I don't feel like eating—it's this damn nausea.'

'Mom, but you have to!'

'Okay, tell Komal to send up a thin toast, really crisp—with very little butter, please.'

'Okay! Come on, Akshay, let's get something to eat!'

'That boy and Trisha . . .' Mrs Almeida remarked, 'they were standing very close together in the landing . . . like they had been, you know . . . *cuddling.*'

Mrs Bhave looked up. 'Maybe they were. Remember Trisha's a seventeen-year-old rather attractive girl and the boy is about the same age, and seems decent. Kids these days will do things like that—and we can't stop them. Remember the time when you were that age?'

Mrs Almeida was appalled. 'But . . .'

'If they were having a cuddle, so be it. Hopefully they're both sensible enough—I know Trisha is. You see, Rita, if I start butting in and forbidding Trisha from seeing him or boys in general, exactly the opposite is going to happen.' She sighed. 'And I can't alienate Trisha—especially not now. Besides, she's going to need as many friends and as much support as she can get, and as far as I can see there's nothing wrong with the Khurana boys.'

Mrs Almeida returned to her cubicle completely outraged. No wonder Mrs Bhave's father had disowned her and thrown her out of the house—she must have been one hell of a teenager. Ran away with a shippie motorbike-wallah, so it was said. And now she was encouraging her buxom teenage daughter to go riding with boyfriends! How times had changed, and what had modern parents become! If anything, they were worse than their kids. At any rate, whether it was her business or not, she would keep a very sharp eye on young Miss Trisha.

And for young Miss Trisha, it seemed the day was only getting incredibly better.

'Can you come back in the afternoon?' she asked Akshay breathlessly as he took his leave. He nodded, his eyes sparkling.

'Sure. Poor Jai has maths and physics tuitions this afternoon from 2 to 5. He flunked them pretty badly and Papa was mad.'

'Great, because Shivi won't be here—Komal and Tikka take her for her dancing class.'

'Is your mom going out too?' he asked.

'No, but she'll be in her office. She's very busy on a project.'

'And that old bat?'

'She'll go home at lunchtime, I guess. We'll be alone.'

'Great!'

'Bring your saxophone,' she said. 'We can make music.'

She must have brushed her hair five hundred times—it was shining like a shampoo advertisement by the time she stopped, and her arms were aching. She debated whether to dab on a bit of the perfume her mom had given her for her last birthday and regretfully decided against it. Perfume was a complete tell-tale. But she did up her eyes carefully and put on just a hint of lip gloss and wore her favourite golden hoops. She'd been going around tidying her study and humming, when Shivi entered and eyed her suspiciously.

'Why are you cleaning you room?' she asked.

'Because it's untidy. Now do you mind going to the other room?'

'Are you going anywhere when I go for dancing class?'

'No, Shivi. I promise.'

'Then why have you brushed your hair so much and put on lipstick? You didn't brush mine.'

'Okay Shivi, where's the brush?'

Shivi scampered out and returned with the hairbrush, and smiled happily as Trisha combed her curls gently. 'There you go, baby,' she said and sent the thrilled little girl off with a kiss. 'You look beautiful.'

'Hi Mom, still working?'

Mrs Bhave looked up from her Mac. 'Yes, dear. I want to finish this before I go to hospital.' She took in the shining hair, the fresh skirt and Trisha's glowing kohl-lined eyes and touched up lips but said nothing.

'Er, I asked Akshay over to play his saxophone . . . is that okay?'

'Sure. Very nice.' She smiled and arched her eyebrows. 'Will you sing?'

'Umm . . . I don't know . . . Okay, see you.'

'See you, darling.'

Mrs Bhave smiled. There was no doubt about it; her lovely daughter had developed a crush on the young fellow—under the circumstances perhaps that was a good thing.

Trisha flew downstairs and looked at herself in her dressing table mirror yet again. She had put on a rose-pink pleated skirt and a matching pink and white top—nothing suspiciously revealing, of course—but it brought out the high colour in her cheeks nicely and hinted at the heavy, gentle swell of her breasts.

Then she heard the short, tentative doorbell and ran to the door. She ushered him in. Again that awkward silence came between them.

'Hi! Come in.'

'This is my study.' She flicked a sideways glance at him.

'Nice!'

Painted dark blue and white, the study had her desk and computer unit and bookshelves along one wall. Just along the large window, screened by the slim-line wooden Venetian blinds, was a sofa-cum-bed with navy blue and purple cushions and a table in front of it; the blinds imparted a warm glow to the room.

She shut the door quietly behind her and drew the bolt. He was looking at her uncertainly, expectantly.

'Are you sure it's okay?'

She nodded. 'We're safe for fifteen or twenty more minutes,' she murmured, as they fumbled clumsily over each other. 'Shivi will be back in half an hour. If Mom knocks, you disappear into the bathroom.'

He sat up and gazed at her. 'You're so beautiful; you're so utterly sexy, Trish.'

She blushed, but was pleased. 'You think so? I think I'm fat, just look at my figure and—my bottom!'

He shook his head and then nodded, confused. 'No. You're the sexiest girl in the world . . .'

'Thanks. That's sweet of you.'

There was a knock on the door and they sprang apart as if they'd been shot.

'Trisha, dear, are you there?'

The door handle was pressed down gently.

'Oh shit, it's the old bat!' Trisha looked around wildly. No time for them to throw on their clothes . . . Besides, the settee was a rumpled mess . . .

'Quick, pick up your sax and play something!' He whipped out the instrument and blatted out (somewhat discordantly at first) the opening notes of the first song that came to his head.

Trisha shook her head in wonder as the first notes emerged: how did the guy know all these ancient numbers? She took a deep breath and closed her eyes and sang.

'It's cherry pink and apple blossom white . . .'

Her voice just quavered a bit in the beginning, but gained strength and resonated deep and clear; it was perfect for the sax.

Outside the door, Mrs Almeida paused. So Trisha and her friend were just 'jamming'. She listened. The girl had one hell of a husky voice, like fine grade emery paper covered with honey. And whoever was playing the saxophone—probably that Akshay fellow—was bringing tears to her eyes with the memories it evoked of dances she had danced a very, very long time ago. How on earth did a modern hip hop teenager know a song like that and play it so well? At any rate, if one kid was playing the sax and the other singing, they couldn't really be up to any close-up hanky-panky. She wanted to listen longer, but needed to go up to Mrs Bhave—she'd really been looking so unwell these days, poor thing. She stole away; she would also, she thought, reassure Mrs Bhave that the fellow seemed all right after all. It didn't strike her till much later, that Trisha's room door had been locked.

Inside the room, the two dishevelled teenagers looked at each other and giggled as they made music.

Later that evening after kissing Shivi goodnight, Mrs Bhave came into Trisha's study.

'Mom, you . . . you look tired,' Trisha said, glancing at her pale mother.

'I am . . .' Mrs Bhave sat down on the settee. 'Trish, you like Akshay, don't you?'

'He's okay, Mom,' she shrugged but the blush had gone a shade deeper.

'Well, he seems to be a nice boy—at least he hasn't got metal studs and rivets sticking out of various body parts.'

'He's quite nice, Mom—and different.' She smiled, 'I mean, he doesn't mind learning how to ride a bike from a girl! And he's pretty talented!'

'Yes. Good. It's nice that you have a boyfriend. But don't do anything foolish, darling, and remember, you have your Boards coming up in March and like it or not, they're very important. Don't get distracted . . .'

'Mom! Please! He's not my boyfriend! We're just . . . well, friendly.'

'Okay, sweetie . . . goodnight.'

'Goodnight, Mom.'

Certainly, it had been one hell of a day.

CHAPTER SEVEN

ERCP

'I don't want to go to school alone!' Shivi bawled, sitting down on the hall floor and flinging her water bottle away. 'I want Trisha to come with me!'

'Baby, come on now . . .' Komal pleaded, 'Trisha will come just now!'

'Why do I have to go to school if Trisha doesn't? It's not fair!' Shivi emitted a huge hiccup. Mrs Bhave walked up to the upset little girl. Any minute now, she would be sick . . .

'Baby, Trisha has to come with me to the hospital,' she said soothingly, as Trisha watched. 'In the evening, Komal will bring you too.'

'But I want to go now! Why can't I go? You never take me anywhere with you! I hate you, I hate you!'

'Baby, you'll get late . . . you don't want the bell to ring before you get there . . . okay, what if Trisha dropped you?'

'No! She has to come inside school and go to her class! She has to wear her uniform too!'

Trisha rolled her eyes and knelt by her sister. 'Listen Shivi, I'll tell you a big secret.' She whispered something in her little sister' ear. Shivi's eyes grew wide. Trisha nodded. 'Shh . . . don't tell Mom, okay? Now come along.'

Sniffing dolefully and casting black looks at her mother, Shivi got to her feet. Trisha glanced backwards at her mother and rolled her eyes again. Then she beckoned to Tikka who was polishing the pickup.

Inside, Mrs Bhave sighed and then frowned as she heard Smelly Beast start up. Oh well, anything to get Shivi to school when she was in this sort of mood. She went to the front door and looked out.

Tikka had ridden the bike up into the back of the pickup, and Shivi, now smiling delightedly through her tears, was sitting on it, with Trisha pillion, holding her around the waist. Shivi gave her mother a beatific smile and wiped her face. Then she put on her helmet and purple stardust shades and waved. She was ready to ride to school. Tikka slowly backed the pickup out of the driveway. Mrs Bhave gave her daughters a flying kiss and wiped a tear that had suddenly rolled down her cheek.

And so Shivi rode to school in style astride the silver Bullet, firm on its stand in the bed of the pickup, and poor Trisha was beetroot red with embarrassment as they stopped outside the gates. The kids swarming in pointed and giggled and sniggered and a group of boys wolf-whistled. (Then Tikka emerged and they vanished, laughing.) But Shivi was all smiles now; the tantrum had vanished like a summer thunderstorm, and she hugged her elder sister goodbye.

'Don't forget your bottle . . . Komal will pick you up after school.' But Shivi had spotted Bobby and had grabbed him by his tie again, chattering shrilly in his ear.

'I came by motorbike! I came by motorbike! I came by motorbike! Did you see me? Did you see me?'

Trisha dived into the pickup, next to Komal as Tikka flashed a smile and teased: 'Baby, you won't go on the bike?'

'Let's go home. We have to take Mom to the hospital now . . . God, what a kid!'

Inside her the cannonball of dread—exactly like she got at the beginning of exams—was getting bigger and heavier. The day had started badly: at 5 a.m. the phone had gone off, sounding like a fire alarm in the silent house. Groggily Mrs Bhave had answered it. It had been Mrs Almeida, in tears because her twenty-seven-year old son, Roderick had been arrested for drunken driving in Mumbai and she had to go there to bail him out. Trisha had been horrified.

'But Mom, we have to go to the hospital!'

'It's okay, darling, we'll manage. Mrs Almeida has to go!'

'Are you all packed, Mom?' she asked when she got back after dropping Shivi.

To her surprise her mother came up to her and put her arms around her. 'You're an angel . . . you manage Shivi better than anyone.'

'Poor thing . . . but Mom, that's the last time I'm doing that. I nearly died!'

Her mother brought out a small overnighter and a folder containing all her medical papers.

'Okay Trisha, it's time we left. Here, take this. There's Rs 50,000 in this,' Mrs Bhave said, taking out a thick envelope from her handbag. 'They'll probably want some advance on admission . . . take my credit card too.'

Trisha looked at the envelope as if it contained a cobra. '50,000 bucks? But what if I lose it?'

'You won't, darling.'

Tikka dropped them at the portico of the hospital and went to park the pickup. Trisha looked around, and eventually went up to one of the security guards.

'Where do we go for admissions?' she asked timidly. Blindly and dazedly she followed the unnecessarily complicated procedures required, filling in forms, paying the advance and collecting the receipt. At last, she was done.

They were handed two yellow 'Visitor' passes and one blue 'Attendant' pass. The girl at the admission waved to a ward boy who had just come in.

'Take them to Room 3934 in the new wing—Dr Phadnis' patient.'

They followed the ward boy across a grassy courtyard swarming with people—several families seemed to be camping in the shade of the bougainvillea bushes and the lemon trees here—into a glass-fronted new building. There was a gift-cum-book shop on one side, and yet another Chinese takeaway and a Nirula's snack bar on the other. Ahead was a large hall crammed with aluminum seats like in a cinema hall. A large flat screen TV on the wall showed a cricket match in progress, and Trisha smiled wanly, remembering the leg-breaks she had bowled at Akshay. She had really bowled him over . . . and well, he had too.

And then their way was barred by a giant of a fellow, with a moustache like a bush.

'Only one can go. Pass?'

She showed him the pass. He nodded, but blocked poor Komal. 'Only one attendant,' he said, his eyes bulging belligerently.

'Komal, sit here, I'll be back,' Trisha said, hastily following the ward boy and her mother to the lifts. It was a stainless steel one, with a peculiar smell, and Kenny G playing.

Again Trisha smiled: Akshay would've made a funny face if he was here . . . He abhorred Kenny G.

It was hushed and cool on the third floor where they got off. Yet another guard with an even more magnificently bushy moustache examined her pass and gave her a token with the room number scribbled on it. 'Give it back when you leave,' he said. The ward boy plonked her mom's file at the nursing station.

'3934, Dr Phadnis' patient. Admitted for ERCP.'

They followed him through a corridor painted a pleasant peach, with white doors on either side, each with a nameplate for the patient and doctor.

'It's like a hotel, Mom,' Trisha whispered. Except that in a hotel you didn't have nurses pushing trolleys full of medication and syringes around and barging into rooms with them. Or that awful disinfectant, antibiotic smell . . .

'It's not too bad, is it?' Mrs Bhave commented as they looked around the room the ward boy ushered them into. One entire wall was a glass window, overlooking the green woody pelt of Delhi's Central Ridge. A black kite winged past laconically, and on the ledge, a couple of doves pirouetted. The ward boy got busy showing Mrs Bhave the bed and its controls and the emergency bell.

Trisha looked around. Apart from the bed and the scary emergency paraphernalia behind it, oxygen tubes and whatnot, there was a drip stand, a bedside table and against one wall, a wide settee, flanked by two chairs and a coffee table.

A plump nurse, with the most gorgeous ebony skin that Trisha had seen, came in with a tray and a blood pressure machine.

'Mrs Bhave, you haven't eaten anything, have you?' she asked, glancing at her papers and smiling at 500 watts.

'No.'

'Who's the attendant?'

'Me,' Trisha said. The nurse looked at her quizzically. Then she turned to Mrs Bhave.

'Okay, lie down.'

She took her blood pressure and temperature, made a note and went out. Trisha glanced at her watch. It was just 10.30 a.m. Another one and a half hours to go . . .

Trisha checked out the room. There were built-in-cupboards, a safe, and behind a partitioned section, on a granite plinth against the wall, a microwave oven and an electric kettle, and a mini-fridge nestling beneath.

'Mom, this is quite swanky,' she said, peeking into the bathroom. She sat down on the settee and picked up the glossy Information Booklet lying there. She scanned through it and looked up sharply as the door burst open and two doctors accompanied by the nurse and another more senior looking nurse came in.

'Hello, Mrs Bhave, I'm Dr Sharma and this is Dr Pradhan. We'll be assisting Dr Phadnis.'

Dr Sharma was only slightly taller than Trisha, and had rather large ears and knockout buck teeth and serious eyes. Dr Pradhan was taller and somehow more aloof; his eyes were black and looked as if they really weren't seeing anything. They scanned her mother's papers and nodded. 'Okay, Mrs Bhave, we'll call you at 12,' they said, and left before Trisha could even think of asking them anything.

Of course, the moment the door sighed shut, the questions tumbled out: Would it really only take fifteen minutes? Was it done with general anaesthesia? When could she go home? Would the procedure hurt? What medication would be needed?

Mrs Bhave had dozed off on her bed. Trisha went to the window and looked out. The greenery stretching to the horizon was soothing to the eye and down below she could see an endless queue of cars enter and leave the car park. She thought about Akshay—and that incredible Sunday. Had that really happened just two days ago?

Mrs Bhave woke up after about twenty minutes. 'How are you feeling, Mom?' Trisha asked.

'Oh well, the same. Is there a pad and pen? I want to write some instructions for Mrs Almeida.'

'She's in Mumbai, Mom.'

'Yes, but when she gets back . . .'

'We'll be home by then.'

12 o'clock came and went. At 12.15, Trisha began pacing the room. Her mom had dozed off yet again. At 12.27, she went to the window and drummed her fingers on the sill. At 12.30 she left the room and went to the nursing station.

'My mother had to go for an ERCP at 12,' she said. What if she'd missed the bus, so to speak? What if Dr Phadnis had taken his next patient? What if she was now last in the queue? What if he said that as she hadn't shown up she had to get re-admitted? Idiot! She was thinking like a moron!

At the nursing station, the sister looked up calmly. 'Dr Phadnis hasn't come as yet. He'll call.'

'Darling, have you brought something to eat for yourself?' Mrs. Bhave asked when Trisha gave her the news. 'Did Komal . . .'

Oh shit, Komal! She'd clean forgotten about poor Komal! She must still be in the waiting area, wondering what the hell had happened.

'Mom, I'll just send Komal home. She can pick up Shivi and return later.'

Trisha bought herself a cheese and tomato sandwich and a Coke at the Nirula's snack bar and went back to her mom's room. It was empty. She stared around blindly.

'Mom?' She rushed to the bathroom. Empty. She ran out into the corridor to the nursing station.

'My mother?' she asked, panic-stricken. Had something terrible happened? Why wasn't she in her room?

'They've taken her for ERCP . . .'

'Where?'

'Old building, Room 205 . . . Gastroenterology Department.'

She was almost in tears when she got to the Gastroenterology Department. The small waiting area was crammed with people, and every time the door to the toilets opened she got a whiff of urine and phenyl. Behind a counter, a slim girl with light brown eyes and tinted hair was speaking on the phone. Trisha waited till she put down the receiver. She had a pleasant face.

'My mother . . . Mrs Bhave, a patient of Dr Phadnis . . . for ERCP . . . she is here?'

Oh God, what if they'd abducted her mom? What if she wasn't here? What if they'd taken her to an operating theatre and removed her appendix by mistake?

The girl looked at her and smiled. 'There,' she said pointed to an adjoining room. 'The ERCP patients are there.'

Trisha entered the room and looked around in disbelief. God, this could not be real! This . . . this was like the bus bay at the ISBT. All along the walls and spaces in between, the gurneys had been parked, each with a patient. She spotted her mother and rushed over.

'Mom, are you okay?' she asked, taking her hand and wiping a tear away. 'They just took you away.'

'I'm fine. Have you eaten, sweetie?'

The packet of sandwiches and the Coke bottle were still in her bag.

Dr Phadnis bustled in at three o'clock and did a swift round of the room, followed by his team of doctors and nurses. Trisha stared at him in relief; he looked as handsome and suave as ever. He stopped by her mother's bed.

'How are you feeling, Mrs Bhave?' he asked, smiling and examining her eyes.

'Tired.'

'Well, I'll see you inside.'

'Doctor . . .?' Trisha started to say . . . but he and the team had vanished in a swirl of white coats and stethoscopes.

At 4, a couple of ward boys wheeled Mrs Bhave out of the bus bay. The receptionist came up to Trisha with a form and asked:

'Relative?'

'Me.'

The girl looked her up and down. 'Only you?'

'I'm her daughter.'

'Your papa?'

'He's dead.'

'Sorry . . . um . . . very well, kindly fill and sign this.'

Trisha scanned the form. Basically, it was something that seemed to let the hospital and doctors off the hook if something went wrong. But she had no choice. She signed and rushed out. At the entrance to another corridor, sealed off by glass swinging doors, was a large board saying 'ERCP Centre. Remove Footwear, No Admission'.

People—hospital staff, doctors and nurses—were going in and out busily; none of them bothered to take their footwear off. And there, in a row in front of a pair of shut doors at the end of the corridor were three gurneys, nose to tail, waiting to enter. Her mom was 3. At 4.45 they took her in, and outside Trisha sat down suddenly. This was it . . . three minutes later, a nurse came flying out.

'The MRCP report and X-rays?' she asked. Trisha looked at her blankly.

'What?'

'The doctor wants them quickly!'

Okay, keep calm; they had brought them, she knew they were in the most bulky of all the envelopes. If they hadn't brought it down with them, it must be in her mom's room. 'I'll get it!' she said and took off.

Trisha ran back with the report. 'Here it is!' she said, weak with relief, handing it to the nurse who was tapping her feet impatiently. Anger sparked. 'You should have got it when you brought her down!' she said. The nurse vanished. And then her phone started playing 'Cherry Pink and Apple Blossom White'.

'Hello?'

'Trisha? Where are you? Nobody here knows anything. Which room is your mom in?'

'Akshay?'

'And you were expecting?'

Through her tears she smiled. 'Idiot, I'll get you! Just come here!'

'Where, baby? Tell me where and I shall be there and you can have me! Even on the operating table!'

'Pervert! Come to the Gastroenterology Department, second floor in the old wing. It's Room 202.'

'Don't elope with an endoscopist, my love! I shall be there! We shall wriggle through intestines of gastroenterology to escape our pursuers . . .'

A few minutes later Akshay turned up, still in his school uniform, tie awry, hair berserk, eyes searching. She rose to greet him and took his hands. 'They've taken her in,' she wailed, pointing to the doors.

And they were wheeling her out! She stared incredulously as the doors swung open and the gurney was wheeled out.

Oh God, had they done it at all? It had not even been fifteen minutes . . . Dr Phadnis and his team strode out, still masked and gowned. He beckoned to her.

'Wait a sec,' she said to Akshay and went in.

'How is she? Did you do it?' She was staring at her mom, lying curled up on her side on the gurney, the horrible drip bottle hanging over her, a cannula in her arm.

'It went very well. She'll be fine.'

For one glorious moment her heart soared and she wanted to sing. 'Then it was not malign . . . the cancer?'

He shook his head. 'Malignant, I'm afraid,' he said.

'How . . . long?' she whispered.

He stared at her and put a hand on her shoulder. 'Eight months to two years,' he said in a flat, expressionless tone. 'She's very fit, so it could be more . . .'

'You can't do anything?'

'No. It's too far gone. Do you have any older relatives? Your father?'

'There's just me . . . my father's dead.'

The receptionist came up with a set of papers and he turned his attention to her. 'I'll look in this evening. She'll be okay.' He nodded and was gone.

She followed the gurney to the lift, Akshay by her side.

'What?' he asked, looking scared. 'You look like a ghost. You're absolutely white.'

'Eight months,' she whispered dully. 'He said eight months to two years . . .'

He took her hand and held it tight. 'He can be wrong,' he said hollowly. 'You never know.'

Upstairs another problem presented itself. Bushy Moustache planted himself firmly in front of Akshay and barred his way. Trisha glanced at her watch.

'It's five o'clock,' she said. 'Visiting hours.'

'Pass?'

Oh shit, Komal had the passes.

'Please,' she pleaded. 'He'll come out in two minutes.'

'No.'

'Fucking idiot . . .' Akshay was beginning to get pissed off.

'Shh . . . listen, wait here, I'll be back, Komal should be coming any minute now with Shivi, you can take her pass.'

Hastily she followed the cavalcade to the room and watched as they transferred her mother to her bed, wincing as they hoisted her up and put her down as if she were a sack of potatoes.

'You have a private sister?' the staff nurse asked Trisha.

'What? No. Why?'

'Better . . .'

'But this is a hospital.'

A little later she spoke to the nursing agency on the phone and fixed up a private nurse. Through the glass doors at the end of the corridor she saw Komal, Shivi and Akshay. Komal seemed to be arguing with Bushy Moustache and was wagging her visitor passes in his face.

'What's the matter?'

'He isn't allowing Shivi in,' Akshay said, his voice tight with anger. 'He's saying children under ten are not allowed.'

'I want to see Mommy!' Shivi was beginning to look mutinous.

'You will,' Trisha said. She picked up the little girl and flung the visitor passes at Bushy Moustache.

'Komal and Akshay, just wait here. I'll be back,' she said, glaring at Bushy Moustache.

'I am taking my sister to see our mother,' she snapped. 'Just you try and stop me!' She turned on her heel and stormed in.

She took a deep breath as she entered the darkened room, with Shivi on her hip. 'Shivi, Mom's resting, so don't disturb her . . .'

Shivi's eyes were big as moons as she gazed around the room.

'Is she all right? Is she alive?'

'Yes, of course, come on, let's say hi to her.'

Shivi leaned forward. 'Hi Mommy,' she whispered, staring at the cannula and drip. 'Is the needle hurting you?'

Mrs Bhave's eyes flickered open. 'Hi Shivi baby! Did you ride here on Smelly Beast?'

'How are you feeling, Mom?' Trisha asked. 'Do you have any pain?'

'My throat is very sore,' Mrs. Bhave said huskily. 'Now I'm sounding like you, darling!'

'What did they do?'

Her mom's eyes flashed indignantly. 'They trussed me up like a chicken and held me down and then stuffed something down my throat. Then I don't know really what happened . . . but I couldn't move a muscle!'

'Just sleep, Mom, they'll give you something to eat and drink soon.'

Right on cue the door opened and a ward boy marched in carrying a tray, with a thermos and two Marie biscuits.

'Chai!' he announced and left the tray on the table.

The staff nurse entered with the blood pressure machine and smiled brilliantly at Shivi.

'Your little sister?' she asked Trisha. 'She's so cute!'

The door opened again and suddenly the room seemed full of security guards; there were three of them including Bushy Moustache.

'Come out!' he said belligerently. 'Children are not allowed.'

'Okay, Shivi, say bye to Mom. She'll be home tomorrow.'

'Come on, madam . . . come on!'

Something snapped; she whirled and said 'Fuck you!'

Shivi's jaw dropped. 'Mommy,' she whispered. 'Did you hear what Trisha said?'

Mrs Bhave opened her eyes and smiled. 'Yes, dear.' She looked icily at the men hovering in the background. 'Get out!' she said imperiously, flicking her fingers in dismissal. 'Now!'

Muttering, they withdrew. The nurse just looked on, her eyes wide.

'She rides a motorcycle, and that too a Bullet!' Trisha told her with a proud toss of her head, her tears glimmering. 'Shivi, let's go. Mom, I'll just leave her with Komal and be back.'

She marched up the corridor to the lobby outside the lifts. Bushy Moustache was barring the way of some other visitor who did not have a pass.

'Komal, you take Shivi home.'

Shivi protested and only agreed to go home after Trisha had allowed her to play games on her computer with Mr Teddy Sir.

Trisha frowned. Like an idiot she had forgotten to pack night clothes and toothbrush . . . that stupid old Almirah's phone call in the morning had completely derailed her. Akshay was staring at her with a reverential look in his eyes.

'Can I say hi to your mom?' he asked.

At the lift, Shivi turned around and looked straight at Bushy Moustache.

'Someone should cut off half his moustache,' she muttered, 'bully!'

Akshay greeted Mrs Bhave and stood awkwardly by the bedside. Mrs Bhave smiled and then closed her eyes.

Trisha took his hand and dragged him to the partitioned section. She wrapped her arms around him.

'Oh Akshay, it's been such a *horrible* day . . .'

They had gone and now she was alone, confronting what Dr Phadnis had told her. *Eight months to two years, maybe more.* Eight months would be February, and she would be preparing full tilt for her Boards. Two years would be . . . well, she would be in college then. But no, nothing like that was going to happen. There came a tentative knock on the door and she looked up.

A lady with an almost circular face and three comfortable chins, resting one on top of the other, peeped in. Her eyes were big and round and strands of hair had escaped the comb. She had a lovely snub nose.

'Trisha beta?' she asked.

Trisha nodded, perplexed.

The lady entered quietly. 'Hello beta, I'm Gullu's mother, Parkash Aunty,' she said. 'Gullu, silly girl, only told me this evening that your mother is in hospital.'

'Is Gullu here?'

The lady shook her head. 'No, she wanted to come but had her music class and couldn't cancel it.' She walked up to the bed. 'Sleeping . . .' she whispered. She stood by Trisha and took her hands in her own soft ones.

'Beta, if there's anything you need, please ask. Don't be shy. How is your little sister?'

'She's okay, Aunty. I sent her home.'

'You have been here the whole day?'

Trisha nodded.

'Have you eaten?'

'I'll order something.'

Gullu's mother delved into her vast handbag and pulled out a plastic box. 'Aloo paranthas with achchaar,' she announced. 'And sooji ka halva.' She marched to the kitchenette. 'Ah, good! You can heat them in the microwave,' she said.

The paranthas smelt divine and Trisha's tummy growled like Smelly Beast.

'Thank you, Aunty.'

And then Gullu's mother gave her the warmest, most-engulfing hug she had ever received.

Trisha walked her to the lift and saw Bushy Moustache scowling at them both.

Gullu's mom gave the fellow a baleful look and snorted.

'Muchchad ke mooch kaat denge. We'll cut off Mr Moustache's moustache,' she said in Punjabi and got into the lift.

Evidently she had won a round with him too. She had entered without a visitor's pass.

At eight o'clock the new staff nurse on duty—a tall girl with a waist Trisha could only ogle at enviously—entered and proceeded to give her mother an injection. Trisha watched like a hawk. It seemed so easy—she opened the cap of the cannula, filled the syringe, squinted at it and squirted a tiny bit—and then just put the nozzle into the cannula and gently pressed down on the plunger. Her mom didn't even open her eyes. Then she took her pulse and blood pressure, noted them down. She checked the intravenous line, tapping it slightly and put the bell near her mom's head as she settled her back.

'Your mummy?' she asked Trisha.

'Uh-huh,' Trisha nodded through a mouthful of paranthas.

'Didn't your papa come?'

Trisha shook her head. 'Dead,' she said softly.

'Oh, so sorry!' Her eyes softened as she looked at Trisha.

'It's okay,' she shrugged. 'Long time ago . . .'

'Now your mummy is sick . . .' The girl's eyes were eloquent. Gently she reached out and patted Trisha's cheek. 'Don't worry, she'll be well soon.' She smiled. 'If you want anything, ring the bell, okay?' She glanced at her watch. 'You called a private sister?'

'Yes, but it's not pakka if she'll come.'

'You ring the bell—okay?'

'Okay. Thank you.' The nurse's name was Flossie, according to the badge she had on.

The girl had barely left when the door opened again. Trisha had been standing at the window, staring out at the dark velvet canopy over the Ridge, and the fire-orange glow of the sodium lights of the city beyond. Dr Khurana entered with Flossie, looking a little bemused.

'Hello, Trisha,' he said, as Flossie turned on the lights and handed him her mother's file. 'I spoke to Dr Phadnis—he said it went off well.'

'Is she going to be all right?'

'She's doing as well as she can at the moment. Dr Phadnis said she could go home in a couple of days.'

'Oh!' Her heart sank. They wouldn't be going home tomorrow then . . .

Then her phone, lying on the coffee table, started playing 'Cherry Pink and Apple Blossom White', getting louder with each passing moment.

Dr Khurana looked askance as she fumbled and switched the blessed thing off. 'Sorry,' she said, blushing.

'That is one of my favourite tunes,' the doctor said, turning back to her mother. 'I taught Akshay that on the sax—he should listen to this version—it's a nice rendering.' He glanced at her and smiled. 'You sing very well—I heard you the other day.'

'Thank you,' she said, going red.

'How are you feeling?' Dr Khurana asked her mother. 'You should feel better by tomorrow.'

Her mother nodded. 'Thank you for coming, Doctor.'

'They've put the stent in place—it should clear the way for the bile. Okay, Mrs Bhave, I'll be going now. I'll see you at home in a few days.' Trisha escorted him out to the lifts. There was a different Bushy Moustache on duty now.

'Doctor . . .' Trisha mumbled, the tears beginning to well. 'Dr Phadnis said she has eight months to two years . . .'

Dr Khurana took her arm gently. 'It's a slow-growing tumour—she could be okay for a while. We'll wait and watch.'

'What exactly is it?'

'It's called cholangiocarcinoma—a rather rare cancer of the bile duct.'

'Oh . . . and they can't do anything?'

He shook his head. 'Not in this case. Chemotherapy and radiation won't help; they'll only make her miserable. Surgery is not possible.'

'Oh!' He was avoiding her eyes. God, she thought suddenly, how must it feel to be a doctor, a crack, cutting-edge specialist like all these fellows were—and be confronted with an illness you were helpless against? 'Trisha, will you be all right here by yourself?'

She nodded. 'Yes,' she said, just as her phone started playing again. He waved as he got into the lift and she waved back.

'Hi!' she said breathlessly into the phone.

'You didn't pick up and then you cut the call—I was shit scared.' She snorted. 'Guess who was here! Your dad.'

'Oh, yeah, he did say he'd drop by.'

'He was here when the phone started ringing and he recognized the tune!'

'Oh! Did he know?'

'Well, he said whoever was playing the sax was playing it rather well and that you should listen to it and maybe take a tip or two.'

'You're kidding me!'

'Seriously! He might ask you to listen to it.'

Within a minute she got another call.

'How's your mom?' Gullu asked. 'Has my mom been to see her?'

'Yes, she came and left me some paranthas. Mom's okay.'

'Sorry, I wanted to come but I had my lesson . . . they charge 350 bucks every time, even if you cancel.'

'That's okay.'

'Anyway, who were you talking to before I called? The line was busy for ages!'

'Oh . . . just some friend.'

'Ahem! Not *the* friend?'

'Who?'

'You know, Trish, the *boyfriend* . . .'

'Who? What boyfriend?'

'Akshay Khurana, sweetie!'

'Oh him . . . yeah, it may have been him!'

'You're blushing! I know it!'

'Gullu, shut up!'

'Gotcha! But it's okay—he's quite sweet.'

'He came here when Mom was inside . . .' she let out unthinkingly.

'*What?* Oh my God, if he's come to see your mom in hospital, he's deadly serious! Be careful, Trish, be careful!'

'You yammer such garbage, Gullu, really!' But she was smiling again.

'Yeah, yeah, I know. Anyway bye—catch you tomorrow.'

'Bye, Gullu. And say thanks to your mom!'

At around 9.15 there was a perfunctory knock and the door burst open, and Dr Phadnis, accompanied by Dr Sharma and Dr Pradhan, strode in, followed by the sister on duty. She put on the lights, and Trisha sat up bolt upright, blinking.

Dr Phadnis nodded and smiled and then all three of them were around her mom's bed, with the sister opening the file and clicking her ballpoint pen.

'Has she eaten anything? How are you feeling, Mrs Bhave?'

Mrs Bhave opened her eyes. 'When can I go home, Doctor?' she asked.

'We're thinking of sending you home the day after tomorrow. Tomorrow we'll just check if everything is okay.' He smiled at her and barked something at the sister.

'She's . . . doing okay, Doctor?' Trisha asked tentatively.

Dr Sharma nodded briefly. 'Yes, she's doing okay.' And just like that, they were gone.

She lay down on the settee and drew up the sheet and blanket to her chin. Five minutes later, she heard her mom snoring softly.

Sometimes, when you wanted to believe in miracles they just happened right out of the blue—as they had just last Sunday in that incredible cavern. Now there was just one more miracle she wanted: for her mom to be well again and everything to go back to normal. If that happened she would be a complete believer in miracles—forever. If they only were able to go back to the life they had had before this, evil, insidious disease had reared its loathsome head . . .

CHAPTER EIGHT

REGRESSION, REMISSION, OBLIVION

It wasn't a miracle Trisha awoke to a couple of hours later, but a nightmare. She had dozed off, after tossing and turning for a good hour and a half, when she heard a groaning sound from her mom's bed. She was at the bedside in a jiffy.

'Mom? Mom? What's wrong?'

Her mom's face was all scrunched up and there was sweat pouring off her. She moved her head from side to side, moaning, her pallor a horrible greyish white.

'Are you in pain? Mom, Mom . . .?' Her mother just opened her eyes, gasped and nodded. 'Yes,' she whispered.

The bell! Where was it? Trisha rang it and rushed to the door. Outside, the corridor was in near darkness, with just the white glow from a tube light at the nursing station at the end of the corridor. The red bulb on the top of their room door pulsed. Trisha rushed back to the bedside.

'I'm going to call the nurse,' she said. What if there was nobody there, she thought, panic-stricken. What if it was too late by the time she found help? Get a grip, girl, get a grip. She gulped and steadied herself. She rushed out, barefoot; to her relief the night sister was already on her way . . .

'Please come, she's in pain . . .' she whispered. 'Hurry!'

'Mrs Bhave, what's the matter? You are having pain?' The sister checked the IV line, took her pulse and checked her blood pressure.

'Please give her something!' Why was the stupid woman not instantly giving her a painkiller?

'I'll have to ask the doctor. Just wait.'

She walked back to the nursing station.

'Mom, hang on, she's just asking the doctor.' She took her mom's hand and squeezed it. Mrs Bhave was moaning now, and Trisha was white in the face. She kept looking at the door. After what seemed like a century the sister came back in. 'Duty doctor says he'll have to ask Dr Phadnis.' she said. 'But it's very late now . . .'

'Wh . . .what do you mean? You can't give her anything?'

The sister looked at Mrs Bhave. It was evident she was in extreme distress.

'Please,' Trisha whispered dully.

'Okay.' The sister left the room as Trisha sank into the chair disbelievingly. She returned with a callow fellow, who strutted in like a courting sparrow.

'Yes . . . what's the problem?'

'My mother is having pain.'

'Oh . . . I'm sorry, I'm not authorized to give . . .'

'But you're a doctor!' She was almost in tears. 'Can't you give her a painkiller?'

'I'll have to ask Dr Phadnis!'

'Then please ask him!'

'It's very late.'

Trisha swallowed the sob that was threatening to erupt. 'Okay, then I'll call him,' she said desperately, taking out her phone. Please, please God let him answer . . .

The doctor and sister exchanged glances. He exhaled. 'Okay,' he said, giving instructions to the sister, who left the room.

'I've asked the nurse to give her an injection that should ease the pain and make her sleep,' he said.

'Why couldn't you have given it to her earlier?' Trisha whispered, wiping her mom's brow with a wet towel. 'Why do you have to wait for this to happen?'

But he was on his way out. The sister came back with a syringe and gave her mom an injection. Fifteen minutes later, Mrs Bhave's face relaxed again, and she slept.

On her settee Trisha sobbed for the next half hour. They weren't doctors here—they were ghouls. They revelled in their patients' pain . . . sadistic bastards, all of them.

She wiped her eyes and looked at her mom. Sound and peacefully asleep. But maybe . . . maybe, they had to be careful before giving her medication . . . especially after this procedure. What if her mom had reacted violently to the injection, or had been allergic to it? What if it had triggered off a heart attack? And Dr Sparrow didn't seem to have a whole lot of experience . . .

She awoke with a start when the nurse barged in at 5.30 the next morning, banging and rattling her tray. She drew the curtains back and switched on the lights.

'Good morning!'

Trisha rubbed her eyes blearily and looked at her mom. Her face was calm and peaceful; she looked rested if pale.

'How are you feeling, Mom? Do you have any pain?'

'No.' She smiled wanly. 'But I thought I'd had it last night.'

'The stupid doctor didn't want to give you the injection without asking Dr Phadnis.'

'I hope he is able to go to the bathroom without having to ask Dr Phadnis!' her mom retorted, bringing a smile to Trisha's face.

The door opened and the doctor entered.

'Here he is, Mom!' Trisha whispered. And added under her breath: 'Dr Sparrow, M. D. Hopeless Case.'

'How are you this morning, Mrs Bhave?' the doctor asked her cheerfully, studying her chart.

Mrs Bhave looked him up and down. 'Doctor,' she said, her voice still gravelly, 'do you always wait until your patients are nearly dead with pain before giving them painkillers? Why couldn't you have given it to me earlier?'

'Um . . . ma'am, you'll have to ask Dr Phadnis about that . . .'

'You can be sure I will!'

'No fever?' the doctor asked the sister.

She shook her head.

'No, sir. Also, BP and pulse are normal.'

'All right, very good.' He nodded and left.

'Trisha, call Tikka—you go home now, darling. You've been here since yesterday.'

'But Mom, I can't leave you!'

'You have school . . . you've already missed a day.'

'I told Ms Sonam I wouldn't be coming for two or three days. It's okay.'

'Go home, darling, and rest . . . you must be dead beat. I don't want you to fall sick too.'

'I'll be fine, Mom!'

'Anyway, ring up and find out how Shivi is.'

Shivi, apparently, was being royally spoiled by Komal and having a jolly good time.

'I'm having chocolate milkshake for breakfast!' she announced gleefully. 'And Gullu and her mommy came over last night and left gulab jamuns just for me! And then Akshay and Jai came and gave me some Toblerone.'

'Wow! Leave some for me!'

'I've left some for Mommy. I want to come to the hospital.'

'Okay, but after school.'

'I don't want to go to school. You're not going to school, so why should I?'

'Here, say hi to Mom . . .'

'Hi Mommy! How're you?'

'I'm well, darling.'

'When are you coming home?'

'Maybe tomorrow.'

'Can I come to the hospital? I've saved gulab jamuns for you.'

'How about you come in the evening . . .'

'I want to come now!'

'Darling, now all the doctors will be coming to see me.'

'Oh. Can I take the gulab jamuns to school?'

'Yes. Tell Komal to pack them up properly so they don't spill.'

There was a knock on the door and the duty sister entered with another nurse.

'You wanted a private sister?' the duty nurse inquired.

'Yes.' Trisha nodded.

'This is Richa.'

The duty sister opened her mother's file and showed it to Richa, explaining her mother's case.

'Okay,' she said, 'I've explained everything to her.' She left the room.

Mrs Bhave was still on the phone.

'Shivi, give the phone to Komal or Tikka, sweetie.'

'Yes, Mommy.'

'Trish, let Tikka drop Shivi to school. Then you go home.'

'Okay, I'll have a bath and come back. Let me ask when Dr Phadnis will come to see you.'

Back at the hospital, bathed and fresh and carrying a change of clothes for both her mom and herself Trisha flaunted her pass under Bushy Moustache's nose and came up.

'Hi, Mom—has the doctor been here yet?' she asked breathlessly. Richa shook her head and she sighed with relief. Her mother was dozing.

'I'll make her fresh now,' Richa said, taking the clothes out of the carryall.

Trisha watched as the nurse expertly sponged her mother. Tomorrow . . . hopefully tomorrow they would be back home and things could return slowly to normal.

She was on the intercom with Nirula's downstairs, about to order chicken kathi rolls for herself when the doctors swarmed in.

'So how are you feeling this morning, Mrs Bhave?' he asked, studying her file.

'Okay.'

'She had a lot of pain last night, Doctor,' Trisha said. 'And they wouldn't give her anything for it . . . at first.'

'Well, your reports are good. Your bilirubin is already coming down; the stent is working well. You should be feeling hungry . . . what have you eaten?' He turned to the nurse.

'She had a little suji and some juice.'

'Good. How's the nausea?'

'Better.'

'Very well! We'll have an X-ray taken and if it's fine you can go home tomorrow. I'll see you again this evening.'

And then they were gone.

'Whew! They're always in such a hurry.' Trisha made a face and picked up the intercom again; then she paused. If Akshay was coming at lunchtime—as he had told her on the phone—maybe they could eat together downstairs in the snack bar.

'Hi, I'm here in the lobby,' he said throatily at 1.15 p.m. 'How will I recognize you?'

'What? Oh you silly ass . . . I'm wearing a bright yellow kurti embroidered with purple fuchsias and jeans!'

'Purple fuchsias? Wow! I couldn't miss that for anything.'

'Mom,' she said, hanging up. 'I'm going down for lunch. Um, Akshay's come over.'

Her mom, who was now sitting up next to her, raised an eyebrow. 'He's bunked school? Dr Khurana will be very annoyed.'

'His school is just walking distance from here, so he said he'd pop over.'

'Okay dear, you go down and have a good time. Ah, now where's my mobile? I'd better call Rita and check if things are okay with her.'

By about 4 that afternoon, Mrs Bhave was feeling considerably better. She even asked Trisha to order her some vegetable spring rolls from the Chinese takeaway.

'I just love the crispiness,' she said, wiping her fingers on a paper napkin.

'But Mom, are you sure you should have these?' Trisha asked. 'They're so greasy!'

'I'm hungry,' her mom replied. Two words which made Trisha very happy indeed.

'Trish, you go home this evening. I have Richa here. I will be fine!' Mrs Bhave insisted.

This time, Shivi had no problem getting through during visiting hours. Bushy Moustache knew he had been beaten. Trisha even flashed him a smile—poor guy, she thought suddenly, what a job, to pick quarrels with people who were already upset and worried and forbid them from seeing their loved ones who were ill; and yes, knowing that about twenty-five would want to visit a sick relative or friend, all at the same time if they could. But to Trisha's consternation, Dr Phadnis and his team hadn't still turned up when visiting hours were over and they had to leave.

'I'm taking Shivi to the park,' Komal announced as they reached home. Komal, Trisha knew, was a stickler for routine; it was later than she would normally have taken Shivi—but there was still plenty of daylight. 'Just for ten minutes . . .' That, Trisha thought with a grin, would put Komal's schedule back on track. Bath at 7.15, dinner at 7.30 p.m. bed at 8.00 p.m. come what may! This hospital business had jiggered up her routine good and proper!

'I'm going to the market, baby,' Tikka said. 'I have to buy vegetables and fruit.'

Now she was home and completely alone . . . something that very rarely happened. Trembling, she punched in Akshay's number.

'Hi, where are you? Can you come over now?'

'I shall be pissing by yer git in phaive minutes on my way fhom my saxphyene class . . .'

'What? Will you stop talking like Peter Sellers, please!'

'See ya in five, baby doll!'

'Idiot!'

She was frantically tidying her hair and doing up her eyes when the opening notes of 'Cherry Pink and Apple Blossom White' floated up through her bedroom window. He was down there, rolling his eyes and playing his sax. She raced downstairs.

'You goof!' She grabbed him and pulled him in. 'The whole neighbourhood will hear you.'

'I play zis not for you. I play zis for ze beautiful old bat that lives in the cave up zere. Hopefully she will fly away . . .'

'She has. She's in Bombay.'

'Zen shall we go to ze bat cave and make love zere, my zweet.'

'You really are a crackpot!' Suddenly she grinned. That would be one up old Almirah's snout. 'Okay,' she giggled, 'let's go up!' She took his hand and led him up.

'Where's drummer boy?' she asked. Akshay rolled his eyes some more.

'Ze drummer boy, I zink he has ze hots for ze Gullugirl!'

'What?' She stared at him, astonished. 'He likes Gullu?'

Akshay nodded and grinned back. 'Yup. Of course he won't admit it . . .'

They entered the 'bat cave' and looked around.

'But zis is hopeless!' The bat cave was austere as a monk's cell, cold, white and uninviting.

Not hopeless, Trisha thought, suddenly crimsoning with shame.

'Not here. Not now. It . . . it wouldn't be right . . . not when she's in hospital,' she gulped.

'Would you like to listen to something?' he asked, as they sat rather self-consciously in the drawing room, eyeing each other. 'Or would you like to sing?'

'Just let her come home, Akshay,' she said. 'Then . . .'

'That's fine by me.'

She got up and walked to the kitchen. 'Would you like something to eat or drink?'

In the drawing room he saw shadows pass the windows; Shivi and Komal were returning from the park. He picked up his sax. The opening notes of 'The Colonel Boogie March' blared out stridently as Shivi rushed in and Akshay began marching up and down the drawing room.

'That's our assembly tune!' Shivi said, marching along with him, grinning. 'Hup—two-three-four, hup-two-three-four!'

The phone rang, startling her.

'Hello? Is that Trisha? This is Richa . . .'

'What?' she whispered, suddenly giddy and sitting down. 'What happened?'

'The doctor came; your mummy can go home tomorrow.'

Then her mom came on the line. 'Hi Trisha—yes, I'll be home tomorrow. The X-ray turned out fine. They'll do a blood test tomorrow morning and give me the final go-ahead.'

'Oh great!'

Relief poured through her. Once her mom was home, things would be normal again.

'Who was that?' Shivi asked, popping her tousled head around the door. 'Was it Mommy?'

'Mom's coming home tomorrow, Shivi,' she said, picking her up and kissing her. 'And now you better go back to bed before Komal finds you running loose!'

Two minutes later, Gullu called.

'Hi, how's your mom doing? My mom says sorry she couldn't visit her today.'

Trisha grinned wickedly. 'Don't you think Jai is an awesome drummer?' she asked innocently.

'Absolutely! What? Oh, yeah, he's pretty good, I guess . . .'

'I think he rocks!'

'You do? Wow! But Akshay's pretty good too. And he plays the piano and the keyboard as well.'

'Yeah, well, they're pretty talented. Jai was saying you're pretty good too.'

'He did? Seriously? You're kidding me!'

'Really!'

'What did he say, exactly?'

'Just that you play pretty darned well, both in plucking and rhythm.'

'Oh.'

'Gullu, I can hear you blushing! There's a roaring in my ears!'

'What? Rubbish!' Gullu ran a hand through her mop top. 'Besides,' she went on tartly, 'have you see yourself when Akshay's around? You tremble like a leaf—weak in the knees, your pupils dilate, you keep licking your lips and passing your hand through your hair . . .'

It was nice to be back in your own bed again, Trisha thought, pulling the sheet up to her chin. Tomorrow, Mom would be back too and everything would slowly return to normal. And maybe that tumour or whatever would also just dissipate of its own accord. What did the doctors like calling it—regress. Yes, maybe it would regress or . . . what was that other term they kept using—go into remission.

Not regression. Not remission. Oblivion. That's where she wanted it to go: into oblivion. Permanently.

Her mother was sitting on the settee having her breakfast—idlis and cornflakes—when she got in the next morning.

'Hi sweetie, how're things at home? You managing okay?'

'Hi Mom! Sure, everything's fine. You got the final go-ahead?'

'Well, no one has said anything to the contrary. So I suppose so.'

'Did a nurse come for the night?'

'Yes dear, her name is Hema . . . I've asked both of them to come home for a couple of days.'

'Good.'

The sister on duty opened the door. 'The billing department is calling for you—Room 102, ground floor.'

'Oh.' Shit . . . she'd clean forgotten to ask her mom about money. They'd already taken 40,000, maybe that would cover it all . . . but . . . but what if it didn't? How embarrassing would that be! They'd probably hold her mom prisoner (strapped to her bed, maybe!) until she got the money . . . Jesus! Oh, but thank God, her mom had given her fifty grand, so the ten grand must still be in its envelope. Also she had her mom's credit card. She rummaged frantically in her bag; yes, there it was. Relieved, she got to her feet.

'I'll see what they want,' she said and went downstairs.

Her mother's total bill was for Rs 65,435. She had paid 40,000 advance and had 10,000 in cash. She was still short by 15,435. She went white. She couldn't pay her mom's bill. She'd had nightmares about being in such a situation and now it was happening for real! They would keep her prisoner until she came up with the cash, which meant there would be more delay before she got out of this railway station of a hospital!

The credit card! What an idiot she was!

'I . . . have 10,000 in cash,' she told the cashier. 'Can I pay the balance by credit card?'

He nodded and put his hand out. 'Yes, certainly.'

At last she clutched the sheaf of stamped bills and receipts and made her way back up. She handed them over at the nursing station.

'The doctor will give the final permission,' they told her.

The doctors bustled in at 11.45 a.m. and did just that.

'You can go home, Mrs Bhave,' Dr Phadnis said, smiling.

'Er . . . Doctor, is there any special diet she needs to be on?' Trisha asked.

'She can eat what she likes.'

'When can she start riding her motorbike again?'

Gotcha! That stopped him in his tracks. He turned, his eyebrows raised.

'What?'

'Mom rides a Bullet, Doctor.'

'Oh . . . I see . . .' He shrugged and smiled his charming smile. 'She can ride it whenever she feels strong enough to. As I said she's made an excellent recovery—she's very fit!'

'Goodbye, Doctor. And thank you very much.'

The discharge summary took another hour and a half to complete. Trisha glanced at it, trying to make head or tail of it. Again, the diagnosis brought a chill: Cholangiocarcinoma . . . Carcinoma— everyone knew was cancer. She thrust it away with the rest of the reports, hoping it would mutate into something harmless the next time she looked at it and began packing her mom's overnighter. 'This is like coming out of jail,' Trisha whispered as they waited for the lifts. 'How're you feeling?'

'I just want to get home and start working again.'

'We have to see Dr Phadnis in his clinic in five days.'

'I'll be fine . . .'

And then they were home. Komal had kept her mom's bedroom spick and span and ready. 'You better rest!' Trisha insisted. 'You can go to the office tomorrow.'

'Okay, dear. By the way, Mrs Almeida is returning tomorrow too. I called her.'

'Oh, that's great!'

And yes, everything would be squarely back to normal now. If not completely normal as in pre-cancer times, at least it would seem like that. For the time being at least, she could imagine that things were normal.

A smile of pure mischief lit up her face. She glanced at her watch and picked up her phone . . .

'Hey Akshay, guess what? Mom's home! Listen, the old bat is due tomorrow morning. I think we have some unfinished business in the bat cave . . . when can you come?'

'I'm on my way, chick, I'm on my way!'

CHAPTER NINE

RIDING UP THE MOUNTAINS

'Kassaulli! Kassaulli! We're going to Kassaulli!'
'What?' Trisha whirled around, startled, as Shivi burst into her study, hyper excited. 'Who's going to Kasauli?'

'Mommy says we are!' Shivi sang. 'In the holidays!'

'What holidays?' She got up. 'Where's Mom?'

'Upstairs in her office. We're going to Kasssaulli, we're going to Kassaulli!'

In her office Mrs Bhave was working at her Mac. She turned around as Trisha entered.

'Hi Mom, what's this about Kasauli?' Trisha looked at her mom. Indeed, it did seem as if a miracle had unfolded; she had more or less regained her appetite, her colour was good and she had been working her butt off on her Kasauli project. True, she did tend to tire quickly and often took catnaps on her settee, but give it time. It had been a little over a month since her 'procedure', and already her bilirubin count—which was an indicator of the presence of bile in the liver—was down to 3, from a scary 9. Of course, normal was around 1, but she'd get there. Dr Phadnis had been very pleased with her progress.

'Hi sweetheart—yes, I thought we could all drive up during the Independence Day weekend. Rakhi is on Wednesday, the 13th, Janmashtami on the 14th and Independence Day on Friday, so you'll get five whole days off. I have to go there for my project, and will probably stay on and call Mrs Almeida up, but you and Shivi can drive back down on Sunday with Tikka and Komal.'

'Oh!' Trisha frowned. 'Mom, but everyone in Delhi will be driving out to Kasauli and Simla during that weekend.'

'I know, darling. We'll leave very early.'

'Where are we staying?'

'At a cottage near the resort site; it belongs to the proprietors.'

'But there'll be hordes of people swarming about.'

'The place hasn't opened yet—we'll probably be the only ones around.'

'Oh.'

'I thought we'll drive up in the pickup and take Smelly Beast with us too.'

'You're going to ride Smelly Beast?' Her heart leapt. Her mom had not got on the bike since her procedure. She grinned. 'Don't tell me you'll be riding up and down the mountains with Almirah pillion; that'll be a sight!'

'Maybe! I should be strong enough.'

Still it couldn't be too bad. If her mom and old Almirah stayed back for a week, she'd pretty much have the run of the house and could have a blast with Akshay. But wait a minute . . . yes . . . why not . . . wow, if it worked out . . .

'Okay Mom, great!' She ran back down to her study and called Akshay.

'Hey listen,' she said breathlessly. 'What are you guys doing for the Independence Day weekend?'

'Hi! Why are you breathless, my love? Pining and panting away for me?'

At dinner, Akshay tackled his parents.

'Papa, are we going anywhere for the Independence Day weekend? We've got five days off.'

Dr Khurana looked up. 'Haven't given it much thought. We'll go somewhere, don't worry.'

'How about Kasauli? We haven't been there. It's not too far and not too rainy and it's quieter than Shimla.'

Jai looked up from his plate suspiciously. Something was up . . .

'Hmmm . . . that's a possibility.'

'The road is excellent. But if we plan to go, we better do our bookings quickly.'

Now his mother looked up. 'Why this sudden interest in Kasauli?'

'Well, it's an interesting little hill station. Full of retired army types and writers and intellectual people like that and lots of schools . . . it has a hundred-year old club, which burned down and was rebuilt.'

'Since when have you developed an interest in intellectual people and schools and clubs?' Jai inquired.

'I'm interested in a lot of things you may be unaware of.'

'Yeah, yeah . . . sure.'

Dr Khurana grunted. 'Okay, if you want—why don't you do the bookings then? Two double rooms at a clean hotel.'

'Dear, do you think he'll be able to . . .?'

'Mom, don't worry. There are two or three good places there: Ros Common, which is the government tourism department place, and the Deodar Hotel and . . .'

'My God, you've really done your research, haven't you?' Jai's eyebrows shot up. He'd have to get to the bottom of this.

'Great, then I'll do the bookings online. Um . . . I might need your credit card number in case they want any advance.'

'Show the page to either me or your mother before you send them any credit card numbers.'

'Okay, Papa.' Akshay could no longer hold back his grin.

Five whole days, well, four, if you discounted the travelling, with Trisha in a pine-scented hill station in the Himalayas! It couldn't get any better. He rang her.

'The bait has been swallowed! Say, where are you staying?'

'At this resort place outside Kasauli that my mom is designing. The owners have a cottage nearby. It's about 4 or 5 km away from Kasauli proper. It's called the Snowview Resort.'

'Is it open for guests?'

'Mom says they've shut down for renovation. They want to get done with all the renovation and redesigning before Dusshera and Diwali, even though this is a stupid time to do painting and stuff.'

'Oh shit!'

'Listen—we can always meet up in town and go for walks and things. We're taking Smelly Beast too . . . Mom wants to ride again.'

'Wow . . . super!'

August 13 dawned cool and breezy. Trisha looked up at the sky; her heart beat faster as it struck her that just across the park, Akshay and his family too were probably up and loading up their Safari. What would happen if they passed each other on the road? It was very likely.

By 5 a.m. the Toyota had been loaded up. In the bed, Smelly Beast was snug under its tarpaulin. Shivi was in a lather of excitement—running up and down to the pickup with her toys, books and packets of chips and bullseyes for the journey.

'Come on, come on, come on, let's go!' she cried jumping up and down and quickly grabbing a window seat as she saw Trisha and her mother approach.

'Mom, will you be riding Smelly Beast on the way?' Trisha asked. Mrs Bhave (smartly turned out in jeans and a maroon jacket) nodded.

'I will, maybe once we're on the highway, let's see . . .'

'That would be great! That would be really great!'

In the Khuranas' Safari, Jai eyed his brother and gnashed his teeth. The bugger had kept his secret well. Ever since this Kasauli holiday had been planned, Akshay had been behaving strangely; he'd be humming under his breath, and picking up his sax and playing snatches of all kind of silly love songs. Something was up and Akshay was keeping a very tight lid on it indeed.

But Jai was smart. If Akshay was behaving so idiotically, it just had to do with the girlfriend. They had gone out on Smelly Beast every weekend during the past month—but all of them (including Gullu) had been present and the two of them—except when riding—had never been left alone. They'd even had a couple of jam sessions which had been great fun. And Gullu played the guitar fabulously. She had natural rhythm. In fact he'd got in a few precious moments alone with Gullu—though all he had managed to do was to brush his hand against hers, seemingly by accident.

Now he stared out of the Safari's windows as they sped down the highway, and sneaked surreptitious glances at his brother.

'Who was that?' he asked when Akshay ended his call.

'None of your business!'

'I'll find out.'

'Hah!'

Half an hour behind them, the pickup turned on to NH 1 and Tikka put his foot on the gas. The road was good—though there was a lot of construction work going on, with flyovers being made endlessly. The black pickup, with its high clearance and bull bars, was quite a formidable sight when it drew up in rear-view mirrors, and most cars allowed it to pass. But the Khuranas were making good time too and maintained their half-hour lead. They appeared to be chasing the rain, because the road was wet, though drying rapidly as a brilliant sun came out behind them and the clouds sailed on ahead.

The Bhaves drove into the courtyard of 'The Haveli', just outside Karnal, about 150 km from Delhi at around 8 and stopped for breakfast. It was famed for its paranthas and great coffee, and was a mandatory stop for travellers on this route.

'Hey, where are you guys now?' Trisha whispered into her phone. 'We've stopped for breakfast at The Haveli . . .'

'We're way ahead . . . Papa says we're going non-stop till Giyani's Dhaba before we turn off for Kasauli.'

'Is it raining?'

'No, but it looks like it's rained earlier.'

'Where are you staying?'

'At the Deodar.'

'Great! We'll probably see you there this evening!'

'Right, Tikka, bring the bike down please!' Mrs Bhave said as they emerged from the restaurant half an hour later, having enjoyed their breakfast of idlis and fluffy omelettes.

'Mommy, you're riding? I want to sit up front, up front!' Shivi was jumping up and down again.

'Darling, you'd better squash between me and Trish,' Mrs Bhave said, strapping on her helmet. 'You could get hit by a flying stone on the highway if you sit right up front.'

Trisha's heart sang. Her mom was riding Smelly Beast again. Everything was back as it ought to be. Mrs Bhave had got on and started the bike, as onlookers stopped to watch. Smelly Beast made its customary thunderous announcement. Trisha helped Shivi on and climbed up behind her. Then she leaned forward and hugged her mom, the tears glimmering happily.

'Here we go, babies!' Mrs Bhave sang and let out the clutch. 'Hang on tight!'

They caused quite a sensation when they rumbled into the parking of Timber Trail at around 11 a.m. for another break. Of course the Khuranas were gone, but the other visitors stared in astonishment as the petite Mrs Bhave and Trisha got off the gleaming silver bike, and the big black pickup halted beside them.

'We'll take a break,' Mrs Bhave said. She took off her helmet and shook her hair loose. Her arms were aching and she was tired; she'd been riding the heavy bike for two and a half hours, which was a lot even for someone who was fighting fit. 'There's no hurry.'

'Mommy, can we ride the cable car?' Shivi asked excitedly.

'Not this time, sweetie—we'll have something to eat and drink though. Now, what would you like?'

'Tikka, please put the bike on the pickup,' Mrs Bhave requested, as they emerged after half an hour. She was still quite fatigued and knew it would be foolish to continue riding. Trisha looked at her in surprise.

'Mom . . . you don't want to ride anymore?'

'I'm a bit tired, dear. Still don't have the stamina I used to have.'

'Okay, then can I ride? Please?'

'Darling, you're not street legal! You don't have a licence.'

'Mom, I look street legal. I look twenty-five! And it's so beautiful and the road is so good.'

'But you've never ridden in the mountains before, or even in traffic, for that matter.'

'Mom, there's always a first time for everything. You said so yourself. Besides, where Tikka's been taking us is pretty up and down too so I have some practice on slopes. And there's so little traffic; it looks like everyone's at home busy tying rakhis!'

Mrs Bhave took a deep breath and looked at Trisha's expectant face. They could get into big trouble if anything happened, but . . . Tikka had told her that Trisha now rode with complete confidence; the controls came automatically to her so she could concentrate on the road and traffic. As for not having driven in traffic, well that had to happen at some point.

'Baby drives absolutely first class!' Tikka had informed her proudly. 'She has no problems!'

'Okay,' she said at last. 'Just for a bit though . . .'

'Yay!' Trisha flung her arms around her, beaming.

'I want to ride, I want to ride too!' Shivi cried.

And so, with Trisha feeling so proud she felt she would burst, they rumbled out of Timber Trail and on to the wide sweeping road leading to Simla. Mrs Bhave, sitting pillion, was pleasantly surprised to see how well Trisha handled the bike and dealt with the traffic as well as the hairpin bends and the odd rocks that had tumbled down the mountainside on to the road. Apart from changing gears smoothly—and being in the right gear at the right time, she kept to her side of the road scrupulously and allowed traffic to pass her without demur. She didn't even get flustered when people hooted at her. She was a natural; she and the bike were a single entity. Mrs Bhave put her arms around her daughter's waist.

'Darling, you're very good! You've bonded beautifully with Smelly Beast.'

'Thanks, Mom! I'm loving it.'

At a checkpoint a couple of cops waved them down. Trisha's heart missed several beats and behind her, Mrs Bhave went 'oh-oh' and prepared to launch her charm offensive. But the cops only wanted to admire the bike and as Trisha burbled past at almost walking pace and began heading for the side of the road to park, waved her on with salutes and grins. Behind them, Tikka snapped a very whippy salute, making both the young men jerk upright to attention and salute back. Trisha was in the seventh heaven of delight. The rains had cloaked the mountain sides with green, the road was beautiful, and if you stuck to your side of the road, there was always plenty of space for trucks and buses (the buses were wicked and came towards you crabwise almost) to pass. Their luck with the weather continued—the rain was ahead of them, travelling up into the mountains as they climbed.

'Okay, baby, slow down, we have to turn left soon,' Mrs Bhave said as they approached Dharampur. They turned off the road to Simla towards Kasauli now. While the road surface deteriorated and it became narrower, it was much quieter, with less traffic. The Bullet went up the steep bends without a murmur, the Toyota keeping a discreet distance behind them.

Meanwhile, the Khuranas had stopped at Giyani's Dhaba, a famous eating place at Dharampur. They spent an hour over their meal and then proceeded towards Kasauli, still ahead of the Bhaves. The Safari roared up and around another bend and Jai gasped.

'Papa, please stop! Look at that rainbow! I want to photograph it.'

Dr Khurana pulled over to the side and Jai leapt off, followed by Akshay. It was a beautiful spot and the rainbow arched over an entire valley. Behind it, the clouds massed, a deep steel grey, contrasting beautifully with the emerald foliage of the forests, now lit up by the brilliant sunlight. Both the boys were avid amateur photographers, with a keen competitive spirit between them. Jai now stepped to the verge, trying to frame his picture properly.

'Jai, be careful!' his mother called, getting out of the car. Dr Khurana, too, got off and stretched his legs; he'd eaten too much. Akshay had crossed the road and was clambering up the rocks on the other side, looking for a high vantage point. Suddenly he paused and cocked his head . . .

No! It couldn't be! The sound throbbed and faded away and then came back. There was only one thing in the world that made a sound like that. He glanced at Jai, but he was concentrating hard on his photography. Okay, so big deal; must be some armywallahs on their bikes . . . nothing more. And then his eye caught the flash of silver on the road looping up from below. Before he realized what it was, it had disappeared round a bend. He moved his eyes away and completely missed the black pickup following it. But the sound, it was now bouncing off the mountain . . . making the pahari crows flap around cawing hoarsely. He clambered down and stood by the road. His parents were leaning against the Safari, enjoying the cool breeze, and Jai had just popped his head over the verge from across the road after having taken his rainbow picture.

The big silver Bullet banked majestically around the bend and came into view. Looking ahead, Trisha spotted the silver grey Safari parked at the side of the road.

Oh, shoot! There was no mistaking the grey-haired gentleman standing against it . . . or Mrs Khurana in her green printed salwar kameez and trim bun. They had both turned to look towards the approaching bike. But where was . . . she scanned the scene and then suddenly saw him—on the other side, looking completely zapped, his hair deliciously awry, mouth open. She thundered past the Safari, followed by the black pickup and raised a hand and waved weakly. Behind her, her mom had dozed off, her head on Trisha's shoulder, with Shivi squashed happily between them.

Holy shit! Dr Khurana hated bikes, and here she was—underage and without a licence—riding blithely past him in the mountains, with her mom and little sister sitting pillion! He would forbid Akshay to have anything to do with her. He might even not see her mother as a patient anymore! This brilliant plan of hers had backfired already!

Dr Khurana raised a hand and an eyebrow and waved back and as for Akshay—he had the silliest grin on his face as they sailed past. Jai could only goggle. But he was sharp enough to raise his camera and take a nice picture of the bike as it went around the bend ahead, framed for a moment by the rainbow, the sun bouncing off its petrol tank.

'Bugger!' he whispered when they were back in the car. 'So that's what you've been cooking all this while! I should have known!'

'The drive-by was not part of the plan, I can tell you!'

'Papa's going to freak!'

'Mom!' Trisha squealed, as they went around the next bend and mercifully out of sight. 'We just passed Dr Khurana!'

'What? Oh!' Her mom opened her eyes and blinked. 'Why didn't you stop to say hello?' she asked, still drowsy. 'Akshay and Jai are over all the time.'

'Dr Khurana doesn't like bikes! He thinks they're too dangerous.'

'They are, if you ride them stupidly.'

'He's going to stop Akshay from coming over now. He recognized me!'

'Don't be silly, sweetheart. Why should he?'

'He'll think I'm some wild Hells Angel type, into drugs and booze!'

'I think he knows you better than that.'

In the Safari there was a studied silence as the Khuranas resumed their journey.

'Wasn't that your friend Trisha on that bike?' Dr Khurana asked at last.

'Was it, Papa?'

'With her mother and little sister sitting pillion . . .?'

'That girl has such a beautiful voice,' Mrs Khurana said dreamily. 'So rich and deep!'

'She does, doesn't she, Mom? We jam really well.'

'How old is she?'

'I'm not sure, Papa . . . must be eighteen or something . . .'

'She looks about sixteen to me.'

'I'll tell her that. I'm sure it will make her happy!'

Jai rolled his eyes at his brother.

'Her mother should really not allow her to ride that bike.'

'It's a Bullet, Papa. Very steady and stable.'

'Oh. And how do you know that?'

'It's common knowledge! That's why all those army fellows do those tricks on them on Republic Day. You know, so many of them on one bike doing handstands and somersaults . . .'

'Hmm . . .'

Mrs Khurana glanced at her husband and touched his arm. He looked at her and she smiled and shook her head gently.

The Kasauli trip had been explained.

'Okay dear, slow down, our turnoff to the resort should be coming any moment. It's supposed to be signposted.'

'Up ahead, Mom, I think I see it.'

A freshly painted signboard in green and blue and white, with an arrow pointing up the mountain, indicated 'Snowview Resort'. A stony track led steeply up the side of the mountain, guarded by a blue gate. Trisha rumbled to a halt.

'It's up there, Mom.'

Tikka had drawn up behind them and was already opening the gate.

'Are you sure you'll be able to ride up that?' Mrs Bhave asked, eyeing the steep path.

Trisha grinned.

She gunned the bike, kept it in low gear and it thumped up the mountain track inexorably. Trisha kept her eyes on the track, trying to avoid the larger rocks. Behind them, Tikka drove the pickup through the gate, shut it and got back in just as the Khurana's Safari drove past.

The proprietor of Snowview Resort, Mr Lamba, and his wife warmly welcomed their guests and were duly impressed by Smelly Beast. Shivi offered their two small children, Sunil and Anita, her bullseyes, and the three quickly became friends. Mrs Lamba showed them to their accommodation: a cottage perched at the very edge of the mountainside, about a quarter of a kilometre away from the resort proper and beautifully hidden away amongst the towering pines and deodars.

'It's quite small, but comfortable,' Mrs Lamba said as she unlocked the front door and a huge hairy spider scuttled away indignantly. It was cosy: a large living-cum-dining room was flanked by bedrooms on either side, both overlooking the valley. All three rooms had fireplaces. The kitchen was at one end of the dining room; it had a modern cooking range and copper utensils hanging from the wall. Jars and bottles gleamed from behind glass-fronted wooden cabinets. The wooden floors creaked as they walked around, inspecting the place.

'If you need anything, please let me know. You'll have to manage your cooking, I'm afraid, as our kitchen staff is on leave—but fresh vegetables and milk are delivered every morning.'

'Thanks so much. This is lovely. Okay girls, which bedroom do you want?'

They settled in quickly. Mrs Bhave walked over and had a brief meeting with Mr Lamba, taking along some of her drawings and plans. Shivi went along with her—she wanted to firm up her friendship with Anita and Sunil. Lying in one of the planter's chairs in the verandah overlooking the view, Trisha called Akshay.

'Hey, this place is gorgeous . . .'

'Our hotel isn't too bad either. When are you coming up?'

'I don't know. Mom's gone for a meeting. Shivi's gone to play with the owners' kids. Probably, we'll come down this evening. Did your dad freak when he saw us on the bike?'

Mrs Bhave got back from her meeting a little later, Shivi skipping happily by her side. Trisha stiffened. Something was up. Her mom's face was tense; she had tight frown lines creasing her forehead.

'Mom, you okay?'

'Hmm.'

'Are you feeling all right?'

That horrible sinking feeling was back in her tummy.

'Oh yes, dear.' Her mother smiled and took her hand. 'I'm fine.'

'Mom, when do we go into Kasauli?'

'Later this afternoon.' Trisha eyed her mother.

'Oh.'

'We'll go and see Nana and Nani first, at about five o'clock. That's before they leave for the club.'

'Nani and Nana? Do . . . do they know we're here? Did you tell them we were coming?'

'No, not exactly.'

'So it'll be a surprise?'

'Yes, sort of. And it's time Nana came to his senses.'

There was a steely look in Mrs Bhave's eyes and the soft lines in her face had hardened. She had written twice to her parents since her illness—neither letter had been acknowledged or replied to. She'd rung them up three times, only to have the phone disconnected the moment her voice had been recognized. Her father, she knew, could be rigidly inflexible: he'd always held that to change one's mind was a sign of mortal and moral weakness. So even if you took a stupid decision, you had to stick by it, come what may. In all likelihood he hadn't even opened let alone read her letters.

'Mom . . . do we have to?'

'Don't worry, Trish, it'll be okay. At worst, they won't see us . . .
that's all, it's no big deal.' That, she knew, was not entirely true: it was
a big deal, a huge deal . . . now more than ever before. A glint came
into her eyes. 'By the way,' she added, 'we're driving to their house
on Smelly Beast.'

'Mom!' Trisha smiled suddenly. 'You're as bad as Nana! He'll freak!'

'Well,' her mom said, ruffling her hair and kissing her on the top
of her head, 'I am *his* daughter!'

CHAPTER TEN

BUNKER HOUSE AND A
HAUNTED BUNGALOW

'Come on, Shivi, hurry up! Mom's waiting! Where are you going now?'

'Coming, just coming! Uff, you're always in such a hurry!'

Standing beside Smelly Beast, Mrs Bhave dangled her scarlet helmet and tapped her feet. Trisha emerged from the cottage shaking her head.

'Shivi's gone running into the garden,' she said. 'Don't ask me why!'

Shivi charged out a few minutes later, clutching a grubby handful of nasturtiums and daisies and one big yellow dahlia. She unravelled her ribbon and began tying the flowers into a bunch. Several had been yanked out by the roots.

'Who are the flowers for?' Mrs Bhave asked.

'Nani!' Shivi said excitedly. 'We're seeing her for the first time.'

'Oh. I see. That's very thoughtful of you, baby.'

'I'm always thoughtful,' Shivi said indignantly. 'Come on, let's go now!'

'Mom, can I ride?' Trisha asked. She had changed into a fresh pink top and maroon capris, and her hair was shining. She'd done up her eyes and touched her lips with gloss too. She wanted to look her best for her grandparents, no matter what they had done and what she thought of them.

'Umm . . . no. Kasauli is full of military police and they'll pounce on you in a second. I'll ride.' She was still a little tired, but would manage; her stamina had really taken quite a beating. 'Fingers crossed it doesn't rain! Take the umbrellas though.'

They rumbled into Kasauli, attracting curious glances from both residents and visitors. A group of schoolchildren cheered as they drove past.

'Right now, we take the Upper Mall. Hang on, babies, it's a bit steep.' Mrs Bhave gunned Smelly Beast and the bike thumped steadily up the steep slope. At the back, Trisha clung on and held Shivi firmly. Suddenly they veered off on to a narrower bumpy track, shrouded by great trees. And then a few minutes later, they slowed and stopped.

'There,' Mrs Bhave whispered, pointing down the mountainside to a clearing in the forest. 'Bunker House.'

Trisha looked down. Surrounded by huge trees and flanked on one side by a wildly unkempt garden was a large house with a sloping red roof and three chimneys. It was built on a cemented platform, and a TV dish stuck out incongruously from one end of the roof. An olive-green Gypsy stood in the parking area.

'That's where you lived, Mommy?' Shivi asked her eyes wide. 'Is that your house?'

'Uh-huh. See that swing at the end of the garden? I used to love swinging.'

'So do I!'

'And see that wooden platform at the end there? I used to practise dancing there. Your nani called me Ghungroo . . .'

'Mom, you never told us that before!'

'Shall we go down and check if anyone's home? The gate's down by the side of the road.'

Maj. General (Retd.) Shamsher Soni sat glued to the television set, his eyes glazed as the heroine emitted shrill shrieks and her boyfriend got bashed up by the goons. Soon the tables would be turned and the hero would be doing the dishoom-dishoom, though hopefully the heroine would be mortally injured by then. The General was a big, thickset man with a hard face and an unpleasantly brusque way of talking; he made you feel like he was sneering at you all the time, and his eyes bulged belligerently as if defying you to contradict him. His wife was a tiny mousy woman who scuttled about the house like a frightened bunny, obeying her husband's every whim. Her sad black eyes had long lost their lustre, and what was left of her curly hair was now grey and hung in tired wisps about her face. But she had Trisha's 'light up the world' smile—not that she had smiled for a very long time now.

'But you know these films are all the same!' the General blathered loudly, as if it were her fault.

'Jee haa,' she said placatingly. She looked at him. He was ogling the heroine who was now magically under some waterfall, singing shrilly, her basketball bosom bouncing almost right out of her tight blouse.

'Jee . . . this, these letters from Ghungroo . . .'

'What letters? We don't know anyone called that. How many times have I told you? We have nothing to do with her.'

'She's not well . . . Sh . . . she has c-cancer.'

'Bah! She's just trying to get the house. I know that girl. And I told you not to read those letters. Why did you?'

'She has two children to look after.'

'Both girls! She ran away with that sailorboy shippie and he could only give her girls! The only sensible thing he did was to drown.'

'Jee, don't say things like that. You wanted her to marry that Namdev boy. He's now in jail.'

'Are you questioning my decision? If she had married him, he would not have been in jail. Now, will you keep quiet and let me watch the film?'

There was a commercial break and the General muted the TV. Patton, their Rottweiler, began barking. He was tied in the courtyard at the back and had been sleeping under a chair. Now he was up, barking ferociously.

'Shut up!' roared the General. 'What's the matter with that damn dog?'

Patton paused. And then the General heard the deep thump of a motorcycle engine getting louder. Someone on a bike was coming down the driveway.

'What the . . .?'

'Must be the courier boy,' his wife said. 'Is Patton tied up?'

The General made his way to the dining room and peered out of the mullioned windows that overlooked the driveway and gate.

A big silver Bullet had nosed its way carefully down the steep driveway, rumbling and grumbling. The General's face turned to granite as the bike stopped and the slim figure riding it got off and took off her helmet. He hardly saw the little girl in the middle, clutching a bunch of flowers in her fist or the pretty young girl behind her with silver hoops in her ears. The engine was switched off and there was sudden silence. Then Patton started up again.

'Kaun . . .?' his wife came by his side.

'Lakhan!' shouted the General, his eyes bulging furiously. In the kitchen, his servant leapt up from his mat. 'Set Patton loose!'

'Ghungroo . . .! It's Ghungroo and her little girls!' The tears flooded into Mrs Soni's eyes and she put a hand on her husband's arm. He jerked it away angrily.

'Stop it! I have told you she is not welcome. She is NOT our daughter. She is a trespasser on my property and will be dealt with as such!'

'She has children!' His wife stared at the silver motorcycle. Mrs Bhave had got off, as had her girls; she looked exactly the same as she had the day she had stood by the handsome sailor who had come asking for her hand seventeen years ago. The little girl was holding the bunch of flowers in front of her like a shield, while her sister stood uncertainly by her side. At that moment Patton bounded around the corner, barking savagely. He meant business.

'Mommy! I'm scared!' Shivi went white as the big dog charged towards them, curling its upper lip and baring its teeth. Trisha too shrunk back and wished they had brought Tikka along. Mrs Bhave held both of them protectively to her and stared at the dining room window. She could see her father glaring out at her, with her mother clinging ineffectually to his arm as always. They had both aged, she thought with a sudden pang. But her father's expression had remained the same: hard, belligerent and unforgiving. The dog charged towards them, growling menacingly. Mrs Bhave glanced at it and then at the window again.

'What kind of a hero do you think you are, Papa?' she said in a level, clear voice. 'You set your dog on your own family?' She turned to Trisha. 'Baby, start the bike and rev it. That bloody dog is going to get a surprise . . .'

White in the face, Trisha hopped on and started Smelly Beast and twisted the throttle. Patton stopped in his tracks. The bike growled and thundered and Patton remembered a recent narrow escape from the clutches of a leopard, which had sounded just the same (though smelled very differently). He gave a yelp, turned around and fled.

'Why don't you come out and face us, Papa?' Mrs Bhave challenged, keeping her voice under control. 'Instead of hiding behind the curtains like a coward?' Trisha looked at her, really alarmed. She'd never seen her mom so angry. 'You're pathetic! You threaten my children with a guard dog. God! What will your precious regiment think of you if they knew?'

'Mom . . .' Trisha urged, taking her arm. 'Let's go . . . please.'

The General opened the window. 'What do you want? I told you, you are not welcome here. You do not belong here. You are trespassing on my property. Now get out!'

'Jee . . .'

'I wanted you to meet your granddaughters . . . and I think you know why. This is Trisha and that's Shivi. And now that you've scared them both half to death, we will go. I don't think they want to meet you now—or ever.' She turned. 'I hope you're feeling very heroic about what you've just done, Papa! I hope you get another medal for it! What a wonderful grandfather you are!'

'Jee, please . . . let them in . . . she's our-'

'She is not our daughter. They are not our granddaughters.' He was talking stonily, like a machine.

'Jee, you don't know what you're saying . . .'

'Will you keep quiet and stop snivelling?' His big hand lashed out and caught her across the cheek. 'Shut up, I tell you.'

They watched in silence, Mrs Soni stifling her sobs and holding her pallu to her face, as the bike thundered up the driveway and out of the gates. On the driveway lay a bunch of nasturtiums and daisies and one big sunny dahlia, tied loosely together with a child's pink hair ribbon.

Just outside the gate, Trisha stopped the bike as her mom tapped her on her shoulder. She dismounted and her mom helped Shivi off. Both the girls were trembling and still looking fearfully down the driveway. Mrs Bhave's face was set; it was everything she could do to keep the tears away.

'Well, that went well . . .' she said in a brittle voice, shaking her head. She looked at the two frightened girls and her face softened. 'I'm so sorry, sweethearts. I should have come alone . . .' She took them into her arms and hugged them. 'I thought that maybe if he saw you both he wouldn't be so obtuse. He's like a piece of granite.'

'Mom . . . was he always like that?' Trisha whispered, thinking about her own happy-go-lucky father. 'Horrible?'

'He's very nice provided things go his way,' her mom replied. 'But when they don't, well, then . . . He just expects everyone to see things from his point of view only.'

'No wonder you eloped! How many times did you try to run away before that?'

'That, sweetheart, is another story. Now come on, let's have a jolly good tea and get the horrible aftertaste of this visit out of our mouths!'

'Yes!' Shivi perked up. 'What a horrible dog they have.'

'Let's go to the Deodar, Mom,' Trisha said, taking a deep breath and trying to get her equilibrium back.

Her mom raised an eyebrow and smiled. 'Any special reason, dear?' she asked innocently. Trisha blushed.

They rumbled down past the church on to the Lower Mall and parked in the lot adjacent to the hotel next to a silver grey Safari. As they walked up to the Deodar's dining room, she punched Akshay's number on her mobile.

'Hello boys! What a pleasant surprise!' Mrs Bhave smiled innocently as Jai and Akshay joined them, five minutes later. 'Come on, sit down, what will you have?'

Trisha was beaming. Akshay coloured richly as he glanced at her, and Jai grinned and beat a knowing tattoo on the table.

'You know, our nana set his huge, ferocious dog on us. Then Trisha started Smelly Beast and it ran away.' Shivi was always ready with the latest news. 'He's mad and looks like an ogre.'

'Shivi!'

'But it happened!'

'Okay, now let's see the menu, shall we?'

They walked down to the market afterwards and ate bhuttas. Mrs Bhave was warmly welcomed by several old shopkeepers who recognized her as 'General Sahib ki bachchi' and were utterly delighted to meet the girls. Of course, all the old-timers knew what had happened; but now Ghungroo had come back with her two daughters, so maybe General Sahib had seen sense after all.

'What's your POA for tomorrow?' Akshay whispered, managing to sidle beside Trisha. Jai, of course, grinned behind his bhutta and cleared his throat ostentatiously.

'I don't know. Why don't you guys come over to the resort? Maybe we could go for a ride . . .'

'Okay. I think Papa wants to go to Chail tomorrow.'

'Then he could drop you guys at the resort . . . it's on the way.'

'Yup, that sounds good.'

Then Jai's mobile rang.

'Yup? Oh, hi!'

He listened, slowing down so that the others walked ahead, his face turning pink. 'Okay, great!' he said softly. 'Just great! Oh man, yes, yes, yes!'

He caught up with the others.

'Who was that?' Akshay asked, staring at him curiously. 'And why are your ears red?'

'They aren't. And it's none of your business.'

'Oh okay . . . sorry I asked. Touchy, touchy!'

'Just shut up!'

Akshay stared at him. 'What is the matter with you?' he asked.

Mrs Bhave bought some bread and ham and eggs and butter and they loaded up Smelly Beast.

'Okay guys, hope to see you tomorrow,' Trisha said, climbing on behind Shivi.

Smelly Beast thundered off down the mountain, its chrome gleaming in the mauve dusk.

While Jai was suspiciously keen on going to Chail the next morning, Akshay managed to wriggle out of the trip, much to his mother's amusement.

'We'll drop you off at Snowview Resort,' she smiled, as Jai winked ferociously.

'Mom, why did Nana have to be like that and set that dog on us?' Trisha asked, as she brushed her hair before bed.

'He's a very proud man, and he hasn't forgiven me for marrying your dad against his will. It was the first time anyone flagrantly disobeyed his orders.'

'But that was so long ago!'

'He thinks I made him look foolish in front of his superiors and colleagues by refusing to marry the fool he wanted me to marry. A colleague's daughter agreed to it and her father was promoted to a position Nana thought should have been his. So he hasn't forgiven me for that.'

'But why can't he see things from your point of view?'

'Darling, if he had, the world would have been a truly wonderful place. Now, don't worry about it. It's his loss. He doesn't know that he's missing out on the company of the two sweetest, prettiest girls in the world.'

'I feel bad for Nani though.'

Her mother sighed. 'I just wish Nani had a bit more spunk and stood up to him. She's let him have his way every single time. That's part of the problem.'

'Do you think he'll ever change?'

'I doubt it, Trish. He's too set in his ways. All right, sweetie, goodnight! And just forget about it.'

But it was a long, long time before Mrs Bhave finally dropped off herself, tired though she was. Maybe she had handled it the wrong way. The girls had been thoroughly upset. One thing she made up her mind about. Before this trip ended, she would see her parents again and talk to them, come what may. They would just have to listen, whether they wanted to or not—period.

'So what do you want to do today?' Mrs Bhave asked Trisha, as they sat down for breakfast the next morning.

'Mommy, you didn't kiss me good morning!' Shivi said indignantly. 'Now you'll have to give me ten kisses to make up!'

'Umm . . . maybe I could ask Akshay and Jai over and we could go for a hike or something,' Trisha said. 'It looks like a clear day.'

'Sure. In fact, there's a lovely two-hour trek from just across the road from here—it winds its way up the mountain, and you get a beautiful view of the valley on one side. There's a lovely old Inspection Bungalow at the end of the ridge too . . . they say it's haunted so hardly anyone stays there now.'

'Great! Let me call the boys.' She took out her phone and called Akshay. 'Hey, why don't you guys come over this morning? Mom says there's a great hike we can go on from here.'

'We're going to Chail . . .' Akshay began lugubriously, grinning into the phone.

'Oh, shoot . . .'

'But . . .' he went on, 'if you want, I could sacrifice the trip and get dropped off by your place.'

'Umm . . .'

'Jai wants to go to Chail. I don't know—he says he wants to see the highest cricket ground in the world.'

'Oh, that means . . . that means . . .' Oh God, that meant it would just be her and Akshay!

'Yup!'

She took a deep breath. 'So have you decided?'

'Decisions, decisions.' She heard his muffled snort of laughter.

'Just wait till I see you!'

'They're leaving at 8 so I'll be dropped off at about five past.'

'You horrible fellow! Just you wait!'

'That's the path you take,' Mrs Bhave explained, pointing to a narrow path climbing up the mountainside from across the road. 'Have a good time, and be careful!'

Akshay glanced at Trisha as he shouldered his knapsack. She was so beautiful; she was wearing jeans and a sky-blue pullover which showed off her figure fabulously. Her thick hair was in a bouncy ponytail, and she had pulled a baseball cap over her head. The ponytail was enough to get his heart racing. She caught his glance and smiled at him. At that moment, Akshay was sure that he was the luckiest guy in the world.

They set off, somewhat self-consciously, knapsacks on their backs, walking sticks in their hands.

For a while neither of them spoke. Then quietly, their fingers brushed and linked.

'Fabulous day,' Akshay remarked.

'Yes. Hope it stays that way. I hope you didn't want to go to Chail too badly . . .'

'Well . . .' he glanced at her slyly. 'I *really* had to think about it. It was a tough decision, I can tell you. I had to do a thorough cost-benefit analysis . . . it was an opportunity of a lifetime to see the highest cricket pitch in the world . . . really tough, you know.'

'Poor boy! Bastard!'

'Hold it!' He jerked her to a halt and glanced around quickly.

'What?'

'This!' he said, dropping his stick and putting his arms around her, kissed her softly all over her face.

'Akshay, someone might come!' But she was kissing him back now, kiss for kiss.

'Wow!' Akshay said at last. 'This is so cool I can't believe it!'

'Like it's too good to be true . . .' She was glowing.

He took her hand and squeezed it.

'Mom said there's a haunted Inspection Bungalow at the end of the ridge,' Trisha said, 'come on, let's check it out.'

'Great!'

At the Inspection Bungalow, the ancient caretaker had just finished sprucing up the place. He locked it with a huge brass padlock and hobbled down the mountain path to the nearest village to buy supplies. Some inspectors from the Forest Department were due that evening and everything had to be shipshape, even though the bungalow was in urgent need of renovation. Still, these days, the sahibs and their shrill, nasty memsahibs insisted on clean sheets and spotless bathrooms and if so much as a cockroach was seen in the kitchen . . . He'd slogged for two days, cleaning the place out, and hoping his efforts would be noticed and they'd transfer him elsewhere. The place had a reputation of being a 'bhoot bungla' though the ghost had not made an appearance in the eighteen years he had been here. Many local people refused to walk past it, especially on cloudy days when the mists came visiting; that's when it was rumoured the ghosts came out and did unspeakable things to anyone who might be there. At the village he was hailed by the operator of the only STD booth here and informed that the Forest Department inspectors had called to say that they would not be coming after all. So much for all his work. Still, it was astonishing that they had called at all; normally they would have just kept him waiting and not showed up. He shrugged—well, fine then, he'd just go and get drunk . . .

Trisha and Akshay stopped by the gate of the 'bhoot bungalow' about half an hour after the old caretaker had left, at around ten o'clock.

'Will you look at it!' Trisha whispered, taking Akshay's hand.

It was a small whitewashed structure with a rusted corrugated iron roof and a verandah running all round it and a small unkempt garden in front. Like many of its kind, it had been located at the tip of a ridge, commanding a magnificent view of the forests in the valleys below, and the snow-capped mountains beyond. Akshay opened the creaking gate. 'Let's see if anyone's home . . . Hello, koi hai?'

'There's no one here,' Trisha said five minutes later after they had gone right around the house. She peered through a window. 'The place is locked.'

'No chowkidar either.'

'Maybe whoever is staying here has gone out.'

'It doesn't seem like anyone's staying here at the moment.'

'Not even the bhoots.'

For a moment they looked at each other.

'It's such a pity it's locked . . .'

'I know.' She sighed. 'Too bad . . . come on, let's carry on.'

They walked on to the edge of the ridge and started back at around noon. Though the morning had been clear and sunny, the clouds were drifting over now, filling in the valleys and nestling on the mountainsides.

About forty-five minutes later they reached the old forest rest house again.

'Look,' Akshay pointed. 'It's nearly completely obscured by mist.'

Hand in hand they walked up the path from the gate. The cloud was dense now, but somehow comforting. From the wooden-floored verandah, the little green gate was no longer visible. The big brass padlock on the front door gleamed at them. Akshay stomped off towards the back.

'Hello? Excuse me? Koi hai?'

'If only we could get in and have a look. These old places are fascinating.'

A faint breeze stirred the mist around them and they heard a door bang gently from the back.

'Someone's here!' Trisha whispered, clutching his hand.

'Hello? Koi hai?' Akshay called again. 'Come on, let's check at the back.'

'Akshay, it could be the bhoot!'

'So let's meet it.'

'It's supposed to do horrible things to visitors . . . strangle them and push them off the edge.'

But he had gone around to the back and was pointing. 'There's your bhoot,' he said, pointing to a screen door which was gently swinging to and fro, and banging softly.

'We're in luck,' he said excitedly, pulling it open. 'The door behind it is also open!'

They were inside in a minute.

'God, it's so gloomy in here,' Trisha whispered clinging to him.

'I've got my trusty Maglite,' Akshay said, 'but I kind of like it like this.'

They went from room to room and then stopped in the master bedroom.

It was simply furnished, with a double bed, a wooden table and two chairs and a cupboard.

'Akshay—look the bed's made. Someone is living here.'

The beds had been neatly turned down and the curtains had been drawn across the windows.

'But there's no sign of anyone's belongings. No clothes and nothing in the bathroom. Maybe they've left.'

He plonked down on the bed.

'This is like the Goldilocks story,' Trisha said, looking around. 'Any minute now the three bears are going to come barging in.'

She lay down beside him and sighed happily. 'You know, I can't believe it, but Mom's almost normal. I mean, she rode Smelly Beast for two and a half hours yesterday!'

'She's great.'

She glanced at him. 'You know, I want to believe in miracles, Akshay, and if Mom gets okay, I will.'

'At the moment, I think it's a miracle that you're here next to me in this bhoot bangla bed!'

'Idiot! You know, that Dr Phadnis said that Mom had eight months to two years. Eight months would be April. I don't believe that anymore. It really is a miracle!'

'Like you are!'

She looked at him. 'Did you bring . . .?'

'Babe, I always carry a Maglite, eclairs, penknife, toothpick, handkerchief, tweezers . . . what do you think? "Be prepared"—that's my motto!' He got out of bed and rummaged in his jeans' pockets. Then he parted the curtains and peered out.

'Just look at the fog, Trish,' he said. 'It's blotted out everything.'

She stood beside him. 'It's like we're the only two people in the entire world.'

'Here,' she said, 'let me . . .' And then they were in one another's arms.

Outside, the mist pressed against the window, thinning one moment and becoming opaque the next. The old caretaker, struggling up the path from the gate, paused and blinked owlishly. It was amazing he had made it up the mountain path from the village without falling down. He looked towards the house and started. The curtains of the bedroom window had suddenly parted, about a quarter of the way—and he had drawn them completely. And, hai Ram, there were two figures silhouetted against it: a male and female. They looked like they were struggling. Suddenly they fell back and vanished.

'Bhoot!' he yelled. 'Bhoot! Bachao, bachao!' He turned and fled, pausing only to take a swig from the bottle in his hands. He plunged down the path, lost his footing and fell into a ditch, knocking himself unconscious.

In the room, Akshay leapt up like a shot rabbit. 'Bloody hell—let's get out of here!'

'The three bears!' Trisha squealed, scrambling up. 'I knew they'd come!'

Frantically they hopped into their clothes, and then, peering cautiously into the mist, snuck out of the bungalow. There didn't seem to be anyone around. They ran down the path and out of the gate, just as the mists began to shift and lift.

They stopped again, after walking briskly for half an hour, and suddenly discovered that they were absolutely famished. They wolfed down the sandwiches and the poha Komal had packed for them, staring at the clouds drifting past.

'Where did you go the whole day?' Shivi demanded crankily as they tramped back into the driveway of the cottage at around 3.30.

'We went for a very long walk. You would have got tired.'

'I wouldn't. You always leave me and go.'

'You were playing with Anita and Sunil.'

'Yes, but they had to sleep in the afternoon.'

'You should too. By the way, where's Mom?'

'How should I know? Everyone leaves me and goes!'

'See what we got you!' Akshay said, digging into his pocket and producing a beautiful maroon pebble. 'And here's a green one too. Rubies and emeralds, only for you, Princess Shivi.'

'Wow, thank you, Akshay!'

'Hi kids, did you have a good time?' Mrs Bhave came out of the cottage, a large drawing pad in her hand.

She looked at her radiant daughter and then at Akshay, her eyebrows rising faintly. He caught her eye and looked away awkwardly. Suddenly she wondered what her reaction would be if he asked her for her daughter's hand . . . of course, they were far too young, but . . .

She'd had her suspicions since that Sunday just after the biking picnic, but then Mrs Almeida had said she thought they had been kissing and she had left it at that. But now, there was no doubt . . . something had happened on the hike. It was clear as daylight on both the kids' faces. Well, sooner or later it was bound to . . . and if it had to be Akshay . . . well, it could have been so much worse. What she had seen of him she had liked. What she was afraid of was that he would break her beloved daughter's heart at some point down the road. They were both so very young.

'Good,' she said gently. 'I'm glad you enjoyed yourself.'

Akshay got picked up by his parents at around 7 that evening.

In the car, Jai and Akshay sized each other up.

'So. How was Chail?' Akshay asked.

'Great!'

Mrs Khurana turned around. 'Jai met his friend there, imagine!'

'Who?'

'Oh, Gullu was there with her family,' Jai said carelessly.

'Aha! Say no more!'

But it hadn't worked out quite the way Jai had wanted it to. First, they had Gullu's nosy brother and sister on their tail as they walked through the pine forests 'to explore'. Finally they decided to 'birdwatch', which the kids found boring, so they ran off, leaving them alone at last.

'Whew, thank God—I was just going to get really wild!' Gullu said explosively.

'Yeah . . .'

Gullu grinned. 'So Trish and Akshay have gone off on a lovey-dovey hike together?'

'Yeah, all very innocent, of course!'

'Of course! I'm going to have a ball teasing Trish.'

'That Akshay gets so mad when I rag him . . . By the way, you play the guitar fabulously.'

'Thanks, and you're great on the drums!'

'Thanks!'

They stared at each other, shifting closer, and Jai wondered whether he ought to just take her in his arms and kiss her all over; her eyes seemed to say yes . . . and he was just revving up his courage, when from up the mountainside, Parkash Aunty suddenly bellowed.

'Bachche, come back, it's going to pour any minute and we're returning!'

They sprang apart.

'Oh shoot!'

'Trust Mama!'

That evening, after dinner Mrs Bhave put her head around the door to the girls' room. 'Trish, sweetie, I need to talk to you.'

Trisha looked up from her book. 'Oh?'

'Not here,' Mrs Bhave said softly. 'In my room . . .' She gestured towards Shivi, who was sleeping on the adjoining bed.

'Little pitchers . . .' she mouthed. Trisha nodded and padded softly out of the room.

'What is it, Mom? You're feeling all right, aren't you?'

'Sit down, sweetie, let me brush your hair.'

'Uh okay.' Trisha sat down on the big comfortable planter's chair. She loved it when her mom brushed out her hair. She looked up at her. 'So, Mom, what did you want to talk about?'

Mrs Bhave took a deep breath and shut her eyes. 'Have you and Akshay been intimate?'

'What?'

'Have you slept with him?'

'Mom! Please! What a question!'

'Darling, you know what can happen if you don't take care! You know the consequences. You're far too young for those . . .'

'Mom!' She didn't know what else to say. She was blushing furiously.

'You neither need to confirm or deny it. But just think of what might happen. You have the rest of your school and college lives to think of. You have to learn to stand on your own feet.' Her mom had come around and was looking at her. 'I know it seems like the most wonderful thing in the world at the moment—and it probably is. But sweetie, please be careful. I know he's a good boy, but if anything happens—it will happen to you alone.'

'Nothing happened, Mom!'

She gulped. But it had very nearly happened; they had both wanted it—and had taken care too, but then they had been too freaked out.

'Goodnight, sweetheart. Your hair is really looking beautiful.'

Frantically she called Akshay.

'What? What's the matter? Missing me already?'

'Akshay—she knows!'

'What? Who? Who knows what? What are you talking about?'

'Mom knows we . . . we . . .!' she gabbled. 'I mean we didn't but we nearly did . . .'

'Holy shit! And you're still alive? You're still allowed to talk to me? Or is this . . .' his voice dropped tragically . . . 'goodbye?'

'No, it's all right! In fact she was . . . um . . . cool about the whole thing.'

'Cool about it? What mom would be cool about her teenage daughter romping around in bed with me?'

'Well, she was. She didn't ask me to admit to anything. Well, she didn't have to . . . she knew. She said it was written all over our faces. All she said was we ought to be careful of what could happen.'

'But shit, how can I face her now?'

'She won't eat you.' Suddenly Trisha grinned. 'I'll bet she's looking forward to that though.'

'I'll bet,' he said dismally.

'I told you she was cool. She sort of said that in case we were sleeping together, we ought to take precautions so as not to screw up our lives more than necessary, and yes, she would prefer it if we didn't go all the way.'

'Whew. We haven't even been all the way!'

In spite of herself, Trisha giggled. 'She said I ought to take precautions whenever and wherever I meet you! Anytime and every time!'

'Wow, man, she thinks I'll ravish you the moment I set eyes upon you!'

'Idiot!'

CHAPTER ELEVEN

SINGING IN THE RAIN

The next morning Trisha awoke to a strange drumming roar on the roof of their cottage. For a moment she was puzzled; she padded to the window and peered outside. It was dark and grey and pouring. Trisha cursed. She had wanted to meet the boys and take Tikka and Smelly Beast to an out of the way road in the mountains somewhere but there would be no biking this morning. The rain just thundered down steadily, neither lessening nor increasing in intensity.

'Well, sweetheart, it looks like we're going to be stuck indoors today,' her mom said, putting an arm around her waist. 'Actually, I'm thinking of going down to see Nana and Nani again this morning.'

'What? But why, Mom?'

'Because they can't behave as if I don't exist! They can't pretend you and Shivi don't exist. Nana can't run away from these facts just because his stupid ego got pricked.'

'Mom, be careful. Remember that horrible dog?' Trisha grinned. 'You're not thinking of going on Smelly Beast again, are you?'

'No, darling, but I'll take Tikka with me. He'll tame the brute in two seconds.'

'Let me call the boys. If it's okay with them could you drop me and Shivi off at their hotel?'

'Remember what I told you yesterday, darling . . .'

'Sure, sure . . . Mom, please! I'm not a kid!'

'Oh great, we're in Room 4, downstairs,' Akshay told her on the phone. 'The only thing is that Jai's going to be here too. I'll try and get rid of him somehow . . . okay, bye, see you!' Akshay put down the phone and nipped across to his parents' room. 'Mom, Trisha and Shivi are coming to spend the morning with us.' He looked at the falling curtain of rain. 'Not that we can go out anywhere.'

'That's nice.'

'Woo-woo,' Jai hooted, opening his eyes wide. 'But you won't have any privacy here.'

'Maybe you can entertain Shivi somewhere,' Akshay said sarcastically. 'She's closer to your mental level.'

'No worries.' Jai looked smug. 'Or maybe we could practise.'

'What?'

'You know, music . . .'

'What?'

'Gullu's family is driving down from Shimla—they'll be spending a couple of nights here.'

'You little weasel! You're a real slimy bastard . . .'

'Look who's talking!'

At around 10, Tikka escorted Trisha to the wing of the Deodar where the Khuranas were staying. The door to Room 4 burst open.

'Hi, come on in. Where's Shivi?'

'Hi Akshay! She didn't want to come. She wanted to play with her friends at the resort. She's formed a gang with them and they run riot . . . Hey, hi Jai, how're you doing?'

'Great!'

'Well, what should we do?' Akshay said, ushering her into the room. The boys' clothes were scattered all over the beds, and Akshay's saxophone gleamed in one corner.

'Umm . . . be back in a second,' Jai murmured, grinning wickedly and making ferocious kissing noises.

Tikka nosed the pickup down the drive at Bunker House; the olive Gypsy was not in the porch. Somewhere inside, Patton began barking again. Mrs Bhave got down and rang the front door bell.

A servant boy, opened the door, holding the dog by the collar.

'Is Sahib in?' Mrs Bhave asked, as Tikka held her umbrella and looked at the dog.

'Sahib's out, but Memsahib is in. Please come in.'

This grimy fellow had better manners than her father, Mrs Bhave thought wryly as she stepped into her own house and looked around. It had been more than seventeen years . . . The mirror through which she had seen what had happened in the drawing room was still in its place in the hall, and everything seemed much the same, if a little more worn out. Except that the family photographs on the mantelpiece had disappeared.

'Nice dog,' Tikka said, squatting on his haunches and petting an astounded Patton on his broad head and chest. 'Good boy.' The servant boy looked shocked.

Mrs Soni entered slowly and stared at her estranged daughter, a hand going up to her mouth.

For a moment they stared at each other and then were in each other's arms, speechless, tears blurring their eyes.

'You've become so thin!'

'Where's Papa?'

'Gone to the club to play rummy.'

'You've become very frail, Ma,' Mrs Bhave said, looking her up and down.

'You didn't bring your little girls?'

'No, not after what happened yesterday.'

'I'm sorry. You know what he's like . . .'

'Ma . . . did you get those letters?'

'Yes . . .'

'You know, if anything happens to me, you'll have to look after my babies.'

'Don't talk like that, Ghungroo.'

'Ma . . . I'm fine now, but . . .'

'You know your father . . .'

'So what will he do, Ma? If I'm not around he'll have no choice.'

'You know how stubborn he can be. He just refuses to accept you or them.' She swallowed. 'I picked up those flowers and hid them.'

'Please promise me that you will look after them, Ma, please!'

'We will. Of course we will. But nothing will happen to you, baby.'

'It's very hard on Trisha.'

'She's such a beautiful girl.'

'She is. In some ways she's very much like me. But she's a lot like Kartik too; she reminds me a lot of him.'

'I wanted to come . . . when he died . . . but your papa put his foot down. He said I wouldn't be welcome back here if I went.'

'Is he drinking a lot?'

Her mother nodded, silently. 'Almost a bottle,' she whispered. 'Every day.'

'He's going to kill himself.'

'I can't do anything.' She got up. 'Just wait, I have something for you.' She left the room and returned quickly, with an envelope in her hand. She handed it over to Mrs Bhave.

'This is for you and your little girls,' she said simply. 'I was going to courier it to you.'

Mrs Bhave stared at the cheque in her hand. 'Ma . . . this is for 20 lakhs! I can't take it. How did you save so much? And how did you keep it from Papa? Surely he knows about it.'

'I sold some useless jewellery. I've been saving this for you since the day you left. Papa doesn't know about this bank account and I get all the correspondence sent to Mangalson's from where I pick it up when I do the stores.'

'Ma, why don't you just leave him and come and live with me in Delhi?'

'I can't leave your father. He's completely dependent on me. He'll go to pieces and probably have a heart attack. We've been married for more than forty-five years. It would kill him if I left and that would be murder.'

'But he's made your life absolute hell.'

'Whatever is written is written. But no, I can't leave him.'

Mrs Bhave got up. 'Well, I'd better be going now. I'll try and see you again before I go back to Delhi. Here's my mobile number.'

Her mother just nodded and wiped her eyes.

Tikka had just seen her into the pickup when the olive Gypsy roared down the incline. Maj. Gen Soni's rummy game had got over quickly, because he had lost his temper yet again and accused his opponent of cheating. Now his eyes bulged as he spotted the

gleaming black Toyota pickup in his porch. He parked right in front
of it, blocking its path, and charged out.

'What are you doing here again?' he bellowed. 'Get them, Patton!'
he roared. Patton had come running out for a last pet from Tikka, who
was now fondling his ears.

'Papa, I'm just going,' Mrs Bhave said. She stared at him. 'I came
here to see Ma and I have a right to do that. She may be your wife,
but she's also my mother and nothing is going to change that.'

'How dare you . . .' Hardly in control, he strode up to her, hand
raised. 'I'll teach you who is boss in my house . . .'

'Sahib, no!'

Tikka planted himself firmly in front of him.

'Papa, will you come to your senses for one second, please?'

'I am in my senses,' the General shouted. 'Now get the hell off my
property before I shoot you!'

'Papa,' she said quietly. 'You're just a pompous old fart, you know
that? You've ruined Ma's life and now you want to ruin ours too. You
and your precious General Namdev and his promotions and hanky-
panky arms deals . . .'

For a second it seemed like the General would strike Tikka. But the
man stood stolidly in front of him, staring unblinkingly at him, his
face expressionless. He backed down, breathing heavily.

'I am telling you,' he said clearly, 'the next time I see you on my
property, I will shoot you. Is that understood?'

'That will make you so popular with your friends, won't it?' she
said, getting into the pickup. 'What a hero! Imagine the headlines,
Papa: Hero of '71 tank battle shoots daughter in cold blood!'

Really, she ought to control herself and not be so sarcastic, she
thought, but he had a way of winding her right up. She was behaving
like a teenager herself. But then maybe, she had never stopped being one.

Tikka dropped her outside the hotel. The rain had thinned now, the
roar was muted and the blue whistling thrush had begun singing
tentatively.

Mrs Bhave sighed and stepped out. She cocked her head and
listened. From the main building came the faint plinking of a piano
and the thump of drums. And then . . . her eyebrows shot up. A smile

spread across her face. It suddenly seemed as though the recent unpleasantness had never happened . . .

At about the time Mrs Bhave had stepped into Bunker House, Jai had had a brainwave.

'Say, I know what we can do!' he said excitedly. 'You know, in the main lounge upstairs there's a piano and a drum kit . . .'

'So?' Akshay raised a quizzical eyebrow.

'So I say, we go up and ask the manager if we can play.'

'They'll never allow it.'

'Why not? There aren't too many other guests, and as long as they don't object, what's the problem? I mean, we'll be providing them with entertainment on this otherwise dark and rainy and boring morning.'

'Nah!'

'Come on, let's give it a bash. If they say no, fine. We'll come down here and you can play the sax and I'll bang on the tables and Trish can sing.'

'Tell you what. You go and fix it up. It's your idea.'

And Jai's charm worked. The manager, a sourpuss, was a thin-faced man of about forty-five, named Francis D'Cruz. He was unenthusiastic . . . at first, but agreed to give the boys a chance when Jai assured him that they could play all the golden hits dating back to the '50s and '60s. His pretty, baby-faced daughter Rosie was simply thrilled.

'Great! Let me fetch the others,' Jai said gleefully when the deal had been done. He ran down the steps and stopped halfway down and stared. A mud-spattered maroon Sumo had drawn up, and out of it tumbled a large roly-poly family. First out was a mop-top girl with round black eyes and a happy grin. Jai raced down the steps.

'Hey Gullu,' he called cheerfully. 'Get your guitar and come to the lounge. We've got a concert audition in five minutes!'

'So what can you guys play?' Rosie asked excitedly, having abandoned her station behind the reception desk. Her father had checked in his new guests and was now pacing up and down disapprovingly. Really, hotel staff should not fraternize with guests, it was unprofessional.

Akshay was at the piano.

'It's in perfect pitch,' he said, amazed. 'You keep it tip-top.'

'Of course we do.'

Jai rolled the drums. 'These are good drums,' he said, 'really good!'

Then Gullu, all tousled and rumpled, entered with her guitar strung around her.

'My God, you've assembled a pop group here in five minutes.'

Trisha gulped. How could she sing here? It was different in Akshay's house, this, this was a public place. And there was that lizard-like manager, and his daughter with those huge expectant eyes. Thank God there were no other guests.

'Okay, Trish,' Akshay said, suddenly taking her hand and squeezing it. 'Listen. Just shut your eyes; blot everything out and sing!'

'What would you like to hear, sir?' Jai asked the manager, eyeing him shrewdly. Play what they wanted to hear and you had them in your pocket. This guy was about fifty years old, so he'd probably like stuff dating back thirty or forty years . . . no problem! Thank Papa for that!

'Do you know anything by Bob Dylan?' the manager asked, raising a doubtful eyebrow. 'Have you kids even heard of him?'

'Mr Bob Dylan? Hey Akshay, Gullu, Trish, do we know any numbers by Mr Bob Dylan?'

Gullu grinned and plucked out the lead of 'Sad Eyed Lady of the Lowlands' and went on to the chords.

'Great!'

Trisha shut her eyes tight, took a deep, deep breath and opened her mouth to sing.

And so she didn't see the expressions on the faces of Rosie and Francis D'Cruz as her voice rang out, deep and clear and resonant, perfectly suited to the song. They went through a couple of verses, and then Jai nodded and hammered his drums.

'Okay guys, let's whip it up!'

Trisha was at full throttle when her mother walked into the lounge. Mrs Bhave sat down quietly in a large sofa at the back.

'Right, guys—"What a Wonderful World",' Akshay said, nodding and playing the chords. Like his brother, he had sized up Mr Francis

D'Cruz and come to the same conclusion. Once you won them over, they didn't mind what you played, but you had to win them over with what they wanted first!

The door of the lounge opened again and the Khuranas entered. They looked around in surprise and quietly sat down beside Mrs Bhave. Then Gullu's mom, in search of the manager, surged in, followed by Gullu's father, aunt, little sister and brother and grandmother. And then, in twos and threes, other guests filed in, drawn by the wonderful resonant voice and the music that accompanied it.

Trisha was facing the band, not the audience, so she wasn't at all aware of the additions to the audience and went on singing. And Akshay didn't stop between the numbers, but merged one into another seamlessly so that the music carried on uninterrupted.

When they stopped at last, with 'Raindrops Keep Falling on my Head', Trisha turned around, surprised by the burst of applause, and went bright pink.

'Oh my God,' she whispered. 'I had no idea!'

Akshay grinned. 'Congrats! You just gave your first public concert, Trish! They're giving you a standing ovation! Take a bow.'

Rosie was staring at her wide-eyed. 'My God, what a voice!' Her father was completely gobsmacked.

'I've never been so embarrassed in my life!' Trisha whispered to Akshay as they all sat down to lunch later that afternoon in the hotel dining room. 'Really,' Trisha went on, 'all those people listening . . . I had no idea.'

'It was only family and some other guests, Trish. Imagine, what would you have done if it was a crowd of 1,00,000 sweaty louts stomping their feet and whistling and throwing their jocks at you!'

'Don't be gross. You are such an idiot! And such a sucker for clichés: you had to do "Raindrops Keep Falling on My Head . . ."'

'You just wait. I bet old Kotkilli Cruz there is going to ask if you'll sing for the hotel on special evenings . . . for fifty bucks a time.'

'Akshay, you take the cake!'

'Is anyone sitting here?' Mrs Bhave asked, as Akshay looked up. Trisha was sitting at his right, and the seat to his left was empty.

'N-no, Aunty . . .' he stuttered, hurriedly getting up and drawing her chair back, his face going beetroot.

'Thank you, beta.' She smiled brilliantly at him and sat down. 'You play the piano and sax very well.'

'Thank you, Aunty.'

Under the table, Trisha's thigh pressed against his. The poor guy was absolutely scarlet.

'You guys really gel well together,' Mrs Bhave said, nodding at the four. 'You make a great group.'

'Thanks.'

'If you can get Trish to sing . . .'

'Mom! Please. I sang! I nearly died when I saw all those people!'

'For kids of your generation you really know some old fogey stuff: stuff that I used to listen to when I was your age.'

'Hello ji, how are you feeling now?' Gullu's mother, in a shocking pink nylon sari and vivid magenta lipstick, had rolled up, and was smiling at Mrs Bhave in her usual friendly way. 'I'm Gullu's mother.'

Gullu went pink with embarrassment. Mrs Bhave looked at her and smiled back.

'I'm very well—and thank you again so much for coming to the hospital.'

My mom, poor Gullu thought, is like a hippo and so, so tawdry. Look at Trisha's mom, slim, and yes, sexy. And Jai and Akshay's mom, she was so poised and sophisticated—a proper lady. Why did her mom have to come over here and make a spectacle of herself? She felt a hand clutch hers and squeeze it. Next to her Jai said nothing and didn't look at her. She squeezed back, her heart beginning to beat faster.

Mrs Bhave looked around the table; it was good that Trisha had made friends—Gullu was a very sweet girl and her mother was a gem. And of course, there were the boys and their parents. And one of those boys had won her daughter's heart . . . and he was not going to go scot-free. She turned to Akshay.

'Trish said you really enjoyed yesterday's hike.'

The colour rose slowly in Akshay's face. 'Uh . . . yes . . .' he stuttered as Jai grinned from across the table and squeezed Gullu's hand again. 'It was a g-great hike.'

Trisha blushed furiously. She leaned over. 'Mom, you're embarrassing him!' she whispered.

'Did you check out the Inspection Bungalow at the tip of the ridge?' Mrs Bhave continued.

'Umm . . . yeah. Trisha said it's supposed to be haunted. It was locked up and there was no caretaker around.'

'Yes.' Mrs Bhave smiled. 'That's usually the case. But usually you can get in—some door or window is invariably left open . . .'

'Mom, would you pass me the salad bowl, please?' Trisha hissed desperately.

Akshay nodded. 'Yes . . . actually we did get in. A door was left open and was banging, so we checked.'

'Here you are, darling. Oh, I see.'

Oh God, Trisha thought, what's got into Mom? Any second now she was going to ask, 'And did you go to bed with Trisha in the bungalow, Akshay?' Really, she ought not to have gone to see Nana and Nani that morning—the meeting had obviously derailed her badly.

Mercifully her mom left it at that and turned, albeit reluctantly, to her plate. But later, as they all got up to disperse, and Akshay leapt to his feet to pull her chair back, she leaned towards him and said softly.

'Akshay, I'd like to talk to you privately, please.' She looked at him. 'I think you know about what. As soon as possible, okay?'

'Y . . . yes ma'am, Aunty, any time.'

Oh heck, he was screwed.

'Say, why don't you guys all come to the resort now?' Trisha said. 'We can hang around and maybe go for a walk or something . . . if it stops raining.'

'Sure, I'll just ask my mom.' Gullu raced off.

'Um . . . we're all not going to fit in the cab of the pickup,' Mrs Bhave said. 'It's still pouring and you can't sit in the bed. Tikka will have to make two trips.'

'Jee, Memsahib.'

'Trish—you, Gullu, Jai and Shivi go first; Akshay and I will follow.'

'Um . . . okay, Mom. Actually, I could wait here with Akshay.'

'I want to buy some stuff, darling.'

'Oh . . . all right.'

Akshay watched helplessly as the others piled into the pickup and drove off. Mrs Bhave had neatly lassoed him!

'Right, Akshay, this won't take long,' she said now, taking his arm and going back into the lounge. 'Sit down, dear, and don't look like a frightened rabbit.' She looked at him. 'You like Trisha a lot, don't you?'

He nodded silently.

'And I think she likes you a lot too.'

'I . . . I hope so, Aunty . . .' he stuttered.

'She does.' She looked at him levelly. 'I guessed what happened yesterday . . .'

'I'm sorry, Aunty, it was my fault. I . . .'

'Trish has had a lot of stress these last few months and is probably going to face a lot more. I don't mean only her Boards. Akshay, don't take advantage of her situation—she'll be very vulnerable.'

'Can I see her, Aunty?'

'Of course you can! And make her sing as much as possible. She's been blessed with a beautiful voice. I'm just saying don't take advantage of her situation.'

'I'll never do that.'

'That's fine.' She smiled. 'Now let's go down to the shops, shall we?'

Trisha buttonholed him the first opportunity at the resort.

'Mom wanted to talk to you, right?' Her eyes searched his face. He'd been rather thoughtful all afternoon.

'Yes.'

'Well, what did she *say*?'

'She gave me the third degree. She said if she caught me with you again she'd come after me with a shotgun and blast off my face . . .'

'*Akshay!*'

'She said you love me very much and would die for me. And she wanted to know if I would do the same for you . . .'

'You . . . you idiot!' She was sitting on the arm of the planter's chair he was sprawled in, staring at him. She grinned and moved her head back.

'And what did you tell her, my hero?'

'If you accidentally fall into my lap now, I'll tell you in your ear maybe.' He pulled her down and stared at her, his arms around her.

'Trisha, why are you sitting in Akshay's lap and kissing him?' Shivi asked from the doorway, rubbing her eyes sleepily, her curls all tangled up.

'Oh shit!'

'It's okay, Shivi, I just lost my balance and fell.'

'You did not! You were kissing him . . . pachak, pachak!' Shivi turned and ran inside. 'Mommy!' she bawled, 'do you know what Trisha and Akshay were *doing*?'

CHAPTER TWELVE

MS TEN PERCENT TAKES FOUR

'Baby, Memsahib has said you have to give the order for the bania.' Trisha looked up from the settee in her study, as Komal looked around the door. She had been texting Gullu. She raised an eyebrow.

'What? But . . .' Trisha swung her legs off the settee and glanced at the list that Komal handed over. 'But Memsahib does this!' she protested. She squinted at the list. 'Besides, I can hardly read this! Where's Memsahib?'

She charged up to the office-cum studio. Mrs Bhave was, as usual, busy at her Mac, and old Almirah was at her computer too.

'Mom, what's this bania list stuff about?' Trisha asked.

'Oh that, yes, Komal's made her monthly list. Will you order the stores on the phone, darling? Please?'

'Mom! You know how badly I speak Hindi . . . and I hate ordering and stuff.'

'You'll manage. Oh, and before you go, there's one more thing I'd like you to do—well, actually two things.'

'I was planning to go to Akshay's and Jai's to practise . . .'

To her dismay, her mom wanted her to check out what they required for Diwali and do the necessary shopping, as well as deposit and cash some cheques at the bank.

'Mom! I'll be running around all day!' Trisha protested.

'I'm sorry, I would have done it myself but the Noida project architects are coming in this morning and the Ratnagarh people this afternoon, so I'm pretty much buried up to my neck.'

'Oh.'

'Thank you, you're an angel.'

'I know that, Mom, can't you see my halo?' Trisha folded her arms across her chest and sniffed. 'So what's in it for me?' she asked, grinning.

'Oh yes, sweetie, I nearly forgot—you'll have to pick up my latest blood report too—so you've got a busy morning ahead of you. The slip is in my bag.'

'Mom!'

Mrs Bhave looked at her and smiled. 'Maybe there will be something in it for you, maybe not. Now off you go!'

Trisha clattered down the stairs, a little exasperated. Damn! There went her morning.

'Write!' Komal commanded, as Trisha clicked her ballpoint. '10 kilos atta; 10 kilos sugar; 1 kg arharh daal . . .'

A few minutes later, Trisha looked at the list in amazement. 'You mean we go through all this stuff in one month?' she asked incredulously.

'Now ring them.'

She dialled the number and proceeded to read out the order in her 'bhelpuri' Hindi.

Komal giggled.

'Baby, you talk in Bombay Hindi, how will he understand?'

Trisha shushed her with a frown. 'And bring the order quickly, please!'

She put the phone down and pushed her hair away from her forehead. Then she picked it up again.

'Hey Akshay, listen, I can't come this morning; my mom wants me to do errands. Would you like to tag along? Oh great! I'll message you before leaving, about 10.45 or so, and pick you up.'

Okay, what next? Oh yes, those paying-in slips. Now where had she put the cheques her mother had given her? Her eyes widened when she saw the sums they were for. Suddenly she smiled. On an impulse she charged out of the room and up the stairs. She propped herself against the doorway of her mom's office, folded her arms across her chest and cleared her throat. Her mom looked up. Trisha waved the cheques and grinned.

'From now on, Mom, I'm known as Ms Ten Percent—that's going to be my cut!'

'Here's your ten per cent up front,' her mom said, getting up and kissing her. 'Now run along, or I'll never get my work done!'

She ran back down to the storeroom and opened the big wooden cupboard. Shivi joined her excitedly.

'Make a list, make a list!' Shivi said excitedly, sitting down on the floor and scattering broken diyas and stumpy candles all around.

'Shivi, don't make a mess. Komal will have a fit. And you've just bathed. What are you doing sitting on the ground?'

'Can I come shopping with you?' Shivi asked.

'Oh, okay.'

'Yay!'

'But I'm not buying you ice creams and sweets and pastries. Then Komal yells at me because you don't eat lunch properly.'

'Uff . . . okay! Are we going to the bank?'

'Yes.'

They picked up Akshay and drove off to the bank.

'Are you guys bursting fireworks?' he asked.

'I hope, a few . . . I haven't asked Mom yet. I'm buying diyas and candles today.'

His eyes shone. 'You know, I just had an idea! Why don't we drive down to the dry lakebed and burst some of our crackers there? It's way out so the pollution won't be such an issue, and it is kind of special.'

She nodded, excited. 'Yes. We can take stuff to eat too. I'll ask Mom.'

'Okay, Akshay, just sit there and wait and try not to rob the bank. I'll be back in a jiffy,' Trisha told him, as they entered the bank. She indicated the waiting area, as Shivi took off for the counters and quickly stood first in the queue in front of one of the counters, completely invisible to the teller. The bank staff knew the two girls well by now; they came twice every month, and Shivi was a favourite with all of them, and

never came away without a handful of sweets. Trisha walked up, and
handed in her cheque. It was for another big amount—Rs 50,000.

Trisha tucked the money safely away in her handbag and returned
to him. 'Come on, let's go!' She grinned. 'I'm a very rich girl, you
know, so treat me nice, I have diamonds on the soles of my feet—and
maybe you can be my bodyguard!'

'Urrgh—and you tell me about clichés! But good, so now you can
buy Shivi and me truffles and Bentleys, or we'll rob you! Have you
put the loot away safely?'

As always, the dread stirred like a waking python, when they
approached the pathology laboratory to pick up Mrs Bhave's reports.
So far, Mrs Bhave's bilirubin had maintained a steady downward trend,
even though some of the other parameters in the report were still
pretty high. Dr Phadnis had not asked for another of the dreaded CA
19–9 test to be done.

'Hello Trisha . . . here's your mother's report.' The girl at the
counter, who had a kind but tired smile, handed the dreaded envelope
over as Trisha paid her.

She got into the pickup.

'Well?' Akshay asked.

'I . . . haven't looked at it as yet,' she said, glancing at him. He was
looking tense too.

'Thanks for coming,' she said in a small voice. 'I hate collecting
her reports alone.'

'Then you call me every time you have to, you hear?'

'Trisha, has Mommy passed?' Shivi asked, staring at the envelope.

Trisha took a deep breath. 'Let's see . . .' she said 'Total Leucocyte
Count 7910—that's within normal, Haemoglobin 11.6—okay . . .'
Her eyes scanned down the report. 'Liver Function Tests . . . S Bilirubin
Total 0.6—pass! Direct 0.3, pass, Indirect 0.3 pass! She's passed, Shivi,
she's passed!' A little way down there were other figures, which were
high and starred: something called S Alkaline Phosphatase at 774 and
S Gamma G T at 837—both way above normal, but . . . but . . . all the
doctors really seemed bothered by was that damn bilirubin—and it
was normal. She was fine. She was cured. It was over.

'That's great!'

She looked up, surprised. Akshay's voice had been unnaturally gruff. She saw him swallow and then pretend as if there was something in his eye. 'Isn't that great, Shivi?' he said, and suddenly hugged the little girl.

'Tikka, Memsahib's report is absolutely okay!' she said, as Tikka nodded.

'It's God's blessing,' he said and folded his hands.

She called her mom straight away. 'Mom, guess what? You passed at last! Your bilirubin is normal! You're fine! Isn't that great?'

She folded away her phone and looked at Akshay. With Shivi sitting between them, she couldn't even hold his hand. Suddenly, she couldn't give a damn. She leaned over her little sister and put her arms around his neck and kissed his cheek.

'Haaw! Trisha, you're kissing him again!' Shivi said.

'And I'm kissing you too . . .' she said, and did so.

'But he's a *boy*!'

'You know,' she said softly to Akshay a little later, 'I surfed the Internet for stuff on what Mom had. It was so scary I stopped after a bit. They say five years is the max you can survive or something like that.' She looked at him, now sitting beside her as Shivi had wanted the window seat again. She went on: 'But I suppose if the disease has gone away and your reports are normal then you could go on beyond that, couldn't you?'

'Come on in for a bit,' she urged Akshay, when they reached home. 'Come on and have lunch.'

'Umm . . . okay!'

She charged up to her mom's office, pulling him along. 'Hi Mrs Almeida!' she yelled popping her head into the cubicle. 'Mom's report is fine! She's cured!'

'Oh!' Mrs Almeida half rose. 'That's good . . . no, Trisha, your Mom is busy . . .'

But Trisha had aheady yanked open her mother's office door, dragging Akshay behind her.

'Mom! Your report! You've passed. See for your . . . oh, sorry!'

Her mom was having a meeting. There were two suited grey-haired gentlemen sitting in front of her, listening to her intently as she presented slides on the screen behind her. They turned as Trisha burst in.

'Oh, I'm so sorry!' Trisha backed out, mortified, right into the arms of Akshay, and clutched at him for balance.

'Babe!' he murmured, stepping back and holding her close as Mrs Almeida emerged from her cubicle and lowered her glasses. 'Babe, your lips are red like wine, you are but totally divine! Be mine till the end of time, or else forever shall I pine!'

'You idiot!' she hissed, dissolving into giggles.

'Trisha, step inside for a moment . . .' her mother called. 'Say hello, sweetheart.'

Scarlet, Trisha disentangled herself from Akshay and walked back in. 'I'm sorry for barging in . . .' she stuttered, holding up the report like a shield. 'I got your report.'

'Mr Srinivasan, Mr Gupta, this is my daughter Trisha. Trish, these are the gentlemen who're in charge of the Noida Expressway Villas project.'

Outside, poor Akshay grinned at Mrs Almeida and shrugged.

'It is good you are making Trisha sing,' Mrs Almeida said suddenly. 'She has a beautiful voice.' He looked up, surprised.

'Oh, yes.' He shrugged again and rolled his eyes. 'It was tough, I can tell you . . .'

'She's very shy.'

'I know.'

'And she's a very sweet, innocent girl . . .'

'Uh-huh . . .'

'She can't bear to hurt anyone. Even little Shivi bullies her.'

'Absolutely! She can't hurt a fly!'

'Which means sometimes she gets hurt by others.'

'I guess—even by flies.'

'She's like that song she was singing the other day . . . Cherry Pink and Apple Blossom . . .'

A few minutes later, much to his relief, Trisha emerged.

'Mrs Almeida, Mom needs you.'

'Okay, dear, I'm just going.'

'Mrs Almeida thinks you're as pink as the cherry tree and innocent as the white apple blossom,' he said solemnly as they walked down the stairs. She stopped.

'What on earth are you talking about? You've been chatting her up, haven't you?'

'Their branches intertwined,' he went on.

'What?'

'In the song . . . the branches of the cherry tree and apple blossom intertwine.'

'What should we do now?' Shivi asked after lunch. 'I'm bored!'

'Why don't you play with your dolls, Shivi? Akshay and I have to study.'

'My dolls are all sick. Four have broken arms and legs and Joanie's head has come off and I can't find it.'

'Let me see them. Maybe I can fix them,' Akshay offered. 'I'm going to be a famous surgeon one day.'

'Akshay, you can't look! They don't have any clothes on! Shut your eyes.'

'Oops! Sorry.'

'I can fix them easily. They got hurt.'

'Oh.'

Shivi spread her dolls and pieces of dolls all over the bed and opened up her 'doctor set'. Suddenly she frowned.

'You know, I think Babita's head will look better on Joanie's body . . .' she said and yanked Babita's head off her body.

'Ouch! But then Babita's body doesn't have a head.'

'Doesn't matter, she'll get used to it.'

Trisha grinned. 'So should I leave you two to play Jekyll and Hyde with dolls and amuse myself some other way?'

'Trisha, you can make brownies. We'll play here.'

But Shivi had lain down and was trying to fix a leg where an arm ought to be. 'Come on, get in, get in,' she said sleepily, and then suddenly put the doll aside and rolled over.

'She'll be asleep in five!' Trisha mouthed as Akshay slowly got off the bed. 'Then we can sneak away. She'll sleep the whole afternoon.'

'Trisha baby? Trisha baby?'

'Oh heck!'

Frantically they disentangled and Trisha just made it to the door as Komal pressed down the handle. Trisha undid the bolt and peered out.

'Yes?' Trisha pushed the hair out of her face, hoping it was not too messy. 'What?'

'Baby, the bania's come, please check the order.'

Akshay lounged against the wall in the storeroom grinning, as Trisha squatted on her heels, ticking items off her list as the delivery boy took them out of his bag and announced them.

'I told you to come in the morning, not in the afternoon when everyone's resting,' she scolded and then bit her tongue. Poor guy, he was just the delivery boy; he just brought the stuff when it was given to him. 'It's okay, I'll tell your boss not to send the stuff at this time. Do you want water?'

Against the wall, Akshay was in hysterics.

'What?' she demanded.

'Babe, your Hindi!'

And then he sweet-talked her into taking part in a cricket match that he and Jai were playing (and Jai was captaining) that evening.

'There's just one thing,' he said solemnly.

'What's that?'

'Jai says you have to improve your batting.'

'I can't bat.'

'I could teach you. Do you have a cricket bat?' He shook his head, it wasn't likely.

She nodded. 'Shivi used to have a plastic cricket bat . . . let me check.'

'And a ball . . .'

'You mean you want to start right now?'

'Why not? I could show you how to hold the bat, and and a few strokes. You can stand in front of the mirror . . .'

'Oh, okay.' She got up. 'Be back in a sec,' she said, 'I'll find the bat.'

She was back soon enough, holding it up. The bat was several sizes too small and bright yellow.

'It's *batter* than nothing,' Akshay said, poker-faced. 'Come on. Here, hold it like this. Babe, your right leg doesn't have to get airborne when you play a stroke.'

'Oh! Now I know why you wanted to teach me how to bat. You wanted to *hold* me close, that's all!' she teased as he stood flush behind her, his arms around her waist, and showed her the grip.

But she was both right and wrong about being able to bat. When her turn came during the match, Akshay, still batting at the other end ran over.

'Just hit it anywhere and run! Got it?' She smiled nervously and nodded.

'Okay, I'll try!'

Vivek, the opposition's crack bowler grinned as he took the ball and walked almost up to the boundary and turned around. This was about twice his normal run up, but heck man, he couldn't miss giving Akshay and his chick the frights. He came pounding in. At the batting crease, Trisha watched in alarm as he bounded up to the wicket. She saw his arm swing over, shut her eyes and swung her bat wildly, the leg following through as usual. She heard and felt the ball slice the edge of her bat, and charged down the pitch towards Akshay racing down from the other side.

There was a roar from their team's 'dugout'.

'Six! Six! Six! She's done a Sehwag on you, Vivek!'

'Oh!' she said. 'Now you get to bat?'

'No,' he grinned. 'That was a six.'

'Clean her up, bugger!' Ravi, the rival captain—and the fellow she had got out previously—snarled. 'Get her. She's clouted you first ball, man!'

'Fluke!'

Again, she gritted her teeth and waited as Vivek walked slowly back and turned. This time she got a glimpse of the ball whistling down outside the off-stump. She swung mightily, made contact and the bat slipped out of her hand and went airborne. The fielder at mid-wicket ducked as Akshay screamed.

'RUN!'

'Oh! My bat!' she squealed and looked around, bewildered. Then she heard and saw it land with a thud and charged towards it.

'Not there!' Akshay screamed desperately. 'Not there!'

The opposition was in splits as Vivek ran her out in slow-motion and Trisha looked completely bamboozled, her bat back in her hands, stranded at mid-wicket.

'But . . . but I thought you had to have the bat in your hand . . .' she protested. Even Akshay suppressed a smile, though what he really wanted to do was to run up and hug her—she looked so completely baffled!

'I'm so sorry! I didn't know!'

'Next time you recruit chicks you better teach them the rules!' Ravi Singh grinned.

Their rivals made a steady start and by the fifth over were 30 for two, with Ravi Singh batting well on 20. Jai had not called on Trisha to bowl as yet; she was his secret weapon and he wanted to save her till it became absolutely necessary; he always liked sailing close to the wind. Fielding on the boundary near their 'dugout' Trisha chatted with Gullu.

'It's a crazy game! They never told me you could throw your bat and run!'

'Catch!' Someone yelled. She whirled and saw the ball heading straight for her like a homing missile. She cupped her hands and waited; it landed and bounced out of her palms and over the ropes.

'Six!' The score was now 36 for two. The rivals needed just 23 in 25 balls and had eight wickets standing.

'What are you waiting for, man? Get her to bowl!' Akshay told his brother.

Jai nodded and tossed the ball to her.

'Go get 'em!' he grinned.

Her mouth was dry and her heart beat nervously as she walked up to the wicket, her ponytail bouncing jauntily. By now, the number of spectators had increased, and Trisha could see Shivi running up to their mom: who had sat down on one of the benches, with both Komal and Tikka standing behind her.

Oh shit, she should've never agreed to play. Her palms were sweaty and she could hardly grip the ball. 23 to get in twenty-five balls . . . It would be easy for them . . . Her first ball more or less slipped out of her hand, and ended up as a juicy full toss. Four!

'Hey, easy, Trish!' Akshay said, tossing her the ball with a wry grin. 'Just think it's me batting.'

Shit, even that didn't work. The damn ball just wouldn't do what she wanted it to. The second delivery landed outside the leg stump and went on straight harmlessly.

'Wide!'

Forty-one, they needed just eighteen.

The next was hit for two runs to mid-on. Sixteen to get in twenty one balls. Too easy now.

And then, three blessed dot balls as thank God, the ball began to turn and the batsman swung wildly and missed. By the end of her over, they needed fourteen from eighteen balls and still had six wickets in hand. It was all but done and dusted.

By the end of the next over the target was twelve from twelve with four wickets in hand . . .

Jai grimaced. He'd run out of bowling options; nearly all his usual bowlers had finished their quotas—Bhaskar, the only one left, had one over left and would bowl the vital last one. His secret weapon hadn't worked so far—she'd been hit. He had no choice. He tossed the ball to her.

'Babe,' Akshay said to her as he handed her the ball. 'Forget the match, just bowl for the heck of it.'

She nodded. 'Okay, I'll try,' she said with a wan smile.

The new batsman, a strongly built fellow called Ranjan, leered at her and lifted his bat menacingly.

She gave away nine in the first two balls—a six and a three. Worse, now Ravi Singh was facing her, grinning and licking his lips. Just three needed now from ten balls; it was over. Only a miracle could save them. She turned and gripped the ball; it was all over but still . . . And heck, she'd got him out twice in consecutive balls the last time he had faced her; no matter how much he grinned now, he must be just a trifle nervous. If . . . IF she got him out again . . . She grinned, and turning with a lithe dancing motion, tossed the ball up.

It floated high and lazily, wobbling on its axis as it spun furiously. Ravi Singh watched it and got ready to sweep. Suddenly it dipped, bounced, and fizzed from wide of leg, cannoning into his stumps as he swatted desperately.

'Bowled him!'

There was a stunned silence from the rival camp as they rubbed their eyes in disbelief. The new batsman walked up warily and tapped the pitch down nervously. Oh yes, they still needed just three from nine balls—three of which this girl would bowl . . . No problem.

Trisha turned and squinted. This time she pitched it just on leg; the batsman stepped way out forward to lóft it over mid-on; the ball jinked away, missed his bat and Jai snapped it up and had the bails off in a flash.

'Howzatt?'

Stumped out by a mile!

Their team were now hopping madly, yelling their lungs out.

Trisha was on a roll; at least she'd made some amends for that spilled catch and embarrassing run out. The match was still as good as gone, so it didn't matter what she tried. She watched the new batsman take guard warily.

This time she didn't spin it at all and pitched it in line with the middle stump. The batsman swung back on his heels to cut, missed and winced.

'Bowled him!'

Hat-trick, hat-trick, hat-trick!' This time Akshay lifted her right off her feet.

'You did it, you did it!' he yelled as the team danced around her in delight.

She had one ball left. They had one wicket left. Three runs to get. But a whole over after that.

The last man swaggered up.

'Abbe, smash her! Smash her!'

Recklessly he twirled his bat and waited. 'I'll show her!'

Trisha squinted. 'Okay, let's see if this works,' she murmured and tweaked the ball in the opposite direction. It pitched outside the off stump as the batsman jumped out to loft it—and then cut back sharply. It missed the leg stump by a whisker, Jai fumbled as he collected it, and the batsman foolishly took off for a run. Jai recovered and had all three stumps down in a flash. Run out! They had won!

'Run out, run out! Four wickets in four balls! We've won!'

They charged up to her and to her acute embarrassment lifted her on to their shoulders for a lap of honour.

'Trisha! Trisha! Trisha!'

'Put me down! Put me down, guys!' she squeaked ineffectually, blushing furiously.

Poor Ravi Singh and his team could only watch in stunned silence.

Shivi was beside herself with excitement. Mrs Bhave smiled and waved madly and Gullu was screaming hysterically and taking pictures.

They put her down at last, gently clapping her on the back and shaking her hand. She pushed the hair out of her face.

'Akshay, you guys just listen . . .' she said breathlessly, holding up her hands.

'What?'

'I'm retiring!'

'*What?*'

Stony faced, Ravi Singh and his team came up to congratulate her.

He extended a sweaty hand and nodded briefly, but said nothing, his face set.

She looked at him. 'Sorry,' she said, knowing he must be feeling godawful. 'Don't feel too bad. I don't know how it happens but it just does.'

Sometimes, when you believe in miracles, they happen.

Sometimes, they don't.

CHAPTER THIRTEEN

CELEBRATIONS

'Mom, our house must be the most beautiful one in the whole colony,' Trisha exclaimed as she gazed at the rows of flickering diyas that gilded the balconies and the terrace. 'Everyone else has those horrid electric Chinese lights that look more suited to some sleazy boudoir.'

'What's a sleazy *boodor*, Trisha?' Shivi asked, busy playing hopscotch on the hopscotch patch Komal had made for her out of rangoli powder.

'Umm . . . a bedroom with lights that can look eerie.'

'It's as if the lights are alive and breathing and *feeling* . . .' Trisha went on dreamily, wondering what Akshay and Jai were up to at the moment. She was resplendent in a shimmering new pink and purple and gold salwar kameez. Her mother, in black and scarlet silk, and Shivi in dark blue and gold, equally stunning. Mrs Bhave had pulled out all the stops this Diwali, buying them all expensive new outfits and decking up the house, with diyas and fragrant garlands of marigolds, roses and jasmine, till as Trisha giggled and remarked, 'It looks like a bride, Mom!'

'Well, it is our first Diwali here, so it must be memorable,' her mother replied, smiling.

'Mommy, can we burst the firecrackers now?' Shivi asked again, getting impatient. This had become a point of contention in the neighbourhood. A few days before Diwali, a group of very sanctimonious looking kids from the colony (some of whom, Trisha had got out first ball) had come around requesting residents not to burst crackers because of 'the noise and pollution and fire-hazard they cause, Aunty'.

'Goddamn spoilsports!' Trisha had complained to Akshay, and added, hopefully, 'Are you guys bursting crackers?'

He had given a hollow laugh. 'What a hope! Do you think Papa will allow us? He keeps going on and on about how horribly you can get burned and be scarred for life.'

'Oh, shit! And now all these wet blankets have come around making us promise not to burst them. I know about the pollution and all, but it's only for one night! I mean, all these do-gooders ride around in their parents' SUVs the whole year and now they say don't burst crackers! They say child labour is involved but they have twelve-year-olds sweeping and swabbing their houses from morning to night. Give me a break!'

'Yes, but, umm . . . we have a Safari and you guys have that hunky pickup.'

'I know. But at least we don't go around with pudding faces and preaching what we don't practise!'

He snorted with laughter. 'Babe . . . pudding faces, you got it right!'

Happily, Akshay and Jai had struck a deal with their parents; they would dutifully visit a couple of close relatives and then be dropped at the Bhaves' for the rest of the Diwali celebrations. Gullu promised she would try her best to get away from her family and come over, but didn't sound too optimistic.

Now, as Shivi stomped around impatiently, Trisha dialled Akshay. 'Hey, when are you guys showing up? Shivi's getting hyper.'

'On our way! We have to smuggle the crackers we bought—Papa will ground us if he finds out we're taking patakas to your place. Hey, by the way, did you ask your mom about the lakebed idea?'

'Yes! She said fine, we'll all go there, but after we've celebrated at home. So we'll be bursting some here first.'

'Oh, great!'

Mrs Bhave had really spent an exorbitant amount of money on fireworks.

'Mom! Aren't we spending too much?' Trisha asked, aghast.

Her mother squeezed her hand. 'Darling, it's our first Diwali here, and my work has done rather well, so I think we can celebrate without being too tight-fisted and welcome Lakshmi properly.'

'Mom!' Trisha looked appalled. 'You really shouldn't say things like that!'

At last, Akshay and Jai drove up with their parents. Akshay stared at Trisha, his mouth agape, until Jai nudged him in the ribs.

'It's rude to stare at visions from heaven!' he hissed, controlling his snort of laughter. 'They may not let you in!'

'Boys, you're having dinner with us,' Mrs Bhave said, smiling affectionately. 'Tikka will drop you home afterwards.'

'Great!'

'Are you sure that's okay and they won't be a nuisance?' Dr Khurana asked.'

'Not at all. It'll be a pleasure to have them.'

Dr Khurana nodded. 'Very well . . . we'd better be on our way. We have a lot of visiting to do.'

They'd just got started with a trio of beautiful 'anars' when a group of youngsters assembled at their gates. Trisha looked up.

'Shit! Akshay, Jai—it's the po-faced anti-firework brigade! Oh God, they're wearing earplugs and gas masks! I can't believe it!'

Akshay and Jai, who were just about to set off a couple of anars, looked at the group, some of whom were waving placards reading 'Stop! Crackers Cause Pollution and Asthma!' The two boys exchanged glances and went to the table where the fireworks had been kept and came out with a long string of ladhis and wicked grins on their faces. They strung it along the driveway, all the way from the porch to the gate. Akshay rushed up and whispered something in Trisha's ear; her dark eyes danced and she nodded. She clutched four phuljaris in her hand as Akshay lit them and Jai collected four more and followed her. She walked up to the group and before they realized what was happening she had handed over the phuljaris to them one by one, with Jai helping out, her sweetest smile on her face. 'Happy Diwali,' she said. Then she bent down gracefully, lit the ladhi and ran back lightly to the porch, a huge grin of delight on her face. It is virtually impossible to refuse a sputtering phuljari from a very pretty girl with sparkling eyes and a drop-dead smile; you just have to accept it, or she might just drop it on your feet and make you hop.

A maroon Sumo drew up at the gate and Gullu, in an emerald green lehenga and a big grin on her face, tumbled out, clutching her guitar case. Jai's face lit up like an anar. 'I got away!' she exclaimed. 'Mama said okay! I can't believe it!'

'Do you guys do puja and stuff?' Akshay asked Trisha. He had a tikka on his forehead, which Trisha thought looked terribly cute. She shook her head.

'No. Mom doesn't like to do that sort of stuff; she says it makes her feel uncomfortable. She says as long as you are good and honest in your everyday life you don't need to do stuff like that; if there's someone up there checking, he or she will see and appreciate you anyway. She thinks it's like bribery in a way, promising to be good so that you can get something in return or begging for favours. Of course, we light up the house and all to welcome Lakshmi, if she would like to visit.' She smiled disarmingly. 'Mom's completely irreverent, you know!'

After a truly magnificent dinner they drove out to the lakebed.

'God, what a beautiful place,' Mrs Bhave remarked as they reached.

'Mommy, it's so dark!' Shivi clutched her mother's hand. 'And the stars are so near!'

'Look Shivi, look at all those diamonds on the ground,' Akshay said, taking the little girl by the hand and pointing out the mica being reflected back. Shivi nodded.

'If they are diamonds you should collect them—then you can be rich and marry Trisha,' she said.

Tikka had rolled down Smelly Beast and lit the half dozen kerosene lanterns he had brought along and set them on the ground in a ring.

'Really dear, it's so peaceful here. And now we're going to shatter that peace with Smelly Beast!'

'Yes!' Trisha said gleefully rubbing her hands. 'Exactly!'

It was, of course, a moonless night; there was just the faint sodium glow of the city lights radiating above the surrounding hills, and above them a sky freckled with diamond point stars. Occasionally, borne on the breeze came the muffled thud of some faraway fireworks.

'Mommy, do you think there are any wild animals here?' Shivi asked fearfully.

'Not once we start up Smelly Beast, darling,' her mother answered, smiling. 'They'll run away!'

'Come on, let's burst the leftover fireworks first!' Trisha said, as Tikka brought the big basket down from the pickup.'

'This is such an unusual Diwali!' Trisha whispered to Akshay, after they finished the second round of fireworks. Tikka had gathered all the empty boxes and collected an armful of dry brushwood and made a bonfire around which they were all sitting. 'This place is so heavenly. I'll never forget it.'

'Akshay, play us something, please,' Mrs Bhave requested as they settled down.

'Okay, but you guys have to join in.'

He started a series of sweet, blues melodies, with Jai softly thumping the drinks cooler box in rhythm and Gullu strumming her guitar, her black button eyes fixed on his face. Trisha started to sing very softly at first and then her notes began to rise and soar. Nearby, Smelly Beast gleamed silently. Suddenly Akshay whispered a word in Jai's ear; he passed the message to Gullu. She smiled and nodded. At the end of the number, the three of them launched into 'On This Night of a Thousand Stars' from *Evita* and grinned at Trisha. She glanced up at the sky and rolled her eyes despairingly.

'You're hopeless, Akshay!' she groaned; which might have been true, but it was also one of her favourites and he knew that. She took a deep breath and started to sing.

'That was lovely, children. Thank you,' Mrs Bhave said. Trisha looked at her, surprised. Her mom's eyes were soft and shimmery. Gullu and Jai were staring at each other as if they were the only two people in the world. Shivi had dozed off in her mom's lap.

'Mom?'

'I'm fine, dear.'

'I think I'll go for a spin on Smelly Beast now,' Trisha said. 'Coming, anyone?'

Akshay jumped up. 'Sure.'

She strapped on her helmet and got astride. 'Come on,' she said.

'Mom, I'm taking the route around the hills that Tikka showed me . . .
I showed you those pictures, remember.'

'Baby, be careful, drive slowly,' Tikka said. Trisha nodded and
gunned the bike.

'Darling, are you sure it's safe?'

'Mom, I know that route by heart, I could do it blindfolded.'

'Should we follow you in the pickup?'

'No, Mom! We'll be back in ten-twelve minutes, I promise!
Besides, for most of the way you'll be able to see our headlight beam
and track us.'

'Okay, but if you're not back in ten, we'll be after you! Have you
got your phone?'

'Deal! Yes, yes, I have it.'

They set off, Trisha accelerating rapidly. The headlight cleaved a
path before them, and Akshay held her tight around the waist.

'What's the hurry, babe?' he shouted as they bounced up the
incline, and onto the track. 'Watch out for the ruts.'

'We have ten minutes,' she yelled back. 'Now hold on, I'm going
to let her rip!'

'Watch it!'

The big bike thundered up the winding track. Trisha concentrated
grimly as the headlight etched the ruts and potholes ahead, which
she avoided dexterously. What she wanted was to revisit the cavern,
but knew that was impossible. If she kept up a good pace, they could
perhaps stop for a few minutes, especially in the section near the
overhang where their headlight beam was not visible from down
below and sneak a kiss. Suddenly, she braked. Akshay clutched her
around the waist.

'What?'

'Shh . . . look at that! On the top of that rock, lit by the headlight!
What an enormous owl!'

'It's beautiful!'

The majestic eagle owl glared back at them, its 'horns' up, eyes
burning golden amber, and its tan plumage beautifully flint marked
and barred in black.

'It's not at all bothered by Smelly Beast's engine or the light.'

At the campfire on the lakebed far below, Mrs Bhave had been following the wavering beam of the headlight as the bike worked its way through the hills. Now the beam was stationary, pointing at the sky and silhouetting a bird on a rock. The kids must have stopped to look at it. She could hear the faint idle rumble of Smelly Beast's engine.

'Tikka, do you have binoculars?'

Tikka nodded and pulled out a small pair from the glove box.

'Oh look, Gullu and Jai, what a magnificent owl. Trisha and Akshay must have stopped to look at it.' She handed the glasses over to Gullu.

She was right. But Akshay and Trisha weren't looking at the owl anymore. 'As long as it's there we're safe . . .' Trisha murmured, 'we have a perfect excuse. They can probably see it from down below too.'

Unperturbed, the owl remained on its perch for a further five minutes, staring unblinkingly at the two young people wrapped in each other's arms by the bike. Then its partner flew down beside it and both of them took off into the darkness. Trisha and Akshay didn't notice the bird had gone (and never saw its mate!) till Trisha suddenly surfaced and looked over Akshay's shoulder.

'Oh shit, we better move. The damn bird's flown! Is my hair messed up too much?'

'You have the roll-in-the-hay look again,' he grinned and kissed her cheek.

'Did you guys see that owl?' Trisha exclaimed breathlessly after they'd ridden back to the pickup. 'We stopped to watch it.'

'Yes. It was beautifully lit up by the headlight. We knew you'd stopped.'

'And then the birds flew away and there was only the searchlight beaming up forlornly into the night sky looking for its lost love!' Jai intoned dolefully. 'For almost five long minutes . . .'

'What birds?' Trisha looked at him askance as her mother put her hand in front of her face to hide her smile.

'Its partner joined it and they were smooching like anything . . . you mean you didn't see them?'

'Oh yes, of course, we did . . .' She was blushing. 'They were so sweet.'

'Yes. And then the owl offered his girlfriend the heads of seven bandicoots tied up with a red ribbon . . . like he was giving her flowers.'

'Eh? Heads of bandicoots? Yes, yes . . . Red ribbon . . . wait, what? Jai!'

'Goodnight, darling, and Happy Diwali again.'

'Goodnight, Mom. It was really great this year. The best we've ever had!'

'I'm glad you enjoyed yourself.'

Mrs Bhave hugged her tightly and kissed her on the forehead. Beside her, Shivi was fast asleep, her arms and legs splayed out in abandon.

'Well, darling, you're going to be seventeen soon. How would you like to celebrate your birthday?'

'It's still a month away.' Trisha grinned. 'I'll let you know, okay?'

Mrs Bhave shut the door quietly and stood with her back against the wall and closed her eyes. Then she took a deep breath and walked slowly towards her own bedroom, putting off the hallway lights as she went.

'Ooof, you sleepyhead, are you going to spend your whole birthday sleeping or what?' Shivi bounced on the bed and yanked off Trisha's blanket. Trisha moaned. 'Come on, get up, get up! Can I open your presents?'

Trisha sat up and turned blearily towards her bedside alarm clock. 'Shivi, it's only 7!' She lay back and looked around the dim bedroom, yawning. They'd gone to see Dr Phadnis yesterday evening again, just a routine appointment, and he had really kept them waiting because of some emergency. Mrs Bhave's bilirubin figure had increased marginally to 1.5, which was just 0.3 points above the normal range but he hadn't seemed at all bothered by that.

'You're doing very well,' he had said, 'believe me, you're doing excellently. How's the appetite and nausea?'

'Almost normal, Doctor.'

'Good! Your mom is doing remarkably well,' he'd told Trisha. 'The stent is working perfectly.'

And may it continue doing its work perfectly, Trisha prayed; it had been four months now and her mom had been almost, *almost* normal. Maybe the growth had been benign after all.

Mrs Bhave entered the room with a gift-wrapped box in her hands.

'I want to give mine first!' Shivi said, charging to her cupboard and scrabbling about. She pulled out a glittering packet and handed it over to Trisha, a huge smile on her face.

'Thank you, Shivi!' She opened the packet carefully, so as not to spoil the wrapping paper. In a basket inside, nestled a presentation pack of toiletries—rose-shaped soaps, two bottles of bath and shower gel, and two embroidered hand towels.

'Thank you, Shivi, they're so sweet . . . you must have saved up for ages!'

'You can have the pink and yellow roses, I'll have the violet and white ones,' Shivi said matter-of-factly.

Mrs Bhave sat on the bed and embraced Trisha.

'Happy birthday, darling!' She handed over her gift. 'I hope you like it.'

Trisha unwrapped it slowly, wondering what it could be; her eyes widened as the wrapping came off the box.

'An iPod! It must have cost a bomb!' She knew it was a high-end model.

'It's been loaded with all the songs you love to sing,' her mom said. 'And here's something else . . .' From the foot of the bed she brought out another large box.

'Wow! It's a helmet!'

'I thought it was time you got a new snazzy helmet,' Mrs Bhave said. 'This one is lighter and stronger than your old one. You'll be more comfortable and less hot in it.'

'It's fabulous!'

Shivi's eyes were huge. Then her mom took out a smaller box and handed it over to Shivi. 'And this is the little present for Shivi,' she said, hugging the little girl. The tradition had been started in the family by their father: the sister of the birthday girl always got a 'compensatory gift'. Within seconds Shivi had ripped open her parcel and slipped on the silver bracelet, holding it up for all to admire.

Trisha's mobile went off and she picked it up, her heart beating fast. It was Gullu, singing 'Happy Birthday' down the line in her froggy croak and twanging her guitar.

'Has Akshay wished you?' she asked wickedly.

'Not yet. Must be sleeping; you know how they like sleeping late on Sundays.'

'What? Not on your birthday! He ought to be outside your window with his sax playing 'Happy Birthday' and serenading you! What a lazy bum!'

'It's okay, Gullu. No big deal!'

'I hope the fellow's remembered. You know what guys are like!'

'It's only 7.30, Gullu. Give the guy a break. You're always so dark and dire!'

'Knowing you, Trish, you'll be saying that at 11.59 tonight! Haul him over the coals, girl, if he doesn't call in an hour.'

Mrs Bhave and Shivi were exchanging glances, and seemed highly amused. Trisha stared at them wonderingly.

'Okay, Gullu, thanks. I got to go. Say, come over this evening.'

'Sure I will.'

'Bye then.' She disconnected. 'What?' she asked her mom. 'Why are you looking like that?'

'Like what?' Shivi could barely suppress her giggles.

'Like that!'

'Why don't you get dressed? Then we can discuss plans for the day—what would you like to do?'

Trisha looked at her mom askance. She shrugged.

'I thought I'd laze around like a bum,' she said. 'No hurry to have a bath and all!'

'None at all, darling! See you at breakfast.'

'Sure!'

She got up, went to the bathroom, brushed her teeth and washed her face. She'd have a bath after breakfast: it was her birthday and it was Sunday so she could do as she pleased. She glanced at her clock; it was getting on to eight o'clock and he still hadn't called. Just wait till his birthday came around; she'd give him the silent treatment for the whole day. Come on, come on, give him a chance, maybe he's overslept, maybe he just forgot, maybe he didn't give a damn . . .

She opened her room door and frowned. She could have sworn she had heard the patter of footsteps scampering away: probably Shivi up to some prank. She went out into the corridor and looked up and down. Shivi came charging out of the drawing room.

'This way, you have to come this way first,' she said, hardly able to contain her excitement. She grabbed her hand and tugged her.

'Shivi . . . but I want breakfast . . .'

'Later!' Shivi dragged her into the drawing room.

A great drumroll of thunder greeted her as Jai beat a tattoo on his drums—she couldn't believe he'd brought his whole drum kit—and Gullu struck the chords, and then Akshay, trim and natty, picked up his sax. Her mom, Mrs Almeida and even Gullu's mom were on the settee smiling as they began to sing and the band began to play.

'Happy Birthday to you . . .'

They'd decked up the room too, with crepe paper streamers and balloons.

'Thank you,' Trisha said, overwhelmed. 'Oh shit, let me change; I'm still in my nightie!'

'I told you but you wouldn't listen!'

Gullu's mother surged out of the sofa and hugged her. Gullu, grinning mischievously, handed over a gift-wrapped packet. Mrs Almeida followed suit; it felt like a book, Trisha thought, and then Jai stepped forward with his offering, a sleek box. Finally, Akshay stepped forward shyly, digging into his pocket and pulling out a decorative maroon and gold drawstring pouch.

'Open them, open them all!' Shivi commanded, jumping up and down.

'Okay, okay, hold on, Shivi.'

Gullu had given her a beautiful Kashmiri silk scarf.

'Thanks, Gullu, this is gorgeous!'

Mrs Almeida's present was a hardcover copy of *Gone with theWind*.
'Thank you,' Trisha said, leafing through the massive tome.

And Jai had given her a smart Parker pen set.

'I didn't know what to give you,' he said apologetically. His eyes
lit up. 'But I'm sure you'll do damn well in your Boards if you write
with this.'

'Yeah, yeah. But thanks, Jai, it's sweet of you.'

She was aware that they were all staring at her as Akshay handed
over his little pouch diffidently. 'Happy Birthday, Trish,' he said, his
cheeks reddening. 'I hope you like them.'

She opened the drawstring and drew out the tissue paper wrapping.
A delicate silver necklace strung with tiny animals—an exquisite
elephant, a delicate deer, two monkeys and a crouching leopard—with
a pair of kissing parakeets as a pendant, along with a lovely silver
anklet reposed in the paper. She took her breath in sharply and her
eyes widened as she drew them out. She had dragged Akshay to the
silver shop where she had seen these, several times, but hadn't bought
them because they were too expensive.

'Akshay! You shouldn't have! Thank you!' So he had observed her
lusting after them and whining that she couldn't afford them and had
probably started saving up for them. Poor guy must have been hugely
embarrassed while buying them for her. Sixteen-year-old guys don't
buy jewellery. (He had taken Gullu with him and sworn her to secrecy.)

'Here, put them on me,' she told him softly, a little while later, after
all the others had left, promising to be back in the evening. 'It's the
done thing.'

She turned and lifted her hair over her neck. He fumbled with the
delicate catch. 'Why do they make these things so small?' he muttered.
'Ah, yes, got it!'

She turned around to face him. 'How does it look?'

'Great!'

She looked at herself in the mirror. 'Don't you think it should be
longer?'

'I don't know.'

'Okay, now the anklet.'

She put up her foot on a stool and raised her nightie over her knees.

If anything it had an even smaller clasp and he struggled clumsily to make it catch. It looked stunning around her slim brown ankle.

'It's beautiful,' she said softly, gazing herself in the mirror. 'It looks sexy as hell!' She turned and put her arms around him and kissed him. 'Thank you, Akshay,' she said staring at him. 'You know . . . I want . . . I want to spend a night with you, Akshay,' she said softly. 'A whole night.'

'Me too . . .'

CHAPTER FOURTEEN

ON THIS NIGHT

'Baby—the gas has finished, you have to order a cylinder,' Komal announced one morning at the end of December. Trisha frowned. During the last few months, her mother had begun handing over the monthly housekeeping money to her—after making her withdraw it from the bank—and Tikka and Komal had been asking her to order whatever was needed for the house. She had even begun paying the servants their salaries.

At the beginning of that month her mom had just handed her an envelope and said, 'Darling, will you give Komal and Tikka and the gardener and Minubai their salaries—I have a meeting in five minutes and it's already the 3rd of the month' and rushed off upstairs, where she was expecting her clients from the Ratnagarh project. The Noida Expressway Villas project had just about got over and her mom had plunged straight into the Ratnagarh one without a break. 'But Mom . . .' she stuttered, looking helplessly at the envelope in her hands. But Mrs Bhave was pretty organized; inside, each person's salary had been clipped separately with their names and amounts written on a Post It. Trisha took the envelope to her room and counted to re-check and then summoned the staff. It was terribly embarrassing, sitting there at the head of the dining table, handing out their earnings; she was just a chit of a girl, after all, only seventeen . . . how would they feel to receive their salary from someone they had seen growing up from babyhood? In effect, she was in charge—of running the house, keeping the daily accounts, checking the bank accounts, ordering the stores, paying the phone and electricity and other bills—virtually everything! Her mom had very sneakily delegated everything to her!

Now she marched up to her mom's office and exclaimed:

'Mom, I've just realized I have been running the house for the last three months! You've gradually handed everything over to me!' She couldn't help feeling a little indignant about it.

He mom looked up from her Mac. Her face was drawn, the cheeks sunken in, the fatigue showing clearly; she'd really been slogging it out these last couple of weeks. 'I know, darling, and you're doing a wonderful job. I just have to put all my time and energy into this Ratnagarh project. It really is a huge job, much bigger than I had anticipated and worth a fortune. So will you be a sweetheart and continue holding the reins for a bit? The project should be done by the middle of January. Then I'll take over again and you can concentrate on your studies.'

The Boards were scheduled to start in the beginning of March (Holi this year would be a complete write-off), and they all had started slogging away. Their music and cricket had all but stopped; they met just once a week now, on Saturday evenings, and that too for just a couple of hours. Akshay, for one, was badly missing his old life.

Jai eyed his brother uneasily, knowing it would be his turn next year; he was suffering too because Gullu (who was in class with Trisha) had also dropped out of the scene. Gullu had bought every guide in sight and was mugging them up cover to cover; she'd been sent to her grandparents' house, which was much quieter than her tumultuous household.

As for Trisha, she was relatively lucky. She had a photographic memory and a quick understanding and the ability to express herself with brevity. Maths was perhaps her weakest subject; but she got around it by grinding through every problem in every paper she could lay her hands on.

There was just a week more and the exams would be on them. But a fortnight later they would be free! She sighed and opened her textbook. Better get cracking again. Her mother looked in. 'Darling, I'm off to see Dr Phadnis.'

'Oh, do you want me to come along?' Trisha got up.

'No. It's just a routine appointment. I'll be fine.'

'So what did he say?' she asked breathlessly when her mom returned, the old, almost buried, dread stirring briefly.

'He said I'm doing fine,' her mother replied. 'Baby, why didn't you have your dinner?'

'I thought I'd wait for you.'

Trisha watched her mother peck at her food desultorily. 'Mom, you're hardly eating anything,' she said. 'Are you sure you're okay?'

'I'm fine, just a bit tired. This project is really wearing me out.'

'So what's your deadline?'

'Well, the grand opening ceremony is on the 14th evening. They're having some fancy inauguration and a party afterwards. I'll have to go to Ratnagarh on the 13th morning. I'll be back a couple of days later.'

'Oh, my last paper is on the 14th.'

'Yes I know, I'm sorry, dear. But maybe we can all go there together sometime later and you can see what I've done to the place.'

'Great!'

As always it was the final week's countdown to the exams which was the worst. The days crawled past, and poor Akshay and Gullu became more and more haggard and nail-bitten. Trisha just hoped she wouldn't blank out when the question paper was put in front of her. The rumours that swilled around just made it worse. Everyone had a question paper that was a sure shot. Their timetable was quite sadistic.

'Maths followed by physics the next day!' Trisha groaned, 'some pervert has made this timetable! I hope he rots in hell!'

It was some consolation that all three of them had the same centre. Pale and tense, they clustered together outside, weak smiles on their faces, trying to ignore the hysterical kids around them cramming frantically at the last minute. Their parents hovered anxiously around them, offering last-minute advice.

'Right Akshay, you know—deal with the easy problems first quickly, so you'll have enough time for the tough ones,' Dr Khurana said as his wife thrust a tetrapack of apple juice at Akshay.

'And make sure you show your working clearly and neatly!'

'Papa!'

Poor Gullu was in a complete state; she hated both maths and physics. 'It's a double whammy,' she groaned. 'If I do badly in these, I've had it for the rest of the papers . . .'

'Tikka and Komal will be here with something for you to eat after this paper,' Mrs Bhave said, her arm around Trisha. 'You won't have enough time to come home and eat.'

'Mom, please, I can't think about eating.'

'Gullu, you have everything? All your pens and pencils and rulers and rubbers, hankies, safety pins?' Gullu's mom hollered as poor Gullu winced.

'Mama, shhh! Yes, I do!'

The bell shrilled, long and petulantly, and the kids jumped. 'Oh shit, here we go!' Trisha squeaked. She smiled wanly at her friends. 'Best of luck, guys!'

They exchanged a rather weak series of high fives, put their heads down and trooped in.

'Look at them go!' Mrs Bhave murmured shaking her head. 'Lambs to the slaughter! No system that does this to children is civilized!'

'But how will they excel otherwise?' Dr Khurana said testily, turning towards his car. 'They must be tested.'

'Where do they get these people from?' Trisha wondered, looking at the dried prune of a fellow walking down the aisle, with a hawk nose and tightly pursed lips. His eyes darted sharply everywhere, full of dark suspicion. He looked like some revolting bird of prey. 'I bet this guy's never smiled in his life. He probably just thinks the worst of people . . . wonder why . . . what happened to him . . . well, look at him, no wonder . . . idiot, think of the bloody exam.'

And then she was staring at the paper, her eyes widening. Surely she had seen—and done—that first problem. It seemed familiar . . . so was the next, for that matter. She glanced down the paper, her heart beginning to sing. She couldn't quite believe it—she'd solved every single problem before! Whoever had set the paper really had nothing original to offer! Gleefully she picked up her pen and put her head down.

They met briefly afterwards, grinning delightedly. Gullu flung her arms around Trisha and exchanged high fives with Akshay.

'I knew everything, thanks to you guys!' Gullu squealed.

'Shh . . . keep it down, Gullu!' Akshay grinned. 'Someone might overhear and think we had the paper . . .'

'Oh shit!'

The physics paper, on the following day, was tough and long—set by some crafty devil who obviously got his kicks by setting nasty traps in his questions. Trisha barely finished in time and looked up wearily as the bird-of-prey invigilator pounced and snatched up her paper.

Gullu was shaking her head dismally. 'I couldn't finish it,' she groaned. 'I left half the last question . . .' Akshay looked pretty grim too. 'I forgot to show the working . . . I just did the calculation in my head and put down the answer; there was no time!'

'They should give you extra marks for that!' Trisha said. 'But whew, thank God those two monster papers are done!'

And then at last, the end was in sight.

Early on the 13th morning, Mrs Bhave entered Trisha's study to say goodbye. 'Well, darling, I'm off, best of luck for your last paper!'

Trisha looked up tiredly from her desk. 'Thanks, Mom. Have a good trip.'

Her mother was driving down to Ratnagarh in the pickup with Tikka.

'Why don't you go on Smelly Beast?' Trisha had teased. 'You'll knock their socks off if you arrive on that bike in black leather and purple shades!'

'Haha, I know, but I'm just a bit tired. This project has really taken it out of me. I'll be back on the 15th evening, darling, and we'll celebrate.' On the settee Shivi stirred sleepily. Mrs Bhave walked over.

'Shivi baby, I'm off.' She bent down and kissed her. 'Bye, sweetheart and be good!'

'Mommy, I'm spending the night at Arti and Ajay's house tomorrow. It's their birthday party . . . remember? You said I could.'

'Yes, I know that, darling, of course you can.'

Gullu's younger twin brother and sister had invited Shivi over for a birthday sleepover and Mrs Bhave had agreed to let her go, knowing full well that at the time Shivi would probably want to come back home.

'You'll be leaving me alone for one whole night!' Trisha had teased Shivi. 'Imagine! What if I have a bad dream?'

'I'll leave you Mr Teddy Sir. You can cuddle with him,' Shivi offered generously. She was thrilled to the core; imagine spending a whole night at Arti and Ajay's place!

Trisha followed her mother out and waved as the pickup drove away. She sighed and went back indoors, drawing her dressing gown close; it was still cool in the mornings. Just one more exam and they would be free!

On the day of the last exam, a mini-nightmare unfolded. An underground water main on an arterial road burst, and the truck bringing their papers to the centre was delayed. The kids were herded and locked into a large hall, while the invigilators paced up and down outside, calling frantically on their mobiles and checking the windows. The paper, chemistry, originally scheduled to start at 2 p.m., finally arrived at 4. The hall was a seething mass of frantic kids; Trisha and Akshay sat side by side saying little and just waiting. This wasn't real; it couldn't be happening. Fortunately, someone had the good sense to chalk up a big notice outside the centre's gates informing parents and guardians that the exam would now get over at 7 instead of 5. Mrs Khurana, who had driven up to pick up Akshay and Trisha, drove home exasperatedly and informed Komal that Trisha would be late.

'It's okay, I have to take Shivi to a party but will be back by 7,' Komal explained.

At a quarter past seven, Trisha and Akshay staggered out of the hall, too dazed to even think straight. Mrs Khurana ushered them into the car as Jai grinned at them.

'You both look like you've been through a blender,' he said. 'So what are your plans to celebrate?'

'I just want to go home and sleep!' Trisha groaned. 'I'm beat.' She looked at Akshay. 'We'll do something tomorrow, okay?'

She entered the house and stood in the drawing room, looking around and switching on the lights. She put her bag down, yanked off her tie and kicked off her shoes. Thank God she wouldn't have to wear those ghastly things ever again.

'Komal! Shivi! I'm home! My exams are over!' she sang. 'Where are you guys hiding?' But there didn't seem to be anyone home. She glanced at her watch; it was a quarter to eight. Okay, maybe the party was going on longer than expected. She dug out her phone and switched it on. It rang almost immediately.

'Trisha baby?' It was Komal. 'Shivi says she wants to spend the night here,' she went on, sounding distressed. Trisha's eyebrows shot up. Well, that had been the deal. She shrugged. If she said no now, there'd be a huge tantrum. 'It's okay, Mummy said it's okay.'

'But you'll be alone.'

'I'll manage, don't worry.'

'Phone Memsahib and let her know. And baby, heat up the food in the microwave; yesterday's leftover do pyaza meat is lying in the deep freezer.'

'Okay, Komal.'

She rang her mom. Mrs Bhave sounded distinctly weary and didn't seem too happy about her being alone at home. Well, she would be tired after all that slogging; soon they would be able to relax and fool around together, go for a long ride on Smelly Beast . . . At that moment, she felt weird. The house was absolutely quiet—maybe she should blast on some music. She walked to the kitchen and opened the fridge. Imagine being home alone on the day your Class XII exams got over. She shut the fridge door slowly, without really looking at what was inside, walked out and plumped down on the sofa in the drawing room. She looked at her phone, her heart beginning to thump like Smelly Beast's engine. Should she? Dare she? What if? She took a deep breath and dialled. Suddenly her fatigue seemed to slip off like a cloak.

'Hi,' she said softly. 'Listen . . .'

She put her phone down and went back to the kitchen and opened the deep freezer. She pulled out the dish in which the meat was lying and frowned. It was rock solid. She'd better leave it out for a while to thaw. She peered into the fridge; yes, there was rice, with diced carrots and peas and corn and a head of frilly pale green lettuce and some broccoli. And there was ice cream. She glanced at her watch; it was nearly 8.15. Better get cracking right away—then she could go and have a shower and change. And then . . . she smiled and blushed. She rushed into the dining room and opened the drawers and cupboards of the sideboard. Yes, everything should be perfect. Table mats or a tablecloth? A tablecloth would be much too formal, so mats it would be: those funky brightly-coloured hibiscus-shaped ones her mom had recently picked up. And yes, candles. She rummaged around in a cupboard and pulled out a pristine pair of tall maroon candles and stuck them into the silver candlesticks. It was already 8.30—she'd better start warming up the meat; then she'd go for a shower. She put the meat on the stove and rushed to her bedroom and opened her huge walk-in closet. Then came the most important question—what should she wear? She stood there, riffling through her skirts and slacks and salwar suits, frowning, when the faint aroma of cooking meat drifted in. Oh heck, she'd better see to it before it caught . . .

She ran back into the kitchen and began stirring the meat vigorously, pouring a little water in. It smelt divine. Ten minutes later, the curry was bubbling aromatically and she was about to switch off the gas when the doorbell rang. Oh shit, she hadn't even showered! She was still in her school uniform, all hot and sweaty and grungy! Hopefully it was just a courier delivery. She peeped through the magic eye and her heart jumped up and down like a yo-yo. She opened the door and smoothed down her dark blue skirt.

'Hi, you're early . . .'

'Should I go away and come back later?'

'Idiot, come in before someone sees you!' She grabbed his hand. 'Um . . . put your bike behind the hedge there, and come in! How did you get away?'

'Jai's covering for me, but now I owe him our National Debt.' He stepped in. He'd changed into a smart dark green T-shirt and jeans and put on some musky aftershave. 'My dad quizzed me about the paper endlessly . . . they've gone out for dinner, thank God.'

'Look at me,' she wailed, 'I haven't even bathed or changed! I must look a sight!'

'But you smell divine, babe!' He leaned over and sniffed appreciatively. 'What exotic perfume is that?'

'I'm reeking of do pyaza meat and ginger and garlic and perspiration and exam hall grunge and you say I smell divine!' She was outraged, but then caught the mischief in his eyes.

'You've been cooking? Dhaba style? Lots of sweat and grime and gutter grease, eh?' He grinned.

'Idiot! Just heating up Komal's divine do pyaza meat; it was frozen solid.'

'Great. God, it seems so quiet without Shivi. Are you sure she'll stay away the whole night?'

Trisha grinned. 'She'd better!'

He followed her to the dining room and stared at the table. 'My God, you've really gone out of your way . . .' He gulped and then grinned. 'Are you sure this is all for me? The candles and flowers and glittering knives and forks . . . wow! You're not expecting someone else, are you?'

'Akshay! I'm warning you!' She stepped up to him and sniffed and screwed up her nose. 'What's that smell?'

He stared at her. 'What smell?' he asked, alarmed, sniffing. 'You mean I have BO?'

'Well, it's coming off you in clouds! Did you spray yourself with mosquito repellent or a weedkiller or is that just your natural animal effluvium?'

'Eh? Effluvium? You don't like it? Oh shit . . . it's an aftershave.'

'You mean you actually shaved before you came? You shaved specially for me?'

Now he was blushing. 'I could wash it off if you like . . .' Good God, the woman didn't like Ralph Lauren's 'Safari'.

She grinned. 'Gotcha, baby!'

'Just wait till I get my hands on you, you horrible girl!'

But she had beaten him to that too; she reached up and held his face in her hands and kissed him tenderly on the lips.

'Even your moustache tastes of do pyaza . . .' he murmured, kissing the tiny pearls of perspiration on her upper lip. 'Delicious!'

'My moustache! Oh you . . . you . . .!'

'Let's eat. I'm starving.'

'I feel like a pig. I'm going for a shower first. Help yourself to a Coke if you like.'

'Thanks.'

She smiled suddenly. 'You can read Gone with the Wind while I'm gone and tell me the story when I come out.'

'I don't want to open a book for the next six months,' he said fervently.

'Do you know,' she said as she stood beside the bathroom door. 'This is probably the last time you'll see me in my school uniform.'

'Ah! Such a sight for sore eyes! I shall remember this divine apparition for as long as I live!'

'I really hate you!' She flashed a smile, curtsied and disappeared inside.

They ate their dinner staring soulfully into each other's eyes and feeding each other from a single plate.

'I can't believe it,' she whispered later in her bedroom, glancing at him sideways. 'We have the whole night together.'

'I wish every night could be like this,' he said.

'In the meanwhile, let's make the best of now. I love you so much, Akshay, it scares me.' She trembled uncontrollably as he caressed her.

'So what should we do in these holidays?' she asked dreamily during an interlude twenty minutes later. 'Are you guys going anywhere out of town?'

'I don't know. Papa hasn't said anything yet. You know what he's like. He'll suddenly announce we're going to Timbuktu for a week starting tomorrow.'

'I'll never forget tonight.'

'Me neither! Anyway, we'd better think about practising too. That audition is in the middle of May. By the way, there's another match coming up too . . . Jai was saying something about it.'

'Oh no! Count me out. I've retired, I told you.'

'Babe, you took four wickets in four balls! You can be in the Indian team if you go on like that! You can't retire . . . you can't say no!' His eyes grew large and serious. She stared at him, suddenly suspicious.

'What? Why?'

He shook his head. 'If you say no, I've had it!' He made a throat slitting gesture.

'What do you mean?'

'I . . . I promised Jai I'd make you change your mind.' He looked apologetic. 'I'm sorry.'

'You promised Jai you'd make me change my mind?'

'Yes.'

She folded her arms across her breasts. 'Well you'll have to tell him that's one promise you can't keep.'

'I can't do that, Trish.'

'Why?' She darted another suspicious look at him.

'Because if I don't keep my promise he said he'll tell Papa about us tonight. He's a stinker, I know, and he will.' He looked like he was about to cry.

Trisha's eyes narrowed. 'And you, Mister Akshay Khurana, can't fib to save your life.' She reached for a cushion and whacked him. 'You horrible fellow, you've been leading me on!'

At dawn, they were lying together in a tangle of weary limbs, fast asleep. The top sheet lay crumpled on the floor. Trisha opened her eyes and smiled sadly. A faint glimmer of light showed through the windows. Oh, oh, time to rise and send him on his way. Shivi was an early riser and would want to come home as soon as she woke up. She lifted her head and glanced at her bedside clock. It was 5.15.

'Akshay, wake up,' she murmured.

'Mmm . . . what?' He blinked blearily. Then he smiled and put his arms around her.

'Akshay, it's morning.'

'I know.'

'We'd better straighten out this room now and open the windows. Both Komal and Shivi have noses like bloodhounds.' She walked to the window, and adjusting the blinds slightly, looked down. Her mouth fell open. 'Oh no!'

'What?'

'Just come here,' she whispered, gesticulating frantically.

He stepped up beside her and looked down.

'Akshay, tell me I'm not seeing this. That's not the Toyota pickup standing in the driveway there, is it?'

'Oh, hell!'

'Mom's back!'

'Your door's locked?'

'Yup.' She took a deep breath, forcing herself to stay calm. Her mom might have returned, but so far at least had not disturbed them. Probably, hopefully, she was sleeping or resting or whatever. 'Go and change,' she whispered. 'I'll check if the coast is clear. Thank God you hid your bike behind the hedge. I have no idea when she got back. She said she was returning this evening. Did you hear anything?'

'No . . .'

She took a deep breath. 'As long as she didn't hear anything . . . my God, we were so loud! Anyway, go and change!'

He was ready in minutes. She opened the door and peeped into the hallway. All was quiet. She tiptoed to her mother's bedroom. The door was shut. She went to the front door and opened it and peeped outside. The pickup gleamed quietly in the porch; there was no sign of Tikka anywhere. She ran back in and beckoned to Akshay.

'Go, baby, go!' she said, stifling a giggle in spite of herself. She reached up and kissed him. Then he pulled his bike out, wheeled it out of the gate and pedalled off like a bat out of hell.

Trisha returned to her room and sniffed critically. She made up the bed neatly; Komal would be pleasantly surprised. She drew her bedcover over and turned Mr Teddy Sir around.

'You can look now, sir,' she said primly, and then turned him around again. 'Yikes! I forgot. I'm still in this ridiculous nightie! Sorry, sir!' She changed into her usual nightie and dozed off with a silly smile on her face. At 6.30 Shivi burst in, with Komal in tow, making a hell of a racket.

'Trisha! I'm home. Mommy's home too! Mommy, I'm home! Did you miss me? See what I got as a return present!' She charged to her mother's room and flung open the door.

'Mommy! I'm home! I made Bobby and Ajay and Arti all sleep on the floor, while I slept on the bed, because I was the queen and they were my slaves!'

Mrs Bhave was fast asleep. She opened her eyes and raised her arms towards her excited younger daughter. 'Hello, Shivi darling, of course I missed you, baby. Where's Trisha?'

Trisha stood sheepishly in the doorway, her heart beating fast; the guilt was beginning to creep all over her like a rash. What time had her mom got in last night? Had she heard anything? A 'normal' parent would have stormed in then and there, but her mom . . . she was different. She stepped into the room.

'Hi Mom, when did you get back?'

'I don't know . . . sometime after 1, I think. I just didn't like the idea of your being alone all night. Also, I was very tired. Were you all right? You forgot to bolt the front door. I walked in with my keys.'

'Yes, yes . . . I was fine, Mom. I . . . er, locked my bedroom door as a precaution,' she added, wondering if her mom had tried the handle, 'but yes, I must have forgotten the front door.'

Her mother smiled wanly. 'I saw your school tie and bag and shoes in the drawing room and knew you were home.'

'Mom, you look dead beat.'

'I am, I think I'll sleep some more.'

She was nibbling her toast dreamily at the breakfast table when Komal stood before her, smiling toothily.

'Baby, you were very hungry last night—you finished all the meat and rice and ice cream.'

'Komal, my exams also got over yesterday.'

Oh shit, between her and Akshay they had put away a considerable amount of food, and he'd eaten at least twice as much as she had. But Komal was still smiling happily at her.

'Okay baby, so what should I cook today?'

CHAPTER FIFTEEN

SACRIFICE

An hour after he had left, Akshay called her, sounding glum.
'Hey Trish, you know I told you that Dad likes springing surprises on us?'

'Yes.'

'We're going to Italy tonight for a fortnight. Just imagine—he goes and fixes everything up without consulting anyone . . . as if no else has a life but him!'

'Italy! Wow! But shit, two whole weeks and just after the exams.'

'Well, come over for a bit. We could practise or just mess around. Mom's already getting after me to pack and stuff.'

'Okay, will do!'

At 9.30 Shivi came barging into her study, all indignant.

'Trisha, it's almost ten o'clock and Mommy's still sleeping. I went to her room and she was fast asleep.'

'She's very tired, Shivi, let her sleep.'

'But it'll be lunchtime soon!'

'Okay Shivi, listen, I've got to go to Akshay and Jai's for a bit of practice. Tell Mom I've gone when she wakes up, okay? I'm taking my bicycle because Tikka's gone on leave.'

Shivi nodded and to Trisha's immense relief didn't go into an 'I want to come along' song and dance. 'Okay,' she said, 'Bobby's coming over to play with me in the morning,' she said.

'Ooooh . . . so you have a date!'

Shivi shook her head violently. 'We're going to play terrorists and commandos,' she said. 'I'm going to shoot him sixteen times!'

'Hi Jai,' she said as Jai opened the door for her. Impulsively she reached up and kissed his cheek. 'Thanks,' she said quietly.

He grinned. 'You're welcome! You can't imagine what leverage this has given me with Akshay! It's changed the whole balance of power in this household!'

'Jai! Heck, I'm going to miss you guys; even Gullu's gone off to Dehradun! It's not fair!'

She returned home at 1.30, wiping her eyes as she rode her bicycle. Hell, she really was a sentimental fool—he was just going away for a fortnight, not forever! When he returned they could plan all sorts of things—the whole summer was stretched before them. Maybe she could invite Akshay and Jai and Gullu to Ratnagarh; surely her mom could swing the deal? But till he came back she would live off the wonderful memory of last night . . .

'Mom? Are you awake?' Trisha asked, stepping into her mother's room. Mrs Bhave emerged from the bathroom, drawing her blue housecoat around her.

'Hello darling, sorry I slept the whole morning!'

'That's okay—I've just come back from Akshay's. They're off to Italy for a fortnight.'

'Oh.' Mrs Bhave sat down on her bed. 'I've just had a bath and all I want to do is go back to sleep. It's ridiculous.'

'Komal will be yelling for lunch any second.'

'I don't really feel like it.'

Trisha drew the curtains. On her bed, her mother looked pale and frail.

'You'd better eat, Mom. You're looking size zero again!'

Shivi came charging in, with Bobby in tow, yelling, 'Mommy! Mommy!' and flung herself on her. 'You slept the whole day!'

'Take it easy, Shivi. She's very tired.'

'But mommies are not meant to get tired,' Shivi said. 'Mommy, we've been playing terrorists and commandoes all morning . . .'

'Come on, Shivi, Komal's yelling for lunch.'

In fact, by the evening, the first wisps of anxiety had begun to clutch insidiously at Trisha. Her mom must have grossly overdone things to have remained so listless throughout the day. Well, she'd better be careful and not take on such huge projects in future. Mrs Almeida came in briefly, ordered Mrs Bhave to rest and put away all her papers and documents.

'Your mother really works far too much,' she said disapprovingly. 'She'll make herself ill again.' She smiled at Trisha. 'Look after her, will you? I'm off to Goa for three weeks—my flight leaves this evening.'

'Oh, you too? Okay, bye Mrs Almeida, have a good holiday.'

'Thank you, dear.'

At 7.30 that evening, Mrs Bhave looked into Trisha's study.

'Well darling, I'm turning in early. I really don't know why I'm so tired.' Trisha glanced at her watch in surprise.

'We haven't even had dinner!'

'Not hungry, dear.'

'You said that at lunch. You've hardly eaten the whole day.'

Those words had a horrible ring of déjà vu. 'Are you sure you're feeling okay?'

'I'll be fine after a good night's rest. I got home pretty late last night . . . and had virtually no sleep the night before.'

Nor had she had much sleep last night, Trisha thought wistfully, but it had been so wonderful. At any rate, she turned in by 10, watching Shivi sprawled in the bed beside her, Mr Teddy Sir discarded on the floor. She picked him up, winked at him and put him back with Shivi.

At 11.45 the insistent ringtone of her mobile woke her.

'Wha . . .' She squinted at it. Maybe Akshay's plane hadn't taken off; maybe they weren't going after all. She frowned.

It was her mom's number being displayed.

'Hello? Mom?'

'Trisha, could you come in here for a minute, please?' her mom's voice wavered. Trisha leapt out of bed.

She could barely believe what she saw. Her mom was lying on her bed, wracked by violent tremors every two or three seconds.

'Th . . . this damn shivering . . . I . . . I can't control it . . .' Mrs Bhave stammered, trying to hold on to the bedstead.

'Mom!'

'Br . . . bring me a b-b-blanket . . .' The tremors were so violent they were rattling the bed now.

'Mom . . . have you got malaria?' Trisha rushed to the cupboard and pulled out a heavy blanket. 'Here.'

'I don't know, darling . . . I've . . . b . . . been feeling itchy too all day.' And as Trisha bent low over her to tuck her in she saw the telltale yellow tinge in her mom's dark eyes again. She put a hand on her brow. It was burning.

'You have fever.' She rummaged in the bedside table drawer and took out the thermometer. Within moments it was beeping urgently.

'Mom, you have 103.6!' She was shocked and frightened now, her heart tumbling down a bottomless well of dread. 'I'd better ring Dr Phadnis.'

Of course his number was unreachable.

She sat down on the bed; this could not be happening, this was not happening, just last night she was lying in Akshay's arms and now . . . and why the hell wasn't that damn Dr Phadnis available when you needed him? She jerked up. 'Mom, where are your hospital papers?'

'Up . . . upstairs, in the filing cabinet . . .'

She grabbed the keys and ran up.

The discharge summary given by the hospital had mentioned emergency numbers. Murmuring a prayer she dialled Dr Pradhan and nearly wept with relief when he answered in his dour way. But to his credit he remembered her mother's case.

'Doctor, my mom's shivering uncontrollably and . . .'

'Fever?'

'She has 103.6 and it seems to be rising.'

'Bring her over to the Emergency immediately.'

Trisha looked around wildly. 'Okay,' she squeaked. 'Thank you.'

How the heck was she going to do that? It was almost midnight, Tikka was not around and Dr Khurana was sitting on a plane to Italy; she didn't dare call for a cab, an ambulance would take hours and she couldn't drive the pickup. For a moment a sickening thought crossed her mind: maybe she was being punished for what had happened last night; she had disobeyed her mom, and now they were all paying the price.

'Mom, we have to take you to the hospital,' she said, dismissing the thought.

'M . . . Money . . . take some . . . from the cupboard.'

Trisha gulped. She opened the cupboard and took out the chunky envelope in which she had brought the monthly household money from the bank.

'I'm just changing and then we'll go,' she said and flew to her room. She shook Komal awake.

'Komal, Mummy's ill. I'm taking her to the hospital,' she said as poor Komal sat up, stunned. 'Pack her things, clothes, toothbrush, hairbrush . . .'

Minutes later, she and Komal propped Mrs Bhave up on to her feet.

'How will you go? Have you called a taxi?'

The solution had come to her almost unconsciously. She took a deep breath. 'On the bike, Komal, we'll make her sit on the bike.'

'Da . . . darling, I'm feeling very cold.'

Komal wrapped another blanket around Mrs Bhave. 'Take this, Memsahib,' she said. 'What'll you do, Baby? Even Tikka is not here!'

'Come on!' Trisha stopped. 'No, not with the blanket.' If the blanket came loose while they were on the bike . . . it was unthinkable . . .

'Komal, bring my sweater and windcheater . . .'

They zipped Mrs Bhave up snugly in a sweater and windcheater and helped her out to the garage.

'Mom, your helmet . . . You'll have to hang on tight to me, okay?'

Her mom nodded.

Trisha got astride. 'Okay, Komal.'

Komal held on grimly as Mrs Bhave got on to the bike and then leant forwards, clutching at Trisha. 'Hold on tight, Mom.'

The engine thundered in the driveway and Trisha threaded the bike past the gleaming pickup. She would have to learn how to drive that at the earliest. She swung out on to the road and opened the throttle. The rasping thump of the engine set the stray dogs off barking, but they were away.

She drove carefully, totally focused on the road, keeping to the left and out of the way of speeding cars and bikes. Her mom was holding her around the waist with a vice-like grip, her head dropping on her shoulder. It was really frightening on the long dark road running through the Ridge. She slowed as they approached a police check post and wondered if she should stop and ask for help. One look at the cops manning the post and she decided against it. For a start, she didn't have a licence and if they asked for it, she'd had it. They stared at her as she passed them, more surprised perhaps by her mom all wrapped up in her windcheater, but didn't hail her down.

She burbled up the hospital driveway into the brightly-lit Emergency portico. Amazingly, it was deserted; an ambulance with gaping doors stood to one side. A broad ramp sloped up inside to a set of swing doors. Trisha put her feet down and looked around. Behind her, she felt her mom's grip slacken. Oh God, was she passing out?

'Mom! Hang on! Please don't fall off!'

She looked around wildly again. From somewhere behind the wail of an ambulance grew louder. Suddenly the siren stopped and a white Omni drew up in the portico. Two orderlies jumped out and opened the doors. A patient in a gurney was lowered and the orderlies wheeled him hurriedly up the ramp, ignoring her.

'Please!' Trisha cried, 'help my mother off . . .' The ambulance was driving off, and a nurse who had got off with it, glanced at her and hurried off behind the gurney. She was alone again, still astride the throbbing bike, feeling her mom's grip slacken even more.

'Mom, hang on tightly please.' Tears streamed down her cheeks as she gunned Smelly Beast and turned it towards the ramp. She rode up and flinched as the front wheel slammed against the swing doors and the bike burst through into the brightly lit waiting hall beyond. There was a stunned hush in the room as she brought the bike to a halt. For a moment its raspy growl echoed in the room and then Trisha switched off the engine. She felt her mom slump against her back. The door leading to the ward opened and out stepped Dr Sparrow M.D. Hopeless Case. He stared at Trisha and the bike, his mouth opening and closing.

'Doctor, my mother's collapsed! Please help!'

And then to her eternal relief the doors opened again, and Dr Pradhan stepped out.

'What the hell . . .' he barked and then seeing Mrs Bhave slumped and barely clutching on to Trisha rushed forwards. 'Nurse,' he shouted, 'don't just stand there!'

As they wheeled her in, he turned briefly to Trisha. 'You brought her on that bike?' he asked incredulously.

'There was no other way, Doctor . . .' she said simply.

'Okay, we'll see to her now. You better park the bike and come inside. Have you brought her case file?'

'Here it is.'

Her mom was already on an intravenous drip when she got back. There were ten beds in the ward, eight of which were occupied. Doctors, nurses and orderlies rushed around, and monitors beeped and winked and patients moaned and called out. Trisha sat at the edge of her mom's bed. Mrs Bhave was awake, looking around her, as if surprised. Trisha dried her eyes.

'You'll be fine, Mom; they'll start your medication.'

But nobody seemed to be in any hurry to start anything. Dr Pradhan had vanished, and Dr Sparrow, who was obviously the duty doctor, was trying to deal with a three-year old who had swallowed kerosene for the third time that month. Sure her mom was on the drip but she needed a doctor to examine her. Trisha got up and approached Dr Sparrow.

'Doctor, my mother . . .' she said when there was a pause in the hubbub. He glanced at her. 'Yes,' he said. 'Dr Pradhan is just coming . . .'

A nurse came up with a tray. 'Mrs Bhave?' Trisha nodded.

'I have to take blood.'

Half an hour later, just as she was beginning to get agitated again, Dr Pradhan entered along with Dr Sharma and a couple of others. Her mom had dozed off, and in the bright light Trisha could see the unhealthy yellow pallor on her sharply etched face. She stood aside as the doctors examined her.

'I've spoken to Dr Phadnis,' Dr Pradhan informed her. 'We'll have to admit her. She'll probably need another procedure. Is there anyone else with you?'

'No.' Akshay was probably somewhere high over the Arabian Sea.

'I see. So you'll stay with her?'

'Of course.'

'They're just making up the room. You can go to the admission office in the meanwhile.'

'Okay.' Well, at least she knew the drill now.

It was 1.30 by the time her mom had been shifted to her room—the same one she had been allotted before. With a sense of unreality Trisha sat down on the settee as the nurses took Mrs Bhave's blood pressure and temperature. Dr Pradhan stepped in for a few moments.

'We've scheduled it for tomorrow afternoon,' he told Trisha. 'We'll do an ultrasound and MRCP in the morning. It appears the stent has been blocked again. We might have to push another one through it. She'll be okay.'

After he left she went up to her mom's bed. 'How're you feeling, Mom?'

'Okay, what are they saying?'

'You need another stent. They said they'll push it through the one you already have. It's got blocked.'

'Oh. Did Dr Phadnis see me?'

'No, Dr Pradhan did. He's spoken to Dr Phadnis.'

'Oh. Trisha, will you ring up Nani tomorrow and let her know?'

'Nani? But . . . but . . .'

'Not at home. You ring up Mangalsons and leave a message and your mobile number. Nani will call you back when she can.'

'But why? She can't and won't do anything.'

'Just let her know, okay?'

'Okay. I'd better call Komal and tell her; she must be frantic.' She rang home and Komal picked up almost immediately.

'Komal, Mummy's okay, but will have an operation tomorrow. I'll come home in the morning.'

She lay down on the settee and stared at the ceiling. 'You up there,' she murmured silently, 'you're doing this to me because of what happened last night, aren't you? But why bring Mom into this? What's she done? Whatever, I'm sorry . . . just let her get better. I'll do whatever it takes . . . not even see Akshay ever again if that's what you want!' Maybe that was the sacrifice she would have to make—give up something she valued the most in return for something equally so, though her mom didn't agree with this sort of bargain bartering.

She was groggy and gooey-eyed when the nurses came in for their morning rounds. She went to the nursing station and fixed up for a pair of private nurses again. As usual they had no clue about when the doctors would come on their rounds, which left her in a quandary. Should she stay on, or go home and have a bath and change? Also there was Shivi . . .

Trisha decided to stay on. Komal could bring her a change of clothes and her toothbrush and toiletries—and most importantly, her phone charger—in the evening. She could manage, grungy as she felt, till then. She glanced at her phone. The battery was halfway down, and it could plummet swiftly. There was a knock on the door, and a fellow from the catering staff barged in with a tray.

'Breakfast, Madam,' he said cheerfully, putting the tray down.

Mrs Bhave made a face. Trisha frowned. Hey, wait a minute . . . She went up to the nursing station. 'My mother's supposed to have an ultrasound and MRCP this morning . . . can she eat breakfast?' she asked. She knew the ropes now.

'You've gone and overdone things, Mom,' she scolded back in the room. 'You take on these huge projects. Maybe you need to hire people to help you . . .'

'I'm just glad I lasted out till the end,' her mother replied with just a trace of her old asperity. She smiled. 'Yes, I will have to expand my staff. Poor Rita can't manage everything.' She turned and looked out of the window. 'They threw such a lavish party—champagne, lobsters, what have you, and there I was, trying to keep the nausea down—couldn't eat a morsel.'

'You need to get well first.'

Trisha read the newspaper cover to cover, and paced about agitatedly when they took her mom for her ultrasound and MRCP. Twice she went to the nursing station to enquire about the doctors; they shrugged and smiled and said they had no clue.

She was dozing on the settee when Dr Phadnis came into the room with his team at around 3 that afternoon. She awoke with a jolt.

'Good afternoon, Mrs Bhave. How are you feeling?' Dr Phadnis bent over her mom. The nurses flurried around, showing him Mrs Bhave's file. 'Has she got any fever?' he asked.

'No sir, not since morning.'

'Very well! I'll see you in the ERCP room in a while,' he said. 'We'll have to put another stent through the earlier one.'

Trisha intercepted him at the door. 'Will . . . will she be all right?' she asked softly.

He turned and smiled as she desperately ran her hand through her hair. God, she must look a sight. 'Yes. We'll push a longer plastic stent through the one she already has and hopefully that should take care of things.' His eyes twinkled briefly. 'I believe you brought her to the Emergency room last night on a Bullet?'

As she waited outside the ERCP room that afternoon, she realized that this time she was completely alone. The last time she had been here, Akshay had turned up and held her hand. Why the hell did everyone have to decamp whenever there was a crisis? She'd really been left high and dry this time. She twisted her handkerchief in her hands, and stared at the wall. She just remembered that there was a phone-charging station in the room. She'd just plugged hers in when she saw the doors to the ERCP room open and her mom being wheeled out. Dr Phadnis followed shortly.

'How did it go, Doctor?' she asked, barely daring to breathe.

'Fine! We'll have to keep her under observation for a couple of days to check everything's all right.'

'Okay, thank you.' She gulped. 'Umm . . . the tumour?'

He nodded. 'We've pushed it to one side.'

'You can't take it out or anything?'

'No, impossible.'

'Then?' She swallowed hugely.

'Sometimes these tumours take a lot of time.'

'But eventually . . .'

His eyes held the reply she hadn't wanted to hear. He touched her arm, nodded gently and was on his way.

Komal brought a change of clothes, both for her and her mom, and she felt much better after she had bathed and changed. Komal had also brought three fat keema paranthas and nimbu achar. Mrs Bhave pulled a face at the semi-solid mush that she was offered, but sucked on a tiny slice of nimbu achar.

'I'll stay tonight, Mom,' Trisha insisted. 'I thought I'd go home early tomorrow. I have to take Smelly Beast back and then I'll come back by auto later.' Hopefully by the day after they would discharge her.

Early the next morning she walked to the parking lot and got astride Smelly Beast. It needed a bit of a wipe down: the petrol tank and handlebars were pearled with dew. She started the bike, bringing the attendants running out of their cabin. They grinned and saluted her as she rode past.

She went to her study and sat down at her desk, trying to think of what she had to do. Okay, first a bath and fresh clothes, then check on how much money she had—they'd taken a Rs 10,000 advance last night—and ask Komal if she needed to buy vegetables and fruit and bread and milk and eggs and . . . God, it was never ending. If her mom came home tomorrow she'd need to get some flowers too . . .

She was on her way back to the hospital by eleven o'clock, hoping the doctors hadn't yet come on their rounds. They burst in fifteen minutes later and crowded around her mom. It always made her nervous when they did that; sometimes you got the feeling that they were examining some object—like a car perhaps—that needed fixing. Dr Phadnis swept out before she could corner him, but Dr Pradhan came up to her.

'We're discharging her tomorrow.' He smiled at her mom. 'Mrs Bhave, you can go home . . .'

And thankfully, the following morning Tikka was back and drove them home in the pickup.

'God, am I glad that's over!' Trisha flopped down with a huge sigh of relief as her mom settled into her room. Much to Trisha's delight, both her old nurses, Richa and Hema had turned up. Richa was doing the morning shift and Hema the night one; she would keep them for a couple of days, until her mom regained her strength.

She had left a message and her number at Mangalsons for her nani, but her grandmother had not called back. She called Gullu as soon as they returned home.

'Hey!' Gullu squealed, 'Where have you been and why haven't you
been in touch? I believe you had one hell of a night . . . Jai told me!
And you've been sitting quiet, gloating all these days!'

'Gullu!' And then it all poured out. 'Gullu, I really thought I was
being punished . . . you know, because of that night.'

'What? Don't talk bullshit, Trish!'

'No really! One night he's over, and the next thing I know I have
to rush Mom to hospital on Smelly Beast!'

'You took her on Smelly Beast? My God! How's she now?'

'Not too great, but okay . . . She's still very weak.'

'Listen, I'm going to be away for another fortnight at least. My
dad's hell-bent on buying a place in the hills so we've been gallivanting
up and down the mountains looking at sites. Have you heard from
Akshay?'

'No. I'm . . .'

'What?'

'Nothing. Listen, I have to go now. I'll be in touch. Bye Gullu!'

'Bye Trish, take care!'

She gulped and wiped a tear as she put away her phone and looked
up. 'All of you up there, you big guns, listen to me—I'll do whatever
it takes to make Mom well again. For a start, I'm going to stop seeing
Akshay . . . how's that for a sacrifice, huh? Now you go and keep your
part of the deal if that's what you guys want! I'm sorry I disobeyed
Mom and slept with him.' She was sobbing and sniffing fiercely as
she lay on her bed, staring up at the ceiling. There was a feeling in
her bones this time that she didn't like at all.

And that feeling manifested itself all too strongly, when five days
later, Mrs Bhave had a fever again.

'It's just 100.8, Doctor,' Trisha told Dr Pradhan. This time she
hadn't even tried calling Dr Phadnis.

'Okay, have a cannula fixed and give her injections of Magnex
twice a day. Get in touch if the fever persists.'

'A cannula?'

'Yes, in her arm for the injection.'

'Oh okay, thank you.' She put down the phone. Where or who
would do that? Dr Khurana was still abroad. She didn't know any
other doctors in the neighbourhood.

She took her back to the hospital and much to her relief, they gave her mom her first injection. Richa and Hema had been dismissed two days earlier.

'You don't have to bring her all the way here twice a day. You can get a nurse or do it yourself,' the doctor on duty at the Outpatients Department told her airily. 'Make sure there are no air bubbles in the syringe.'

'How can I give her an injection?' She was appalled. That evening she called the local hospital; they were dismissive and brief. They did not send nurses to people's houses for injections.

At 7 that evening, her mother still had 100.2. Trisha took a deep breath. Okay, so she would do it herself. She had watched closely, when they had given her mom the injection at the hospital, and it hadn't really seemed too difficult. She took out the small squat bottle from the fridge and removed its seal. Then she plunged the needle into the rubber bung and sucked up the medicine in the syringe, surprised by how hard she had to pull at the plunger. Shivi, who had been following her, looked at her wide-eyed.

'Trisha, what are you doing?'

'I have to give Mom her injection.'

'But you're not a doctor!'

'There's no one else. I have to do it.'

'Poor Mommy.'

Trisha held up the syringe to the light and lightly pushed up the plunger. Suddenly the medicine spurted out like a breaking string of pearls.

'Yikes!' She squinted at the syringe and flicked its sides smartly as she had seen the nurses do. Well, that was it. Heck, Akshay was probably lolling on some beach eyeing bikini babes while she was here preparing to give her mom an injection. Well, whatever he did was no longer any concern of hers . . . she wiped the tears that had suddenly welled up.

'Mom?' Her mom was reclining in her Lazy Boy, watching TV. 'Mom, I have to give you your injection.'

'Okay. . .' Mrs Bhave said tiredly.

'Here goes . . .' Trisha knelt by her side and snapped open the cannula. She fit the nozzle of the syringe snugly and began pressing the plunger, one eye fixed on her mother's face. The plunger didn't budge. She increased the pressure and suddenly it broke free and squirted them both.

'Oh shit!'

'Trisha, it's like a pichkari!' Shivi was thrilled.

She gritted her teeth and tried again, gently rubbing her mom's arm so that the medicine could travel more easily through the vein. This time the plunger went down steadily and smoothly.

'Does it hurt?'

'No,' whispered Mrs Bhave, 'not at all.'

But the injections didn't seem to do much good either. The fever came and went apparently at will along with the shivering fits and the itching.

'Have a blood test done—complete blood count and liver function tests and the CA19-9—and let me know the results,' Dr Pradhan instructed.

Trisha looked at the blood test report white-faced with horror: her mom's bilirubin was now 11.9 and nearly all the other parameters were starred, indicating abnormality. Her CA19-9 figure was an appalling 14,398.

Ten days after she had come home, Dr Pradhan told Trisha to get her admitted again.

'We'll have to do a more exhaustive procedure, when her fever subsides. Also the bile is beginning to collect and getting infected. We might have to drain it out.'

She was better prepared and organized this time. 'Not this room again,' she said, shaking her head as they entered Room 3934. 'It's becoming our second home. This is our third time here.'

She had more support too. For one Tikka was back and around for doing errands and ferrying her to and fro. Mrs Almeida had cut her holiday short and visited the hospital every evening. Trisha got into a grim routine. She'd awake by 6.30 a.m. and ring the hospital immediately. At first she was cheered when her mom would say that she had had a good night, but learnt all too soon how quickly that could change. She'd leave for the hospital at 8.30 every morning and could find her mom pale and drawn, already exhausted. Sometimes of course, the surprise could be happier; her mom might sound dead beat first thing in the morning but be quite chirpy by the time Trisha reached.

'Darling, I'd like some cold coffee,' Mrs Bhave said one morning and Trisha scurried down happily to the canteen to fetch a foaming glass. But after two days, she'd gone off coffee completely.

She'd stay the whole day, waiting for the doctors, and ordering her lunch from the cafeterias, reading *Gone with the Wind* and dozing or just staring out of the window at the wheeling pigeons and kites, and watching her mom lying there on her bed, drawn and mostly asleep. Mrs Bhave's eyes were beginning to assume an alarming orange hue and the bones in her face jutted out sharply. At 5.00 p.m. Komal and Shivi would arrive and stir things up, with Shivi chattering non-stop about what she had done all day. Mrs Almeida would turn up too, and talk softly with her mom, while Trisha distracted Shivi, occasionally taking her to the gift shop downstairs; she felt bad that the little girl had to spend the whole day at home, with Komal. Often, Mrs Almeida would bring papers which her mom had to sign. At 7.00 when visiting hours got over; they'd all return home, dropping Mrs Almeida home on the way.

'Mrs Almeida, what are all those papers Mom signs?' Trisha asked one evening as they drove back.

'Dear, it's her financial affairs.'

'Is she taking on more projects?' Trisha was incredulous. With her mom you just didn't know.

'No, dear.'

'Mrs Almeida, do you think Mom will get well again? I mean back to normal?'

'I hope so.' But she was looking out of the window, a handkerchief clutched in one hand. At the hospital, even Bushy Moustache had begun smiling at Shivi and raised his cap respectfully at Trisha when she arrived and left; but there was a sadness in his eyes as he ushered them into the lift. Once home, Trisha, too tired for anything, would check the day's post (nothing from Nani yet, but often stuff for Mrs Almeida to look at), bathe, change, eat, make a list of the things she had to prepare for the next day and go off to bed. Not that she slept very well.

'She's strong,' Dr Phadnis had told her, during one of his lightning visits, 'so she'll fight. She has to.' But he looked grim and angry and frustrated. 'We'll make her as comfortable as possible,' he had said quietly before leaving the room. Was that a tacit admission of defeat?

And then, a week later came the call Trisha had unconsciously been steeling herself for.

'Hey, babe! God, you don't know how much I've missed you!'

'Akshay!' How she loved the sound of his voice.

'Babe, listen, we're going on to Greece for a week ... Papa swung some bargain deal with a tour company. So we'll be back in Delhi about twelve days from now.'

'Akshay ...'

'What?'

'Mom's in the hospital. She's had another procedure and needs yet another. She's not too good.'

'Oh shit, man. Listen, are you all right?'

'Akshay, she fell ill the night after we ... we ... you know ...'

'Oh ...'

'I can't help feeling we're ... I'm being punished. She had told us we shouldn't, and we did.'

'What? You can't be serious, she was ill before too.'

'Not like this. She got okay. She was riding Smelly Beast. She was fine ...'

'Trisha, it can't have anything to do with what happened that night. There's no connection ...'

'Akshay, we had a great time, we weren't supposed to, but we did, and what happens immediately afterwards? Mom falls ill.'

'She might have fallen ill if we hadn't ...'

'We'll never know that.'

'But there's no connection between the two! There's no logic! You can't believe that!'

'Akshay, I don't know what to believe anymore. I'll do anything for Mom to get all right again.'

'You're obviously stressed out. Listen, I could try and fly back ...' He was sounding desperate.

'No! That's just it. I thought that maybe if I gave up something I hold precious, Mom will get better.'

'What? What are you talking about?' There was a note of panic in his voice.

'About us, Akshay,' she said quietly, the tears beginning to spill down her cheeks again. 'I think we should stop seeing each other.'

'What? But . . .'

'Maybe that will make the pendulum swing in Mom's favour . . . I don't know, Akshay! I love you very much, so maybe that's what I have to give up!'

'Trish, don't think like that! It's just this awful disease that no one knows how to deal with and your poor mom has got it. It has nothing to do with us!'

'I'm going to give it a shot anyway,' she said dully and put down the phone. She was sobbing uncontrollably.

'What is it, Akshay?' Mrs Khurana looked at her son, as he slumped down in his lounger.

'It's Trisha's mom. She's in hospital again. And Trisha . . . she doesn't want to see me again.'

'Why?' Jai eyed his brother, suddenly alert.

'Not a good thing that, cholangiocarcinoma,' Dr Khurana remarked. 'Very unusual, but not good at all.'

'I don't know. She just said . . . she didn't want . . .' he faded away into a whisper.

'Want me to call Gullu and check with her? Maybe she'll know.'

Akshay shook his head. His parents got up. 'We're going for another dip, want to come?'

Akshay shook his head. 'No.'

'Me neither.' Jai waited as they walked off and turned to Akshay. 'What's up? Don't tell me she's found another dude?'

'She thinks she's being punished because of . . . of that night . . . and if she stops seeing me her mom will get okay again.'

'But that's bull!'

'She likes to believe in miracles. Obviously she thinks the two things are linked.'

'What's got into her? She's nuts!'

'I don't know. I wish we hadn't come here.'

'I'll tell Gullu to talk some sense into her. She's due back in Delhi in a day or two. Trisha must be totally stressed out.'

'I guess.'

'Besides,' Jai said in a hollow voice. 'We can't lose her; she's the best leg break bowler in Delhi!'

The rocket from Gullu, still gallivanting in the mountains with her family, came the next day.

'Trisha! Why didn't you tell me your mom was in hospital again? Are you nuts? When I told Ma, she was hopping mad and so am I.'

'Gullu! I've . . . I've been so tied up . . . running around . . .'

'Huh! Don't give me that. I'm your friend, aren't I?

'Gullu, I'm sorry, I really am. Mom's not doing well and I don't know what to do anymore!'

'Hang in there, Trish, we're returning tomorrow . . .'

'It'll be great to see you. I've missed you like mad.'

'Yes, and hey, what's this about you and Akshay?' Gullu was getting truculent again. 'Jai called me and I've never known him to sound so down and out!'

Trisha took a deep breath. 'Yes,' she said dully. 'I think I'm being punished for what we did that night and so must make amends . . . I don't want to talk about it, really.'

'Trisha, have you lost it totally?'

'I thought maybe if I gave up something, you know, made a sacrifice, Mom might get better. That's how miracles happen, don't they?'

Gullu snorted. 'Fine, you go and make a martyr of yourself then, but why make poor Akshay the sacrificial lamb? What'll you do to ease his suffering? What's he done to deserve this?'

'Gullu, I just want to see if it'll work. You know I'm nuts about him . . . you don't know how much it's hurting me.'

'Hah! Just wait till I meet you tomorrow. I'm going to beat some sense into you, girl. By the way, your mom is in the same hospital?'

'Yes. Same room even.'

'Okay, Ma and I will be there tomorrow. See you and stop thinking all this nonsense!'

'Bye Gullu!'

She put the phone down and thought about what Gullu had said.

But all too soon, she had to get organized for the next day. The doctors had scheduled her mom's 'draining' procedure for the following morning. Her fever had persisted, and she was being fed virtually intravenously. She got into bed and stared up at the ceiling. How would they live here alone, she and Shivi, if her mom didn't come home? It was unthinkable. The house *was* her mom; every square inch of it was stamped with her personality. She'd chosen the happy sunflower yellow of her and Shivi's room, the sky blue for her own, and the bright tiles and light wicker furniture, again painted in bright, cheerful colours. Beside her, Shivi snuggled up and put her arms around her. Ever since their mom had gone to the hospital, Shivi had got Komal to join their beds together. Trisha hugged her warm, thin frame tightly and tried to sleep.

CHAPTER SIXTEEN

'HEY DUDE . . .'

For the tenth time in five minutes Trisha glanced at her watch, and stared at the door of the room they had wheeled her mom into— it was different from the one where they had done her previous ERCP procedures. Both her previous procedures had taken between fifteen and twenty minutes, but now it was getting on to almost an hour and there was no sign of her mom emerging. Dr Sharma was doing this particular procedure—and he had looked pretty serious when she met him briefly.

'We'll do our best,' he had said somewhat grimly, which really alarmed her. 'There's always a 10 per cent chance . . .'

At least she had Mrs Almeida sitting upright beside her.

'It's never taken so long,' Trisha said at last. 'She's out in twenty minutes usually.'

'Maybe it's a different method.' And maybe, Mrs Almeida thought cynically, maybe they'll do it properly this time; any 'medical procedure' that was done and dusted in fifteen minutes flat couldn't have been done properly, according to her. And frankly that flashy Dr Phadnis, who she had met just once, was far too good-looking to be a doctor delving into people's gall bladders and livers.

'I hate this waiting! It's the worst part . . .' Trisha glared at the door, willing it to open. In the corridor where they were waiting, people rushed back and forth, shouting, looking worried and harried.

'I know, dear, we just have to be patient.' She squeezed Trisha's hand. 'Your mother is a fighter.'

224

'I know,' Trisha said in a small voice. 'But . . .'

The second hour ticked past and there was no sign of Mrs Bhave or her doctor emerging. Even Mrs Almeida was beginning to get concerned.

Almost two hours after she had been wheeled in, Dr Sharma came out. Trisha sprang up.

'It went okay,' he said quietly. 'I'll see her in her room.' He looked a little guilty as he walked off.

It didn't seem all right when they eventually wheeled her mom out, ten minutes later. Trisha looked in horror at the two transparent bags hanging by tubes from her mother's sides, into which a slime green liquid slithered, drop by drop. Her mother's face was grey with pain.

'Mom?'

Mrs Bhave opened her eyes. 'Where's that bloody doctor?' she whispered. 'I want a word with him . . . I'm going to throttle him.' She glanced around and then closed her eyes again.

'Mom, did it hurt?'

The answer was all over her mom's face. Mrs Almeida took Trisha by the hand.

'Come along, dear, at least it's over.'

'She looks like she's been hit by a truck,' Trisha whispered. 'What have they done to her?'

Dr Sharma came up to the room an hour later.

'She must be very angry,' he said to Trisha, a trifle sheepishly. 'But we've put in a couple of tubes to drain out the infected bile. We'll only be able to put in another stent once the infection is taken care of.'

'Another stent? What about the plastic one you just put in?'

'That's no longer in position.'

'Don't tell her that now, Doctor.'

He was leaning over her mother, examining the tubes and checking the bags. 'How do you feel, Mrs Bhave?' he asked.

She opened her eyes. 'You have the guts to ask me that after what you did to me there?' she whispered hoarsely.

'I'm sorry, but we had to.'

At 5, Shivi burst into the room and came to a dead halt when she saw her mom.

'What's that hanging out from Mommy?' she asked Trisha, taking her hand.

Trisha swallowed her tears. 'They're Mommy's new designer handbags, Shivi,' she said, 'well, saddlebags really.'

'What?'

'Hi Shivi, come here and give me a kiss, darling!'

'Mommy! You've got two new handbags.'

'Hey Shivi, take it easy. You can't bounce all over Mom anymore.' Trisha's mobile rang.

'Hey Trish, Ma and I are out here by the lift. Bushy Muchchad here won't let us in because we don't have passes!'

'Gullu! Hang on, I'm just coming.'

'Mom, Gullu and Parkash Aunty have come . . . I'll just fetch them.' Trisha raced out.

Gullu, looking slightly plumper and tanned, stood next to her mom, who was trying to tuck in her untidy hair. As Trisha emerged, they both converged on her.

'Trish!'

Gullu had her usual healthy, fresh smell while her mom smelled of kitchen spices. They enveloped Trisha.

'I missed you,' Trisha said at last, drawing back. Gullu's eyes narrowed.

'Would you like to meet Mom?' Trisha added hastily, 'I'll just tell Shivi and Komal to step out—they don't allow more than two visitors at a time.'

Bushy Moustache raised an eyebrow and indicated faintly with his hands that they could go in.

'Shukriya—thank you,' she said, 'come on, Aunty, we can go in.'

Gullu's mom surged up to Mrs Bhave's bedside and took her hand. 'Jee, don't you dare worry about anything—we'll look after your bitiyas—you just get well and come home!'

Mrs Bhave looked at the big, concerned eyes, the untidy hair and the quivering double chin; behind the bluff manner, was a kind, caring person.

'Thank you, thank you for coming.'

Gullu meanwhile had lost no time in cornering Trisha.

'Well?' she hissed.

'Well what?'

'Well . . . Akshay!' Gullu said sibilantly.

Trisha shrugged. 'I don't know . . . they've gone to Greece or something.'

'Greece or *something*? Trish, just listen to yourself!'

'Gullu, please. Drop it.'

'I will not. He's my boyfriend's brother and you've devastated him, and you're my best friend so I cannot let it be!'

'Gullu!'

Gullu's eyes narrowed further. 'Hey,' she whispered, 'all this antagonism . . . you're not pregnant, are you?'

'Don't be silly.'

'Then why? Why are you pushing him away? You need him max now!'

'We're being punished and I must make amends.'

'And you're talking like a dimwit from the Middle Ages.'

'So let me. I have the right!'

'As long as you don't smash up someone else's life in the process.'

'Well, she told us both to lay off and we didn't. Now she's ill as hell. So now we must pay the price.'

Gullu stormed on: 'When will you get it into that thick head of yours that there's no connection between the two things? God, Trish, you're supposed to be the brilliant one, the topper. You're talking like some illiterate village cretin!'

'What's a cretin?' Shivi wanted to know. 'And what are you two phus-phussing about. Secrets are not allowed!'

'Hey Shivi, see what I brought for you from Dehradun!' Gullu dug into her jeans and pulled out a fancy drawstring pouch. 'These bullseyes were specially made for you, and here's a cute rag doll, which looks just like you!'

'Thank you, Gullu!' Shivi opened the pouch and popped a bullseye into her mouth. Then she went around offering everyone else in the room a bulls eye each, the doll tucked under one arm.

'See Gullu, nothing's changed,' Trisha whispered desperately. 'I just think that if I give up something I value the max, whoever is up there might relent and make Mom well again.'

'And if that happens, then what?'

'I . . . I don't know . . . I haven't thought about it.'

'Will you go back begging forgiveness?'

'I haven't thought about it. If Mom gets well . . . that's all I want now.'

The question was there, in Gullu's eyes, in big bold capitals, but she never said anything.

What if . . . what if her mother didn't get okay . . . what if that miracle didn't happen, what then? It was unthinkable.

'Will you show me around, Trisha?' Gullu asked suddenly.

'What? You want a tour of the hospital?'

'Yes.' Gullu glanced at Shivi who was busy on the settee bandaging up her doll. 'Richa, she needs an injection, will you give her one, please?' Shivi said.

'Ma, Trish and I are just going out for a walk . . .'

'Yes, take Trisha out of here,' Mrs Bhave nodded. 'A little fresh air will do her good.'

Gullu tucked her arm firmly into Trisha's and led her out of the room. 'I saw a nice park downstairs just outside, we're going to sit there and thrash this out, madam.'

'There's nothing to thrash out.'

'There is too.'

They bought hot roasted channa and sat down on a bench. There were children from the neighbouring colonies running all over the place, on the swings and slides; Komal could bring Shivi here, Trisha thought. She looked around; it seemed amazing that life was so normal just outside the gates of the hospital. Children played, their mothers gossiped and screamed, the traffic roared up and down the road, people did their shopping and ran their errands.

'Now,' Gullu said, fixing her with a look. 'You seriously think that whoever it is up there is punishing you for having the best night of your life by making your mom seriously ill? And that if you dump the poor guy, they'd relent and she would get well again?'

'I just want to give it a shot. That's all. I told you, I'll do anything to get Mom well again.'

'Well it hasn't worked so far, has it? Your mom has two bags of guck hanging out of her sides, poor thing. Seems to me whoever is up there has a pretty sadistic sense of humor!'

'But she's still being treated.'

'Listen, how do you know if there's a big gun up there in the first place?'

'I'm covering my bases.'

'So if there is, then why do so many people—why do babies and children die—horribly and unnecessarily? Why do people die anyway? Why would someone who is so great want to make people suffer? If he or she really gave a shit we wouldn't be sitting outside this hospital because there wouldn't be any hospitals because no one would ever get ill or hurt.'

'Gullu, please . . . I don't know. I can't think of all this stuff.'

'But you have to.' She gestured expansively. 'Think of how lucky you are to have someone like him at a time like this. Any normal guy would have been over the horizon the moment your mom fell sick. He bunked school and came to the hospital, remember?'

'Listen, I'm tired. Let's go back up.' She glanced at her watch. 'Anyway visiting hours will be over in ten minutes and Bushy Moustache will be getting all antsy.'

'So promise me you'll at least think about it,' Gullu said as she got into the lift with her mother a little later.

Trisha pursed her lips and nodded, more to get rid of the subject than anything else.

'See you tomorrow.'

She went back into the room, where Shivi was stuffing some of the cotton wadding back into her doll's stomach.

'She's just had an operation and I'm stuffing her insides back,' she said. 'Just a minute.'

'Come on, Shivi, we better go.' She went up to her mom. 'Bye Mom, see you tomorrow, ring me if you need anything from home.'

How many more days would she be saying this, she wondered.

Tikka's eyes were big with concern as he held the door of the pickup open for her. 'How's Memsahib?'

'She's okay . . .'

She stared at the traffic, hooting and juddering, and shut her eyes. She was glad Gullu was back. And Gullu's mom—she really was wonderful. But soon, Akshay and Jai would be back too.

As usual the house felt strange and silent without her mom. She eyed the vacant Lazy Boy, switched on the TV and stared at it glassily. Shivi wandered up to her, looking lost.

'Trisha, when will Mommy come home?'

'Maybe in a week.'

Shivi went off to the kitchen looking for Komal. Trisha eyed the drinks cabinet. Everyone in the films swigged back drinks when they were stressed. She opened the cabinet and stared at the glinting bottles.

She pulled out a tall glass and glancing around guiltily opened the bottle of gin and poured two fingers into the glass, filling it up quickly with a can of tonic water from the mini-fridge.

Fifteen minutes later she was on her second gin, smacking her lips and feeling better. She raised her eyes to the ceiling and jabbed a forefinger at it:

'You up there, you've made a real balls-up of things down here haven't you? Why are you putting me and poor Shivi through all of this—we've already lost our dad—and that was totally unnecessary too, thank you very much—and poor Mom had to shoulder that all by herself. And what do you do, just when things start going so well for her? Give her bloody cancer? Thank you very much, so nice of you! So what have you got against us? Sure, we don't get down on bended knees and prostrate ourselves and worship you the way others do, but so many of those who do that only do so because of all the horrible things they do in normal life, like selling drugs or throwing bombs, or is it that all you want is for people to worship you? Egotist! Sorry, I didn't mean to call you names, but your Highness or Godliness or whatever, if you really care do something nice for a change! Excushe me while I get another drink . . .'

She sloshed a little more gin and clattered some ice into the glass and flopped back into her mom's Lazy Boy.

'Yesh! Let's see you pull a real rabbit out of your hat, eh . . . get Mom well and bring her back home—then I'll really believe in you and your miracles; I'll worship you from head to toe, 24×7. People keep saying you can perform miracles, but why are you so choosy? Why don't you perform miracles for everyone; all those innocent people who you condemn to death much before their time? And you can start with Mom! Otherwise, you suck. I've already sacrificed poor Akshay at your altar . . . so you owe me big, you hear? What am I going to tell him, poor fellow, when he looks at me out of those huge black eyes of his and says I've chopped up his heart into little pieces and flung the bits in the gutter? Because, you know, that's exactly what I've done! You like people worshipping you and bowing and scraping before you don't you? Look at how many miserable people there are around. You're useless at your job . . . I'm sorry . . . I'm sorry . . . I didn't mean to be rude . . . and I think I'm repeating myshelf . . .'

She took a deep breath. 'So sometimes you screw the wrong people . . . Okay, okay but I'm telling you now, here's a mishtake you can fix.' She gulped. 'I mean, I'm just seventeen, for Christ's sake, and my whole world has just come crashing down . . . And look at Mom . . . she's barely forty and poor little Shivi . . . Why are you screwing our lives up like this?' She hiccupped like a pistol shot, startling herself and then suddenly the tears flooded in. 'Just get Mom well, that's all I ask.' She sniffed and flopped back into the Lazy Boy as sleep overwhelmed her.

'Trisha . . . Trisha, you've fallen asleep . . . you're like Mommy!' Somewhere faraway Shivi was yelling at her . . .

She jerked awake. 'Wha . . .?'

'Dinner's ready, dumbo!'

'Oh.' She struggled to her feet and weaved uncertainly towards the table.

'Why are you walking like a crab?'

'Becaushe I feel like . . .'

She managed to help herself without spilling anything and avoided Komal's eye.

'First you were talking to yourself, then you went to sleep and now you're walking like a crab!'

'Of not courshe! Just eat, Shivi.'

'Oh okay, what a grouch you are!'

'Am not!'

'Are too!'

'Am not, I'm shweet and reasonable!' She giggled.

She was having trouble negotiating her spoon of prawn curry from her plate to her mouth; there seemed to be so many spoons and so many plates. Suddenly she didn't care. She put her spoon down and flopped face down into the plate.

'Trisha!' Shivi started giggling. 'Komal, Trisha's gone to sleep in the prawn curry!'

Komal came hurrying out of the kitchen. 'Trisha baby, what have you done?' She was horrified.

'Trisha baby bewda peeyela—Trisha baby's drunk booze!' Shivi said in glorious Bombay Hindi, rolling her eyes. She pointed gleefully to the gin bottle that Trisha had inadvertently left outside after her last top up.

Komal summoned Tikka and together they took Trisha to the bedroom, with Shivi following.

'It's okay, I'll look after her now,' Komal said as they put her down gently on the bed after having taken her to the bathroom and washed her face. Tikka left, looking quite worried.

'Komal, Trisha is all right, isn't she?' Shivi asked in a small voice, suddenly scared.

'Yes, she's okay, she'll have a headache tomorrow, that's all.'

Komal put Trisha to bed, thankful that she hadn't been sick. Then she put the gin bottle back in the bar. She locked the cabinet and put the key down her blouse. That was the last drink Trisha baby was going to have; she'd keep an eagle eye on the poor girl henceforth.

Trisha woke up in the middle of the night with a pounding headache. Her tongue felt like a block of wood stuck to the roof of her mouth.

'Komal!' she groaned. 'Some water!'

Komal jerked awake and put on the light.

'Please, put off the light. My head! Do we have asprin?'

Komal came up to the bed. 'Baby, don't do things like this.' She lifted Trisha up gently and gave her a glass of water. 'You don't solve anything by drinking, you only get a headache!'

'I was drunk?'

'Completely!'

'Oh, I don't remember . . .'

'Now try and sleep.'

She was a little better and completely mortified by the time she drove to the hospital with Tikka the next morning; there was both concern and amusement in his eyes.

'You okay, baby?' he asked as he ushered her into the pickup. She nodded sheepishly. Her head was still throbbing, but the headache was receding. But what a complete dope she had been! At breakfast, Shivi had eyed her strangely, but not said anything. Now they would drop Shivi and Komal at Gullu's house for the day before heading for the hospital. As for her, she couldn't remember anything about last evening. Time and again, she put her palm to her face and smelled her breath; it seemed all right (she had brushed her teeth furiously and rinsed with a full glass of mouthwash). She walked down the familiar hospital corridor and pushed open her mom's room door.

'Hi, Mom, I'm here. How're you feeling?'

Mrs Bhave turned towards her and smiled. 'Okay,' she said huskily. Trisha eyed the hateful bags, slung on either side of the bed. They were one third full of guck.

'Would you like some cold coffee?'

She had to be as clear-headed as possible.

'Okay, dear.'

'Be back in a jiffy!'

She dozed through most of the morning. Dr Sharma came on his round and said her mom was doing as well as could be expected, whatever that meant. Around lunch, Gullu rang.

'Hey Trisha, I hear you got pissed last night?' She sounded shocked.

'Don't be nuts!' Trisha looked exasperated. Obviously Shivi had been broadcasting.

'Listen, I don't care whether you did fall asleep in your prawn curry or not. But from tonight I'm spending the night with you until your mom returns home.'

'Gullu, I'm fine. I really am.'

'That doesn't matter. Besides, I've been given orders by my mom!'

'Oh, okay.'

'Great. Bye, see you then. Oh, by the way, in case you're interested, Jai and Akshay are returning tonight . . . they cut their trip short, and I'm wondering why.'

'Not interested.'

'Suit yourself.'

'Sure.'

She switched off and stared at her phone. So tomorrow, he would probably call, or worse, come over. Then what?

Mrs Bhave was much the same the next day; she had a bout of fever early morning, but it kept around the 100 mark and she didn't have those frightening shivering spells. Dr Phadnis seemed satisfied.

'We'll schedule her next procedure as soon as she's free of fever for a couple of days,' he told Trisha.

'Doctor, will she ever get well?'

He shrugged. 'You can't say with these things . . .' was his noncommittal reply.

At 5, Shivi came bursting in with Komal.

Then Gullu called.

'Ma and I are outside,' she said.

'Okay, I'll send Komal out, then your mom can come in. I'll be with you in a sec.'

Gullu's mom entered, smiling all over her cherubic face. 'Go,' she ordered Trisha, 'Gullu's waiting for you outside.'

She went out and opened the door to the lobby, where the lifts were.

Gullu stepped forwards to greet her. Behind her on the chairs lined against the wall, sat Akshay and Jai, their eyes big with trepidation.

He was tanned, wearing his favourite dark blue T-shirt and khakis. He'd obviously tried to tame his hair, with little success; it still stood up in those hilarious spikes she loved so much. His eyes were huge and liquid and questioning.

'Er . . . hi, Gullu.' Her voice faded away as she stared at Akshay. 'Hi Trisha,' he said softly getting to his feet, glancing uncertainly at her.

She turned on her heel. 'I'd better go back in, Mom might need something,' she mumbled. Gullu came after her and caught her sleeve.

'Trisha—don't be such an ass!'

'Why did you bring them here?' she hissed, as she opened the lobby door.

'Well, it's visiting hours and they wanted to come. Don't be so silly, Trisha!'

'I told you, Gullu, I don't want to see him anymore!'

'Okay, dammit. But just remember what you're doing to him!'

'I'd better go to Mom . . . see you, Gullu . . . no need to come tonight.'

She nearly bumped into Parkash Aunty coming out of her mom's room. 'Gullu will stay the night with you, beta, to keep you company, until your mummy comes home,' she said, smiling.

She went back into her mom's room.

'Has Gullu gone? I thought . . .'

'Umm . . . no, I think she's still outside, talking to her mom.'

'Okay. I'm so glad she's spending the nights with you.'

There was a discreet knock on the door. She whirled. Akshay had put his head tentatively around it like a nervous hedgehog. Her mom smiled.

'Hi Akshay, so nice to see you! Come in! How was your holiday?'

Mrs Bhave glanced at him and then Trisha. 'Why don't you two go off for a walk?' she suggested. 'I'm sure you have some catching up to do!'

Akshay looked at Trisha imploringly. She had turned her back to him and was staring out of the window. She shrugged.

'Okay.'

They stood awkwardly in the corridor outside.

'Trisha, what have I done?' he was absolutely bewildered and, to her horror, seemed very near to tears.

'You know what we both did. Listen, I think you better go.'

'But . . .'

'We did wrong. Now Mom's being punished and so are we! That's all there is to it.'

'But . . .'

'Just go, Akshay,' she whispered. 'Please!'

'Papa's coming to pick us up from here at 6.30,' he said in a dead voice. 'He wants to see your mom too . . .'

'There's a big waiting room on the ground floor. With TV and all.'

'Okay . . . but what about the music competition?'

'You'll have to find someone else, that's all. Now please . . .'

He walked away slowly, his hands in his pockets. In the lobby Gullu and Jai were in animated conversation, their heads nearly touching.

She went back inside, feeling monstrous.

'Darling, is everything all right between you and Akshay? You're not having a tiff or anything?'

She shook her head. 'No, of course not.'

'Hmm . . .'

Shivi was suddenly jumping up and down. 'Mommy, I nearly forgot . . . You know, last night Trish got drunk. She almost finished the whole gin bottle! She was walking funny and fell asleep in her food!'

'Shivi!'

Mrs Bhave's eyebrows shot up and she glanced at Trisha. Her beautiful daughter was bright scarlet.

'You must have had a terrible headache this morning . . .' she said dryly.

Trisha nodded. She was very near tears. 'I'm sorry, Mom,' she whispered, taking her hand.

'That's okay, sweetie . . . just don't make it a habit.'

She shook her head vigorously and cast a murderous look at her little sister.

'I won't,' she said. 'I felt like such a fool afterwards.'

'Good.' Her mom smiled tiredly and shut her eyes.

Of course, Gullu did come home with her, though in the pickup they both looked out of their respective windows in silence. They reached home and went to Trisha's study; the silence between them stretched inexorably. At last Gullu could bear it no longer.

'Listen . . .'

'I won't. I don't want to talk about it.'

'Well, I do.'

'You'll have to find someone else to talk to then.'

'Trisha!'

She whirled. 'Why don't you leave me alone?' she shouted. 'Do you have any idea how I feel? Mom's probably dying—dying do you hear—she'll probably never come home again and I'm trying to make a bloody miracle happen. Have you seen what she looks like? All yellow and grey and bones sticking out everywhere! She used to drive that Bullet, dammit. All the way up to Kasauli. Now look at her!' She ran to the bathroom and slammed the door.

Gullu ran to the bathroom door. 'Hey, Trisha . . . take it easy.'

'Just leave me alone, all of you! Stop bugging me.'

'Okay, okay . . . sorry! But please stop crying and come out.'

They ate in near silence, with Shivi's frightened eyes moving from one to another. At last she asked:

'Trisha, did you and Gullu have a fight?'

'We did, but we're okay now,' Gullu said. 'Right, Trish?'

But Trisha only nodded.

What was poor Akshay doing now, she wondered. Was he wandering about the streets, contemplating suicide? Would he jump in front of a bus or the Metro? If he did something silly, she'd be to blame for that too. Really, was there no end to it?

'Er . . . Gullu?' she said tentatively as they got ready for bed. 'I'm sorry I yelled like that.'

'That's okay.'

'About Akshay . . .'

'What?' Gullu brightened up instantly.

'You don't think he'd do something stupid, do you? Like jump in front of the Metro?'

Gullu shrugged. 'How should I know? He's your boyfriend. You should know.'

'Well, I don't. He had this horrible dead glaze in his eyes.'

'Well, you were a frozen fish too, remember?'

She shook her head. 'I had to be. It nearly killed me but I had to do it. It's got to work.'

'Again the same rubbish.' Gullu rolled her eyes.

'It's got to work,' Trisha went on stubbornly. 'It must!'

Mrs Bhave's fever came and went irregularly for the next three weeks. Her bilirubin had dipped to 9.5, but never went below that. Her nausea was better but her appetite was still poor. Some days she'd show flashes of her old energy, on others she'd sleep most of the time, her face drawn and grey.

Trisha's routine was firmly established. She'd ring the hospital first thing in the morning to check how her mom had been that night (and had begun to loathe the signature tune and sing-song recorded voice on the phone). Then a quick bath, a glance at the list she had made the previous evening—things to do, clothes to take . . . She'd drop Shivi and Komal off at Gullu's house and arrive at the hospital usually by around 9.30 a.m., hoping the doctors hadn't yet come on their rounds. Sometimes she went to the bank before coming to the hospital, especially if there was a bill to be paid. Her mom would be dozing most of the time and often Trisha would doze off on the settee too. Occasionally she would stand at the big glass window and stare at the cars filing into the car park below or at the vast expanse of the Ridge stretching to the horizon. There was always a queue of glittering cars waiting to get in. How long would she be doing this, she wondered. When and how would it all end? Would she be here next year at this time too?

And then suddenly, the silence would be shattered as the doctors burst in and gathered around her mom's bed. If she needed to ask them something she had to be quick to pounce, for they vanished in a trice. She had started listing her questions and kept the piece of paper handy in her pocket.

'Doctor, her tumour is definitely malignant?' she asked Dr Pradhan one morning, slipping out into the corridor after him.

He looked at her with his basset hound expression. 'Yes, I'm afraid so.'

'So, there's no chance . . .'

'There's always a chance. She's done very well so far. We can only hope and make her comfortable as possible. At least she is not in pain.'

At least . . . 'How long?' she whispered.

He shrugged. 'No one can really say.'

She had made friends with some of the nurses on duty. By and large they were a cheerful bunch, mainly from Kerala, with flashing eyes and brilliant teeth and gorgeous ebony skin.

'Such a pretty girl you are, no? You must be having how many boyfriends!' they teased her. And then, kindly: 'Don't worry, your mummy will get all right!' Even the Bushy Moustaches had begun opening the doors for her and smiling.

Shivi, Komal, Gullu and Parkash Aunty (and Mrs Almeida) would turn up at 5 p.m., livening up matters considerably. Gullu would come home with them at 7. While the subject of poor Akshay was still off limits, Gullu would breach the unspoken agreement from time to time. One evening about a week later she stood in front of Trisha arms akimbo.

'Have you ever peeked into that big waiting lobby on the ground floor?' she asked.

'No. Why should I?'

'Well, maybe you should.'

'Why on earth should I do that?'

'Because, Madam Frozen Fish, Akshay has been spending the whole bloody day there for the past week.'

'What?'

Gullu shook her head exasperatedly. 'He's such a fool. I've never seen such devotion! He must have been a Labrador or a cocker spaniel in his last life. You have no idea how lucky you are! You kick him out and he sits outside your room with the patience of a saint. Jai thinks he's seriously bonkers.'

'I don't want to talk about Akshay,' she said woodenly.

But the next morning, just after the doctors had done their rounds, she went downstairs and peeked into the big waiting hall. It was crowded with people, and every now and then the PA system would crackle hideously to life and ask for someone to report to reception or page a doctor. She scanned the room and to her relief couldn't see him anywhere. But there was the other—more comfortable—hall, where the relatives and attendants of the ICU patients waited. She stood halfway in the doorway and peered inside.

Her heart gave a sudden lurch as she saw him, sitting in the second row, watching some hysterical T20 cricket match on TV. There was a grim determination in his expression, as if he had made up his mind to stay here for as long as it took. She backed away and went back upstairs to her mom's room.

He was still there at 3 in the afternoon but had dozed off, his head thrown back, his hair sticking out at mad angles as always. Why didn't the stubborn fellow go home and forget about her? Why was he giving her such a hard time—she was having a bad enough summer anyway. She'd have to be careful she didn't bump into him in any of the snack bars or the gift shop; she couldn't trust her own reaction if that happened. And why the hell was he keeping this vigil anyway?

One morning, to her delight, she found her mom propped up in bed, eating porridge, slowly and loathfully but still spooning in the stuff. Mrs Bhave smiled. 'Trisha, we need to talk. Come here, darling.'

She approached nervously and sat down. Her mom took her hand.

'Trish, you know what I have, and so do I, so we both know that there's a chance that it won't work out.'

'Mom, don't say things like that. You'll be fine.'

'I sincerely hope so!' The familiar raspishness was back in her mom's voice. She took a deep breath. 'Darling, I've settled most of my affairs; you and Shivi will naturally get everything: the house, the pickup, ah—Smelly Beast will be yours exclusively when you're eighteen. Also, there will be more than enough money for both of you to live on till you're twenty-one; then you'll get the big bucks and can have a blast . . .'

'Mom! Please don't say these things! I don't want to hear them!'

'I know they're scary . . . but it's better that you know about them, darling. Mrs Almeida has been a real godsend—she's taken care of all the legalities and so on. I've appointed her as your legal guardian until you are eighteen.'

'Mom, stop! What about your business?'

'Well, I didn't take any projects after the Expressway and Ratnagarh ones, and both were completed.'

'But . . .'

'Darling, this is just so you know. Now, have you heard anything from Nani?'

Trisha shook her head. 'I rang twice and both times they said they'd given her the message but she hasn't called back.'

'Darling, there's just one more thing: take care of Shivi.'

'Of course!' She smiled suddenly. 'Though, knowing Shivi, it'll be the other way around. But Mom, nothing's going to happen.'

'I hope not! Now dry your eyes and sing me something!'

A couple of mornings later, Dr Pradhan informed her that they would be removing her mom's 'saddlebags' that afternoon. Her procedure had been scheduled for a couple of days after that—they would be putting in another stent, which hopefully would drain away the bile more efficiently. It was now the fourth week of April and Mrs Bhave had spent over a month in the hospital.

Two mornings later, Trisha was sitting outside the now unpleasantly familiar ERCP room, alone again. Whisking in and out of the room, Dr Phadnis' secretary smiled at her sympathetically as she went about her work. Her mom had just been wheeled in after having waited in the 'bus stand' for forty-five minutes. Mrs Almeida had called to say she would not be able to make it in time—she had to meet her mom's bank manager and lawyer, and the meeting had been delayed.

'I've told Gullu to sit with you, dear,' she told Trisha. 'I'll come as soon as I can.'

And there was no sign of Gullu; well, she always tended to run late. And then, five minutes after her mom had been wheeled in, Akshay entered the waiting room and walked up to her tentatively.

'Sorry,' he said. 'I got an SOS from Gullu. She can't make it and told me to come here. I hope you don't mind . . . I was . . . er, waiting in the lounge anyway.'

She shook her head dumbly. The door of the ERCP room burst open and Hema came flying out. 'MRCP! The doctor wants to see the MRCP report and the X-rays.'

Trisha handed over the huge envelope she had been holding. 'Here,' she said calmly, as Akshay's mouth dropped open.

'You had that ready?'

'It's happened before.'

'Oh.'

She was glad both the seats next to her were occupied; he'd have to sit across her. He sat down quietly.

Gullu had plotted this, she was sure, feeling angry.

'How long has she been gone?' Akshay dared to ask.

'Ten minutes.' She picked up a magazine and began leafing through it.

The door of the ERCP room opened again and she looked up. Dr Phadnis walked up to her.

'Will you come this way, please?' He looked around. 'Are you alone?'

'I'm with her.' Akshay stood up, before she could say anything.

He led them to a small room, where Dr Pradhan and Dr Sharma were also present, looking very grim.

'I'm afraid your mother had a heart attack in the middle of the procedure. We were almost done, when her heart just stopped.' He sounded surprised. To Trisha, it seemed like his voice was coming from very far away.

'Is she . . .?' The words barely left her mouth.

'Sit down, miss, would you like some water?'

She hardly realized it, but Akshay was holding her upright, his hands firm around her waist. He lowered her gently into a chair.

'We've revived her . . .' Dr Phadnis said. 'But she's on the ventilator. We'll shift her to the ICU as soon as she stabilizes.'

'Will she be . . .?'

Akshay was holding her hand tightly, squeezing it.

'At the moment, we can't say anything; we'll have to wait until she gets off the ventilator and breathes on her own. Is there anyone you would like to call?'

She nodded and fumbled with her phone. He took it from her.

'Mrs Almeida,' she whispered. She looked at him. 'And Komal and Gullu's mom . . . please . . .'

'Umm . . . there's one more thing.'

'What?'

'You'll need to vacate her room before we can take her up to the ICU. We're shifting someone down from there to make room for her.'

'Oh, okay.'

So much for her sacrifice, she thought bitterly.

'So the procedure?' Akshay asked.

'We couldn't complete it.' Dr Pradhan shook his head decisively.

She looked at the three of them standing defensively behind their table and with a shock realized that Dr Pradhan had tears in his eyes.

'We're sorry,' Dr Phadnis said, his bluff bonhomie manner gone. 'It was totally unexpected. She has no history of heart trouble.'

'What are her chances?'

Dr Phadnis shook his head. 'I would have said, quite bright, but now . . .'

'How long will she be in the ICU?'

'We move her only after she comes off the ventilator. It could be two or three days.'

'Can we see her now, please?' she asked, automatically taking Akshay's hand.

'Yes, of course.'

He led them into the ERCP room, where another bed was being readied by cheerfully chatting attendants for another patient. On her plank—for that's what it seemed like—Mrs Bhave lay, still and puce-coloured, the oxygen mask and ventilator over her face, her black jamun eyes jammed shut like they would never open again.

'Mom!' Trisha whispered. 'Mom, can you hear me?'

She was leaning against Akshay now and he held her up. 'She's unconscious, Trish . . .'

Suddenly she wanted to run out of that dreadful room. 'Come on,' she said, 'let's get her things.'

They entered her mother's now silent room. 'I suppose she'll never come back here,' Trisha said, shutting the door. 'Oh Akshay, there are no miracles here. I wanted so badly for a miracle to happen, for her to get well but . . .' She shook her head tears filling her eyes. He said nothing but his Adam's apple bobbed rapidly as he swallowed.

'I'm so sorry about what I did to you,' she whispered. 'Can you forgive me?'

'How can you say that, Trish? You did it for your mom.'

A few minutes later they parted.

'Come on, let's pack her stuff and get out of here.'

Up on the third floor it was hushed and dark and they had to get a new set of passes. Only one person was allowed at a time, for a maximum of ten minutes, once in the morning and once in the evening, depending on the condition of the patient. When Trisha went in to see her for a few minutes, she looked around the ward in horror. There were patients here, moaning with pain, bandaged from head to toe, victims of burns and road accidents; this was no place to recover from anything.

'Get well, Mom,' she breathed, watching the ventilator hiss as it pumped air into her mom's lungs. There were tubes and pipes going in everywhere. 'You've got to get out of this place.'

Komal, Shivi, Gullu and Parkash Aunty arrived together about an hour later.

'We're downstairs in the lobby,' Gullu called her. 'They won't let us go up to the ICU.'

It was comforting to be amongst familiar faces: Mrs Almeida tall and upright as a heron, Gullu with her round face and shocked eyes with Jai by her side, Parkash Aunty looking hugely concerned and carrying Shivi, and Komal, round and rosy-cheeked as ever, but red-eyed.

And of course, by her side and still holding her hand, was Akshay.

'How is she?' Mrs Almeida asked.

She recounted what had happened.

'You should go home, beta,' Parkash Aunty said suddenly. 'There's nothing you can do here. You can come and visit her during visiting hours, but no point sitting around here all day. It's in God's hands now.'

'But I can't leave her, Aunty.'

'Then Gullu will stay with you.'

'Don't worry Aunty, I will stay,' Akshay said.

'Good. You must not be alone at such a time, beta.'

'Actually, we'll all stick around,' Gullu said. 'Those chairs in that special lounge for relatives of ICU patients are pretty comfy and they've got TV and we can eat . . .'

'Akshay,' she said suddenly as they settled down, 'you're still holding my hand!'

'I'm scared to let it go.'

She smiled at him and wiped a tear. 'Idiot!'

'Who? Me or you?'

'I'm sorry. I just thought . . .' She gulped. 'It's not going to happen; there is not going to be a miracle. Mom's going to die and that's about it.' She put her head on his shoulder. 'I'll never say a prayer again in my life.'

'Hey . . .'

She looked at him expressively. 'I don't know how we'll carry on after she's gone,' she said simply. 'I just don't know. I try to imagine it and just can't.'

'Listen, Trish, that hasn't happened.'

'But it will.'

'I guess we just have to keep chugging on then somehow. What else can we do?'

'I can't imagine life without Mom.'

And then a small faraway voice piped up from deep inside her: 'Ah yes, but you've more or less done so all these months. Ever since she fell ill . . . somehow you've managed . . . you'll get by.' She shook her head vigorously to expel the thought.

CHAPTER SEVENTEEN

ON THE BOULEVARD OF
BROKEN DREAMS

'You're Mrs Bhave's relative?' the nurse outside the ICU asked Trisha next morning looking her up and down.

'Yes.' Trisha felt the blood run out of her face. 'Is she . . .?'

'She wants to talk to you,' the nurse said. 'Bed No. 12. Please take off your shoes before going in.'

'What? She's conscious?' Hope flared. 'How's she doing?'

The door opened and the doctor on duty came out.

Trisha pounced. 'I'm Mrs Bhave's daughter. How is she doing, Doctor?' she asked, planting herself firmly in front of him. He lowered his spectacles.

'Mrs Bhave? Much better than we expected. She's off the ventilator.'

'Oh great! Can I see her please?'

'Certainly. She can't talk as yet, so take a pen and paper . . .' He looked at Trisha. 'You're the girl who brought her mother to the Emergency on the back of a motorbike?'

But Trisha had already gone in.

She glanced warily at the patient in the bed next to her mother's. The poor fellow had been bandaged virtually from head to toe and was unconscious. Then she was at her mom's bedside.

'Hi, Mom . . .' she whispered, gently taking her hand, 'how're you doing?'

Her mom gestured for the pad.

'What the hell am I doing here?' she scrawled in her loopy slanting handwriting. 'Why am I not in my room?'

'You had a heart attack during the procedure.'

'What? When are they going to shift me back?'

'I don't know. I'll ask.'

'How's Shivi?'

'She's well. Bobby and Arti and Ajay are spending the day at home with her today.'

'Good. And how are you, darling?'

'Fine, Mom, just get out of here; it's a horrible place!'

'I will. When are they going to take out all these bloody tubes?'

'I'll ask—probably as soon as possible.'

Outside, Akshay, Gullu, Jai and Parkash Aunty, who had all arrived together, were waiting anxiously.

'She's better,' she said happily. 'She's off the ventilator.' She looked at them. 'I'll wait for Dr Phadnis or whoever to see her; you guys go down!'

'You keep your courage, beta!' Parkash Aunty hugged her. 'Your mummy will get well.'

'I'll wait with you here,' Akshay said.

'Akshay, there aren't even any chairs here . . .'

He grinned sardonically. 'That's okay. I've sat around long enough. I can stand for a bit now.'

'Idiot! I told you I'm sorry!'

He grinned magnanimously. 'And I told you all is forgiven!'

'Thank you, Your Lordship!'

Mrs Bhave was shifted back to her old room the following day.

'She's made a remarkable recovery,' Dr Pradhan said. 'If she continues like this she can go home in a couple of days. She has no fever.'

'So you won't be completing the procedure?' Trisha asked. It was a double-edged sword: if they did they ran a terrible risk (and anyway the outcome would probably be the same); if they didn't, well . . . that was equally bad.

He shook his head. 'No. We can't take that risk.' He smiled thinly. 'She's warned us off!'

'So . . . so there's nothing more you can do.'

'We can make her as comfortable as possible—but that's all. The tumour appears to have spread.' He shook his head.

If all went well, fingers crossed, they would be home in two or three days and away from this awful place with its stink of ether and sickness and antiseptic and blood and pus and pain. That would be one huge step. Whatever happened thereafter would happen . . .

Two days later, the doctors gave Mrs Bhave the all-clear to go home the following morning. Trisha and Shivi were beside themselves with excitement.

'Tikka . . . I want to fill the house with flowers,' Trisha exclaimed.

He nodded. 'We'll go to the wholesale market.'

They bought flowers by the armload—roses, gladoli, gerbera, carnations, jasmine, tulips and narcissus, trumpet lilies and swan-river daisies—filling every room with colour and fragrance.

Mrs Almeida was to meet them at the hospital, as were Gullu and Jai and Akshay. To Trisha's relief, Mrs Almeida took charge of settling the final bills and went down to the billing department. Ten minutes after she had gone, she called:

'Trisha dear, will you come down a moment? There seems to be a problem.'

She rushed down. 'What's the matter?'

'They seem to have charged us again for this procedure.' Mrs Almeida frowned at the receipts. 'It's here in the printout but it's apparently not on their computer.'

Trisha poked her head in the window. 'Excuse me,' she told the man at the counter. 'We have already paid this bill for Rs 24,400, you're charging us again!' The man glanced at the receipt and then at his computer.

'I told Madam there's no entry in the computer.'

'Then where the hell do you think I got this receipt from?' Trisha demanded, her temper beginning to rise. 'What are you suggesting?'

'Trisha . . .'

She waved the receipt in the man's face.

'Are these, or are these not receipts from this hospital?'

He glanced at the paper. 'Yes-'

'It says clearly "payment received" and is stamped and signed!'

'But there's no entry in the computer . . .'

'Then your computer screwed up! Could I see your boss?'

The man pressed more keys on his computer and shook his head. 'It's not here.'

'I don't care! I have this receipt!'

'The receipt number is not there!' The man looked at her woodenly.

Trisha took a deep breath. Okay, he was only doing his job, but if they screwed up it was their problem. There was no way they were going to keep her mom in this place one second longer than necessary and there was no way they were going to pay that amount again.

'We are paying the balance amount minus Rs 24,400 and we are walking out of this hospital. You can play with your computer till you find the missing entry, but we're not hanging around here!'

'Trisha!' Mrs Almeida took her arm, alarmed.

The man shook his head. 'But Madam, until all bills are cleared the patient cannot leave.'

'So clear them, or let me talk to someone who can!'

She counted out the balance amount and handed it over. 'This is the Rs 48,000 that's pending. I would like a receipt, please.'

He was busy jabbing the keyboard. He looked up and shook his head. 'This previous amount has to be paid!' he said stubbornly.

'And I am telling you I've paid it!'

The man in the adjoining counter came over. 'What happened?' he asked.

'She has the receipt but there's no entry in the computer here.'

The man laughed. 'Oh, that machine's defective. Sometimes it eats up the data. One minute.' He went to his own machine. 'Your receipt number?' he asked. He entered it, and nodded. 'It's okay, Madam, the payment was made.'

'Why don't you get your stupid machines in working order instead of accusing people of cheating?' Trisha kept her voice level, but she was scarlet with anger and close to tears. 'Do you think we don't have enough problems without being accused of cheating?'

'Trisha, it's okay, it's been resolved. Let's get out of here.'

She glanced at Mrs Alemeida in the lift, feeling mortified. 'I'm sorry I lost my cool,' she said.

To her astonishment, Mrs Almeida (who Trisha had thought had never intentionally touched another human being in her life) put her arms around her and patted her head. 'You were amazing, wait till I tell your mother, she'll be so happy!' she said. 'For a moment I thought you were going to hit him!'

'I felt like it. Bloody idiots!'

And then, at last, they were wheeling her mom out of her room and to the lifts.

'It's so wonderful to be home again after so long,' Mrs Bhave said looking around, as they drove into the porch, 'I feel like a stranger, almost!' Just outside the garage, Smelly Beast gleamed; Tikka had washed and polished the bike and its chrome dazzled in the bright sunlight.

They ushered her inside and her eyes widened when she saw the flowers lighting up the rooms with their vibrancy and fragrance. She squeezed Trisha's hand and hugged Shivi.

'They're beautiful,' she said, 'thank you.'

A new routine started; Richa and Hema would remain on duty (Richa in the morning, Hema at night) until Mrs Bhave was strong enough to manage on her own.

Trisha would wake, usually with a start at around 6 every morning and gently disentangle herself from Shivi. The dread in her belly would stir uneasily, as she brushed her teeth and ran a comb through her thick, tangled hair. Then she'd pad quietly over to her mom's room. She'd push open the door and peek tentatively inside. Usually her mom would be propped up in the armchair, staring out at the garden, as Hema bustled about, stirring the thick dietary supplement that was slowly becoming her mom's only source of nourishment.

'How was she last night?' she barely dared ask.

'She was all right' or 'She had a little fever last night' would be Hema's usual reply.

She would sit there for some time, having her first cup of tea and then Shivi would burst in noisily, making Mrs Bhave open her eyes and smile again.

At around 8, Richa would turn up for her shift.

'I get so nervous,' Trisha admitted to Akshay. 'By quarter to eight I'm already thinking what if Richa doesn't come . . . and it's ten times worse at night.'

She'd bathe, have her breakfast and Komal would list out the things that were needed for the house. She would check on her mom's medicine inventory—invariably something or the other had to be ordered.

Mrs Almeida would arrive by 10, sort through the mail, send off emails and sometimes call her up to the office. It seemed so strange to see her mom's lovely white Mac sitting quiet and blank in one corner.

'Mrs Almeida, do you think Mom will ever use her Mac again?' Trisha asked one morning.

'I hope so, dear. Now, let me explain these fixed deposits to you. Your mom has transferred most of her investments in yours and Shivi's name, so both of you will get a very good income every month.' Mrs Almeida put an arm around her as the significance of what she had just said began to sink in.

'Oh . . . that . . . that means . . .'

'It means,' Mrs Almeida said with sudden asperity, 'it means that you and Shivi are very well-off young ladies and will have to fend off the attention of layabouts and scoundrels who will want to get their greedy paws on your money.' She smiled and hugged Trisha. 'But don't worry, that is my job.'

And then, invariably every other day or so a bout of fever would strike. Richa or Hema would pop their heads around the door and tell her, 'Madam's feeling cold.' The bouts of shivering were terrifying to see, and when they subsided the fever would soar, leaving her mom weaker than ever.

She had also begun to dread mealtimes. She'd put a tiny portion of whatever had been made into her mom's plate, and watch with a sinking heart as Hema or Richa brought it back virtually untouched.

'Mom, you have to eat! You ate just five peas and half a carrot. I counted!'

Mrs Bhave would look at her plate with absolute loathing. 'Take it away, it's making me sick!'

'How well can your mom manage on her own now?' Akshay asked her one day.

'Well, she still walks around a bit, she goes to the living room and relaxes in her Lazy Boy and now she's talking about going upstairs to her office. But she has no stamina; she gets tired very quickly. She has a bath and falls asleep straightaway! Every bout of fever leaves her weaker, it's like she's coming down this horrible spiral staircase.'

'At least she hasn't got any pain. That's amazing.'

'I was so scared about that. I asked Dr Pradhan what to give her if she did have pain. But he said that apparently there are two kinds of this horrible cancer: in one kind you don't get fever but you do have pain, in the other you tend to get fever and shivering but no or less pain, which is the one Mom has. Imagine, she has cancer and she's managing on paracetamol!'

'Trish, have you thought about the music competition again?' Akshay asked hesitantly, one morning. He still wasn't quite sure of his ground with her.

'I don't know. I just don't feel like singing.'

'Okay, no problem. Forget it.'

'I'm sorry!'

'It's okay!'

But that same morning Mrs Bhave, while flipping through a magazine on interior decoration, glanced at Trisha who was frowning over a list of medicines that needed to be ordered.

'Darling, how's your band practice coming along? I haven't heard you sing for a long time. Isn't your competition coming up soon?'

'Mom, I don't quite feel up to it. We're not taking part anymore.'

'Oh?' There was a sheen of metal in her mom's jamun eyes. 'Give me the phone, sweetheart.'

'Okay, who're you calling?'

Her mom smiled. 'You'll see. Hello? Ah, is that Jai or Akshay? Jai, could I speak to your brother, please?'

'Hi Akshay, this is Trisha's mom. Listen, could you and Jai possibly come over here and play me some music? I think you guys should be practising for that competition and anyway, I'd like to hear some live jazz.'

'Mom!' Trisha shook her head vigorously. 'I told you I don't want to sing!'

Mrs Bhave smiled into the receiver and spoke. 'Yes, I know, she told me that, but I still think you should. So could you bring your stuff over—I'll send Tikka in the pickup. Will this afternoon be all right? At about 4? Thank you, dear, you're very sweet. I'm looking forward to it.' She smiled again and put down the receiver. She looked at Trisha. 'Okay, now what's Gullu's number?' she asked.

'Mom!' Trisha was outraged.

'Come here, baby.' Mrs Bhave patted the armrest of the Lazy Boy. 'Well actually, come here and squeeze in beside me—there's enough space, I'm size zero again.'

'I'm not!' But she squeezed in anyway, looking mutinous.

'Where's Shivi?' she murmured. 'If she finds us like this, we've had it!'

'She must be playing somewhere. Why did you . . .'

'Hush. Baby, just because I'm not well doesn't mean you bring your own life to a standstill. The last few weeks must have been hell for you. You have to get on with your life and your normal activities, darling.'

'But . . .'

'And I want you to sing for me.'

And it was there unspoken, but in her eyes, large and bright as a neon billboard. 'What if something happens and I can't be aware of your presence anymore or hear your voice? I want to hear you while I still can.'

Trisha nodded silently. 'Okay, Mom.'

'Good girl. Now tell Tikka to take the pickup over to the boys' place this afternoon.'

'I've been so scared all these days . . . still am.'

Mrs Bhave kissed her and ran her hands through her hair. 'It's okay to be scared, sweetie, I'm scared too, but you shouldn't let that take control of your life. You've managed so wonderfully through all of this! Remember that time we went to Big Chill and you panicked when you had to order and pay the bill, and then again when I asked you to go to the bank? Well, look at you now; you settled that hospital bill problem without baulking. Rita told me you nearly clobbered the fellow—and I've seen how confidently you count out the notes and run the house; it's no less a miracle!' She kissed her again and grinned. 'You've come a long way, baby!'

'I just wish I didn't have to learn this way,' Trisha said in a small voice, clinging on tightly.

'Darling, sometimes we have no choice. We just have to deal with what comes our way, like it or not, and how happy or unhappy we make ourselves and those around us, depends on how we deal with it.'

At 4.15 that afternoon Akshay, Jai and Gullu rolled up in the pickup with all their paraphernalia. Mrs Bhave had retired to her room to sleep. Trisha opened the front door.

'Hi, come on in.'

Akshay's eyes held hers. 'Great!' he whispered. 'This is great!'

'It was Mom's idea.'

But there was that old familiar excitement rising in her too. They spent a busy twenty minutes setting up and tuning their instruments in the drawing room. Then Trisha peeked into her mom's room. Richa was sitting at her bedside, knitting. Her mom was still fast asleep.

'She's still sleeping,' she told the gang. 'Let's start softly.'

'With what?'

'"Boulevard of Broken Dreams"—I love that one.'

Akshay hunched over his keyboard and Jai softly thumped his drums as she began to sing.

'My God, Trish, you still give me goosebumps!' Gullu said as they wound down. 'You make the hair on the back of my neck stand up.'

'That was beautiful, guys!' Mrs Bhave was leaning against the doorway, frail and ethereal.

'Mom! Did we wake you up?'

'No, Richa did! I told her to. Now keep on playing.'

She settled down in her Lazy Boy and smiled at them.

Hearing the music, Shivi too leapt out of her bed and came charging in. 'Why didn't you tell me you were having a concert?' she demanded, squeezing in beside her mom.

It became a sort of ritual after that, and for Trisha it became the only part of the day she actually looked forward to. She simply gave herself up to the music, feeling the tension and stress and emotion drain out of her as her voice soared.

In the evenings, Komal would take Shivi to the park, and Trisha would accompany the boys and Gullu, and they strolled around, discussing which numbers they needed to practise more and which were likely to impress the judges the most. By 7 she was back home and looking tentatively at her watch again as eight o'clock approached and the nurses' shift changed.

'How's your mom doing?' became Akshay's first question to Trisha every morning when he called.

'Okay, I guess, but she seems to be getting weaker every day. And sometimes she seems sort of spaced out and disoriented; at other times she's still sharp as a tack!' She had not taken her mom back to Dr Phadnis but had kept in touch with Dr Pradhan.

'Akshay . . .'

'Yup?'

'You know yesterday evening, after I got back from the park, she asked me to start up Smelly Beast.'

'What?'

'She said she just wanted to hear the sound of its engine.'

'Oh . . .'

'So I did . . . I sat there for about ten minutes, letting it rumble and revving it from time to time. The neighbours thought I was nuts. But . . . sometimes I think I really am going nuts!'

'Take it easy, Trish.'

'You know, apart from her vitamin supplement she hardly eats anything. She's sleeping more and more.'

'Listen, Trish, let's go the Lodhi Gardens or the zoo or wherever tomorrow. It's rained this evening so it should be cool.'

'Okay, let's see how Mom is.'

'She'll be the same.'

'Okay, but just for a little while.'

'Sure!'

'What's up?' he asked her the next morning, tucking her arm into his as they strolled into the zoo. Another downpour early that morning had left deliciously cool breezes behind. 'Is she okay?'

She shook her head. 'I don't know. She held my hand and gave me such a sad smile this morning, Akshay—I ran into the bathroom and howled. She knows, of course, she's known for months . . . and yet . . . and yet, there are times when it's like she doesn't know. She says she wants to take me and Shivi out on Smelly Beast and that one day, when she gets "200 per cent fit", as she put it, she will . . .'

'What?'

'It's like she's forgetting . . . it's like her mind has started to unravel. I've noticed this in the last four or five days.'

'Oh!'

She smiled bleakly, her eyes full. 'And yesterday Hema asked me to get adult diapers for her. You should have seen Shivi's face! "Mommy needs nappies?" She was shocked, poor thing! Actually so was I.'

'I guess she's still lucky she hasn't any pain. Papa was saying that normally you have to give morphine to people who have cancer. By the way, our results are due on the 15th. And then the mad rush for admission into college will begin.'

'I can't even think about that and I don't care anyway.'

'And our audition for the competition has been fixed for the 16th. I tell you they couldn't have chosen a closer date!'

'Shit!'

'How's Shivi?' he asked. 'How's she taking all this?'

'I don't know. She spends a lot of time in Mom's room playing around her bed quietly by herself or with Richa, but yesterday she said she didn't like the smell coming from the room and fizzed a room freshener all over the place. The other day she asked me, "Trisha, is Mommy the same person she used to be or has she become somebody else?"'

'Poor kid! Smell? What smell?'

'It's the stench of sickness, Akshay; it's like something has begun to decay and putrefy.' She looked at him, her eyes stricken. 'You know sometimes I feel we're completely trapped.'

'That's why you've got to get out . . .' He smiled and pointed to the pacing jaguar. 'Though even the poor animals here are completely trapped.'

'You know . . . there are times . . . when . . . when I just want all this to be over and not drag out like this. And then I feel so guilty about feeling that way; it's bad enough for me but can you imagine what it must be like for Mom? All day she sits there, staring out at the garden, semi-comatose most of the time, or lies in bed, staring at the ceiling and listening to us play all the tunes that used to make her happy. She used to ride Smelly Beast, for God's sake, up into the mountains, and look at her now—she needs diapers! Sometimes I'm just so glad she's still with us, no matter in what condition. But I'm getting scared now that I'll forget the fun person she used to be, the person she was and is, if only this wretched illness hadn't screwed up everything. I'm scared I'll only remember her as this skeletal yellow person lying in that bed with not enough strength to sit up on her own! That seems like a dream now . . .' She was weeping quietly.

He said nothing, but held her as close as he dared in this public place. Fortunately there were few people around.

'Come on, let's look at the pelicans; they always make you laugh,' he suggested gently.

'Yes,' she said, giving him a small smile. 'Sometimes they remind me of you.'

June 15 was one of those horrible hot-wet-towel-in-the-face days that come before the monsoons break. At eight o'clock, Gullu turned up in a complete state.

'Trisha, I need to go to the bathroom!' she squealed, 'I've been three times already!'

At her computer Trisha shook her head in exasperation. 'They said the results would be on the Net from 7 a.m. onwards, but the bloody server is down! We'll have to go to school now!'

Tikka dropped them and parked just down the road. A crowd of shrieking, jostling students thronged the big noticeboard at the gates where the results would be put up. Gullu's hands were clammy as she clutched Trisha's. 'Please, God,' she moaned, 'please let me pass!'

'Don't rely on Him or Her or them or whatever,' Trisha said sardonically. 'You'll just be let down and disappointed!'

'Trisha, don't say things like that! They'll hear you! I've been praying all night!'

'Gullu, you'll do fine!'

The babble suddenly increased. A functionary approached the noticeboard with a sheaf of papers in his hand.

'Make way, move out of the way!' he waved his arms at the kids. One by one, he pinned the sheets up on the board and stepped away.

'Let the stampede get over,' Trisha said, hanging on to Gullu. 'Nothing will change.'

'Look! The media's here too!' A couple of OB trucks belonging to a well-known news channels had pulled up.

There were whoops and yells, and also tears and faces filled with shock, as the kids scanned the lists for their numbers.

'Come on, Gullu,' Trisha said as the throng thinned a bit. 'We might as well get it over with.'

'I don't want to look!' Gullu shook her head vigorously. 'You look and let me know.'

Trisha walked up and craned her neck, scanning the list. Shit, her name and number didn't seem to be anywhere! She frowned. Just what was going on? Ah . . . yes, but there was Gullu's name and number; and she'd got 97 per cent overall! Wow!

But her name? Where the hell was it?

'Hey Trisha, how did you do?' one of the girls in her class asked, beaming. 'I got 95 per cent and I thought I would flunk!'

'I don't know; I haven't found my name or number anywhere.'

'What? Not possible!'

'Just see if you can find it,' she begged. 'I think I'm going to faint.'

Rima, who was a good head taller than her, approached the board.

'Holy shit!' she exclaimed.

'What?'

'You're up there. Right at the top! They've printed out the results score-wise.'

'Eh?'

'There, don't you see it?'

She looked. She'd topped the school with an incredible 99.5 per cent!

'Look!' Rima said, her voice suddenly hushed in awe. 'You've topped the school and are tied first overall in Delhi!'

'What?' Trisha felt a little faint.

Rima was already screaming out the news.

Gullu came charging up. 'What happened?' she asked.

'You got 97,' Trisha told her. She still couldn't believe her own score. But yes, there it was—Trisha Bhave: 99.5 per cent (later she found she had maxed maths and physics and got 99 per cent in biology and got 98.5 in that delayed chemistry paper!).

'And you?' Gullu asked.

'Up there,' she gestured.

'Trisha!'

A cameraman and a girl reporter were converging rapidly on them. She was already on the phone.

'Richa? Could I speak to Mom? Oh, she's sleeping? Okay, when she wakes tell her I've passed.' She grinned in spite of herself. 'I got 99.5 per cent.'

And then Akshay called. 'Hey, how did you do?'

'I can't believe it! I got 99.5, Akshay! What about you?'

'What? Oh, wow!'

'What did you get, tell me!'

'I'm going to have a great deal of fun waving my result under Papa's nose,' Akshay said gleefully. 'He was convinced I'd get around 70!'

'Idiot—what did you get?'

'98!' was his gleeful reply.

'Okay, tell Jai that Gullu got 97 and is at the moment doing bhangra for the media!'

'We need to do some serious celebrating, babe!'

'Yes . . . but . . . sure!' If her mom had been normal, she would have been over the moon, she thought. She swallowed and found a mike stuffed in her face.

'Congratulations, Miss Trisha. You've topped the school and tied first overall in Delhi. So how do you feel?' the reporter asked, grinning.

'Fine,' she said, 'I feel fine.'

'Was this a surprise to you?'

'The results are always a surprise.'

'How many hours a day did you study?'

She smiled. 'Enough, I think.' And added sweetly as her mom might well have done, 'don't you think so too? Now, please excuse me.'

'How's Mom?' Trisha asked as she entered the dim, air-conditioned bedroom.

'She's asleep,' Richa said. Trisha walked up to the bed. Her mom was fast asleep, pale and gaunt.

'Mom,' she said softly, sitting by the bed. 'Mom, wake up! Listen . . .'

Mrs Bhave opened her eyes and smiled faintly.

'Mom, I got 99.5 per cent! I topped the school AND I tied first in Delhi!'

Mrs Bhave smiled and squeezed her hand. 'Wonderful,' she said so softly Trisha had to crane her head to hear her. 'Wonderful, darling!'

'Mom, I'm going for the audition now,' Trisha said, early the next evening, fingering the necklace Akshay had given her. 'How do I look?' Her mother smiled. Trisha, in a long, wine-red skirt and a sleeveless black silk blouse, looked stunning.

'You look beautiful.'

Trisha wagged a finger. 'Now don't go to sleep when I sing!' she teased. 'But I'm so nervous!'

She hardly remembered the rush and bustle in the TV studio; people kept dashing about in every direction, trailing cables and wires and flapping sheets of paper, looking as if the world were about to end, reminding Trisha of the white rabbit in *Alice in Wonderland*. Three other groups from the northern region were competing.

'So how come you guys are into retro and jazz?' the moderator asked Akshay. He was a smooth-cheeked, glossy-haired fellow whose name, astonishingly, was Pedro. 'Most kids your age are into hip hop and rap and fusion and stuff like that.'

'Because we like it,' Akshay said. 'We can also do the other stuff, but we like this better.' Somewhere in the audience, Dr and Mrs Khurana were gratified to hear that.

Parkash Aunty had decided to sit with Trisha's mom. 'With Ma there, your mom will have no chance to fall asleep,' Gullu said earnestly. 'She'll be gossiping away the whole time!'

The four groups were to first play the audience's choice, then the judges' selection and finally their own. The requests from the audience came in a babble of suggestions; they were jotted down on slips of paper which were put into a goldfish bowl and mixed up. Trisha blinked at the razzle-dazzle, multicoloured lights of the set; in a way they were good, because you couldn't really see the audience sitting in the darkness beyond.

'Right. Are we ready?' Pedro grinned and put his hand into the bowl. 'I'm going to pick one number from these at random. If the group knows it, they'll play it. But they have a maximum choice of three.' He shook the bowl and pulled out a slip and handed it to one of the judges.

And then, at last it was their turn. Trisha smiled at the gang nervously and stared at the rafters. What if she fluffed it? What if they knew none of the three numbers? What if Gullu and Akshay didn't know the chords?

'Team D, your first choice, from *The Wizard of Oz*, "Over the Rainbow!" Can you do it?' Pedro smiled dazzlingly.

So, sometimes miracles (albeit minor ones) did happen, after all. Trisha nodded at the group. 'Let's give them three versions—Judy Garland's, Eva Cassidy's and our funky, honky-tonk one,' she said.

The lights dimmed; purple, green, blue, red and yellow spotlights pulsed on her in turn. She shut her eyes and thought of her mom and Shivi listening raptly.

The faint murmur and buzz in the audience choked off as her

first deep, resonant and crystal clear notes rang out. By the end of
the third version, the judges were looking at her askance; there was
gigantic talent here, they knew that, but they were trying very hard
not to show how stunned they were. The other participants stared,
their hearts sinking; this girl, she needed no special effects or backup,
she had that voice . . . and that perfect accompaniment.

The judges picked 'Return to Me' which, again, suited Trisha fine.
She smiled delightedly as the cheering went on and on. The audience
was quite a mixed bunch, but even the teenyboppers in their noodle
straps and tight, tattered jeans were stamping their feet and whistling.

'Right, that was wonderful,' the moderator said, new respect in
his voice. 'What is your choice now?'

'Diana Krall's "Boulevard of Broken Dreams",' she said, as Akshay
played out the opening notes on the piano exquisitely.

They won the audition hands down. As they took a bow, the audience
was on its feet, yelling, 'Encore, encore, another one, please!'

'Well . . .' Pedro smiled, glancing at the set's clock. 'I think we have
just enough time for one more. So will you? Please?' The girl was a
sensation, no question about that. Trisha and the gang exchanged glances.
She nodded and whispered something to Akshay and the others, an
impish smile lighting up her face as she handed him the mike.

'Right,' he said, 'we're going to play you guys something from way
back of beyond. It's a song that became a big hit with troops during
the Second World War, so maybe your grandparents will remember
it. Actually, we're playing it here for someone special.' He returned
the mike to her and picked up his sax and let rip the first notes of
'Cherry Pink and Apple Blossom White' as Trisha began to sing.

In her tiny flat, Mrs Almeida, who had been watching riveted,
suddenly stiffened, and then the tears flooded in and blurred
everything up. That Akshay fellow had said 'someone special . . .'

And in the audience, Mrs Khurana grabbed her husband's hand.
'Did you hear what he said? Someone special!' The doctor could only
nod and fiddle with his tie.

After the show, a representative of FM Forever approached them.
'Listen, you're on regardless of whether you win the finals or not.

We'll be in touch! Now can I have your mobile numbers, please? That was awesome!'

'Hey Mom, did you listen to us?' she asked when she reached home. Mrs Bhave opened her eyes and squeezed her hand.

'You were wonderful, baby. I'm so proud of you!' she whispered.

'Akshay played really beautifully tonight. And so did Gullu and Jai . . . it came together so well! I was so nervous in the beginning, but then it was all right . . .'

Hema was looking at her with reverence. 'Trisha miss, I never knew you could sing like that! You should make a record!'

But at 2 that morning, yet again Trisha was awoken by the ringtone of her cell phone.

'Trisha miss? Please come here a minute . . .' It was Hema.

In the bathroom, Hema was struggling to shift Mrs Bhave from the pot to the chair she had dragged her over in. Mrs Bhave's eyes were closed.

'She collapsed. She refused to take the bedpan so I had to bring her here.'

'Oh my God . . .' For a moment she looked around wildly. 'I'll get Komal,' she said, and then changed her mind and began helping Hema.

They laid her down on the bed. 'It's okay, miss, you go back to bed, I'll see to her now,' Hema said firmly, pushing her gently to the door. 'She's asleep now.'

'Should I ring the doctor?'

'No, she'll be all right. She just doesn't have any strength.'

'Okay, but call me if you need to.'

She peeked into the room early next morning. Hema was sitting by the bed, watching Mrs Bhave intently.

'How is she?' she whispered, tiptoeing in.

'She had some fever.'

'Shivering?'

Hema nodded. 'It was 102.'

'I'll ring Dr Pradhan . . .'

He listened and then prescribed an antibiotic. He didn't sound too hopeful.

Akshay rang at 9. 'Hey Trish, so how should we celebrate?' he asked.

'Listen, could I speak to your dad?' she asked. 'Mom's not too good.'

'Oh shit.'

Dr Khurana was over by 9.40. He examined her, his face neutral. In the corridor he shook his head slightly. 'She's gone down rapidly since I last saw her,' he said softly. 'I'm sorry.'

'How much time does she have, Doctor?' Trisha hardly dared to whisper, half not wanting to know the reply. He shook his head and walked off to his little white Zen.

Akshay, Jai and Gullu stayed with Trisha the whole day.

'She seems to have slipped into a coma,' Trisha said, holding her mother's hand. 'Mom? Mom? Can you hear me?'

There was no response. Richa, who had taken over, was now sitting by the bedside, watching with the same intentness that Hema had shown.

An hour after Akshay, Jai and Gullu had returned home—Hema knocked on Trisha's door.

'What?'

Hema merely nodded and indicated that she follow her.

'Try to talk to her,' she said, fixing the blood pressure wrapping around Mrs Bhave's arm.

Hema pumped the bulb and the mercury rose. Then she listened carefully and repeated the process twice. At last she lowered the stethoscope.

'What's her blood pressure?' Trisha asked.

'60 . . . I can't get the lower one . . .'

Shivi wandered into the room. 'Trisha, when are you coming to sleep?' she asked, rubbing her eyes.

'I'll come, Shivi, you go back.'

'I can't sleep without you.'

'Where's Komal? Tell her to lie down beside you.'

'I want you.' Shivi came up to her and stared at her mom. 'She's fast asleep, isn't she? Why does she sleep all the time, Trisha?'

'Because she's very weak, Shivi.'

Shivi shook her head. 'She's not like Mommy used to be. I liked that one better . . .'

'She's very sick, Shivi. It's not her fault.'

Shivi clambered up into Trisha's lap and stared at her mother. 'Will she get better, Trisha?'

Trisha looked at her little sister, her eyes filling up. 'No,' she whispered, 'Shivi, Mom's not going to get well.'

'Trisha miss, she's awake.'

'Mom? Mom, Shivi's come to say goodnight!'

She squeezed her mother's hand and felt the slight increase in pressure in response. Her mom opened her big jamun eyes, the whites were a virulent orange now, and smiled faintly. Then she closed her eyes again; her mouth opened and shut as she sighed quietly for air a few times, and then the gentle breathing stopped. Hema had her stethoscope on her chest and now lowered it. She shook her head, tears in her eyes, and looked at her watch. It was 8.56 p.m.

Trisha put her arms around Shivi and hugged her hard, tears beginning to stream down her cheeks.

'Why are you crying, Trisha?' Shivi asked, staring at her.

'It's over, Shivi,' she whispered, weeping softly. 'It's over for her. She's gone. Shivi, we're alone now.'

She hardly remembered the rest of that night. She fumbled with her phone and called Akshay.

'Hey, what's up?' he started blithely.

'Akshay, Mom's gone.'

'Trisha . . .'

'Will you tell your dad and Gullu too?'

'Hang on, we're coming.' Dr Khurana and the boys arrived within minutes, followed by Gullu—completely stunned—and her mother. Half an hour later, Mrs Almeida arrived. Hema had called up Richa, who had just reached home away and she came straight back. Komal had tried taking Shivi but without success. She held on to Trisha like a limpet, fright in her eyes. Tikka squatted on his haunches in her mom's room, like some hobgoblin sentinel.

'It's okay, Shivi, Mommy's happy now.' What a bloody lie that probably was. 'At least she's not ill anymore.'

Mrs Almeida, sniffing into a delicate handkerchief, took control. 'I've ordered one of those refrigerated caskets,' she told Trisha. 'But I think we should do the cremation as soon as possible.'

'I don't want any mumbo jumbo ceremony,' Trisha said, glad to have something practical to think about. 'Mom hated that.'

Dr Khurana had written out a temporary death certificate. 'You'll have to get a proper one from the municipality,' he said. 'Don't worry—I'll put someone from the clinic on it. But you will have to go there at least once to sign.'

They sat around in near silence.

'Trisha, dear, I think you should try to sleep. You should get as much rest as you can,' Mrs Alemeida said, as Shivi finally agreed to go to Gullu's mom.

'There's just one more thing I have to do,' Trisha said suddenly. She picked up the phone.

It took a while for the call to be picked up.

'Hello? Nana? This is Trisha, your granddaughter. Nana, Mom died tonight . . .' She took a deep breath, trying to keep down the rising sob. 'I hope you're happy now, you bastard!' She slammed the receiver down, breaking down as Parkash Aunty took her into her arms.

'Baby . . . hush . . .'

Trisha took one look at the rattling, unwashed hearse that turned up to take her mom away the next morning and shook her head.

'No way! She's not going in that filthy contraption. We'll take her in the pickup.' She watched, with Shivi in her arms, biting her lip, as they took her mom out of the house for the last time and laid her down gently in the bed of the pickup.

'Akshay, Jai and Gullu—will you ride with her, please, if you don't mind,' she whispered.

'Come, dear,' Mrs Almeida opened the door of the pickup. Trisha shook her head and put Shivi down.

'Shivi, get our helmets,' she said. 'We're going as Mom would have liked us to.'

Shivi nodded and ran inside.

'Trisha, my dear, you can't be serious. You're in no condition to ride that motorbike!' Dr Khurana was stunned.

But Trisha had already strapped on Shivi's helmet and then her own. 'Mom loved Smelly Beast,' she said. 'So it's only right that we take it along.'

Dr Khurana opened his mouth to protest once more but Smelly Beast had already made its thunderous announcement.

On the following day, they collected Mrs Bhave's ashes and drove north to the banks of the Yamuna several kilometres before it entered Delhi.

'I'm not taking her to some place where those fat priests fall upon you like vultures!' Trisha exclaimed. 'Mom didn't believe in all that and I don't care what people say.'

And so instead they went to the riverbank, flanked by green fields stretching to the horizon, with the river wide and silver and the sky clean and blue. As she sat in the pickup with her mom's ashes heavy and still warm in her lap, she stared out of the window, her mind blank. She sat between Akshay and Gullu, both as red-eyed as she was. Mrs Almeida sat stolidly in the front, next to Jai and Tikka. Shivi and Komal had been dropped off at Gullu's house again.

'This was Mom,' she thought disbelievingly, feeling the crumbling bones and warm ash through the cloth they were wrapped in. 'This was our mom . . . I wonder where she really is now. With Papa?'

In a way, she thought, it was a perverse sort of miracle too: one moment you were alive, a whole person with a life and baggage and issues, the next you were just 'a body'.

'Hey . . .' Akshay squeezed her hand. 'How're you doing?'

She squeezed his hand back and felt the tears run down her cheeks.

They took a boat and there, mid-river, let Mrs Bhave slip into the waters, scattering the rose petals and jasmine in her wake.

'Bye, Mom,' Trisha whispered as the flowers floated away reluctantly, and then gained momentum as the current caught them and bore them away.

CHAPTER EIGHTEEN

RESURRECTION

'What the . . .?' Trisha stared in amazement at the road outside their house. It was jammed with media vans, and a battery of reporters pounced on the pickup as it nosed its way through the gates. Tikka kept one hand firmly planted on the horn.

'What's going on?' Mrs Almeida pushed away a mike that had been thrust through a window. 'Get that thing out of my face!'

'You topped! That's why they're all here,' Akshay said suddenly, gripping Trisha's hand.

'Miss Trisha Bhave, you topped Class XII! Congratulations! How does it feel?'

Mrs Almeida got off the car. 'Excuse me, will you step back, please?'

Trisha climbed out, holding Shivi's hand firmly.

A barrage of questions shot out at her.

'Miss Trisha, your school principal told us that you lost your mother recently. It must be a difficult time for you. But how will you be celebrating your results?'

She pushed her way through, the tears beginning to blind her.

'How would your mother have wanted you to celebrate?'

Mrs Almeida held up her hand. 'Will you kindly make way? At the moment Trisha does not want to speak to anyone.' She swallowed. 'We have just returned after immersing her mother's ashes, so we would like some privacy!'

For a moment there was a hush, and then the babble broke out again.

'Trisha, is it true your mother had cancer? So how did you cope with your mother's illness and preparing for your exams at the same time?' The question came from a particularly obtuse reporter from a leading news channel who had bulldozed her way right up to Trisha. She smiled with mock concern, displaying a lot of highly polished teeth. 'This must be a difficult time for you, but our viewers would be interested to know how you coped, and managed to do so brilliantly.'

'Please, there is a time and place for everything. Trisha is in no condition to answer your questions just now.' Mrs Almeida's eyes were flinty.

'Did your mother know your results?'

'Or did she pass away before that? Our viewers would be interested in knowing . . .' Akshay snatched the mike out of the reporter's hands. 'Ask yourself that question when your mother dies, you thick bitch, and see how you feel!' He was scarlet and breathing rapidly, his eyes welling. He flung the mike away and grabbed Trisha's hand. 'Come on, let's go in!'

'Hey, sir, you can't just . . .'

There was confusion as the mike was retrieved and the reporter regained her composure and tidied her hair. 'So, Miss Trisha, he is a friend of yours?' she asked suggestively.

'Hut! Besharam! Niklo! Shoo—get out!' Tikka sprang on the crowd, his eyes glinting with anger, waving his arms threateningly. The reporters took a step back, holding up their mikes to fend him off.

'Arre . . .!'

'Hey!'

And then they were inside, the front door slammed firmly shut.

'Bloody hyenas!' Akshay muttered. 'Hey, are you all right?'

Trisha nodded and smiled through her tears. 'Wow, Akshay, you actually lost your cool!'

'Trisha, have you thought about your mom's chautha? What would you like to do?' Mrs Almeida looked at Trisha enquiringly.

Trisha shook her head. 'I . . . I don't know. Mom never believed in any organized religion and she hated religious ceremonies. I mean, does there have to be a chautha at all?'

'Look at it this way, dear; it's a memorial service . . . so that all the people who knew your mother can pay their respects to her memory.'

'But she never liked all that religious stuff. It made her uncomfortable.' She was breaking down again.

'But she loved music, didn't she?' Mrs Almeida put an arm around her. 'Okay, don't fret yourself over it now. I'll arrange something. Now get some rest.'

'Thank you, Mrs Almeida. I don't know what I would have done without you.' She looked up at the tall, spare lady. 'You know . . .' she went on quietly, 'actually I don't know what I would have done without all of you . . . Gullu, Jai, Parkash Aunty, Akshay . . . Komal and Tikka . . .

'Come on, dear, you lie down now and try to sleep. Your eyes are all red and puffy, and you're exhausted.'

Trisha sat quietly with Shivi, Akshay, Jai and Gullu in the front row, staring at the huge picture of her mom—surrounded by a sea of pink and white lilies. It was a picture she had taken on their Ladakh trip, her mom astride Smelly Beast, her helmet dangling from her hand, the shades up on her head, smiling into the camera, with the mountains in the background. In the hall the fans hummed, and people began trickling in one by one. At exactly 5, Mrs Almeida went up to the dais.

'Good evening,' she said in her firm clear voice. 'It has become fashionable these days at occasions like this, to say that we have gathered here to "celebrate" the life of the person who has passed away, rather than to mourn their death. I asked Trisha how she would like it to be, and she said, "Let's just remember her." So that's what we will do. Now Mrs Bhave did not believe in religious ceremonies, and so we will respect her beliefs this evening. What she did have was a feisty and fierce spirit of independence, as you can see from her picture; there was nothing she liked better than to set off on a road trip on her monster bike with her two daughters. It frightened me, it frightened everyone and raised eyebrows and invited comment, but it didn't frighten her. There was one other thing that she loved and I have some of that here for you to remember her by: it's a recording of the music Trisha and her friends played for her over the past few weeks, while they practised.

This is the music Mrs Bhave loved and listened to. I think this is how we can remember her best.'

'Oh my God, she's got the CDs we made of our rehearsals!' Trisha whispered to Akshay.

'Shit, we shouldn't have fooled around so much!'

She clutched his hand and shut her eyes as her voice filled the hall and the murmur of people hushed.

And at the end, when the family had to stand in a line to accept, it was a pathetic little line of two: her and Shivi. Trisha shook her head; this was just not right.

'Mrs Almeida, Parkash Aunty, Akshay, Jai and Gullu, come on here,' she said, beckoning to them.

There were a surprising number of people: her mom's clients, including Mr Surinder Lamba and his wife from Kasauli, the gentlemen from the Noida Expressway Villas project, friends and acquaintances from Gurgaon and Delhi, Mrs Krishnan, Ms Sonam and a whole bunch of teachers from school and then . . .

Trisha stared at the tiny grey-haired, sparrow-like lady standing in front of her, her pallu drawn over her head, eyes streaming.

'Nani?'

Her grandmother nodded.

She looked around for the ogre General. 'Nana?'

Her nani shook her head and gave a bleak smile. 'He didn't dare! He's afraid of you!'

'What?'

'Like he was scared of your mother!'

'But he . . . he set the dog on us . . .'

'Because he was afraid, beta.'

She stepped forward and hugged her grandmother tightly. 'You should stand with us, please!'

Her grandmother shook her head. 'I don't deserve that. I do not have the right—I didn't help Ghungroo when she needed me.'

'Where are you staying?'

'I'm going back to Kasauli tonight.'

'Oh.'

She hugged her and Shivi again and moved on.

'Who was that?' Akshay asked her.

'My grandmother,' she said wonderingly.

She woke up early that first morning after everything was over, feeling weird. Gullu had gone back home, and it was just herself and Shivi again in the bedroom. At first, she felt the familiar heavy dread in the pit of her stomach and then realized that there was no reason for it to be there anymore. With a stab of guilt she felt a sense of relief and release. It was over, both for Mom and herself. Outside, a magpie robin sang sweetly on the laburnum, just as it had done yesterday and the day before and last week. She heard the bicycle bell of the fellow who came to deliver the milk to the houses on the street. Regardless of what happened, these things just carried on. She got up quietly, gently pressing Mr Teddy Sir into Shivi's arms and padded softly to her mom's bedroom.

It was quiet and dim, and the smell of sickness still hung about it. It was strange to see that big bed empty and pristine, and not to have Hema or Richa bustling about, stirring her mom's supplement. The nurses had cleared her mom's dressing and bedside tables of all the leftover medicines and stored them in a carton. How many times had she and Shivi romped on that bed with their mom, giggling and squealing, planning their next crazy expedition on Smelly Beast? Yes, that was what she ought to remember, not the skeletal yellow person who had lain in this bed in diapers, too weak to talk. The tears had begun filling up again when Komal came up to her and put an arm around her.

'Come on, baby,' she said softly, leading her away. 'Everything will be all right.'

'I'm all screwed up,' she told Akshay, who would invariably land up shortly after breakfast and stay the whole day. Often Gullu and Jai would come too. 'I feel relieved and then I feel guilty and then I feel so sad. I can't believe we won't see or hear her voice again. I've walked into her room and almost said "Hi Mom!" so many times . . .' She looked at him. 'You know, Mrs Almeida told me that "with every door that shuts, a window opens . . ."'

'And?'

'Well, I was just wondering that if it hadn't been for Mom's illness, I probably wouldn't have met you—and Jai—of course. I mean you wouldn't have been trying to steal Smelly Beast while your dad examined Mom, and so maybe a window did open then . . .'

'Stealing Smelly Beast? Hey, wait a minute!' He glanced at her, and grinned. 'Well, you are right, actually . . .'

'Of course I am, but what do you mean? You've got that look in your eye again!'

'Simple, I thought the bloody door had slammed shut when you discovered us in the pickup and that you'd go running screaming blue murder and Papa would crucify us, but instead you helped us, gave us Coke, and later in the pond you showed me what Shivi calls your big boobies.' He grinned. 'The window sure opened then!'

'Showed you my what! I'll show you something else right now, mister!'

For days there was an endless stream of visitors—friends and clients of her mom's, Ms Sonam and Mrs Krishnan from school (which gave Shivi a fright) and the neighbours, of course.

'You have been amazing, my dear,' Mrs Krishnan told her, clasping her hand. 'You're an example for the whole school; Ms Sonam kept me informed about your mother . . . and I thought about letting you take a year off and appear for your Boards this year, but look at you! You did us proud!'

'Trisha,' Mrs Almeida said one morning, about a fortnight later, 'You should look through your mother's things and decide what you want to do with them.'

'You mean her clothes and bags and shoes and stuff?'

'Yes.'

'I don't know!'

And occasionally, Shivi and she would open their mother's cupboard and sniff hard at the hanging clothes, still imbued with their mom's familiar musky smell.

'They smell of her,' Shivi said. 'I wish she was here!'

'So do I, Shivi. I miss her too.'

They would sit side by side on the big white bed and leaf through the fat photo albums full of birthday and holiday pictures.

Her mom's dressing table was still crowded, with its bottles of perfume and make-up stuff. Nothing had been touched.

'I can't bear to change anything,' she told Gullu. 'It's like she's going to walk back in any moment.'

Mrs Almeida continued to come every morning and sort through the mail as always. But it wasn't going to be a permanent state of affairs.

'Trisha, your mom paid me three months' salary in advance to come here and settle things after she had gone. But after that, I'll have to get another job. I'll still come over, of course, but it won't be every day . . .'

Trisha nodded. 'Sure,' she said, 'so I'll just list all my urgent queries and email them to you!'

Mrs Almeida had called over Mr Bhatnagar, who had been her mom's lawyer, to read out her will. Mrs Bhave had willed nearly everything she owned to Trisha and Shivi while she was alive, so there was no real problem.

'Your mom divided her jewellery for the two of you,' Mrs Almeida said, handing over two large velvet boxes, each labelled with the girls' names. 'This is yours, Trisha, and this one is Shivi's. She listed everything also, so you can have a look and then we'll take these to the bank.' But yes, Smelly Beast was Trisha's exclusively. 'When Shivi's old enough you can buy her a bike of her own,' her mom had written in the note. 'Whichever one she wants! And then go for a holiday to the mountains!'

And then one morning, she opened her mom's cupboard again and stared at the clothes hanging silently there. Okay, Mom was not coming back . . . these clothes would just be infested with moths. Some she could keep—though she would have to open them up or get them altered so that she or Shivi could wear them—the others she would give away. Her make-up stuff and perfumes, well—she smiled bleakly—both she and Shivi could use those.

Shivi was still fragile and followed her older sister around like a shadow. Trisha had sat down in the Lazy Boy one evening to watch TV when Shivi came into the room.

'That's Mommy's chair,' she said accusingly. 'You're sitting in Mommy's chair, Trisha!'

'I know, Shivi, but I used to sit in it before too. So did you.'

'But you can't sit in her chair now. Where will she sit then? You can't!'

Shivi ran up to her, her face crumpled, flailing her arms. 'You can't, you can't.'

Trisha fended off the angry little girl. 'Hey, watch it, Shivi!' She held her arms. 'Listen, it's okay for us to sit in her chair. She won't mind.'

'I don't want to talk to you; I want to talk to Mommy!'

'So do I, Shivi.' Her eyes were filling up too. 'Very badly.'

'What?'

'So do I! I want to talk to Mom very badly too. I miss her like anything!'

Shivi gulped and swallowed a sob. She wiped her eyes with the back of her hand and sniffed. 'Don't be sad, Trisha, I'll look after you.'

'Thank you, baby. That's what I told Mom you'd do!' She picked her up and sat down with her on the Lazy Boy. 'Now let's see that DVD of our music show again, shall we?'

Shivi fiddled with her hair. 'So when are you going to marry Akshay?' she asked.

'What?'

'You're going all red, which means you are!'

'Shivi, please!'

'Will you ask him?'

'I'll have to go to college first.'

'But afterwards? You can marry him afterwards, can't you? And then you can go for your honeymoon on Smelly Beast!'

Smelly Beast! She hadn't gone to the bike since she had driven it to the crematorium. Tikka had kept it sparkling and fiddled with it, but hadn't started it. Well, the bike was hers now, and she could legally ride it the day she turned eighteen and got her licence.

Mrs Almeida had informed Dr Pradhan of Mrs Bhave's death some days later. Trisha approached her one morning.

'Mrs Almeida, I'd like to give Dr Pradhan something to thank him for taking care of Mom.'

'To thank him? That's very considerate of you. But what about the others?'

'No, not the others,' Trisha shook her head firmly.

'This is so strange!' Trisha said clutching Akshay's hand as they waited in the Gastroenterology Department for Dr Pradhan. 'Any minute I expect that door to burst open and Mom to be wheeled out . . .'

'Should we come back another time?'

'No, it's weird, but it's also a relief. I don't have to worry anymore like those poor people have to. I feel guilty about that too, but still relieved.' She looked up. 'Ah here he is at last! Come on.'

Dr Pradhan looked embarrassed as Trisha handed over the neatly packed Sheaffer pen set she had picked as a gift. 'Thank you, Trisha but the others too . . . I can't . . . besides we couldn't do . . .'

'No, Doctor,' she said firmly, 'you were the only one who was always available when we needed you. You don't know how much difference that made.'

'Well, thank you.' He looked at her and smiled. 'You know, they're still talking about you in the Emergency. It was quite an entrance.'

The days sped past; a week, a month, three months, six months . . .

'It's like you're in this fast flowing river that just will not stop for anything, you get carried away by it, no matter what happens,' Trisha told Akshay as they bustled about madly with college admission forms. 'You're just forced to think about other things . . . and this . . . this huge thing that happened, this humungous, most horrible thing that could happen to anyone ever, just moves one inch further into the background. I never thought I'd be able to cope, I couldn't imagine life without Mom around. But even Shivi's begun rushing around in her usual madcap way. She does throw the occasional tantrum, but she's always done that, Yesterday I told her that Mom wouldn't like to know that she'd bashed up two boys in her class and she shot back, "But Mommy isn't here, Trisha, so how will she know?" What a kid!'

And then Shivi's birthday came around.

'I don't know what to do,' Trisha told Akshay. 'Should we organize a party for her or not? It'll seem so strange without Mom.'

'Depends on how you feel. I guess the first time will always be strange.'

She rang Mrs Almeida and asked her. 'But of course you should have a party, dear,' Mrs Almeida paused. 'You know, there's this group, "If We're History, You're Toast"—have you heard them? You should get them to play for her.'

'Mrs Almeida! Okay, thanks so much . . . yes, I think she'll enjoy that!' She put down the receiver and stared at Akshay. 'Mrs Almeida, *Mrs Almeida* just cracked a joke! Can you believe it?' She took a deep breath. 'You know . . . Mom's studio and office are empty . . . we could have the party there—there's tons of space and they won't wreck the house.' She hadn't really been up to the studio much, just occasionally when some letters or papers needed to be filed. It was just too full of her mom's presence. But now, now she thought, Mom wouldn't mind Shivi's party being thrown there. She'd probably like it.

To her immense surprise, she found herself enjoying organizing the party—sending out the invites, deciding on the return presents and games and decorations. It was nice to be in charge—even though she had to agree with all of Shivi's decisions!

With fifteen six and seven-year olds running rampant all over the place and dancing wildly to their music, the party was a raucous success.

'I got some great gifts!' Shivi exulted, 'look what Bobby gave me!'

Trisha hooded her eyes. 'Hmm, maybe we can keep some of them away, so you can give them as gifts to your friends.'

'No way!'

Her own birthday she celebrated more quietly, though, of course, the gang turned up. 'Come on,' Akshay said, grabbing her hand. 'We're going to Big Chill—our treat, but you'll have to order!'

And then Diwali came around again . . .

'We're not celebrating Diwali this year,' Trisha decided. 'The ones up there have been horrible to us. I don't want them to visit our house.'

'You know,' she said to Gullu. 'It's on special days that it's the most difficult, and now I know why Mom blew all that money last Diwali and went all out. She *knew*. And that's why she made me go to the bank and run the house and all that stuff too. I used to get annoyed about it, but well now I don't have a problem with those things.' She nodded. 'And now Komal's trying to teach me how to cook. Mom didn't know the first thing about cooking, but Komal insists I learn. "If something happens to me who will cook the food?" she says.'

But it was pretty bleak and lonely, sitting in a dark house on Diwali night with Shivi all restless and fidgety, and returning all the mouth-watering boxes of sweets that turned up and remembering the fun they had had last year.

'Heck, I might as well join the killjoy anti-cracker brigade.' she said to Akshay that evening. 'Poor Shivi's having a hard time.'

'Come over,' he invited. 'We'll be doing our usual round of relatives and then coming back home.'

'Umm . . . okay, so give me a buzz when you get back.'

'Okay.'

But then at 7, Gullu's mom turned up like the tornado from *The Wizard of Oz*.

'What are you pretty girls doing pining in the dark like this?' she scolded, sweeping them up into her arms. 'Do you think this is how your mother would have wanted you to celebrate Diwali? Come along now, you both are spending Diwali with us—no arguments! Go and change into something nice right now!'

Six weeks after she turned eighteen, she had her driver's licence in her hand. Tikka had taught her to drive the pickup too—on the lakebed—and she passed her test with flying colours.

'You should have seen that inspector's face when I told him I wanted to do my bike test on Smelly Beast!' she told Akshay. 'He freaked! He looked at me as though I were mad and said, "But Madam, it's a Bullet!" I think he was ready to give me the licence the moment he saw me climb on. Tikka was laughing so hard I thought he'd give himself a hernia! I really miss Mom at times like this!'

And gradually she found that she could talk about her mother more easily, without having to bite her lip or wipe her eyes.

'We're getting by,' she emailed Mrs Almeida a little after a year had passed. 'I never imagined we could. It's been just over a year now since she died.'

'Well, dear,' came the sardonic reply, 'you always said you wanted to believe in miracles. Here's one for you . . .'

At about that time too, she decided to move into her mom's bedroom. It was still full of vibrant memories, but they didn't hurt so much anymore. Besides, Shivi had always assumed that their shared bedroom was really hers, because she had the study.

'But I don't want to sleep alone!' Shivi protested, when she put the suggestion to her sister. Her eyes sparkled suddenly. 'I know what! You give me our room but I'll only sleep with you in Mommy's room! Then you won't be alone either and I'll have a room of my own too. Wow! Wait till I tell Bobby and Arti and Ajay. They'll be so jealous!'

'So much for a room of my own . . .' Trisha told Akshay wryly. 'She's got the better of me as usual. Still at least we have the whole of upstairs for our practice.'

'Yes, the acoustics are just great there.'

Her mom's studio had been perfect as a venue for the group to play in and that's where they now assembled while rehearsing.

She'd heard nothing more from her grandparents. Several times she had approached the phone call, but had baulked at the last minute. And then eighteen months after her mom's death, she received a phone call from Mangalsons.

'The General Sahib has died,' the voice on the phone informed her. She rang her nani immediately.

'Yes . . . he had not been well for a while . . . in fact, ever since your mother passed away,' her nani said tearfully. 'He just went downhill after that.' She heard the stifled sob. 'I think he died of guilt more than anything else; he couldn't forgive himself for what he'd done.'

'Are you okay, Nani? Should Shivi and I come over?' She was thinking rapidly. Maybe Shivi and she could drive up to Kasauli on Smelly Beast, with Tikka and Komal following in the pickup as usual.

'Nahin, beta—it's all right.' Her nani paused again. 'Trisha, he made a new will. He's left the house and everything to me as long as I'm living and after that to you both. There's also something he wanted to give you, which I'll send by courier. You should get it in a few days.'

'Shivi! Come on, hurry up, you'll be late for school!'

'Uff, always in a hurry you are!'

'Bring your helmet and shades!'

'What?'

'Your helmet! We're going on Smelly Beast!'

'What? Wowee! Let's go, baby!'

With Shivi clinging to her waist, Trisha gunned the bike out of the driveway and waved to Tikka. The pickup was due for another service. Carefully she burbled up the narrow road that ran past their school and stopped the bike at the gates.

'Bye Shivi, be good and don't bully Bobby too much!' She helped Shivi take off her helmet and kissed her.

'Trisha! Not here! I'm not a baby!'

Behind her a turquoise Swift had drawn up, and a few wolf whistles rent the air.

'Good morning, Mrs Krishnan!' Trisha greeted her old principal with a smile and a shy wave.

Then she got back on the bike. She would bunk college, she decided. She would pick up Akshay now, and they would drive to the cavern again and spend the whole morning there, swimming and messing about.

Tired but happy she picked up Shivi from school that afternoon and rode back home. There was a courier boy ringing the doorbell as she thundered up the driveway.

'Ms Trisha Bhave?' he asked.

'Yes, thank you.' She signed for the packet and took it inside; it felt like a large cigar box.

She opened it and gasped.

It was a beautifully polished box made of walnut wood. Inside, resplendent on wine-red silk, nestled a row of glittering medals, fourteen of them in all. Gently she picked one up and squinted at it. It was made of silver, circular with a five-pointed star with a raised chakra in the centre in gold, on a dark blue and saffron ribbon.

It was the Maha Vir Chakra.

She opened the accompanying envelope.

In a handwriting that resembled her mom's so much it brought quick tears to her eyes, there were three lines:

For Trisha,
You deserve these more than I ever did.
Nana